NOT YOUR AVERAGE BEAUTY

MICHELLE HELLIWELL

ISBN: 978-0-9940357-1-4

Cover Design: Selena Blake

Editor: Nancy Cassidy

❀ Created with Vellum

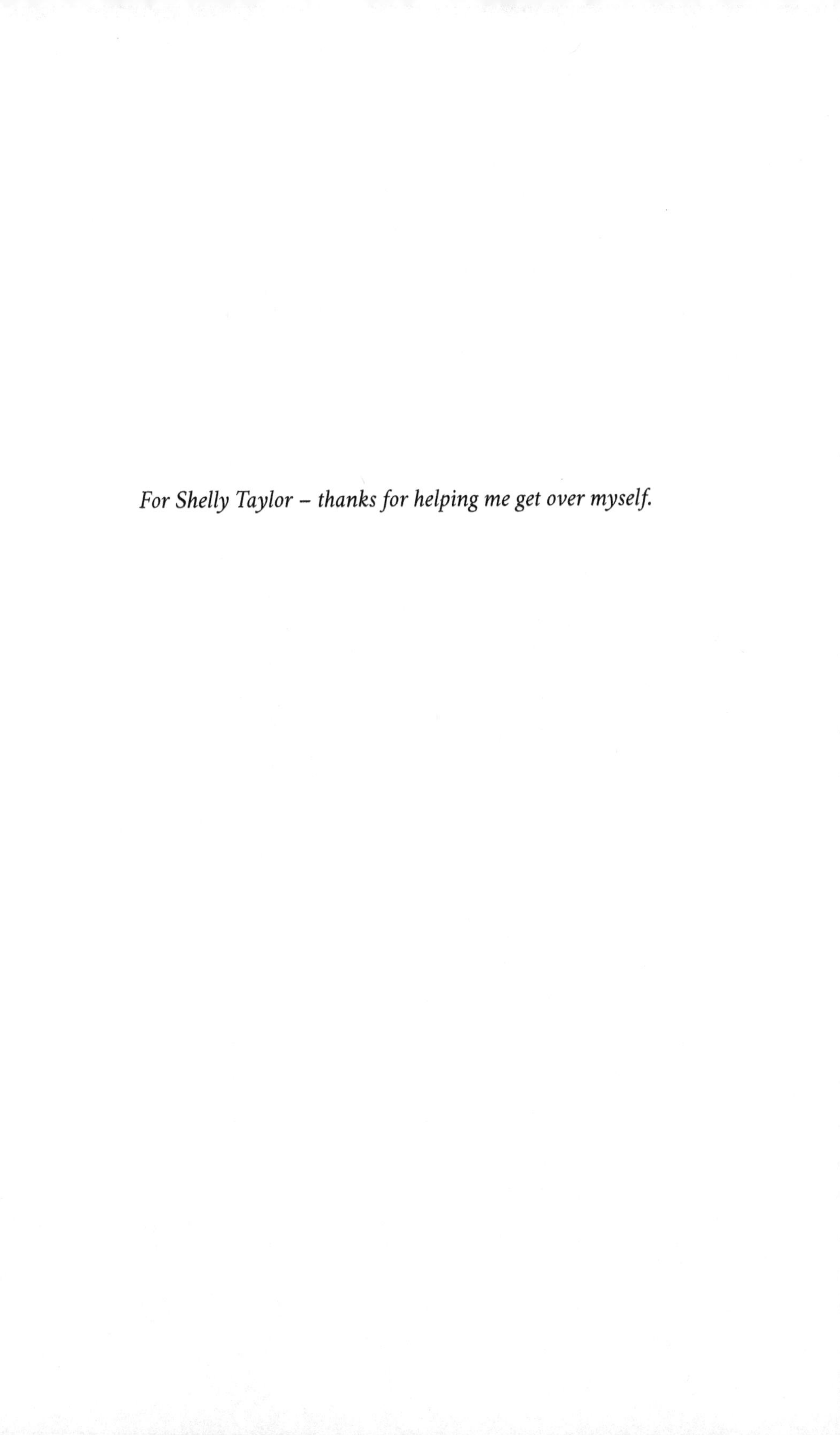

For Shelly Taylor – thanks for helping me get over myself.

ACKNOWLEDGMENTS

Writing might be a solitary venture, but creating a book is the work of many. I would like to take this opportunity to acknowledge everyone who has helped me on the journey to authorship.

First, I want to thank my husband Rob. He has been, from day one, spectacularly supportive in every way. Writing at home with young children is always a struggle but Rob's been there to distract and detain kids when my mama guilt complex was ready to relent. And thanks to my boys, because they have taught me how fierce love can be.

Thanks to my mum, who encourages us in everything to do our best, and my dad, who challenged me to shoot for the stars. The more I write, the more I understand what "my best" is, and that means working harder. The stars are in my sights every time.

To my circle of friends who have held my hands and made me laugh through the raging self-doubt and some of my darker days – Deanna Beck, Melanie Belliveau and the entire crew at Eastern Kings Memorial – thank you. I'm blessed to have you in my life.

You would not have this book in your hands if it were not for the excellent support and mentorship provided by my writer's group, Romance Writers of Atlantic Canada. It is not an understatement to say I have learned something valuable every time we meet. While it is hard to single out any of them, I would like to acknowledge Kelly Boyce, Julianne MacLean, and Deborah Hale for fielding my questions and giving answers generously.

To my critique partners, Anne MacFarlane, Annette Gallant, and Nikki Figeruido, who's guidance and encouragement helped shape this book, thank you. To Nancy Cassidy, my first critique partner, and now my editor, thanks for challenging me to be the best I can be. To Shelly Taylor and Racheal Surette, thank you for being my first readers.

CHAPTER 1

Yorkshire, October 1790

There was blood on his hands.

Who—or what—it belonged to, he didn't know. His temples pounded as he attempted to drag himself up onto his bed. He lifted a shaking hand, sticky and stinking of the drying blood, to his brow, but the act brought the putrid smell too close to his nose. Already weakened, his stomach lurched in protest, and he heaved violently onto the floor.

Glorious. Just bloody glorious.

Was it not but a fortnight ago he'd subjected himself to another session of incomprehensible incantations and bitter potions by a so-called magician? More money and time wasted. And, perhaps, one more thread of hope unraveled in his never ending quest to be free of the Beast. Priests and scholars, alchemists and magicians from every corner of Europe and even beyond had been consulted. No distance had been too far, nor any price demanded too high. For the cost of this horror—waking up in a soup of filth and blood, causing terror among the people it was his duty to protect—was higher still.

The jangle of keys in the lock of his bedchamber door announced help was on its way. In the next instant his butler Hanley, who had served his father before him, entered the room, bringing relief along with a heavy dose of humiliation. He was vaguely aware of Hanley's calm and measured voice directing the small parade of house staff that dared to remain in his employ. They took care of the mess as if cleaning up after a dinner party. As he was hauled up onto his bed and a warm cloth brought to his face, he silently made a note to talk to his steward about giving Hanley a raise in his salary.

Gripped by thirst, he lunged for the jug brought for washing, pulled it out of the hands of the young and no doubt terrified maid, and gulped it down. He motioned for more, and only after he downed another, did he feel sated in any way.

Only after his ablutions and a cup of the blackest coffee, soundly fortified with whiskey, could Stephen Pembroke, Marquess of Pembroke, finally focus on his surroundings. His footmen righted the armoire, and the maids cleared away the bloodied bedclothes and scurried away. The broken mirror, the tenth he'd smashed over the years, was picked up and his room brought back to some sort of order. Between mirrors and broken windows, if there was no one else in the area pleased about the Beast of Barronsfield; the local glazier was no doubt grateful for the business.

"Hanley," Stephen managed to croak at last. Despite the water he had drunk, his throat was like dust.

"My lord?"

"Do you know...?" God, how he hated asking this. "Have you heard—"

"The vicarage," the butler began, then cleared his throat, pausing long enough to let Stephen know there was more.

"Out with it man," Stephen barked. A stabbing pain forced him to close his eyes. He allowed it to pass, and let out a long breath, remembering some line about not shooting the messenger. "My apologies, Hanley. My head is pounding like the devil. Please, just tell me. Is anyone missing?"

"The vicar is missing most of his hen house, his dog—"

"Oh my God."

"I believe that is what the vicar said, my lord."

Mr. Darling, the vicar, owned a Scottish terrier who followed him happily around the village and was visitor and friend to the invalids and foundlings tended to at the small village infirmary. Stephen's lips twisted in disgust. How could he have killed such a harmless creature?

"Anything else?"

"That is all the news that has reached me, my lord."

A shallow relief set in, but he was entitled to none. It had been five years since the curse had claimed a human life. But it had. Long before his family curse had taken this darker, sinister turn, it had claimed five. There had been blood on his hands for years.

Gripping the side of his bed, Stephen forced himself onto his feet, then signaled for Hanley to help him get dressed. "Right. I will meet with the vicar to discuss compensation for his losses. Has Schofield returned?"

"Not yet, my lord."

"Send word I wish to speak with him as soon as he arrives." Stephen stood, his gaze fixed on the bedchamber door while Hanley tied Stephen's cravat to the butler's exacting standard. He felt like the devil, but he needed to look like a marquess, especially when he was about to go out among his tenants. After a few minutes of Hanley's fussing over collars and cuffs, Stephen waved the man off. He had a parson to speak to. Another set of wrongs to be righted. Another set of rumors to face. It had been months since the old woman's curse had reared its head, but he still felt unprepared for the horror of it. Stephen raked a shaky hand through his hair, and tried to collect himself. Tried to shake off the grip of the Beast.

It was becoming harder and harder to do.

ROSALIND SCHOFIELD HAD VISITED the bright blue waters and pink sand of Bermuda, and once—though she could barely remember it—the rolling tobacco fields of Virginia. But it had been sixteen years since she'd last visited England, and the winding journey from Devon to Yorkshire allowed her to become reacquainted with much of it. Her father, Captain John Schofield, had long promised to take her back, but it was a promise he kept only in death. Both he and his crew had been lost at sea in the North Atlantic. She'd left her late mother's sister and family in the colonies to come into the guardianship of her uncle and take possession of an inheritance that would give her a very comfortable living.

"I am sorry that our meeting is by way of John's passing—he was very proud of you, my girl. Very proud, and I can see why. You are a fine young woman, Rosalind," her uncle said, sitting opposite her in the well-sprung carriage spiriting them to her new home. His countenance reminded Rosalind so much of her father it both pained and comforted her. "I am glad to see you after all these months of waiting since the news." He paused then smiled. "Of course, the last time I saw you, you were naught but an imp, reaching no taller than the last button on my waistcoat."

"It is good to be with you, Uncle." A curious sort of joy bubbled inside her. The unfamiliar feeling begat quiet tears and a smile all at once. Her uncle's genuine pleasure in her company was a new experience. She'd lived most of her life in a bustling household in Halifax with her Aunt and Uncle Stanhope and their three daughters, where there was plenty of company to be had, little of it amiable. Rosalind learned early that a crowded room could be a very lonely place, indeed.

"We are not long now from Barronsfield," her uncle continued in low, rumbling tones. "When we arrive, I will show you to your rooms, and leave you to rest and become acquainted with your new home. Later, if the mist clears, we can take a tour of the grounds, if you so wish."

"I would very much, thank you." She saw the nervousness in his eyes, and reached forward to take his hand. Having a niece to care for, even if she was a grown woman, was new for her uncle, and probably just as nerve-wracking as learning of the death of a beloved brother.

"Barronsfield is one of the most beautiful estates in all of England, and the steward's cottage is very comfortable. I think you will be well pleased with it." Her uncle brightened as he spoke. "I had some assistance from Mrs. Darling, the vicar's wife, as to what would be suitable quarters for a young lady. In fact, she has invited you to the vicarage for tea tomorrow to meet some of the other ladies in the neighborhood. Some of the younger ones will be going on to London too, no doubt, once the season starts, so you will have something in common."

"I am looking forward to all of it." All except going to London. The idea of standing in a ballroom, being looked over—or worse, over-looked—did not appeal, especially at her age. Twenty-eight was well past the prime for having a season.

Rosalind had already spent far too much of her life with people who didn't truly care for her, and to be bound in marriage to one was hardly an appealing fate. Her inheritance had given her an unexpected choice. The large sum could fetch her attention she might not other-wise receive at her age, and a reasonable match. But if she didn't marry, by thirty she would inherit the total amount. She could travel, or own a nice cottage with a beautiful little library, and not have to tie herself to anyone. She settled further into the cushioned bench of the carriage and let out a little sigh. Two years was not so very long a time to wait.

The countryside rolled along, and beyond the stone hedges and fields, the trees were giving up their green color for fall's golden hues. Passing into Yorkshire, the landscape changed, growing wilder with every mile. Craggy rocks and fields abundant with soft heather met a sky that seemed to have reached down from the heavens to touch it. Eventually, rolling fog and mist enveloped the landscape. Occasionally she could make out the ghost of a lone tree in the miasma, and it felt like she was on the road to some otherworldly place.

The carriage lumbered on until it reached the market town of Elmsdale. Thick gray clouds blanketed the tops of the stone and wooden buildings built in the time of Elizabeth. It was similar in appearance to many of the villages they'd already passed, and yet something about it left Rosalind a little disquieted. Lonely signs hung from deserted shop fronts, creaking on ancient iron hinges. Windows were shuttered, and the only sound was the rumbling of the carriage wheels on the cobblestone square.

A quick study of Uncle Reginald's face told her something was amiss. The pink that had colored his cheeks a moment ago had disappeared, leaving a pallor that matched his graying beard.

Ahead, the steeple of an old stone church pierced the mist. Past the church was what looked like a parsonage, where a large group of men had gathered, clearly agitated. Her uncle pounded the top of the carriage with his walking stick, and Rosalind lurched in her seat as they came to an abrupt stop.

"Please stay here, my dear," he said. "I shan't be long." Without giving her the chance to protest, he hopped out of the carriage and was immediately accosted by a rough sort of man, younger than her uncle by perhaps a decade.

"Coming to check out your master's handiwork?" the stranger jeered.

"I have no idea what you're talking about, Tom."

"Don't you start your blubbering with me. We know something is up—something evil, and we mean to do something about it, see?"

Rosalind peered out the window, catching her uncle's gaze. He started walking away from the carriage, but he was soon surrounded by several others who were far too threatening for Rosalind's liking. Her hackles rising, she jumped out of the carriage. A damp breeze wafted a putrid odor in her direction. Overcoming the assault on her senses, she strained to make out the worried, angry voices talking over one another.

The approaching thunder of hoof falls silenced the crowd. Seconds later, a huge black horse appeared, coming to a halt near the gathering. Two dozen heads turned in unison to the rider, who dismounted and strode in among the villagers. The man was taller than her uncle by several inches, and the breadth of his shoulders gave him a commanding presence. His hair, tied back in a hasty queue, was the color of straw in an August sun, contrasting with the heavy, black, woolen cape that hung about his shoulders. A flutter stirred in her belly and she abandoned propriety to strain her neck to get a closer look.

Her uncle immediately went to him. If Uncle Reginald was unnerved by whatever had happened here, he hid it well.

"My Lord Barronsfield."

"Schofield," the rider acknowledged. Rosalind studied the man who she knew from her uncle was his employer, the Marquess of Barronsfield.

The marquess spoke calmly with the vicar, who appeared anything but as he motioned wildly to the carcasses of fowl strewn over the yard and the remains of what looked to be a small poultry house. The upset on the man's long, gaunt face was clear, even at this distance. She tried to pick out the man who'd been so angry with her uncle a moment ago, but there was too much frantic activity to focus on any one person.

"—six geese and at least a dozen chickens."

"—last night. Horrible howling sound. Chilled me bones, it did."

"—heard young Jack Gates saw the whole thing, 'cept he's too scared to talk."

The discordant voices continued unabated. She shook her head. What manner of beast could have caused such destruction and sparked such fear among men of hardy farming stock?

"Gentlemen," the marquess called out with an unmistakable air of authority, and the din quickly settled. The crowd was silent, but the expressions on their faces spoke volumes.

Rosalind watched the marquess as he listened with what seemed like genuine interest to the vicar's tale. The village men were appraising his actions as well, some obviously approving of the way the marquess confronted the ordeal, though far more were hanging back, clearly undecided.

"I assure you this will be dealt with to your satisfaction, Mr. Darling." He shook hands with the vicar, who seemed to have calmed somewhat.

"Our wives are scared, your Lordship." The voice came from the crowd, and several men stepped aside to let one from their ranks take center stage. The man, who looked to be a farmer, removed his cap and took what Rosalind felt for him to be a rather daring step forward. "Folks have been sayin' some horrible things 'bout what goes on at Barronsfield, my lord."

Horrible things? Rosalind stood a little straighter, cocking her head, doubting for a moment what she'd heard. Her uncle had yet to mention anything unusual about Barronsfield. And certainly nothing *horrible.*

"And what things might these be?"

"Just talk, your Lordship," the man said, daring to look the marquess in the eye.

"Look, Harrison," Lord Barronsfield replied, exasperation and fatigue in his voice. "I know you're frightened. There is no man more angry than I about this situation. Everyone should know there hasn't been a lord who dared to call himself the Marquess of Barronsfield who would let any harm come to his tenants or servants." Lord Barronsfield's voice rose above the crowd. "The truths and the falsehoods have all mingled to make this a murky tale, but I tell you Harrison, and every other soul under my protection, that I am doing everything within my power to end this." He put out his hand to the farmer, who took it after a brief hesitation. They exchanged a firm handshake, seemingly satisfying some of the men nearby.

After they were done, the marquess and her uncle started walking toward the carriage, deep in quiet conversation.

Eager not to be caught disobeying her uncle, Rosalind hopped back inside, straightened her skirts, then pulled on the door to shut it. Before she'd had the opportunity to let go of the latch, the door flew open, pulling her off-balance. Rather unceremoniously, she tumbled out of the carriage, landing on the graveled park with a thud.

"Oooh!"

Almost as quickly as she fell, she found herself pulled to her feet by a set of large hands.

"Are you hurt, my dear?" Her uncle asked.

She shook her head, dusted her skirts as best she could while trying to reclaim her dignity.

"Sorry, Uncle. Aunt Stanhope always said I wasn't the most graceful of creatures. I was hoping to prove her—"

"My dear," her uncle began, clearing his throat. "I have the great honor to introduce you to my employer and your host, Stephen Pembroke, sixth Marquess of Barronsfield. My lord, my niece, Miss Rosalind Schofield."

Rosalind's head snapped up, and she stifled a groan. Rosalind had imagined her eventual meeting with the marquess. She'd practiced what to say a thousand times on the journey to Yorkshire. She'd envisioned her graceful address. Yet here he stood, having just picked her off the ground while she prattled on unawares. Heat flushed into her cheeks.

She dipped quickly into what she hoped was the ladylike curtsey she had originally planned for this occasion. The marquess said nothing at first, but stood there, examining her as if she were a new species of cabbage.

Rosalind waited for him to say something—*anything*—to her. She clasped her fingers together and willed her herself still. She shouldn't have been so nervous, but then she'd never met someone of his rank before. This was the devil the townsfolk had spoken of? He looked to be an ordinary sort of man. Well, perhaps *ordinary* was not quite the right word for him. Handsome, more like. His eyes were an incredibly dark brown—nearly black in fact—with an intensity that might have been off-putting if not for the gentle line of his brow. His cheeks were ruddied, and there was a haggardness to him that was unexpected for a man of his stature, yet it leant an air of wildness she found at once appealing and a little dangerous.

"Thank you for letting me stay with my uncle, my lord. It is very generous," she said at last as she tried to control her nervousness.

"Think nothing of it, Miss Schofield," he replied. "Allow me to extend my condolences to you on the loss of your father."

"Thank you," she said, surprised he would stoop to comment on her circumstances.

An uncomfortable silence followed. Every rustle of fabric, every shuffle of boots over the dirt begged for a response. Rosalind's mind raced for something to say, but nothing of consequence was forthcoming.

He pressed his lips together, giving Rosalind the impression he wished to be miles away. Gone was the easy manner present when he spoke with the men in the village, or any hint of the smile she saw when he spoke with her uncle a few moments ago. He was guarded, and even a tad awkward. The tension stretching across his brow suggested he was suffering some discomfort.

"Are you cold, Miss Schofield?" he said at last.

"No, my lord," Rosalind replied, confused.

She cast a glance over to her uncle who casually bounced once or twice on his toes, then with the slightest of nods, gestured to her feet. Rosalind, embarrassed, took the hint. She hadn't realized she'd been bouncing on her toes, an old habit she'd tried without success to banish. "My apologies, my lord. The journey has been long. I can be a horrible fidget when I am forced to sit for any great length of time."

"I was extolling the beauty of Barronsfield on the journey. She is quite eager to explore the grounds, and the village as well," her uncle said.

"Especially the bookshop," she continued, her nerves taking over, speeding up her speech. "I probably should not own to it, but I adore novels and fairy tales, though I suppose they have the admirable quality of keeping me still."

"No Fordyce's Sermons, or Mrs. Chapone's Letters?" the marquess asked.

"Heavens no. I have tried, you see, but then I fidget even more."

His only reply was a smile, but Rosalind caught something in his face that took her breath away. And then, as magically as it appeared, it disappeared.

A whiff of not-so-freshly killed hen brought her back to the mess around her. Trampled feathers littered the damp ground. A flash of brown fabric nearly escaped her notice in the hardening muck. Removing her glove, she bent and pulled the object out of the ground.

"What is that?" the marquess asked.

"I'm not certain. It looks to be a reticule, though a very modest one. Perhaps it belongs to the vicar's wife?"

The marquess motioned to her uncle. "Schofield, perhaps this might be useful to your investigation?"

"Here my dear," her uncle took the mud soaked purse. "I will inquire with Mr. Darling." He exchanged an uneasy glance with Lord Barronsfield before leaving to find the vicar.

Rosalind returned to her scrutiny of the trampled ground, and scrunched her brow in concentration "Do the authorities have any idea of who or what did this?"

The marquess started, surveying her with a new interest. "You have not heard of me."

"I don't—"

"Interesting." The tension in his brow lifted, and something approaching a smile teased his mouth. "Very interesting."

Confused, she cast a glance over each shoulder then back to Lord Barronsfield. His hands were on his hips, his dark gaze fixed on her. Swallowing deeply, she tried to ignore the excitement rising in her chest and push aside any idea that she might be the object of his attention. Feelings like that only ended in disappointment. Luckily, her uncle returned before she could allow herself to be distracted by them.

"My lord, if you would permit me, I will see my niece home and then return to assist with the clean up," her uncle said.

"Of course, Schofield," the marquess said. "I do not wish to delay your journey further, Miss Schofield."

"I hope the villain will be found."

The marquess's mouth hardened into a line. "I assure you, the villain is paying for his crimes." He bowed politely. "I bid you good-day."

Rosalind watched the marquess mount his horse and ride off until he disappeared down the road. A lightness carried her steps as she climbed into the carriage. She settled in, smiling at nothing in particular until she caught sight of the worried look on her uncle's brow as he took his seat opposite her. He smiled, but distress kept the joy from reaching his eyes. The carriage moved along as before, but silence was no longer easy. She had a dozen questions for him.

"Uncle," she said at last, no longer able to contain her worry. "I could not help but notice the rough manner with which some of the villagers were treating you."

"Pay no mind to that, my dear." He shuffled on the bench. "'Tis nothing but the foolish superstitions of simpletons, fueled by bad luck and ale."

The obvious false bravery her uncle put forth didn't make her feel any better. "Does his lordship know?"

"Heavens no, Rosalind. My dear, you must understand. The marquess is a very important man. Now, let's get you home and think of more pleasant matters, shall we?" With that, he continued on about the details of her new parlor as if nothing unpleasant had happened. Rosalind chose to relax and allow herself to be swept up in her uncle's enthusiasm once more. But somewhere in the back of her mind, the threatening voice from behind the carriage lingered.

So did the marquess's intoxicating gaze, a look laced with sadness. She shook her head, chiding herself for even daring to give him a second thought. Though he was flesh and blood, she had a better chance with a mythical prince from one of her books. Or a fortune hunter. That would surely be her fate in London, where a plain girl with a good dowry might find marriage, but not love.

Better to have no marriage at all.

THOUGH THE MORNING fog had dissipated by the time Stephen returned his mount to the stables, the gloom was more reflective of his mood. What a mess. He'd forced himself to stand still when Mr. Darling showed him the broken body of his beloved little terrier, even while it tore at Stephen's insides. And when he heard about Jack Gates, a stone had dropped in his gut. From what Stephen could discover, the lad was hurt, but would recover. Another night like this and even the most loyal of his tenants might turn their backs on him.

Walking across the fields of his estate, the small meandering lane that led to the steward's cottage caught his attention. After years of absolute loyalty and dedication, it was very little for him to grant Schofield the favor of allowing his niece to stay at the cottage with him. But after this morning, he wondered if Schofield might change his mind.

He strode past the rose gardens, their blossoms long spent, thinking about the girl who had traipsed through the Darling's poultry yard, her skirts rumpled from travel. That unceremonious exit from the carriage onto his boots pulled his mouth into a smile every time he reflected on it. He hadn't spent much time around women in the past five years, but Miss Schofield was undoubtedly one of the more unconventional ladies he'd met. Unconventional was fine, but beauty was another matter. Beauty, he had discovered even as a boy, was dangerous for him. And far more dangerous for the ones he'd dared to love.

Miss Schofield would be safe from the Beast's curse. She was neither too short nor too tall. Her figure was pleasant enough; she wasn't thin, nor was she overly plump. Her complexion was neither drab nor brilliant; she had a light sprinkling of freckles across her nose that some might consider charming. Her eyes appeared unable to make up their mind as to color; at one moment they attempted blue, then seemed to settle on a greenish-gray. Her hair was not golden, like Catherine's, neither was it raven black like Anne's. Rather it was a shade of non-descript brown, worn back in the conventional fashion.

She was, without a doubt, one of the plainest girls he had ever seen. She lacked title and privilege and she was perhaps a few years older than the ideal, though still young enough to bear him an heir. At one time he might have been more particular, but he was running out of time. He was willing to forgo his scruples on that point. Barronsfield needed an heir.

He needed the most unremarkable woman he could find. And here she was.

There were no fireworks, no arrows to the heart, no rapturous pangs of any kind, nor even the hint of a note from a choir of angels singing above proclaiming she was "the one." His breath did not catch in his throat at the sight of her, nor did he feel his palms tingle when he picked her up off the ground.

Still, her smile was pleasant. Nothing that set him into raptures, but warm, and even comforting. She spoke as if she had a brain in her head, which might make for pleasant conversation. By the ease of her manner with him, it was clear she was unaware she was speaking to the Beast of Barronsfield, or that such a creature even existed. It had shocked him into silence, and opened him up to the possibility that he would not lose Barronsfield after all.

Yes. She would do. Buoyed by hope, Stephen raced back to the manor, quite certain he could shortly have this whole marriage business neatly sewn up.

By tomorrow.

CHAPTER 2

After a day spent settling into her uncle's cottage, Rosalind returned to the vicarage, this time by invitation. She was eager for the opportunity to meet new acquaintances, and perhaps discover more about the previous day's commotion. Between getting settled in and having her first decent night's sleep in weeks, she'd hardly had a chance to ask her uncle about what had happened. For his part, Uncle Reginald was thrilled she'd already received such a welcome, and insisted upon driving her to Elmsdale himself. The bright blue October sky and crisp air was a stark contrast to the gray damp that had greeted her yesterday. The sturdy cart was not as well-sprung as the carriage she'd arrived in, but her uncle effortlessly guided them along, all the while pointing out various local attractions.

Uncle Reginald gestured to a modest building near the vicarage that looked to have been recently improved. "This is the local infirmary. It is small, but no one in Elmsdale or the surrounding area is in want of a doctor."

"Remarkable," Rosalind replied. An extensive garden lay on one side of the building, rimmed by what looked to be a hedge of roses. "Does every village in England have such facilities?"

"No," her uncle said. "His lordship built it several years ago, in

"

honor of his late mother and sister. They died of typhus when the marquess was a lad. Mrs. Darling helps with the foundlings who arrive at the doors."

Rosalind's gaze stayed with the small hospital, thinking about the powerful man who'd chosen this particular way to honor his loved ones. She suddenly found herself wondering if the marquess, great man that he was, had the same empty spot in his heart left by loss that Rosalind had in her own.

The cart trundled on toward the vicarage. As they approached, she noticed a great deal of the debris in the yard had already been cleared away, and in the brilliance of a sunny afternoon, the two story abode looked as charming and welcoming as any she'd seen.

Uncle Reginald brought the horses to a gentle stop, then hopped to the ground to help Rosalind down.

"You have a lovely time, my dear. I'll be back in about an hour to fetch you."

She bid him adieu, and watched him drive off before entering the Darlings' home. After leaving her bonnet and pelisse with the servant, she was led to the parlor.

"Ah! Miss Schofield. It is a pleasure to meet you at last. May I introduce a few of our neighbors?" The clergyman's wife gestured to the five ladies of various ages already seated around the room. "To your left is Miss Eleanore Martin, our parlor-boarder, and on my right, Mrs. Perkins, and her daughters, Miss Mary Perkins, and Miss Caroline."

Rosalind nodded to the ladies as she took a seat next to Miss Martin. "Thank you for inviting me, Mrs. Darling."

"You are very welcome," Mrs. Darling replied with a warmth that felt sincere. "I hope your journey to Yorkshire was not too taxing?"

"It took many weeks, and I am pleased to be settling in at last. The steward's cottage at Barronsfield is wonderfully situated, and the parlor you helped my uncle decorate is lovely." Rosalind gestured to a nearby window. "The country here is very beautiful, and I am looking forward to exploring Barronsfield."

Her innocent comment was met with a small fit of laughter from the Misses Perkins, while Mrs. Darling and Miss Martin exchanged a look of thinly veiled disdain at their display. The outburst was quickly silenced by a thunderous glare from their mother.

"Please excuse my daughters, Miss Schofield," Mrs. Perkins clucked. "They are excitable things, as young ladies can be. We are all still in a bit of a flap after the unfortunate business yesterday."

"Of course," Rosalind smoothed out her skirt, ignoring the girls' outburst. "Mrs. Darling, I happened upon the destruction on my way to my uncle's. Are there any more clues as to what happened?"

The rattle of teacups and the exchange of awkward glances filled Rosalind with a mix of dread and curiosity. On more than one occasion she'd been scolded by her aunt for asking an impertinent question. Sensing she had done it yet again, she took a sip of her tea and endured a moment of uncomfortable silence.

"Not yet, Miss Schofield," Mrs. Darling said at last. "I have it from my husband that the hen house will be rebuilt and restocked from Barronsfield's own stores by next week. But can we speak of more pleasant topics? Your impending arrival has been the topic of many conversations between your uncle and myself."

"Very many," Miss Martin piped in. "I have been looking forward to this day since the spring, though I am very sorry for the circumstances that brought you here."

"Thank you, Miss Martin," Rosalind said. "Thus far, everyone has been so welcoming, it has dulled the ache somewhat."

Miss Martin was striking in appearance. Her hair was a burnished gold color, and hung in ringlets down her back. She was about the same height as Rosalind, but more slight in her build. There was almost an ethereal quality about her, though nothing in her manner suggested frailty. She was dressed simply in a print cotton dress—a marked contrast to the lace and muslin worn by the Perkins girls, though she appeared to be the same age as the younger of the two sisters, perhaps fifteen or sixteen years old.

Polite conversation about nothing in particular went on for some time. There were careful inquiries after the death of her father, and his record in the navy, the latter of which Rosalind related happily.

The conversation then moved on to life in the colonies, the condition of the roads, new fabrics in dresses, and the hopes for the Misses Perkins' upcoming season in London.

"Are you to have a season, Miss Schofield?" Miss Caroline Perkins asked, clearly caught up in the excitement of the idea.

"I am far past the prime for one," Rosalind replied. "My uncle wishes me to go to London, but after all the traveling I've done, I think at the moment I am quite content to stay in one place."

"But you are an heiress now," Miss Mary Perkins, the elder of the two, chimed in. "You will no doubt have beaux seek you out, even in the wilds of Barronsfield."

Rosalind forced a smile. Of course, they didn't know that men never sought out the attentions of Rosalind Schofield. And with the promise of independence so near, she no longer cared if they did.

Before long, an hour had passed, and the ladies gathered their coats and bonnets, prepared to take their leave. Taking full advantage of the lovely afternoon, they waited in the front park of the vicarage as each of their transports arrived in turn.

"It really has been lovely to meet you at last, Miss Schofield," Miss Martin said, holding a basket on her arm. "And I hope you will call me Eleanore."

"And you as well. I insist you call me Rosalind if we are to be friends," Rosalind replied.

"I would like that very much, thank you." The sound of a clock chimed in the distance, and Eleanore patted the basket she carried. "I should be going. I promised some of the extra biscuits to the kitchen at the infirmary."

Rosalind watched Eleanore exchange a few words with Mrs. Darling before departing. Rosalind felt no particular attachment to any of the ladies, though she did feel she had been welcomed. Eleanore seemed a lovely girl. The Misses Perkins were young and frivolous, though perhaps no different from her own cousins. A small twist of longing settled in Rosalind's chest as Mrs. Perkins fussed over her daughters. The pang of loss flared anew. Recollections of her mother were becoming more distant with every passing year. When she lived with her family in Halifax, memories of her mother and letters from her father were her protection against the loneliness. But the memories were fading. Letters from her father would be no more. Her uncle was her last real connection to him.

Mrs. Darling and Mrs. Perkins stood in the small front park of the parsonage, while the Perkins girls huddled away to one side, clearly knee-deep in gossip. Rosalind stood off a couple of paces, waiting for her uncle to return. The word "Barronsfield" caught her ears, and unable to help herself, she took a few steps closer.

"Caroline!" Mary Perkins scolded her younger sister. "Mother said we weren't to speak of it, you ninny."

Rosalind's curiosity piqued, she walked over to the girls. "Speak of what?"

Their countenance was akin to that of a child caught doing something they shouldn't. Caroline looked beseechingly at her sister.

"Well, I think she can hardly be living on the same grounds and not know of it," the younger one said, hands on her hips. She looked around and seeing her mother and the vicar's wife safely out of earshot, she leaned in closer to Rosalind. "The Beast of Barronsfield."

Rosalind shook her head and the girl's eyes widened in response. Caroline leaned in closer. "The Beast of Barronsfield. I can't believe you don't know of the curse."

"I can scarcely believe your uncle would let you live on the estate," Mary said, then looked Rosalind up and down. "Then again, perhaps a plain woman like you need not be worried. Father won't let me anywhere near him, even if he is frightfully rich. He's spoken more than once of moving us out of the neighborhood."

"I don't understand," Rosalind said, forcing a smile while she tried to gather her thoughts, scattered by Mary's insult. "Beast? Who?"

"The *marquess*, Miss Schofield," Caroline replied, eyeing Rosalind as though she was witless. "He is a monster. He was the Beast who killed the Darling's poor little dog and destroyed their hen house."

"And roughed up one of the mill worker's sons," Mary added in a hushed, excited whisper. "I heard the maids speaking of it."

"Impossible." Rosalind thought back to the day before, when she'd first laid eyes on him trying to calm a clearly distraught Mr. Darling, and the crowd of men who had gathered to see the carnage. "I was introduced to him yesterday. He may have been a bit distant, perhaps, but not monstrous in any particular fashion."

"You spoke to him?" Caroline regarded her with a mix of horror and awe.

"Were his eyes red?" Mary whispered. "Olivia Welsford says his eyes glow red, like a demon from hell."

"No. They were dark. Just dark brown." Deep, dark brown, Rosalind remembered. He had certainly looked haggard, but nothing approaching demonic. Indeed, if anything, there was an aura of sadness about him.

Her companions hardly seemed to be bothered by the actual color of his eyes.

"You must be very careful, Miss Schofield," the younger Miss Perkins implored. "Make sure your bedchamber is secure before you sleep. You don't want to end up like the mistresses of Barronsfield."

"Caroline, you ninny, she's never going to be mistress of Barronsfield. She's barely a gentleman's daughter, for heaven's sake," Mary lectured her sister, though Rosalind had to stop herself from laughing at Mary's self-important display. "Lord Barronsfield has twice taken a wife, Miss Schofield, and each of them lived barely a year before meeting a ghastly end at the hands of the Beast of Barronsfield. They say he is cursed, and every time the marquess falls in love with a beautiful woman, the Beast destroys her."

"So there is a monster living in Barronsfield?"

"The marquess *is* the monster, Miss Schofield," Caroline said in a low voice. "He turns into a horrible creature at night, and does terrible things in the village. An old woman hexed him when he was a boy, and his mother and sister died not long after. They say the night his first wife died, he cursed the witch who'd been the source of his family's ills, and she turned him into the Beast. He nearly killed his valet that very night. Two years ago the Beast attacked our own farmers' fields at Dungate lodge. I wasn't allowed to go near it, but I heard from the maids it was horrifying. One of our stable boys was nearly killed trying to stop him." She grabbed Rosalind's hands, her concern earnest. "Miss Schofield, I beg you to be careful!"

"Girls!" The shrill voice of Mrs. Perkins broke the spell of the intrigue. They turned to see a black carriage pull up.

"I thank you for your concern, ladies," Rosalind replied, not sure whether to be amused or unsettled by the force of emotion set on her by Caroline Perkins. "I am certain my uncle will make every effort to ensure my safety."

The girls bid her farewell, leaving Rosalind alone with her thoughts. The marquess? A monster? She caught her bottom lip in her teeth as she recalled everything she'd seen the day before. She stood not fifty feet from the destruction that had been her introduction to the so-called Beast of Barronsfield. A man who destroyed beautiful women? A creature that attacked his neighbors? What sort of ridiculous story was this?

As the Perkins' departed, a handsome carriage made its way to the front park of the vicarage and stopped near the door. Rosalind glanced over her shoulder, trying not to stare. Who on earth would be traveling in such an elegant transport? When the driver jumped down and opened the door, apparently waiting for her, Rosalind turned to her host and gasped.

"My goodness, is that for me?"

"I think your uncle has decided to give you a treat, Miss Schofield." Mrs. Darling smiled, clearly impressed. "This is quite the indulgence!"

"That it is," Rosalind replied, more eager than ever to talk to Uncle Reginald. How he spoiled her so! "Good-bye, Mrs. Darling. Thank you for a lovely afternoon."

"Thank you, Miss Schofield, it was a pleasure. I hope to see you this Sunday."

Rosalind smiled and forced herself to walk, not run, to the carriage, where she accepted the driver's gloved hand as he helped her onto the plush seats. She'd barely settled into her seat when the scent of bayberry—followed by the sight of a set of rather large black boots —caught her attention.

"My lord!"

"You will excuse me, Miss Schofield," the marquess replied in a low, cool voice. The timbre of it as he said her name created an unnerving sensation in her belly. "Your uncle is consumed by his duties at the moment. I am doing him the favor of seeing to your safe return."

Rosalind shuffled in her seat. Was she expecting to see claws or snarling teeth? Glowing red eyes? Of course not. But she'd not been expecting to see the marquess, either. Being in such tight quarters with his lordship—especially when he was so serious and dashing and so close—was a little exciting. Maybe even a little dangerous.

"I am also here for my own particular reasons," he continued. "Perhaps we might take this moment to get to know each other better." She watched him hesitate, looking for a moment like a caged animal, a curious mix of utter confidence and nervousness.

She pasted on a smile, and folded her hands in her lap to force herself still. "Thank you," she said, while her mind raced for what to say next. Just as she was about to ask about something benign like the weather or crops, he cleared his throat, and leaned forward.

"Miss Schofield, I am here to ask you to consider a proposal of marriage."

"Marriage?" she blurted out. "From who?"

"From *me.*"

"My lord, we—" Rosalind stammered, dumbstruck. "We are barely acquainted. Is this not a hasty move for a lifelong commitment?"

"I assure you, I deliberated quite carefully before making this proposal."

When? Sometime between dinner and brandy?

"My lord, we are complete strangers. Have you not considered, even for a moment, that I might be a wretched choice for your wife?" Her mind raced. "I might have a horrid temperament or other faults that would make me difficult to live with."

"I am sure your faults are quite minor," he grumbled.

"And—please take no offense," she held up her hand, causing Lord Barronsfield to look as though he might take it, "but you may have some insufferable qualities that might make your Lordship unsuitable to be my partner." Like turning into a monster, perhaps?

He stilled, his expression guarded, as if confounded by her answer. But then, Rosalind supposed, invitations to be elevated in society through marriage were probably not often met with protests such as hers.

"Miss Schofield, simply put, I am in need of a wife, and a mother to any future children. I am the sole offspring of my parents' union, and it is my duty to produce an heir." He regarded her closely—too close for Rosalind's comfort. "You seem like a sensible woman, and your father was a naval hero. Surely these are qualities that bode well for any future sons. I realize this appears highly unusual, but I have much to recommend in such an alliance. The name of Barronsfield is one of the most important in Yorkshire and indeed, in England. I offer a great estate and the protection of my name and place in society. Your fortune is of little consequence to me—you may use it as you see fit. I am not a treasure seeker, as I am sure others will be. Surely we can come to some mutual agreement that might suit us both?"

Was this a cruel joke? "But you are—"

"A marquess, I know. And you are the product of a naval captain and a solicitor's daughter. That is of no matter to me, I assure you."

"That is not what I meant, your Lordship." Infuriating man. Insulting man. She fought to keep her exasperation in check. "You are the Beast of Barronsfield!"

Anger flashed in his eyes, and fear prickled at the back of Rosalind's neck at his gaze. Almost immediately his hard glare melted away, and Lord Barronsfield sank back into his seat, his shoulders not quite as square as they'd been a moment ago. He looked a tad deflated, and just a little vulnerable. My goodness—had she hurt his feelings?

The marquess looked over to the window before he continued. "I had hoped to get to you before the stories did. I should have foreseen your uncle would have told you."

"*Get* to me? You may be thrilled to know your loyal steward told me nothing." The regret, along with any unease she'd felt at wounding him, vanished, replaced with anger. Anger at his lordship, and even a little for her uncle. She might have laughed if it were not all so ridiculous. "Forgetting the beastly business for a moment, I believe even a half-hearted attempt at some romantic words might have been in order for a proposal of marriage. You have spoken about nothing but alliances and breeding."

"Romance is best left to books, Miss Schofield. There is little place for it in real life. And as for the magic…" His voice laced with bitterness, he looked as if he were about to swallow something unpleasant.

"The Beast destroys the beautiful women he loves. I assume you believe I would be safe." Rosalind thought back to the stories of his wives, the two beautiful women Caroline and Mary Perkins had told her about. The dismissive look Mary Perkins had given her jarred her memory as humiliation burned into her cheeks. *A plain woman like you need not be worried.*

"Miss Schofield—"

"Please." She summoned up every last bit of restraint she had, even as he trampled her dignity. "I have stood up with my cousins for long enough to know that I am no beauty. But if I marry you, it will be confirmed that I am so—so plain and wretched and unworthy—"

"I need an heir, Miss Schofield. You need protection. Surely we can come to some mutual agreement to suit us both? You must know that once we are married, you will want for nothing."

"I will want for my self-respect." He did not comprehend, did he? The man *was* cursed. Cursed with blockheadedness. "No."

"No?" he choked out. "Miss Schofield, do not be so hasty. This is a great opportunity for you. For your family. And it is not impossible that we would be friends. Indeed, I had hoped that would be the case."

"I am not," she paused, curling her hands into fists at her side, "*breeding stock,* my lord. If that is the arrangement you desire, you will have to look elsewhere. I have no wish to spend my days in a loveless household, or to bring children into such a place." She knew that particular fate all too well.

"I assure you madam," he said in an indignant tone, "I did not view you as 'breeding stock.'"

"No? You just stated that is what you require." She turned away, willing her voice to steady, purposefully unclenching her hands and folding them on her lap. Blinking back the tears, she faced him again. "I have my own fortune. In a few short years, it will be mine to do with as I please, if I do not find a suitable partner. You will have to find greater inducement for me to marry than simply the honor of providing a Peer with a legacy. A legacy at the expense of my future happiness."

He watched her intently, holding her there with nothing but the simple force of his gaze, which softened ever so slightly. He opened his mouth, as if to say something before he turned away.

"Damn," he said under his breath, so low Rosalind barely heard it.

In the next moment, the marquess was sitting beside her. Shocked, she turned to him, but before she had a chance to ask him to remove himself, he lowered his head and put his lips to hers. It was gentle at first, the merest brush of skin, sending a shiver down to her belly. As his kiss began to deepen in intensity, she was shocked by her own need for it. Aware of nothing but his caress, it took all of her presence of mind to remember exactly where she was, and who was kissing her. And why. That was enough to break the spell.

Putting her hands on his chest, she pushed him away.

"Do you take me for a fool?"

"Excuse me?" The confusion in his expression was evident as he sat back, looking almost as shocked as she felt.

"You know exactly what I mean. Do you think I am so starved for a little masculine attention that I could be swayed by a kiss?"

"I beg your pardon, Miss Schofield," he returned, indignant. "I was trying to...to..." It seemed he was at a loss for words.

"Ooooo..." Infuriated, Rosalind closed her eyes, and started counting silently to herself.

"What in heaven's name are you doing?"

"Counting to ten."

"Whatever for?"

"To distract myself from looking for something to throw at your head."

"You wouldn't dare."

"I will if you don't stop talking."

"Me? Oh, that is—"

"Seven. Eight. Nine. Ten." Rosalind let out a long low breath, and opened her eyes. "I believe, my lord, it is clear that we have different expectations from marriage," Rosalind said, in her most polite, businesslike voice. "You must agree that we would not at all suit."

"No." Lord Barronsfield sounded deflated. "You are right, Miss Schofield." He turned his gaze for a moment out the window. "Please understand that my proposal was not meant as an insult. The curse upon me is not something I take lightly. I am only trying to balance duty with certain—realities." He looked up and once again, for only a passing moment, Rosalind could see sadness in his eyes, and her anger lessened slightly.

"Are you certain of these realities, my lord? Perhaps they are tragic coincidence?"

"I am certain that the women I have loved are dead." He sat back, his shoulders sagging slightly. "It is not worth the risk. You should read more Fordyce and less fairy tales, Miss Schofield," he replied, quiet and bitter. "Otherwise, you will find yourself an old maid, still searching for your elusive happiness."

"Every plain girl knows that fairy godmothers are only for their fairer, younger sisters. We have to make do on our own. And so I will, and be quite satisfied." It was a brave front, but inside, her pride was rapidly crumbling. She had always known in her heart she was plain. It had been alluded that she'd failed to inherit her mother's wild beauty, or even her father's handsome features. But not even Aunt Stanhope had chosen to speak it so plainly as this.

The carriage had pulled past Barronsfield Manor when, blessedly, Rosalind saw the lane that lead to her uncle's cottage come into view. She signaled for the driver to stop.

"We are not yet at your home," the marquess replied, now sitting on the opposite end of the carriage, which for Rosalind's taste was still not far enough away. "I should see you to the front park."

"Why? So I can sit here and be further insulted?" The carriage barely came to a halt when she jumped out and onto the dirt road.

"Thank you for sending the carriage for me. I will be quite fine from here."

"I have told you, it was not my intent to insult you." The man actually looked apologetic when he said it.

Her face was heated from the emotion that threatened to spill over into tears, but she was not going to let Lord Barronsfield see the depth of her humiliation. She supposed he could have turned into a monster and ripped her to pieces. Instead, the Beast had torn at her pride. Without looking back, she ran down the road toward home. Could a season in London be any worse than this?

That had not gone as he had expected.

Stephen stood by one of the large windows in his study, a glass of brandy in his hand, still smarting from his provocative encounter with Miss Schofield. On the large oak desk behind him was a half-written letter to his solicitor, and a ledger book that needed to be reviewed, but they lay there, ignored.

The last two times he undertook a proposal of marriage, there were flowers. No doubt the sun had been shining and, if he remembered correctly, birds sang in the trees. He'd been a young lovesick fool with Catherine, though that had faded over time. And Anne had stirred him too, years later, though the sensation was somewhere lower than his heart, he'd later admit. Regardless, two beautiful, gently born women had accepted him.

The third time, however, was most definitely not a charm.

He tried to rationalize away Miss Schofield's rejection, but there was nothing for it. Maybe he should have brought a bouquet today. Then again, it would have hardly mattered. He had not expected such a passionate confrontation. He had not expected confrontation at all.

It had been his idea to ask the girl to marry him, although only a moment into the encounter he began to question his sanity on this point. Maybe he was lucky she had said no. Imagine the noise at Barronsfield. She was looking for a partner. Good lord, he needed a wife. A mother to produce children. Not a partner. At least he would now be spared the awkward conversation with his steward about dashing in and scooping up his niece for reasons Reginald Schofield would know all too well.

Yes, a lucky escape indeed.

Except perhaps for the fire in her eyes as she told him about her hopes and dreams. And the way her bosom flushed when she grew angry with him after that rather ill-advised kiss. He hadn't even intended to touch her beyond a chaste touch of the lips to her hand after she'd accepted him. She'd looked so damn forlorn, and it had been his fault. Kissing her seemed like the right thing to do. And from the way she first responded to him, he'd thought it was. It had certainly felt right. Until, like everything else in his life, it fell spectacularly apart.

Who knew such an unremarkable woman—in terms of birth and appearance anyway—could have such remarkable pride? Such a remarkable sense of her own needs? She spoke about a future for herself. He had never known a woman who thought about her own life in this way.

Turning away from the window, he went back to his desk. Back to the work that made sure Barronsfield continued on, even though his fumbling in the past hour had accomplished nothing but help ensure the estate he cared for so deeply would continue to slip away from him. He lowered himself down into his father's chair, the leather creaking underneath him, and went back to work. Duty bound him to do so, and it was the one thing he had left.

His father had instilled in him from his earliest years—with stern looks and a switch if necessary—the absolute importance of duty. Duty to one's family. Duty to one's past. Duty to the estate. To the Crown. Even his duty to be a father. Thus far, he had failed in that regard. Failed Catherine and their daughter, who had not even taken a single breath before she went with her mother into the next life. It had been with them as with his mother, his sister Imogene, and with his fiancé, Anne.

His love had doomed them all.

CHAPTER 3

Thomas Pembroke was not by nature a patient man, but he prided himself on being a pragmatic, calculating one. If he hadn't been, he would have missed his opportunity to wed the daughter of a Viscount and boost his fortune. Of course he didn't get the title, though the money was a consolation. As for the title he deserved—Marquess of Barronsfield—that was more complicated. Murder, of course, was frowned upon, and aside from the rather unpleasant business of an execution, the title and estates would be forfeit, should such an act be discovered. So he had to be creative, in a ruthless sort of way. That, at least, came naturally to him. Second sons had to do what they must to get ahead.

Ruthlessness was a quality lost on his own second son, Edmund, who seemed happy to be a ne'er do well. Word had reached him only that morning that the boy had been caught in a duel, no doubt over the honor of some female he'd been caught in a dalliance with. So be it.

The focus of Thomas's attention remained on Geoffrey, who was everything that a first son should be. Not everything, perhaps. Thomas had spent much of the morning dealing with a Mr. Newcastle, the father of one of Geoffrey's gambling companions, Roger.

Apparently Roger had the good fortune to win a bunch of money from his friend. Unfortunately for Roger, Geoffrey returned the favor by beating him senseless and breaking at least two of his ribs. In bloody full view of a packed room. It cost Thomas two hundred pounds to persuade Roger's father not to go to the magistrate.

"You called for me?"

Thomas glanced up to see his eldest standing in the doorway. Geoffrey wore the look he had mastered as a boy—a dazzling charm and smoothness in his delivery that belied any other emotion he might be feeling. Thomas would have admired it on another day.

"I did. Where the hell have you been? I trust you've had the good sense to stay away from King Street." Anger reached up into Thomas's throat. He forced it back.

"Staying with friends. A few of them thought it might be better if I made myself scarce." Geoffrey replied as he helped himself to a generous drink and sauntered over to the chair on the other side of the desk.

"Your friends have much better sense than you at least."

"It was not my fault, father. Roger cheated. He needed to learn that he shouldn't cheat a friend."

"And you need to learn to control that bloody temper!"

An uncomfortable silence followed. At least, Thomas thought, Geoffrey had the good sense to know when to shut up. He settled back into his chair.

"I've had a bit of news from the north. Your cousin has a new tenant."

"And this concerns me how?" Geoffrey asked.

"Schofield's niece has arrived. It seems the steward's brother had a rather successful naval career—until recently. The man had a daughter, his only child, and she has come into a tidy fortune."

Geoffrey sat down, stretched out his legs and took a sip of brandy. "She's rich, father, but she's a nobody—a servant's ward. What about bloodlines and all that?"

"My bloodline is likely to end up in the cesspool at the rate you are managing to reproduce." Thomas's jaw tensed as he struggled once again to keep his anger in check. He tried a different tack. "Barrons-field made an offer for her. Her bloodlines were blue enough for him."

Geoffrey was silent. Good. It was about time he paid attention.

"Lucky for you, the girl refused him."

"Well, I guess she wasn't as hard up as he thought," Geoffrey replied, sitting up a little straighter.

"You will be if you don't start paying attention!" Thomas could feel his blood rising. "Pack your things and haul yourself up to Yorkshire at the earliest opportunity."

"Excuse me? I thought you said it wasn't a good idea to be seen to be seen anywhere near Barronsfield."

"Circumstances have changed my mind."

Geoffrey stood, pacing now. "Do you have any idea how bloody miserable that place is this time of year? Any time of year."

"*That place* is the home of a marquess, and if you play your cards right it could be yours," Thomas replied. "Miss Schofield will be staying with her uncle on the estate for the immediate future. So she will be right there, under your cousin's nose. Once she gets a better look at the place she might be inclined to change her mind. You need to convince her otherwise. Besides, it might be better for you if you leave town for a while. In case Mr. Newcastle comes back here and decides he wants more satisfaction than a couple of hundred pounds."

Pembroke saw the flicker of assent in his son's eyes. He was lazy, yes, indulgent, yes. But he understood the stakes. Why settle for being a mister when one could be a marquess?

"Very well, sir. I shall make plans directly," Geoffrey replied.

"Take your brother with you."

His son walked over to the sideboard, drained his glass and deposited it with a *thunk* on the heavy oak. "Afraid I'm going to cack it up?"

"Your cousin—for reasons that escape me—tolerates your brother. And Edmund's indulgences could be useful to us." Thomas said, ignoring Geoffrey's petulance. "While you are there I want you to check in with our man in the village. See what the state of things are.

I've had letters, but I need to know how bad it really is. You're to leave today."

He caught Geoffrey's hard glare, one he recognized with some pride as his own, as Geoffrey straightened his jacket and turned to bid his father good-day. Thomas dismissed his son with no more than a look. Geoffrey would do as he was bidden. In the end, he always did.

❦

ROSALIND SAT ALONE in her bedchamber, wrapped up in a woolen shawl to ward off the chill, idly turning the pages of a small volume of French fairy tales. These were normally among her favorites, but since her encounter with the marquess nearly a week ago, she'd lost a bit of her appetite for them. Stories about beasts and fair-haired beauties, bewitched princes falling in love with the wrong princesses—they did not appeal at the moment.

A gentle knock at her door roused her. She stretched, pulled her shawl tightly around her shoulders and opened the door.

"Uncle, good to see you." Rosalind hadn't seen him most of the day, and found she missed him. "Is there something wrong?"

"Not at all, my dear. I wanted to know if you'd had a pleasant day. I feel like I've been neglecting you," he replied.

In all her years with her Aunt and Uncle Stanhope, Rosalind could never recall them ever making a point of asking her if she'd had a good day. She reached out and gave his hand a gentle squeeze.

"Uncle, you have duties to attend to. I understand you cannot be with me every evening, and besides, Mrs. Irving is pleasant company."

He patted her hand, then let it go. "Well, I will let you continue with your reading. I did not wish to disturb you."

Rosalind bid him good night, then closed the door behind her, her heart lifted with contentment. While she would go back to Halifax tomorrow if her father could somehow return to her, she uttered a small prayer thanking him for uniting her with her Uncle Reginald, even if Lord Barronsfield and his insulting proposal was part of the bargain. As far as she could tell, her uncle had no knowledge of the marquess's proposal, or her rejection of it, and she had no plans to inform him otherwise.

Busy though he was, Uncle Reginald lavished practically every spare moment on his new charge. They took tea together every afternoon, and when he wasn't working in the evenings, they would sit and talk about her father, what she liked to read, and about her life in the colonies. He actually seemed to enjoy her company. And she was coming to enjoy his, very much.

As much as they talked, neither her uncle nor Mrs. Irving spoke a word about the so-called Beast of Barronsfield. Rosalind, still stinging from the proposal, warred between curiosity to learn more and the desire to forget she'd ever heard of the marquess and his curse. The entire thing seemed simply ridiculous.

The marquess clearly believed it, else he would never have stooped to ask for her hand, would he? A fresh wave of humiliation prickled at the memory, churning in Rosalind's stomach. Though she knew very little about him—and was perfectly inclined to have it remain that way—she couldn't imagine how a man like him could be so superstitious.

Casting aside her woolen shawl and robe, Rosalind pulled back the coverlets on her bed. Gently she pulled out the warming pan and crawled under the blankets, wiggling her toes against the sheets, then leaned over and blew out the candle by her bed. The only glow came from the fire in the small hearth across the room, lit to help chase away the October chill, creating shadows that danced on the wall. Still, her bedchamber was cozy, like the cottage itself. If it weren't for its location on Lord Barronsfield's estate, it might be a very nice place to spend the rest of her life. Still, she'd had no occasion to see him since. Perhaps she'd be able to hide away here after all.

With the crackling from the fire to lull her, she felt herself drifting off to sleep.

"Rosalind."

Her name floated on the air, repeating several times, each repetition tinged with greater urgency. Rosalind opened her eyes and searched for the voice in the wind, but the sky was heavy with gloom. Shapes and shadow were her landscape. She stood in the midst of an old ruined church, nearly buried in lush overgrowth. The flutter of white cotton around her legs made her realize she was clothed only in her thin nightdress. A dream, then.

A hand reached out of the blackness, landing heavy on her shoulder. Dream or no, it felt terribly real. So did the terror that ran down her spine.

"Do not be afraid."

The voice, barely above a whisper, did not feel threatening. She turned to see who it belonged to, but in the shroud of night, the man's face was little more than a shadow.

"Were you the one calling me? I can't see you."

"I think that is best for now," he said, a hint of sadness in his voice.

"Who are you? What do you want?"

"Help. He needs help. He's about to give up. He can't, or all is lost, and the Beast will have won."

"He? Who? My uncle?" Panic rose in her throat. "Tell me!"

"Not your uncle. But he will be caught up in it, if we do not help him."

"He who? I don't see why you have to be so terribly elusive," Rosalind insisted. "This is my dream. I would never go gallivanting outside in my nightclothes."

"The secrets are not mine to tell," he said. "And maybe this is real, and everything else is a dream."

"Now that is nonsense. Or, I've been having a really long, exceptionally boring dream," she said, pondering the last few years of her life.

"Is this not real?"

He took her gently by the shoulders, grazing his lips along the length of her neck, and up to her lips. The warmth of his breath on her skin sent a rush of dizzying heat into her belly and down between her legs. His kiss was soft, teasing.

She knew she was dreaming—she had to be—and yet, the shock of feeling the rough, warm, masculine skin against her own, and the urgent but tender crush of his lips on hers brought her to the tips of her toes. Was there one of her waking moments that felt as wonderful as this?

Perhaps one.

He released her. He said nothing, but he stiffened, his stance guarded.

"What is it?" Even as the whisper escaped her lips, she could feel the heat between them being stolen away by some distant threat.

"The Beast," he said in a harsh whisper. "He is getting stronger. I have to go."

"The marquess you mean? Is he coming for you?" she said in a feeble attempt to sound annoyed rather than scared.

"No. The Beast is coming. You have to wake up, Rosalind."

"I don't understand. You are in danger."

"Do not concern yourself with me." He kissed her one last time. "Wake up, Rosalind. Now. Wake up."

Rosalind's eyelids fluttered open. The house was as silent as the dim gray shroud of dawn that surrounded her. She lay in her own bed —not, of course, that she'd actually left it. The only sound was her own breathing. The air was cold and she pulled the blankets over her head to keep warm. She put her fingers to her mouth, the taste of the stranger's lips lingering on her own.

Her uncle was in danger. Was that what the man in her dream was telling her? Restless, she kicked off her blankets, threw her robe over her nightgown and pulled on her slippers. Shaking off the chill, she walked to the window and opened the drapes wide enough to rest her nose against the cool glass. The memory of her arrival in Elmsdale loomed in her thoughts. The threats of those horrid men, whoever they were. They thought Lord Barronsfield was a beast. For heaven's sake, everyone seemed to believe it.

She drummed her fingers on the window sill, trying to ignore the call of the birdsong on the other side of the glass. Dawn started to make its appearance, and soon enough the sun would burn through the mists, and no doubt, her weary thoughts. A walk would be just the thing. She turned away from the window, and found a simple frock, wool stockings and a cape to protect herself against the morning chill. She left her hair down in its braid. She'd only be gone a few moments. Just long enough to clear her head.

She swung the kitchen door open. The morning was damp, and still. She walked along the lane, breathing in the fresh air, allowing it to lift her mood and quicken her steps. Dark forest girded the lane, which seemed to guide her toward the sunrise.

The path curved ahead, and before her the wood fell away, revealing a clearing, and a gentle slope leading up from where she stood. A stone building, wrapped in heavy vines and cloaked in mist, rose on the horizon as she reached the peak of the slope. It was about the size of her cottage, and appeared to be girded with hedges. Three massive windows stretched to the building's full height.

Intrigued, Rosalind meandered through the paths leading up to the structure. Though they were faded now, the gardens she walked through must have been impressive in their full glory. In the low light with the ground fog, there was almost a magical quality to them. The stone path eventually led her to a large wooden door, which stood partially ajar. Gripping the heavy iron ring on the door, she gingerly pushed it open and slipped inside.

She found herself inside an orangery. She'd heard of such things of course, but never dreamed she would actually see one. The air inside was warmer, and heavy with the scent of greenery. Squinting in the dark, she spied exotic plants of all kinds, including fruit trees bearing oranges and lemons.

Past the verge, the soft yellow blush of sunlight crept over the horizon, illuminating a second, smaller room, comprised almost entirely of glass and iron. The heavy scent of roses in bloom guided her to the entry.

Beyond was the most remarkable sight Rosalind could recall. A single rose bush stood as tall as she, covered in heavy, red-pink blooms. She put her nose to one of the blossoms, drinking in the scent, its soft petals caressing the tip of her nose. It would be so tempting to spend an entire day here, hidden away.

The sound of boots on the stone floor jarred her, and she realized she wasn't alone. Peering around the plant, she spied the tall figure of a man approaching. Even though he was simply clad in a wrinkled, untucked shirt, breeches and boots, she knew instantly it was Lord Barronsfield. And he was coming in her direction.

Afraid even to breathe lest she make a sound, she ducked back behind the rose bush, and prayed it was large enough to hide her. He spoke quietly to himself, and she realized to her relief, he had no idea she was there.

"Once again, I have made a spectacular mess of things." There was a pause, and a low chuckle. "I guess I should have read up on a few sonnets. You put your faith in me and I've tried my damnedest to do my duty, and I will to the end. I've tried everything I know to make things right, and…well, maybe it means nothing in the end. My uncle and his line—they are still Pembrokes. That should count for something, shouldn't it?"

This was not the snarl of some demonic creature. Lord Barronsfield's voice was soft, even warm, tinged with a hint of melancholy that touched her. Then, to her horror, she heard the sound of his boots moving around the bush. Toward her.

Heart pounding, she stepped softly in the opposite direction, inching toward the entry as the shuffling of the marquess's footsteps approached. As soon as she was close enough, she bolted through the entry way, hiding in the thicker greenery of the orangery. To her relief, her escape seemed to have gone unnoticed.

At least to the marquess. From among the plants burst a small mutt, leaping enthusiastically up on her legs with muddy paws, wagging its tail and generally happy to make its presence known. Rosalind, who most definitely wanted to keep her presence here unknown, bent down to quiet the canine. She bolted upright again, peering over her shoulder to see if she had been discovered. Seeing no sign of him, she closed her eyes and let out a small breath of relief. Without another word, she turned to get away when she was stopped by two large, very masculine hands holding her firmly in place.

"What in the name of hell are you doing here?"

The words, cut with anger, pinned her in place as firmly as his grip. She was almost afraid to look up, lest she discover she was in the clutches of the Beast after all.

"I said, what are you doing here? You have no business here! Answer me!"

Rosalind opened her mouth, but her voice deserted her. Lord

Barronsfield had a firm grip on her shoulders, his partly exposed chest only a foot from her, and his gaze, dark and thunderous, bore down from above. His face was rough from a day's growth, his hair dampened and askew, and in his casual dress he looked more like a laborer than a Peer of the Realm.

Fear welled inside, and in a moment of panic, Rosalind struggled against his grip and kicked him in the right shin. The shock of it caused Lord Barronsfield to loosen his hold enough for her to break free, and she bolted.

Her moment of triumph, however, was quickly spent. She had probably not gotten ten feet when he grabbed her from behind and picked her up as easily as if she was a rag doll.

"Let me go!" she yelled, flailing in his arms. The dog, now barking madly at the marquess's feet, only added to the mayhem.

Seconds later Rosalind found herself on her feet, turned around, still firmly in the clutches of the Marquess of Barronsfield.

"Are you finished?"

At the sound of his voice—commanding, but lacking the anger of only a moment ago, Rosalind stopped. Nervous energy still coursed through her, but trying to outrun him was pointless. He knew exactly where she lived. Goodness, he *owned* the place where she lived.

Rosalind nodded in reply, then felt his grip loosen, but she was still being held firmly in place by his powerful hands.

"Now, I will ask you again," he said, his tone more measured. "What were you doing here, and at this early hour?"

"I was out for a walk. That is all."

"You were following me."

She narrowed her eyes. "Believe me when I say that you are the last person I wish to follow."

His gaze was soft but unreadable. He let her go and raked a hand through his hair. "Your uncle can give you a proper tour at a more reasonable time. Just stay away from the roses."

"I wasn't going to hurt them. They are lovely."

He shook his head and turned away. She wanted to ask why he was so protective of them, but the marquess hardly seemed in the mood for conversation.

"I apologize for intruding on your privacy." She darted ahead of him, making for the door.

"Have you suddenly become familiar with the grounds?" he called out to her. "I will walk you some of the way back to the steward's cottage. Let's hope we are not discovered, Miss Schofield, or you may find yourself a bride after all."

A pit opened up in Rosalind stomach as she looked up at him with not a small degree of panic. He approached, his dark eyes fixed on her. The memory of his kiss came back with full force. A kiss of desperation, she reminded herself.

"You are not going to tell him, are you?"

"Your secrets are not mine to tell."

Startled, she looked up at him, the phrase catching in her memory. She wanted him to repeat it, but he looked straight ahead, and continued walking toward the door. Rosalind tried to find something to say that didn't sound like inane babble, but soon gave up, deciding to endure the silence. All the while she couldn't resist the temptation to steal a glance or two up at him, studying his profile with a new found interest. Trying not to stare, she considered the way he'd tilted his head when he spoke, and noted that the top of her head came to the same place on his shoulder as the stranger in her dreams. *Impossible.* She tore her gaze away, and walked along side.

And wondered.

CHAPTER 4

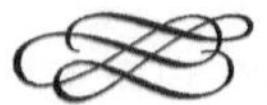

Embarrassment replaced the anger that had gripped Stephen a moment ago. For days following an episode, sleep eluded him until his body forced him into oblivion. He'd risen early, escaping the manor in a vain attempt to clear his head. He should have known he'd find his way back to the antechamber of the hothouse.

It was hard to say what unnerved him more—that Miss Schofield had been watching him, or that he'd been so involved in his own turmoil he hadn't noticed.

He was furious when he found her near his roses. He'd been followed in the past, spied on by servants and others trying to get new stories about him. As he towered over her, he'd seen the utter panic in her eyes. Panic, which dissolved into shame. Shame that she was intruding, that she was somewhere she wasn't supposed to be.

But never fear. She did not swoon or faint at the sight of him. Didn't dissolve into tears. She didn't even scream. She looked him straight in his eyes. There was a vibrancy about her, a sort of restless energy he had never before encountered in a woman. Catherine had only seemed to have energy when she was having an angry fit, and Anne had kept her vibrancy for her lover.

He cast a glance over at her. Miss Schofield kept a careful distance from him, looking straight ahead as they walked toward her home. A long, thick braid of hair curled over her shoulder and down her front. The silence, Stephen decided, was uncomfortable, though he was at a loss for what might constitute pleasant conversation at such a moment. Of course, Miss Schofield seemed perfectly content to ignore him. They left the hot house, and he led past the gardens to an ancient pathway skirted by an old crumbling wall and stands of trees.

A warble of a whistle rose up from beside him, mimicking the birdsong coming from the trees. Apparently Miss Schofield found the silence uncomfortable as well.

"I've never met any ladies with that particular skill."

She stopped.

"My lord?"

"You can whistle."

She paused a moment. "My father taught me. Does it bother you?"

He shook his head. "It's an interesting thing for a father to teach his daughter." The tentative smile on her face stalled, and wondered for a moment if he had given offense.

"My aunt wasn't happy he taught me. She used to lecture me all the time on how it was particularly important for a girl like me to exhibit as many ladylike qualities as possible." She faltered slightly.

"A girl like you?"

"My mother was a very beautiful woman, my lord. She was quite renowned for that, in fact." She paused for a moment. "She had bright green eyes, a lovely little nose and lustrous, red hair." She let go a sigh, as if caught between a memory and a wish. "My aunt never failed to remind me that I should concentrate on developing other qualities that might attract a husband."

"I see." Did he ever. He found he was suddenly rather uncomfortable with himself. He'd behaved like a bloody cad, hadn't he? He knew absolutely nothing of her when he'd proposed, except that her arrival had been a selfish opportunity. No better than the treasure seekers that would soon be circling her. Was this the depth to which he had sunk?

Ever so slowly the sky began to brighten, enveloping the two in a swath of soft mauve mists. It was a magical, peaceful moment, walking along the lane that led to the steward's cottage. The naked branches of hundreds of trees rose about them. The air was still, and there was no sound between them except the movement of their feet on the dirt underfoot. She had even stopped her whistling.

"Miss Schofield." He paused, struggling with his words. "I believe I owe you an apology."

"Please—do not feel obligated." Miss Schofield turned toward him. "I should be the one to apologize."

The sun started to rise and it seemed that ribbons of its fiery glow were caught in her hair.

"No." He shook his head, and felt himself about to reach out to her, then suddenly thought the better of it. "I—"

"I didn't know about the roses."

"No, I—"

"For tackling me then?"

"No." Dear God, could he finish a sentence?

"—because again, that really was my own—"

"Miss Schofield!" He couldn't help it.

"Why does everything you say come out as a growl?"

"Excuse me?"

"Everything—well, not quite everything—comes out as a growl or a snarl. I don't understand. Your voice can be quite gentle and civil on occasions." He could see she was scanning her memory. "Like—at the vicarage, for instance."

He started, amazed by her appraisal and, frankly, that she dared to share it with him, although he was quickly learning to expect that from her. "Thank you, Miss Schofield. I trust I didn't snarl too much with my tenants."

"Not at all. Or, at least, not too much. Would your uncle be the snarling type?"

"Excuse me?" Miss Schofield, he could not help but notice, was brilliant at taking sharp left turns in conversation.

"Your uncle. I heard you speak of him back there. He would succeed you as marquess, would he not?"

Stephen nodded.

"And would he snarl at his tenants if he were in your place?"

As a boy Stephen had watched his uncle take a walking stick to the back of a gardener that dared to look him in the eye as he strolled past.

"Some would say that my uncle is not as indulgent with those beneath him as others might be."

"As you might be, you want to say." The sensibility in her words belied the playful manner in which she spoke. "Are you having an attack of modesty, my lord?"

"Perhaps." He couldn't help but laugh.

"I wonder how your tenants would feel about having your uncle as their master," she continued, thoughtful in her address. "I am far from a radical, but I would think that happy tenants and a good, fair master are the key to a successful estate."

"Assuming I die tomorrow—which I have no intentions of doing, Miss Schofield—even then my uncle would probably not be marquess for very long. He is older than I by many years, and not in the best of health. It is more likely that my cousin would be the next Marquess of Barronsfield."

"And is he a good, capable sort of man?"

No. As much as Stephen wanted it to be true, it wasn't. Unless Geoffrey had calmed the temper Stephen had witnessed when they were younger. Edmund maybe, Geoffrey's younger brother. He was barely out of school, but seemed to have a good head about him. If he'd been free to bestow his title there, Stephen might not have invested so much time and energy into finding a remedy for his curse. But he was not about to air his concerns to her. "It is not for me to say. Perhaps."

"But you are. So it is a good thing you are marquess, then."

"A marquess without hope of a legacy, Miss Schofield."

"My lord, there is always hope if you wish there to be."

Perhaps he was tired, or maybe his patience was wearing thin. Or maybe he had spent the last five bloody years chasing down every possible end to this madness without any satisfaction. Maybe he was simply tired of failing.

"You wish for me, Miss Schofield. I am done with hope."

The girl, for once, went silent. Stephen watched as she turned away from him, and he found himself needing to continue to talk to her.

"Miss Schofield." He stopped and touched her shoulder. As she looked up at him, he could see the discomfort in her eyes. Gently, he took her hands in his own. She did not pull away, but stood there with great hesitation. "I wish to apologize for the proposal I made to you earlier, and for any hurt you may have suffered on my account."

"But—"

"Would you please let me finish?" Now that probably came out as a growl. No matter. It seemed to do the trick, as she was stunned back into silence.

"I told you my reasons for singling you out. But they were *my* reasons. There are many other viable, eligible young men in England and I am sure that many of them would find you a lively, attractive partner." And probably a much better one than I, he added silently.

"My lord, please."

"Do not feel slighted as a result of my actions. My curse."

He inadvertently held her hands to his chest, desperate to force her attention on him. Her hands were cold from the chill air, and her cheeks were flushed. When he first met her, he couldn't remark on her eyes. In the growing light he noticed they were the most remarkable shade of green, marked with bits of brown and rimmed in blue. They reminded him of some fine Venetian glass beads he had seen in Italy years ago. But those eyes were hiding something from him, and her countenance became one of studied nonchalance.

"I care not. I have barely thought of it since. I have not the slightest intention to marry." She pulled her hands away, and bent down to quiet the dog that barked at his feet, then looked down the road. "Well then, I see the cottage is just yonder. I will make my leave. Good morning to you."

He watched her go, at first walking, then bolting down the lane, her new canine follower at her heels. By the time she got back, he was sure she would be breathless. A boon for Schofield then—he might get to eat his porridge in peace.

By the time she reached the cottage, Rosalind was out of breath. She pushed down on the iron latch of the kitchen door, wincing at every creak as it swung open. The dog had followed her home and darted inside.

"Good morning, Miss."

Rosalind whipped around, mortified at being discovered. "Emily!" Blowing strands of wayward hair out of her face, Rosalind attempted a nonchalant smile. "Good morning! I went for an early walk and found this fellow on my travels." She gestured to the mutt at her feet.

"He's a cute little thing, but so dirty!" Emily frowned, looking at the small brown and white spaniel with its pug nose, ears too long for its little face and a tail that never seemed to stop wagging. "I'm just getting Mr. Schofield's breakfast ready. Why don't you put the pup outside, Miss, and I'll bath him later on. Looks like he left half his dirt on your dress."

Rosalind glanced down. If she'd been caught at home like this, she'd have been forced to do all the mending for a week. But this was home now, wasn't it? An intense satisfaction at the notion settled in. She patted the dog, and put him outside with a promise of scraps and a walk later in the day.

"You must be chilled to the bone, Miss Schofield." Emily clucked, beckoning Rosalind to sit by the fire as she poured her some hot chocolate.

"Thank you, I'm fine. I hadn't gone far." Not too far, anyway. Rosalind accepted the steaming cup of chocolate and savored the thick, rich liquid as it warmed her insides. "Has my uncle been asking for me?"

"He's just sat down, but I believe he has plans to go into Elmsdale this morning. I'm sure he would be pleased if you wanted to go with him," Emily replied as she took a pan of bread out of the oven. "Why don't you go up to your room and I'll bring up some warm water for washing."

Rosalind bounded up the stairs and ducked into her room.

She pulled off her cloak, looked down at her dress and sighed. Indeed, she was a fright. She sat on the edge of her bed and plucked at the odd yellow leaf clinging to her hem.

What must Lord Barronsfield think of me? The question popped into her head, unwelcome as it was. She would much rather the marquess forgot the entire unpleasant business of his proposal, which clearly made him as uncomfortable as it made her. She'd been flabbergasted to discover, as he stood there alone, speaking to his own ghosts, that it was still very much on his mind. Maybe even more so. She wanted to put the entire humiliating business behind her. When he did apologize, he'd gripped her hands so earnestly, holding them close against his chest. The feeling of his skin under her hands had so distracted her it had taken all of her wits to think straight.

It shouldn't have been so comfortable to be with him. Firstly, he was supposed to be cursed, but she was having a hard time swallowing the idea. More to the point, he was a marquess and she was a nobody, but as they'd walked together, she'd nearly forgotten it. There was something…familiar, if that was the word, about him. The tilt of his chin in the shadows, the way he walked. Something.

Rosalind plopped down on the edge of her bed, absentmindedly twirling her long plait of hair as she tried to remember the dream that had woken her. No doubt it was her own bit of wish fulfillment. A lonely, plain girl wanting to be romanced by a handsome stranger. And seeing how the marquess was the most handsome man she'd ever met, perhaps she unconsciously thought about him in that way. *Ugh. How pathetic is that?*

A quiet knock and the sound of the door opening interrupted her thoughts as Emily bustled in with a pitcher of warm water and towels. While Rosalind washed, the housekeeper tided up her room and made her bed, then helped her to dress.

"If you'd care to sit, Miss Schofield, I'll fix your hair."

"Thank you, Emily." Rosalind sat at the dressing table while the housekeeper undid the braid and began brushing out Rosalind's tresses.

"You do have lovely hair, Miss Schofield, if you would permit me to say," Emily said.

The comment made Rosalind start.

"Really?" Lovely? One of her cousins had once referred to it as the color of weak tea. Never, ever, was it or anything about her…*lovely*. Solid, maybe. Or polite. Whatever epithets people saved for the girls destined to spend assemblies holding up the walls.

"Aye. It just needs a good brushing, is all," Emily continued.

The sound of the bristles moving through her hair soothed Rosalind. She closed her eyes, and, in spite of herself, her mind wandered back to her earlier encounter with the marquess. It wasn't his eyes her thoughts lingered on, dark and sad though they were. Nor the little lines around his mouth that appeared when he was clearly trying not to say what was really on his mind. No. It was something else.

His hands.

They were large and powerful, yet gentle. When Lord Barronsfield had taken her hands in his, the gesture had startled her at first. The earnestness in his touch felt genuine—as if the weight of his words wouldn't be enough. They were perfect, like his dark eyes and the smooth, deep timbre in his voice that sent a shiver through her each time he said her name.

His intentions for marrying her, certainly, had been far from perfect. But his hands?

She held up her own, which were marked all over with small scratches from the dog who'd been struggling in her arms only a short while ago. There was a little cut on her left thumb from when she'd tried to escape from the marquess and fell.

His hands were perfect. Perfect for a man who only two nights before had supposedly destroyed the Darling's pet and hen house. A sturdy wooden structure, fowl with sharp beaks and feet, and a dog, perhaps small, but with teeth and claws of its own.

"That doesn't make any sense."

"Excuse me, Miss?"

"Sorry, Emily, I was thinking aloud." Rosalind sat up a little straighter, suddenly full of questions. "Do you mind if I ask you something?"

"Not at all."

"I want to ask about the Beast of Barronsfield." She could tell, as she gazed into the mirror at Emily's reflection, that the housekeeper was taken off guard by the directness of her request. "Excuse me for the question. I am a curious soul by nature—to a fault, I have been told—but I am not a gossip. I heard stories at the vicarage yesterday, and I want to know the truth."

Emily waivered, then continued, her voice a little less booming than before. "You might as well hear it from me, as I've no doubt you'll hear plenty a tale in the town, each wilder than the last. I shan't lie to you—strange things have been going on in Barronsfield for near about seven years. It started not long after her ladyship died. After Miss Wickwire's accident, it has become much worse. That was near five years ago."

"Miss Wickwire?"

"The master's fiancé."

"I thought the marquess had two wives." That was what Mary Perkins had told her. But then, Miss Perkins was also certain Lord Barronsfield's eyes glowed red.

"No, Miss. He was married to a Lady Catherine Hazleton. A real beauty she was too. She died birthing, along with the babe." Emily paused a moment, as if in respect. "He was engaged to Miss Anne Wickwire about two years after. Hair like black velvet she had. Men from all over England wanted her."

"And how—" The words caught in Rosalind's throat. The question had escaped her before she could help it, and she scrambled to correct herself. "Sorry. Not my business."

"Carriage accident. It was a horrid night."

Rosalind couldn't help but notice there was less sympathy in Emily's tone, but left it.

"What happens when the Beast comes out?" Rosalind asked. "Things like what happened with the parson's hen house?"

"Aye. Like that. Or worse."

"Does it happen often?"

Emily stopped for a moment, tapping the hairbrush to her chin while searching her memory. "It used to be once, maybe twice a year, but it's much more often now."

"And has anyone ever laid eyes on the creature?"

"Tom Gates—he works down at the mill—claims to have caught a glimpse of it once. And Jim Harper, but when he's not smithing he's as drunk as a lord, so I wouldn't put too much salt to his words." Emily said.

"So how do they know that the Beast is the marquess?"

Emily pressed her lips together, and Rosalind could see at once that the housekeeper was having difficulty choosing her words.

"It's what happens to the master. That's the nasty part of it all, Miss Schofield. No one can explain that away. We all tried at first, your uncle most of all."

"Explain what away?"

"The next morning he's a frightful mess. His room is half in pieces. Clothes torn, furniture broken, and blood everywhere." Emily shook her head, as if she didn't want to believe it. "It was so the night before you first arrived. I heard it from the cook himself. Horrible screaming in the night from behind the master's door at times, then nothing." Emily shook her head. "It took four servants hours to clean the room. The carpet was so drenched in blood, it was completely ruined."

"That's horrible!" Indeed, it sounded dreadful. "Does anyone ever try and stop him?"

"His valet left years ago. Hanley, his butler, tends to him now, and he wouldn't say a word. And he'd be too old to stop the marquess, be he a beast or not." Emily shook her head. "They lock his lordship in his rooms, at the master's orders. They've even tried tying him down, but none of it seems to matter. He's tried potions and spells, but it's only gotten worse. And the poor master is always sick afterward, his eyes all red, and feeling low for days and days. Like it's stealing a bit more of his soul every time."

I have blood on my hands, Miss Schofield. The morning Rosalind had come to Elmsdale, according to Emily, he'd awoken in that very state, hadn't he? As she thought back to when she first saw him, he had seemed flushed, and a bit drawn.

"And everyone knows." It was supposed to be a question, but it came out of Rosalind's mouth as a statement. Servants talked. Everyone knew that.

"It used to be a much bigger household. Servants—some—fled, terrified they would become a victim. People started to talk. Only those most loyal stay now. We lost another just days ago—a scullery maid. Just a young thing, so maybe it was no surprise. There's barely enough of us to keep the house running. Half of it is shut up as it is."

"How on earth did this happen?"

"Haddie Walton. She was a local healer woman, and a very practiced one. She lived in a cottage on the edge of town, and had a garden that housed many plants to ply her trade, including roses. Even Barronsfield had nothing to rival her little gardens." Emily paused a moment, as if searching back into her own memory. "The marquess, then but ten years old, stood outside Haddie's cottage, aloft one of his ponies, holding a wooden sword, swinging it over his head for all the world to see, demanding a rose from Haddie, as was his right as marquess."

Rosalind couldn't help but smile at the image.

"Haddie was furious. They were her prized roses—a special sort, supposedly brought to her by some French nobleman when she was young. Hard to grow in Yorkshire, but she managed it. She stood on the stoop of her door, brandishing a broom, and said 'You are naught but an imp, and you have no rule over me.' And with that, his little lordship trampled through her herb garden, and hacked away at her bush with his little wooden sword, taking what he believed was his to take."

"You speak as if you were there," Rosalind answered.

"I was, Miss Schofield. I was a young woman then, perhaps a little older than you are now. My mother had sent me over to fetch a potion for her. Woman's troubles, you know. I watched as the young Master Pembroke destroyed Haddie's beloved rose bush. She couldn't touch him, you see. Not her place. But when he was done, she looked at him, pointed an old, boney finger in his face, and gave him a look that would have drained the fire from even a dragon's heart."

"'You did not heed me, young master,' Haddie said in that cracked old voice of hers. 'I curse you! Curse you for stealing my beautiful roses! Do you not see that by plucking that beautiful thing, you have doomed it to an early death? I curse you, Stephen Pembroke, that you shall no more be able to keep that which is beautiful—it too shall perish at your touch. Enjoy your rose, for it is the only beauty that you shall be able to keep. The rest is lost to you.'"

"Heavens me," Rosalind whispered. "I think I would have fainted dead away."

"It did seem a little harsh, even for Haddie. Two days later the marchioness—his lordship's mother—fell ill from typhus and died. His sister too. Haddie was horror struck," Emily recalled.

The women were silent, the only noise coming from the bristle brush going through Rosalind's hair.

"What happened to her?" Rosalind asked after a moment.

"Haddie?" Emily said. "She died some years later. Her cottage was not far from where the infirmary is now, but it burned. There's nothing left of it now, save the roses. The master took those. He protects them like nothing else on this earth, but you should see if your uncle can sneak you to the hothouse, Miss Schofield. They are a sight."

Rosalind grimaced. She'd sneaked herself in, and the marquess had been furious to find her there.

"Do you think there was any magic in her words Emily?"

"Haddie was a strange and wonderful woman. She had a great knowledge of herb lore and healing. Beyond that, I dare not say. She was an outspoken woman, an eccentric and even occasionally an angry one. But vengeful?" Emily shook her head, then paused for a moment. "I can't ever recall that. I think she would have been happy if she thought she had scared a wee bit of respect into the marquess, young as he was. Beyond that bit of satisfaction…no."

"Do you fear the marquess?" The question came out almost as a whisper.

"Not at all." Emily's back straightened as she spoke. "He is as fine a master as ever was at Barronsfield. Looks after his servants and his tenants. He's a good man, the marquess. Maybe even a cursed man. But still a good one." Emily looked down at Rosalind and smiled as she put the last pin in her hair. "There you go, miss. Very pretty."

Rosalind took the woman's hand. "Thank you Emily, I promise not to utter a word."

Rosalind waited for the Emily to leave, then let out a long breath and slumped in her chair. What a tale. Could it all be true? It must be.

Rosalind shook her head. His hands were unmarred. And he didn't seem particularly vicious or beastlike. Nor did he feel evil in any way.

Maybe she didn't want to believe it. Maybe Rosalind found it kinder to believe everyone else was a little cracked than to believe she was that homely.

Because that's what Lord Barronsfield needed, didn't he? An ugly wife. An unlovable wife. He needed her.

CHAPTER 5

By ten o'clock, Rosalind and her uncle were on their way to Elmsdale. Whether it was the brilliance of the clear blue sky, or the normal commotion of a market day it was hard to tell, but the place had lost the pallor that had hung about it the day she'd arrived. There was the bustle of a typical morning in a small town—traders coming to bring their wares, the brewmaster haggling with a man in the street over the price of hops. Several ladies were out buying ribbons and bolts of fabric for dresses. She even saw Mr. Darling leaving the bakery, a loaf of fresh bread tucked in his arm. Her uncle pointed to a stone building on the corner of the square.

"There's Turner's—that's the probably the first place you'll want to see."

"Is that the bookshop?" Rosalind's heart leaped in excitement. She studied every detail of the red and gold sign that hung above the door. "My own selection of reading materials is woefully thin."

"Indeed, it is a small circulating library. The collection is modest in size, but rich in content. Barronsfield has supported it for some years now, though I admit I rarely use the place." Her uncle brought the cart to a halt, then hopped down before helping Rosalind onto the cobblestone square. He gestured to a shop window down past the bakery where she'd seen the vicar. "Now, I have to run some errands. Do you see that shop there? That's Oliver's—the best teacakes in all of Elmsdale, if I do say so myself. What say we meet there by eleven?"

"Sounds perfect, Uncle." Rosalind had spent half of the trip allaying her uncle's concerns about being unchaperoned and the second half listening to the litany of places that she should not go to unattended. She set off, excitement and anticipation nearly lifting her feet off the ground.

Rosalind watched the cart disappear down one of the small lanes of the village, then turned her attention to the square. There were plenty of shops worth exploring, but Turner's Circulating Library was first on her list. Determined to come out with at least a couple new stories to read, she made her way to the front door.

Through a dusty window, Rosalind spied row upon row of books. More, in fact, than she'd seen in a very long time. An hour hardly seemed enough time to browse them all. The door groaned as she pushed it open, fresh air rushing past her to greet the stale air inside the shop. The odor of tobacco and dust tickled her nose, and Rosalind fought the urge to sneeze.

There was no one in sight. She took a couple of steps forward, flanked by bookshelves laden with tomes of every size and description, and, she could see, in several languages as well. As she walked through the shelves she scanned the titles—*The Aeneid, The Odyssey,* Greek Tragedies, and on through to Chaucer, Milton and John Donne.

Turning the corner, her jaw dropped a little as she discovered long sought after books that started her heart racing—*The Castle of Orantano,* and *An Arabian Tale.* But one volume, its spine of red leather with gilded detail, caught her attention. Gently, she slid the book off the shelf and opened the cover. It was old and worn, its cover brittle at the corners. The book's spine creaked in complaint she opened the book to reveal its title. In an elaborate script it read: *On Mythik Creatures and Beasties.*

Gently, she thumbed through the thick, hand-sewn pages, carefully examining woodcut images displaying every type of beast imaginable, and even a few that she couldn't have imagined—or wanted to —before. Each was more fantastical than the next. There were dragons and faeries, massive snakes and creatures that looked to be the amalgam of several animals all at once. As she thumbed through the pages, she caught a glimpse of a strange creature that looked to be half-man, half-wolf. Hmmmm.

The were-wolf is a—

Before she could read the next word, the book was snatched from her hands and snapped shut.

"Not suitable."

Rosalind looked up, mouth opened to protest, when she came face to face with a sharp set of eyes that peered out from under the most remarkable set of eyebrows she had ever seen. Two gray masses of hair that should have softened the pronounced brow line only served to highlight that the wig he wore, which had no doubt seen better days, sat a tad forward, so that his forehead appeared almost non-existent. Sunken cheeks, a pronounced chin and an almost total absence of lips made his appearance even more ridiculous.

The brusqueness of his actions took her so off guard it took her a moment to find her voice. "Excuse me?"

"This book," he said in a voice that managed to sound bored and irritated all at the same time, "is not suitable for ladies."

"Why ever not?"

"Because it is full of information that is too excitable for the female temperament. That is why it is in the *gentlemen's* section," he replied in an officious tone that grated on Rosalind's good mood.

"I see," Rosalind replied, careful to keep her voice polite. "And where, pray, is the ladies section?"

"This way." He led Rosalind over to a bookshelf immediately to the right of his desk. "All the suitable books are here. All specially chosen." He seemed particularly pleased with himself on that last point.

Rosalind blinked.

She scanned the meager display. *The Compleat Housewife. A Letter of Genteel and Moral Advice to a Young Lady. Female Conduct: being an Essay on the Art of Pleasing.* The list went on. A few she remembered as being particular favorites of her Aunt Stanhope. "Eleven books? And two are the same title!"

"Fordyce is particularly popular with young ladies," he said, pulling a copy off the shelf. "Would you like to borrow it? Of course, you will have to get a subscription, and you'll need your husband's permission to—"

"I'm not married," Rosalind said, forcing an exaggerated smile if only to keep from screaming.

"Then your father—"

"My father is dead."

"Well, you must be in the care of some—" he started to insist before Rosalind's patience was spent.

"Thank you sir, but I've read Fordyce. Once was more than enough." She pointed at the old red book in his hands. "If I had my guardian sign my subscription, could I borrow this?"

"Absolutely not!" He replied, quite taken aback by the very notion.

"Why not?"

"As I said," he eyed Rosalind as if she was either deaf or an imbecile, "it is not suitable. Women are too excitable, too delicate, for subjects such as these."

"Actually, sir, what gets us 'excitable' are dodgy old men trying to tell us what makes woman 'excitable' when they clearly don't have the foggiest idea about a woman's constitution in the first place!"

"Miss Schofield."

Rosalind stiffened at the voice coming from behind her. The sound of the marquess's boots on the wooden floor quickened her heart as they drew closer and closer. "Please don't abuse Mr. Turner for his ignorance on the subject. Understanding a woman is one of the great mysteries yet to be solved by man."

"Good morning, my lord," she replied, a little puzzled by his presence, yet relieved to see him. If anyone could help her with Mr. Turner, it was the marquess. Didn't her uncle say that his estate supported the library?

"Good morning. I saw you come in, and hoped Mr. Schofield might be with you."

"My uncle had some business to attend to, but I am meeting him at eleven o'clock. Is there a message you wish me to take to him? I can seek him out now, since I am apparently not going to get anything useful from here."

"It is nothing urgent, Miss Schofield," the marquess replied, looking back and forth between her and Mr. Turner, who took Lord Barronsfield's silence as an invitation to speak.

"My lord," the proprietor named Turner said, with deference. "It is an honor to have you grace the establishment after such a very long time. I have been educating this young lady as to our subscription and lending policies."

"Lending policies?" Rosalind choked. "One hardly needs lending policies for such a paltry reading list. Surely Mr. Turner can keep track of ten titles?"

"I believe there are eleven," Lord Barronsfield replied, looking past her to the small shelf.

"I see. Eleven. That is so much better than ten." Rosalind fumed. "I believe I have read all of the books that are in the so-called ladies section. And more than a few of the titles sitting over there, as well." She pointed over to the shelf behind her which housed a number of classics.

"Those books are not suitable for females. Look what it does for their temperament. Makes them quite unladylike," Mr. Turner said, his face reddening.

"My temperament is fine." Was she spitting? She was almost mad enough not to care.

"Miss Schofield—"

Rosalind turned back to the marquess, who seemed almost amused by her outburst.

"Mr. Turner has run this establishment since my father endowed it."

"And no one has bothered to check in and see if he is doing a proper job of it?" Rosalind ignored the gasp she heard escape Mr. Turner at her outburst. "I cannot imagine why a man of your character would wish to support an establishment full of volumes denied to Elmsdale's women."

"Are you questioning my judgment, Miss Schofield?"

Her eyes locked on the marquess's and for a moment she couldn't pull away. He seemed to have gotten closer—so close, she could almost feel his breath on her skin. For a moment it felt like they were the only two people in this small space. The sound of Mr. Turner's voice reminded both of them they were not.

"I think eleven volumes are quite sufficient," Mr. Turner said, his voice cracking slightly. "Enough for a well bred lady."

"If you would care to read those titles, my lord, you would notice that two of these volumes are copies of the same book." She pointed at the shelf. "My education was sufficient enough to do simple calculations like that."

Rosalind closed her eyes and started counting to ten under her breath. She could be reasonable, couldn't she? As her eyes opened, however, she could see the look of faint amusement in Lord Barronsfield's dark eyes suddenly harden, scuttling her efforts.

"I have little doubt a woman with your temperament can count, Miss Schofield," the marquess answered, his gaze still fixed on her, robbing her of her confidence. "How else could you get by in polite society without keeping your mouth closed and counting to ten?"

Rosalind opened her mouth, but her voice deserted her. She felt herself redden as a queer sensation—a sort of a dull ache astonishingly like disappointment, crept into her chest and squeezed. It was if Aunt Stanhope stood before her, belittling Rosalind regardless of who looked on. Years of being subject to such censure had trained Rosalind to respond. She shifted her gaze from the marquess, unable to bear his censure. With as much dignity as she could muster she turned to Mr. Turner, and tried to ignore the look of triumph on his face.

"Mr. Turner, I am sorry for taking up your time."

Head up, not caring to spare Lord Barronsfield a glance, she walked away. For a moment, she almost wished herself back among her cousins. With them, she had been simply ignored. While not the most enjoyable of sensations, at least it hurt less.

CHAPTER 6

Rosalind stood outside Turner's Circulating Library, humiliation and disappointment prickling under her skin. Wanting a moment to collect herself, she turned to make sure the marquess wasn't behind her. Through the shop window, she watched what looked like an intense, and perhaps uncomfortable, conversation between the marquess and Mr. Turner. *What on earth?* As their faces turned in her direction, she darted away. The last thing she wanted was to have the marquess right on her heels. Facing him again was more than her already wounded pride could cope with.

She squared her shoulders and decided to get on with her morning. She walked two doors down to *Mrs. Darymple's Fine Goods*, deciding it as likely a place as any to find a distraction. She was about to grab the door handle when a white gloved hand beat her to it.

"Allow me," came a warm male voice from behind her.

Rosalind glanced over her shoulder, about to say a quick "thank you", when the words caught in her throat. The owner of the gloved hand stood behind her, giving her the most dazzling smile.

"Thank you," came her reply at last. Hopefully, this handsome stranger wouldn't find her completely daft. She'd probably been making doe eyes at him.

"It is my pleasure, I assure you," he said, a cheerful expression on his face. "It is always a pleasure to be of service to lovely young ladies."

His eyes, which were of the clearest blue Rosalind could recall, were stunning. So stunning in fact, the awful encounter with the marquess and Mr. Turner evaporated under the man's appreciative gaze.

"Excuse me," she said once she managed to recover herself. "I am in your way."

"I could never imagine that being the case." He stepped back and with a flourish, gestured to the door, allowing Rosalind to enter as if she were being ushered into a grand salon.

She stepped inside, her heart newly aflutter, unsure of what to do or where to look. It was difficult to concentrate on her surroundings while being preoccupied with the task of recalling when any man had ever looked at her in such a way as this gentleman stared at her now. And he was *still* watching her. She walked over to the far side of the counter and absentmindedly began looking over a display of bonnets. Sensing he was behind her, she turned to greet him.

"We meet again, sir."

He bowed deeply. "Geoffrey Pembroke, at your service."

"Rosalind Schofield." *Pembroke?* The name put her on her guard, and she opened her mouth to ask him about his connections to Barronsfield when the gentleman took her hand and lightly kissed it in greeting. The kiss was quick enough, but he lingered with his eyes in a way that threatened to rob her of her senses.

"A pleasure," he replied. "Now, which of these bonnets will you be taking? Or will you be like my mother, and unable to choose, take them all?"

My goodness, he was so artless. It was hard to know whether to distrust his smooth manner or let herself be swept away. After the bruising she'd just had at the hands of the marquess, Mr. Pembroke's attentions were more than a welcome salve. Thankfully, she managed to hold on to her sense of propriety. "I do not think I will be taking any."

"Well, let's see shall we?" Mr. Pembroke pronounced with a comically exaggerated air, plucking a straw bonnet from the rest. "Try this."

Rosalind accepted it and fitted it on her head. She looked in the mirror, and could see him smiling back at her.

"Well?" she asked, unsure of what to think.

"Beautiful."

The word hung in the air. "Really?" Her response slipped out unintentionally, released by her own disbelief. The bonnet looked pretty, certainly, but beautiful?

"Absolutely," he replied. "As a connoisseur of bonnets, I would stake my reputation on it."

Rosalind looked again, not entirely convinced. Suddenly conscious of the time, and how much she was enjoying this shameless flirtation, she felt a new urgency to leave.

"I really must be going," she said.

"May I be so bold as to ask if you would allow me to show you some of the highlights of Elmsdale?" he said.

He looked so sincere, she relented.

They strolled toward the village square, where Rosalind spied Eleanore Martin, laden down with an overabundance of packages, waiting patiently by the small trickling fountain in the square. She looked to be in need of an extra set of hands.

"I thank you for the offer of the tour, Mr. Pembroke," she said, then gestured to her new young friend. "But I really should see to Miss Martin."

"Of course! Let me assist," he replied brightly. "A damsel in distress is my weakness."

Rosalind laughed at Mr. Pembroke's enthusiasm, flattered by his attentions. She walked toward Eleanore and waved to catch her friend's attention. To her delight, Eleanore smiled brightly in return, though her attempts at a wave were scuttled when one of the many packages in her hands started to fall. Before it could hit the ground, Mr. Pembroke bounded ahead and caught it.

"Thank you sir," Eleanore said. "That was very kind of you."

"Let me help you, Eleanore." Rosalind helped herself to several of the packages in Eleanore's arms. "And allow me to introduce Mr. Geoffrey Pembroke. Mr. Pembroke, this is Miss Eleanore Martin."

"It is a pleasure, Miss Martin," Mr. Pembroke said. "I am not thirty minutes in Elmsdale and I have been introduced to not one, but two lovely ladies." He turned again to Rosalind, looking at her in such a way that sent heat rising into her cheeks.

"I have some news you both might find pleasing," Eleanore said. "There's to be an assembly on Saturday evening."

"Really! That is…delightful." Rosalind could see the excitement on Eleanore's face at the idea, but after a steady stream of disappointment at such assemblies, Rosalind had learned that keeping one's expectations low was the best defense against the inevitable disenchantment they invoked. However, judging from Mr. Pembroke's smile, her feelings on the matter were not shared.

"It sounds like a capital way to spend an evening," Mr. Pembroke said, looking rather expectantly at Rosalind. "Miss Schofield, I have it in my head that you should dance the first two dances with me, and I can be a terrible whinger if I don't get my way."

"That would be lovely, thank you," Rosalind said, certain she going to float away with excitement. Dancing. And not pity dances. Not dances to be endured because someone forced their brother, son, or nephew to dance with her because they felt sorry for her. Deliberately looking away lest she appeared too eager to receive the attentions Mr. Pembroke gave, she stared out into the square, trying her hardest to keep her feet still, when she noticed a familiar face in the crowd. Rosalind groaned inside as she recognized the marquess. Despite the frivolity of the past few minutes, Lord Barronsfield's conduct at Turner's still stung, but it was too late to hide from him now. He was heading straight for her, as if on a mission. Mr. Pembroke broke into a smile.

"Well, isn't this a pleasant surprise. Here comes my dear cousin and lord of the manor." He held up a hand, waving. "Barronsfield!"

Cousin. Of course they were cousins. It would be her luck that Mr. Pembroke would have Lord Barronsfield as a relation. She wanted to disappear.

The marquess strode through the square, trailed by a succession of curious looks and whispers directed his way. He stared straight ahead in that impervious way of his, but it must have been worn on him to be the subject of so much rumor and fear.

"Pembroke," the marquess said, his voice polite and businesslike. "I received your message this morning. This is a pleasant surprise." Rosalind frowned; he didn't sound pleased at all, only surprised. "How was your journey?"

"Rough as always," Mr. Pembroke replied in the same bright manner he'd displayed with Eleanore and Rosalind. "But a trip to Barronsfield is always worth the wear and tear, especially when there are such lovely sights to see." He looked at Rosalind, who tried hard not to blush though she was certain she failed.

"Miss Schofield, Miss Martin," the marquess bowed slightly.

"Lord Barronsfield. An unexpected pleasure to see you again so soon." Rosalind said it as politely as she could manage, which was, on the whole, not terribly polite at all.

"I was in search of you, but I see that you have found other company."

In search of her? Why? To insult her further? Rosalind pressed her lips together, glancing up at Mr. Pembroke, and then to Lord Barronsfield, whose gaze darted from Rosalind to his cousin. His manner disquieted her. He seemed almost disappointed, though with what, she couldn't begin to say.

His presence, even in the open air, was daunting. He loomed on one side of her and Mr. Pembroke on the other, both looking down on her. For a girl used to being surrounded by men and not being of consequence to any, it was suffocating to realize she was being keenly watched by two of them. Not to mention confusing.

"I was becoming acquainted with your cousin, my lord. By chance we met after I left Turner's," she replied, watching him carefully.

"Well, I do not wish to interrupt your morning. I—" he stopped short and looked over at his cousin. His expression stiffened. "I was hoping to speak with my steward, and thought that he might be in your company. I see he is not. I will leave you now."

Curious. He'd already asked her about her uncle when she was in the library. Had he forgotten? She was about to call attention to his error when Lord Barronsfield bowed, then hesitated, apparently waiting on Mr. Pembroke.

"Do you wish to accompany me?" he asked his cousin.

"Of course. I should be off then, ladies, given that my illustrious host has arrived. I look forward to seeing you both this Saturday." Mr. Pembroke bowed to Rosalind and Eleanore.

"Saturday?" Lord Barronsfield stopped. "What happens on Saturday?"

"An assembly, my lord," Rosalind replied.

"I don't dance," the marquess blurted out. The words hung in the air for a moment, awkward. If Rosalind didn't know better, she would have thought he was nervous.

"Good lord, Barronsfield, you must get out more," Mr. Pembroke said. "But perhaps the good people of Elmsdale prefer it otherwise." He laughed at his own joke.

Rosalind started. Though the marquess's stance never changed, she caught his flinch as Mr. Pembroke spoke. She didn't know what to think of Mr. Pembroke's intent, but it felt wrong. And familiar. Like every sly, backward compliment she'd been handed during afternoon tea by her aunt or her aunt's friends, the so-called friendly jokes at her expense, dealt by well dressed women with polite smiles on their faces.

"Perhaps," she said, consumed by the need to answer Mr. Pembroke's charge, "Lord Barronsfield has been much occupied with his duties, making it difficult for him to get out as much as he would like." She cast a quick glance at the marquess. His mouth dared to turn up for a moment as he caught her eye, before looking away again.

Her thoughts were interrupted by bells from the local parish ringing out. "I promised my uncle I would meet with him by eleven," she continued, looking to Eleanore. "Eleanore, perhaps I can help you search out Mrs. Darling?"

"Perhaps, Miss Martin, I can send someone for you," the marquess offered.

"Thank you, my lord, but Mrs. Darling will be here for me shortly."

"Well then," Lord Barronsfield continued. "I will take my leave."

"Good-day to you," Mr. Pembroke said, bowing to the ladies once more. "I look forward to our dance on Saturday, Miss Schofield. And to you too, Miss Martin, if you are so fortunate to attend."

"Thank you. So do I." Rosalind felt the weight of the marquess's dark gaze as his cousin spoke. She grabbed the edges of her cloak, fiddling with the ribbon, suddenly self-conscious. She watched the two men depart, and let go an audible sigh of relief.

A moment later, her uncle appeared, perched on his cart, Mrs. Darling beside him.

"Here you both are!" he boomed as he hopped down. "Rosalind, we have been invited to the vicarage for some nourishment."

Uncle Reginald helped them into the cart, and they were off. As they trundled farther away from the square, Mr. Turner's Library, the red book and Lord Barronsfield dimmed in Rosalind's mind, replaced with the promise of a dance.

STEPHEN UNSTOPPED the brandy and poured three glasses, feeling ever so slightly put upon by the company in his study. He handed heavy crystal glasses to Geoffrey and Edmund, who had joined his brother for a visit. Edmund dropped in on him occasionally, but rarely stayed for too long a time, and didn't need much tending to. Geoffrey, on the other hand...Stephen had been shocked by his cousin's visit. Pembroke thrived in London—the women, the cards, the clubs. Certainly, Geoffrey and Edmund were family, and Geoffrey was practically next in line, but Stephen rarely received guests since Anne's death and he'd become accustomed to being alone in the house.

"Excellent," Geoffrey said, taking what Stephen thought was a rather large sip of the expensive liquor. "So tell me, Barronsfield, why did the Schofield girl turn you down?"

If Stephen had been less familiar with his cousin's ways, he would have blanched at the boldness of the question. Geoffrey had always been less than mannerly. He could thank his father for setting the example. Still, it nagged at Stephen. *How the hell did Geoffrey know?* He couldn't imagine Miss Schofield making his proposal public knowledge. Of course, Geoffrey could have charmed it out of her. He was gifted that way. Still, the idea that Miss Schofield might have fallen under his spell was…disappointing.

"That is between myself and Miss Schofield," Stephen said. "I expect there are at least three different stories making their way to London as we speak, each one more ridiculous than the rest."

"Four, actually," Edmund piped in with a smile that told Stephen his cousin had his normal sense of humor about him. "Don't worry, I've told everyone they are all lies. Pistols at dawn to anyone who besmirches the name of Barronsfield."

Stephen almost laughed aloud at the carefree loyalty of his young cousin, the only relation whose regard he could abide for any length of time. "And have you had any challenges?" he asked.

Edmund shrugged. "Everyone knows I'm a crack shot," he boasted with the confidence of youth, then held up his glass in salute.

"So Miss Schofield is free then?" Geoffrey asked. Geoffrey's persistence on the subject of Rosalind Schofield was a little off-putting, but Stephen couldn't decide what was more bothersome—Miss Schofield's refusal, or Geoffrey's interest in her.

"As far as I know," Stephen replied. "Unless she's managed to snag a few more offers in the past week. The girl's got ten thousand pounds to her name. That's liable to attract more than a few suitors." Stephen quieted for a moment. "Do you intend to make her an offer?"

"Me? Don't know. I hadn't given her a thought until I met her today." Geoffrey shrugged, downed his brandy then got up to help himself to another. "But she does seem to be a rather charming sort of woman. You don't mind, do you?"

"I have no claim on her," Stephen gripped his glass a little tighter.

"Good. Far be it from me to try and scoop up one of your paramours," Geoffrey turned with a flourish, the challenge in his expression unmistakable.

"Careful, Geoffrey."

"Anne meant nothing to me, Stephen. It wasn't you're fault she went after your title. That's all women want, you know. Ready to throw their lives away for one." Geoffrey took another long sip on his glass, then cocked an eyebrow. "Except Miss Schofield. She might be a little less fussy, given her plain looks and respectable fortune."

Stephen sat riveted to his seat, fighting to keep his temper under control. It had been five years, and still Geoffrey knew exactly what buttons to push. "I never knew you had designs on Anne. If I had, I would have never made an offer. You know that." Not that it mattered. Anne didn't really want either of them. What he'd seen in her, beside the brilliance of her eyes and the luster of her hair and skin, he couldn't recall. Beauty had been his weakness. It was still his curse.

"Well, it's all past now, isn't it Barronsfield? Gone. Dead and buried, actually. Time to move on to more lively subjects, like Miss Schofield, and her fortune."

Geoffrey was savoring this, damn it. Stephen watched Geoffrey in silence for a moment. Then, with more control than he remembered having, he smiled back at his cousin. "How's your luck been at the gaming tables, Pembroke?"

Stephen watched his cousin's placid face contort for a hair of a second before returning to its normal carefree expression.

"You know how it is Barronsfield. You win some, you lose some." He walked over to the window and looked out over the expanse of roses that rimmed the manor.

"How about win some, lose more?" Edmund said with a laugh.

"Not all of us are content with a staid life of study, Edmund," Geoffrey snapped. "Some of us need challenge, excitement in our lives."

"I can ask father to buy you a commission, Geoffrey, and you could go find some challenge in India, or the Canadas," Edmund replied.

"We both know who father would rather see at the wrong end of a Frog's rifle," Geoffrey sneered.

Stephen sipped his brandy, watching Edmund carefully, but the younger Pembroke gave his elder brother no satisfaction. Stephen had known for a long time that among the two brothers, Geoffrey was the preferred son. Edmund had grown up his entire life knowing it. Stephen was amazed that a man so young—Edmund was barely into his twenties—could handle his situation so maturely. Still, the flush of blood in his cousin's face did not escape Stephen's notice.

After Hanley showed his visitors to their rooms, Stephen went to his library, his personal entrance ingeniously hidden behind a wooden panel in his study. The library was his sanctuary—the place where he conducted no business except the pleasure of reading. Absentmindedly, he paced in front of the massive bookshelves lining the walls. His father was an avid collector of books, and Stephen, nursed on Homer and medieval tales, had grown to appreciate the wonder, and lately the refuge, he found in a good book. It was his father's idea and funds that helped set up the circulating library in Elmsdale.

He paused for a moment, recalling Rosalind Schofield's argument with Mr. Turner about the rather pathetic selection of "suitable" books available to her. The man had been unquestionably rude to Miss Schofield.

And, he pained to think it, so had he.

It wasn't supposed to be that way. The very last place Stephen had wanted to be today was in the streets of Elmsdale. The encounter with Miss Schofield in the orangery still played on his mind. Her innocent question about his uncle's manner with his tenants had shattered Stephen's carefully constructed rationale about giving up. He was still marquess, and he needed to be out where his tenants and neighbors could see him. Even if they feared him.

When he'd caught a glimpse of Miss Schofield looking through the window of Turner's library, he'd thought to maybe say hello, and in a friendly way, inquire about how she was enjoying her stay. But none of that had gone as he'd imagined it would.

He'd found himself faintly amused by Miss Schofield's outrage with Mr. Turner. When she'd challenged him about his reading habits, he'd been contemplating the freckles across her nose. In her excitement at Stephen's comments she had moved closer and closer to him. So close, in fact, he could see the errant strands of hair kissing her flushed cheeks. To his shock, he had to restrain himself from the overwhelming urge to brush those strands of hair away behind her ears.

Fight the need to know how soft her skin might be as he brushed it with his lips.

It scared him half to death. She wasn't beautiful—how could he even have those thoughts? True, he'd barely touched a woman in years. And he did have needs, passions. Love had nothing to do with those.

But he had to put a stop to those passions before they got the better of him. So he'd turned his thoughts elsewhere, and allowed himself a moment of cruelness. It was safer that way. For both of them.

She'd said nothing, but the humiliation on her face was plain enough. He would have rather she had yelled or struck him, but she did neither. Instead, he'd cut the voice right out of her. Regret gnawed at him as he watched the girl swallow what little pride remained, say a few kind words to Turner that the man didn't deserve, and leave.

Bastard, he was.

Stephen stood in front of one of the many bookshelves that lined his most treasured of places. He scanned the shelves—no Fordyce's sermons to be found. He vaguely remembered a conversation with Turner, probably two years ago now, who had been so pleased to have acquired not one, but two copies. He wondered if any of the young women in the village —Eleanore Martin, for example—ever dared darken the door of the library.

He didn't know. Over the past few years he had increasingly shut himself off to all but a handful of people. As the curse manifested itself, he only came out to clean up the messes—not to be among the people whom he, as the Marquess of Barronsfield, had sworn to look after. His father's legacy, indeed.

Stephen strode to the window. It was early afternoon, and the shadows were already lengthening. There seemed to be less and less light in his life, but he could acknowledge that he was partly to blame for the shadows.

His gaze fell to a heavy oak stand that held a huge, red, leather bound tome. Turner had held that big red book in his hands, the one he had kept from the curious eyes of Rosalind Schofield. When

Stephen left Turner, quaking in his boots and under threat to re-think his lending policies, that big red book left with him.

He sat down at a small writing desk, and rooted around for ink and some paper. He never conducted any business in the library, but this wasn't business.

It was so much more.

CHAPTER 7

*E*mily and Rosalind were in the garden, where they had spent most of the late afternoon gathering cabbage, parsnips and apples. Uncle Reginald was attending to business at the manor, and would not return until dinner. Even Dreyfus, Rosalind's newfound furry friend, had wiggled under the gate and disappeared.

"You're not going to tumble out of that tree now, Miss Schofield?" Emily called out.

Rosalind looked down through the branches of the apple tree and saw the concern in Emily's eyes. Since Rosalind first arrived at the steward's cottage, the housekeeper had fussed over her in a way she could hardly remember having experienced. It was not the urgent, anxious fussing about making sure one's hems were ramrod straight, or that her hair was pulled back so tight she thought her head would ache. She'd had plenty of that and more to spare back in Halifax. No, this fussing was something new, and surprisingly welcome.

"I'm fine, Emily. Just a few more apples and you'll have enough for a lovely pie." Rosalind reached up for the plumpest of the apples still hanging on the branches of the grand old tree.

"Be careful, my dear. I'll go see to the stove and then be right back out to help you down," Emily said, then went inside the cottage.

Rosalind focused on her task, pushing through the leaves, pulling on the branches as they gave up the last of their bounty. The autumn breeze brushed cool up against her skin, and there was little noise except what nature provided. This was such a pleasant place. Except, she frowned, for those horrible men who'd cornered her uncle when she'd first arrived. And all the nasty whispering about the marquess and his curse. It was some queer secret that everyone knew of, but no one spoke of beyond a hush. She still didn't know quite what to make of the whole affair. Thus far it seemed that everyone was convinced of their own version of the truth. Was there something wrong with her that she could find so little to believe in any of it?

Barking pierced the quiet, startling Rosalind. Dreyfus must have gotten tired of chasing rabbits and returned.

"Dreyfus," she called out. "I'm right here, you silly thing."

The dog answered with more barking. Rosalind shook her head, plucked another apple, and cradled it with the others in her apron.

She examined one of the fruit, then took a bite, savoring its tartness while Dreyfus ran around below. She propped her back up against one of the larger branches and enjoyed the sounds of the birdsong and the wind through the drying leaves. Less enjoyable was the barking, which was growing louder by the minute.

"Dreyfus!" Rosalind scolded, her patience tested. "I promised Lord Barronsfield you'd be no trouble. You cannot make a spectacle of yourself."

Silence was the dog's reply. Pleased at having been listened to—if only Mr. Turner could have been as obliging—she started down out of the tree, which was proving a much more difficult proposition then getting up into it. Her boot slipped on one of the branches, causing her to lose her grip and drop a few of the fruit.

"What on earth?" A disgruntled voice exclaimed from below. A familiar, disgruntled voice.

Rosalind froze, then closed her eyes, and wished Lord Barronsfield away. What on earth was he doing here? She stiffened, suddenly unsure of herself, grasping onto the tree with one hand, and her apron with the other.

"Hello?"

"Miss Schofield," he said, peering into the branches. "Why on earth are you up there?"

"Getting apples. Mrs. Irving and I thought we'd surprise Uncle Reginald with a nice apple tart. I'll come down." She fumbled for a moment, trying to figure out how to do it with one free hand and an apron full of fruit.

"Are you in need of assistance?" He looked up at her, a curious expression on his face.

Rosalind grimaced. There was no way to jump down without dropping all the apples, or making a less than graceful spectacle of herself. "You don't need to trouble yourself. Emily will be in here in a moment to help me down."

"Put your hand on my shoulder." He stood near her feet, and held out his arms to her. Carefully, Rosalind bent her knees, and lowered herself until one of her hands rested on his shoulder. A moment later, he took her at the waist, and lowered her to the ground.

"Thank you," she said, a little breathless, though she knew it had nothing to do with any exertion on her part. A tingling sensation rippled through her, lingering at her waist where his hands still rested. "You saved the apples."

He paused, then let her go, and stepped back, looking around the little front garden as if he didn't quite know what to do with himself.

Dreyfus ran back through the yard, jumping up on Rosalind's skirts.

"You've found a friend," he said. "I hope you are comfortable here." There was a vulnerability about him that disarmed her. He looked as bewildered as she felt. It made Rosalind's heart ache just a bit, almost against her will.

"Very much, thank you. It is more lovely than I could have imagined," she said, and she meant it.

The marquess surveyed the cottage, the dog, and Rosalind. She put a hand to her forehead, smoothing a stray lock of hair. What was he doing here? And what was she to do with him?

"Shall I ask Mrs. Irving to bring out some refreshment, or would you like to come in?"

"No. No thank you. I am intruding." He pulled a small envelope out of his coat. "I only came to bring you this."

She hesitated for only a few seconds then took the envelope from his hand. It was hard to look him in the eye. Unlike Geoffrey Pembroke's dazzling gaze, Lord Barronsfield's dark stare touched her in a way that stirred a fire in her belly.

"It is an invitation to come to the library at Barronsfield Manor," he said. "The collection is quite extensive, and I believe you will find the lending policies to your liking."

She ran her fingers over the fine paper and the wax seal. "Thank you."

"I also wanted to apologize for my comments to you earlier today. It is not a normal part of my character to be so rude. It was beneath me, and I am sorry. I went off in search of you after you left Mr. Turner's establishment to beg your forgiveness, but you were already engaged."

"Honestly, my lord, I had no idea that it wore on you so." She remembered the single-mindedness in his approach, and the discomfort as he stood there, watching Mr. Pembroke making her and Eleanore smile with promises of dances and assemblies. Her pride still stung from the marquess's proposal, and it was easier to remember he was the cause of that pain when he was being obnoxious. But his apology today rang true. Clearly he'd been troubled by his behavior, and she gained no satisfaction knowing he was in distress. "There was no need to go to such lengths to apologize." She held up the envelope, and offered it back to him.

Lord Barronsfield held up his hands. "Please, Miss Schofield. There are some parts of my nature over which I have little control and yet they do a great deal of damage. But rudeness? That, at least, I should be able to manage." The disgust in his voice was tangible. He bowed, then turned to leave, when curiosity got the better of Rosalind.

"My lord!" she called out. "Please. Don't go. I have something to show you." She untied her apron and set the apples down on the ground, then taking in a quick breath, she reached out and took one of his hands in her own. The shock on his face was evident, though he did not pull away.

"Miss Schofield—"

"Shhhh." Rosalind busily examined his right hand, then his left. She heard a small sigh of exasperation escape the marquess, and tried not to be distracted by the heat and intense masculinity radiating from his skin. She dared not look up until she had completed her task. After a minute of examining every part of his broad, strong hands, his long fingers—and ignoring the persistent desire to bring them up and cradle her face in them—she looked at him with a satisfied smile.

"Ah-ha! I knew it. My lord, look at these." She held his up hands, then reluctantly released her hold on him, the echo of his touch lingering.

"They are my hands, Miss Schofield. I look at them everyday," he said, clearly not understanding her enthusiasm.

"But you do not see them. Have you noticed how perfect they are?" Rosalind held up her own for inspection. "Look at mine. See this scratch? And here, here's another one from when I fell out of the carriage a few days ago. And this mark on my thumb, that's getting Dreyfus out of a barrel—"

"Pardon me, but I don't—"

"Look." She took his hands again, silently relishing the warmth of his skin. He watched her intently now, and the fluttering in her belly continued. "Not a scratch, not a mark, except for a little scar on your left thumb that looks like it's been there for ages."

"A fight when I was at Oxford. I fail to see—"

"My lord, I don't know how you—or any creature—could rip apart a wooden hen house with its bare hands and not even have a splinter."

The marquess stopped, and pulled his hands away. He looked anew at his fingers, as if he'd never seen them before.

"The thought occurred to me this morning. And—I wondered if you had ever noticed that," she said, looking up at him for recognition and receiving none, trailed off. He was too engrossed in his examination.

"No," he said at last. "No I hadn't." His gaze found her, and held her as motionless as if he had his arms around her.

The creaking of the front door opening jarred their attention.

"I have intruded upon your privacy long enough," he said. "I hope my offer to visit the library is an appealing one."

"Yes," she nodded. "Very appealing, thank you."

His face broke into a smile, the same beautiful smile she'd seen in the vicar's yard and she could not help but return it. He picked up the bundle of apples wrapped in Rosalind's apron and gave it to her. "I should go. I would not want to deprive my steward of his dessert."

He left, leaving Rosalind flustered and nervous. She wanted to drop the apples and run along the lane with Dreyfus to burn off the energy coursing through her. Instead, she let go a long, steady breath and dared to look over the hedges, but he'd already disappeared.

She shook her head, trying to knock some sense back into herself. He was a marquess, for heaven's sake. His interest in her had been based on desperation, and she had handily dispatched any notions of being his wife, his confidante or anything else. And yet he'd done something with her that precious few people had ever bothered.

He'd listened.

STEPHEN SAT in his study with a copy of Tacitus's *Histories* in his lap, the book open to the same page now for nearly half an hour. He kept looking at his hands, and remembered the sight, the feel of her hands on his.

Miss Schofield's touch was gentle and more comforting than anything he had experienced in a very long time. She's run her fingers over every line of his palm, every crease in his fingers.

"My hands are perfect."

"Are you so dull you must give yourself compliments?"

Stephen looked up to catch Edmund walking into the room.

"Well you must be very dull if the best you can do for entertainment is spend an evening here." Stephen replied with a smile. "Why aren't you out amusing the local ladies?"

"I've had my fill of company in recent months. I have to save what charm I have left for the upcoming assembly." Edmund held up a bottle of claret and poured two glasses.

"I thought you had charm in abundance." Stephen accepted the drink. "You certainly advertise that fact to every fashionable young lady worth a look or two."

Edmund chuckled with a hint of bitterness that did not escape Stephen's notice. "I'm afraid my dear brother is much more gifted in that regard."

"I don't think so. Where is he now?"

"No doubt he is out visiting in the drawing room of one of your neighbors—being charming to the ladies and trying to scare up a gaming table," Edmund replied.

"Is he winning or losing?"

"I've given up trying to find out, and frankly it's easier for me to be out of his way. There are some things I'm happier not knowing." Edmund shrugged. "Father can deal with him."

Stephen paused. He so rarely had a confidante of any kind, it was odd to voice his thoughts aloud. "Can I ask you a question? Or rather, if I ask you the question, will you give me an honest answer?"

"Of course," Edmund answered without delay.

"Do you think I'm mad?"

"Do you?" Edmund asked in return.

"I don't know. And the funny thing is, until a couple of hours ago, I would have given you an unqualified yes."

"What's made you change your mind?"

"Miss Schofield."

"You've lost me, cousin," Edmund admitted.

"She was going on about my hands—how they should be quite marked up if I'm spending nights tearing up buildings and livestock."

Edmund cocked an eyebrow, and leaned forward in his seat. "Am I hearing you correctly? You discussed the Beast of Barronsfield with someone who wasn't trying to bleed you or bless you or God knows what else?"

"What of it?"

Edmund shook his head, incredulous. "I've heard countless words spoken about your curse, but barely twenty of them have come out of your mouth. Since when do you speak of it to someone you've just met? Frankly, I'm not sure if I should be insulted."

"I didn't want to burden you when it started. And later on there were other things more interesting to discuss."

"I was nearly seventeen when Catherine died, Stephen. Hardly fresh out of the nursery. I had friends joining the army and getting themselves killed at seventeen. Perhaps I would've too, if father wasn't such a damned snob. That's Thomas Pembroke for you. Too cheap for the army, too blue blooded for the navy."

Stephen let out a breath. If there was one thing he supposed he could be grateful to his Uncle Thomas for, it was keeping Edmund out of a reckless career in the military. "Perhaps at last I have come to my senses. As you say, I have been whispered about, gossiped about in hushed corners of some of the finest parlors, and I have no doubt, the meanest London alleys. I think, finally, I am tired of the darkness and the secrets. They shield nothing, help no one. And, perhaps—" he paused, "I am weary of carrying this alone."

Edmund took a sip of his wine, eyeing Stephen with more scrutiny. "So what did Miss Schofield have to say about your hands? Unmarked, I take it?"

Stephen held them up for inspection. Edmund had a rather satisfied look on his face.

"I think I might attend the assembly just to make her acquaintance." Edmund settled further into his chair. "I know Geoffrey is certainly interested in her."

"Really." Stephen tasted the smallest bit of bile in the back of his throat. "What did Pembroke say?"

"Just this and that—about her ten thousand pounds of course, that she's newly returned to England, her father's a naval hero but otherwise she seemed ripe for the picking." Edmund stopped to take a sip of his claret.

"Ripe for the picking?" Stephen sat up, stunned. "Pembroke said that?"

"Or something like it. You know how he is, Stephen, all talk," Edmund said dismissively.

Was this all because of Anne? Or Miss Schofield's fortune? Either way, it bloody well unsettled him. "Do you think he's setting his cap for her?"

"Why Barronsfield, are you interested?"

"No," he said, probably too quickly. "No. She is Schofield's niece and I feel…responsible for her."

"If that is what you want to call it."

"I do."

"Well then, I hope you are planning to go to the assembly," Edmund said. "Geoffrey most certainly will be there—no doubt testing the waters with your Miss Schofield."

"She is not my Miss Schofield, as I am sure she would be pleased to tell you," he replied. The memory of Geoffrey fawning over her in the village square soured Stephen's gut. His cousin had been already 'testing the waters', hadn't he? "As for the assembly, I have little choice but to make an appearance. I will endeavor to make it short—shake a hand or two, spare the ladies any smiles lest they fear they will be dead by morning, then make my leave. An hour should do it—then the gossips will have hours to spend on their intrigues and I'll have the rest of the evening to myself in my library."

"Listen to yourself, Stephen," Edmund said in a way that reminded Stephen of his own father. When did Edmund grow up? "This estate supports a great deal of the people that will attend that assembly. People who are your friends, if you would bother to notice. And you need friends, especially now. Never mind that you could stand to have a bit of fun. Even Colin Middleton goes to assemblies, and he's even more unsocial than you. Of course, he's actually getting married soon, poor chap, so I suppose he has no choice. Besides, isn't it the duty of you titled folk to make a display of yourself for the rest of us?"

Colin Middleton was the heir to the title Duke of Weymouth, and Edmund's school friend. The young duke-in-waiting had been affianced before he could walk.

"It is not the duty of a marquess to have fun." Stephen knew how that sounded, but he was feeling petulant enough not to care.

"You can't shut yourself up in here and roam the halls like a hermit. Your tenants, your neighbors need to see you."

"You sound like Miss Schofield."

"Then I like her already. She sounds like a woman with uncommon good sense."

She did, didn't she? She'd given Stephen the smallest scrap of hope, the first in a long time.

But he knew how devastating hope could be.

CHAPTER 8

"*Rosalind.*"

Rosalind opened her eyes, listening for the voice that had summoned her in her sleep. She peered into the woods, lit by the ripening moon which highlighted the soft moss carpet below the trees. Rosalind took a few cautious steps off the path, compelled by her own curiosity and the sense of urgency in the mysterious voice on the wind. Up ahead, not a dozen more steps, the figure of a man came into view, but despite the bright moon, the shadows conspired to hide his face.

"I feared you might stay away." The relief in his voice was palpable, though his breathing was labored and heavy. He was unsteady on his feet.

As she drew nearer, she could tell his shirt was torn and open, and if she wasn't mistaken, he looked to be wounded. "Oh! You are hurt. I should fetch some help."

She turned to go when she felt his hand take hers.

"No." The urgency in his voice kept her from resisting. "I would rather you stay. Please."

She ran her thumb gently over his hand. His stance relaxed and the strain in his brow disappeared, though for Rosalind the feeling of his skin on hers excited her heart.

"My dear sir, we really should—"

He put a finger to her mouth, startling her into silence. "'Sir' is rather formal."

"What should I call you then? I don't know your name, which isn't entirely fair, since you know mine."

He took a step forward, the moonlight stretching across his cheeks. "How rude of me. My mother would deplore my lack of manners."

"Lord Barronsfield!" Rosalind took a few steps back, throwing her hands up in exasperation. "Am I so absolutely pathetic that I am having fantasies about you in my sleep?" She buried her face in her hands, disgusted with herself. How utterly weak she was. He reached out and took her hands away from her cheeks, bringing her back to him.

"While I am flattered at being called a fantasy, I do not believe for a moment you are—what was the word you used?—pathetic. In fact, you are rather charming." He broke into that beautiful smile of his, which only made her feel worse.

"I wasn't talking to you, my lord. You are a figment of my insipid imagination."

He reached out to her and ran a finger along her temple. Such a simple gesture, but so incredibly wonderful. "My touch is real enough, is it not?"

"No," she protested, though it sounded weak even to her ears. "This is all a dream."

"Perhaps you are in my dream, Rosalind. Have you not considered that?"

No. She hadn't, and the very notion of Rosalind playing a central role in a man's dreams—especially a man like Lord Barronsfield—was even more ridiculous. She was about to tell him so when he silenced her with an achingly tender kiss. For a moment, she was aware of nothing but the feeling of his skin brushing against hers. And then, as her fingers touched the ragged edge of his torn shirt, she remembered he was injured.

"You are hurt, my lord," she said, taking a step away and breaking their kiss. "You need aid."

"You are all the help I need—do you not see?"

He took her fingers and pulled aside the bloodied white linen, placing them on this chest. The wound had disappeared.

"Impossible!"

"This is your dream, as you like to keep reminding me."

Rosalind closed her eyes, wracked by warring emotions—desire and sheer enjoyment fighting against distrust and fear.

I don't have dreams like this.

Rosalind opened her eyes. It was still early, but the smell of coffee and bread from below told her that Emily had been up for a few hours. A fire burned in her hearth. She sat up and swung her legs over the edge of the bed, staring absentmindedly at her feet. She tried to capture the image of Stephen—Lord Barronsfield—in her head. Was she going mad? Or was she infatuated with him? If so, she knew the answer to the first question. Being near him was dangerous. She could not allow herself to have feelings for a man who had none for her, nor ever would.

After breakfast, Rosalind walked to Barronsfield Manor, gripping her invitation to the library like a talisman. The dream that had troubled her earlier had faded enough to allow the curiosity at seeing the place to trump any reservations she'd had about going. To refuse the invitation would perhaps not only reflect poorly on her uncle, but also deny Rosalind a chance to see a truly magnificent collection of books. Besides, Lord Barronsfield didn't know anything about her dreams. That humiliation would be her own. The mists that had been remarkably resistant to the sun's growing warmth when she first awoke had finally retreated. Birdsong broke the silence, and gave the morning a lovely, soft feeling as she made her way along the paths to the manor.

Through a treed lane, Rosalind spied the massive stone face of the manor rising from the landscape. She walked along one of the elegant pathways toward the front of the house. Touched by a hint of hesitation as she approached, the gravel crunched under her feet, and she slowed her steps as she gazed up at the tall windows. Surrounded by a wall of rosebushes, their blossoms long spent, the place looked almost lifeless.

Rosalind walked up the stone steps and held a hand to a rather large knocker at the door. She had barely had time to knock when the door opened.

"Hello?"

"Come in, Miss," came a rather ancient voice from behind the door.

She took a step into an entry that could have comfortably fit the entire cottage she now called home.

"I have an invitation," her words seemed to bounce from every wall, and she lowered her voice. "I have a note from the marquess inviting me to use the library. I hope this is not an inconvenient time."

"Right this way." The butler, who Rosalind judged to be approaching seventy, smiled as if he'd been expecting her. He took her bonnet and cloak, then proceeded up a huge, dark, wooden staircase directly ahead of them. As they reached the top, he shuffled along, leading Rosalind down a long hallway that looked over the main gallery below. The manor was deathly quiet—she doubted if anyone but the few servants who lived here would be awake.

The house was exquisite, but a veneer of despair hung about the place. Draperies seemed faded, and most of the rooms were shut. Below, a series of impressive portraits of former tenants stared out into the gallery, each set of eyes more mighty and imperious than the one before.

At last, they came to a massive set of doors. The butler turned the ornate doorknobs, pushed them open, and motioned for her to enter. Rosalind stepped inside, her breath catching in her throat as the splendor of the library revealed itself. On three of the four walls, bookshelves stretched up higher than she could possibly reach. Thick, brilliant red carpet lined the floor, leading to two of the largest windows she'd ever encountered. Through them there lay a spectacular view of the gardens. To her left, a black iron staircase wound its way up to a second level that held still more little alcoves full of books. To her right was a hearth with a small fire, several chairs, and in the corner near the window, a small, exquisitely carved writing desk. Along the windows were several benches covered in sumptuous fabric. It looked like a place to do nothing at all but read.

It took a second for Rosalind to catch her breath. "Pinch me."

"Excuse me, Miss?" The butler asked.

She turned around and smiled. "I wanted to know if I was still in the land of the living. I believe I just walked into heaven."

"Yes, Miss," he replied. "I shall return with some refreshments. I am instructed to make sure you feel at home, so if there is anything you require, please call." He motioned to a thick velvet pull, then left.

Rosalind stood still for exactly ten seconds before closing her eyes and letting out a quiet yelp, doing a little dance where she stood. It was almost as much excitement as she could bear. Even with her ten thousand pounds, she could never imagine anything as spectacular as this. It was beautiful beyond compare.

She strolled up and down the length of the room, scanning the shelves, not knowing exactly where to begin. Near the hearth, she spied a large red tome on a stand. On it was a note addressed to her.

Miss Schofield,

I am pleased to inform you that Mr. Turner has amended his circulation policies. I have taken the liberty of signing this book out for you. Please return it by October 23rd.

Yours, B.

"Pinch me," she whispered again. Gingerly, she opened the book, the thick pages and stiff binding releasing the scent of aged leather and paper. She inhaled deeply, savoring the moment, so engrossed in her surroundings she didn't notice who had brought a tray with a steaming pot of chocolate and biscuits.

Rosalind picked up the book and took a seat near the hearth. She started turning the pages of the volume when the woodcut engraving of a half-man, half-wolf again caught her eye. It was a tall beast with ferocious looking teeth and claws—certainly a creature that could rip apart a henhouse. This was the page she'd been reading when Mr. Turner had closed the book on her fingers.

She reached out for her cup of hot chocolate then stopped, and sat perfectly still for a moment, her senses newly alive to every sound. Lowering the book into her lap, she looked warily over her shoulder, having the distinct feeling she was not alone.

STEPHEN HAD BEEN WATCHING Miss Schofield from the moment she entered the library. He wanted to see the expression on her face, looking for the joy he so hoped would be there. She didn't disappoint him. From a small alcove on the second floor of the library, he heard her squeal of delight as Hanley left, and his heart almost flipped as she'd done a little dance about the room.

"Miss Schofield."

"My lord!" She bounded out of her seat, clearly spooked.

"My apologies," he said as he descended the stairs. "I did not mean to startle you."

"Were you spying on me?"

He supposed he was, but wasn't going to tell her that. "I was doing a bit of reading up there when Hanley let you in. He did not know I was here, and in truth, I didn't wish to interrupt your solitude, but you noticed me."

"Your presence is hard to ignore," she said simply.

His foot landed on the last step and paused ever so briefly, unsure what to make of her statement.

"The library is breathtaking," she continued, her smile quickly turned into a wince. "I suppose my expressiveness a moment ago did not escape your notice."

"No, it didn't," he grinned, thinking of it. "If it makes you feel any better, that is how I feel almost every time I walk into this room."

Nonchalantly, he grabbed a book and sat in a nearby chair. Once she appeared to recover from the shock that he was staying, she sat back down and resumed her study. He peered over trying to see what page she had the book open to. Her cheeks were still flush with color which highlighted the freckles around her nose. She must have sensed his attention, for she looked at him with a mix of bemusement and annoyance.

"Did you have a question?" she asked.

"Ah—no." Pause. "My apologies. Please, continue."

She looked appraisingly at him for a moment, before her gaze strayed to the book in his hands. "May I ask what you are reading?"

Stephen found himself looking down at the pages of his book, before discreetly looking at the frontispiece of the slim volume in his hands. What was he reading?

"The Republic. Plato."

"Ah, yes! Have you read the parable of the cave? It's my favorite part."

"The cave?" A lock of her hair hung loose down the back of her neck. Damned distracting.

"The parable of the cave. I find the idea that we have to prepare ourselves to find truth—no matter how painful a journey it can be—a rather good lesson, don't you think?"

"I, ah—" He flipped aimlessly through the pages. "I am disturbing you. Please continue."

She shrugged her shoulders, took a sip of her hot chocolate, and returned to her reading as if he were no longer in the room, which was how he preferred it. At least, he preferred it for a minute or two. Curiosity got the better of him. He stood and walked over to the hearth, then past her chair, trying to get a better view of what she was reading, without, of course, *appearing* to get a better view of what she was reading, which on the whole wasn't terribly easy to do.

"Find anything interesting?" he asked at last. He'd scanned the book late last evening, but discovered nothing. Still, he was most interested in Miss Schofield's opinions.

"Very. For example, look at this—isn't this a wonderful thing?" She pointed to a picture of a small pony with a wet mane. "It's a kelpie."

"Looks like a horse," he replied.

"It's a water spirit. It lives in Scottish rivers. Sometimes it disguises itself as a beautiful woman, and lures men to their deaths by drowning them," she said a little too brightly for discussing a rather sordid beast. "A little like a Siren I suppose. Men always seem to be led astray by a pretty face."

Would it be unseemly to agree with her on this point? He thought about Anne, her beautiful raven hair, and brilliant green eyes. Eyes that rarely looked on him with even the smallest bit of affection, even after she agreed to be his wife. Especially after that.

"I think I found something that might be of interest to you, too,"

Miss Schofield continued, unaware of his wool-gathering. "Here we are…Ly-can-thro-py," she said, sounding the word out.

Stephen peered even lower over her shoulder, trying not to be preoccupied by the view of the top of her bosom.

Miss Schofield looked back up at him as if he had two heads, or at least a very poor set of manners. "Do you often read over another's shoulder?"

"Sorry," He sat back down in the chair opposite her and started wolfing down a biscuit to keep himself from saying something he might regret later.

"A lycanthrope is a man—or a woman too, I suppose, it doesn't say —who shape-shifts into a beast that is half-human, half-wolf. It is a condition that is brought about by being bitten or scratched by another were-wolf, or by a *curse*." Miss Schofield looked up then, and the word brought Stephen's full attention to her.

"Miss Schofield, before we begin, you should know that I consulted a French priest about were-wolves over a year ago. I said thousands of Hail Marys, bathed in holy water and left a good chunk of blunt in his coffers for his time. It didn't work." Why on earth was he telling her this?

"So are you telling me that you are a were-wolf and the remedy didn't work?" She asked all too matter-of-factly. "Or that you aren't a were-wolf? When you change into this beast, what happens?"

"I don't know," he blurted out.

She nearly dropped the book on her feet. "How can that be?"

The shock on her face at his answer flustered him, and he realized, perhaps for the first time, how ridiculous that sounded. "I feel like I am in a waking nightmare. Nothing is as it should be. As to my own appearance, I can only guess. All I know is that I go to bed, and when I wake up in the morning, I feel like I've been pulled head first through the eye of a needle and my bed chamber looks like it's been run through by a pack of wild dogs. I have all these scattered images in my head, and none of them are pleasant, but I can't make sense of them."

"So you have no memory of this at all? Hmmm." She picked up the tome and settled it back into her lap. "Still, it would have to be very rare to be a were-wolf, especially in England. No wolves, you see." She was talking, but not really to him. Rather like she was thinking aloud. Somewhat charming…except for the subject matter. "Well, there is only one way to verify this. Let's see if you have any of the signs, shall we? You don't mind, do you?"

Stephen held up his hands. "You've given me more to think about in the past day than most of the experts have in years. Continue."

"Excellent." Her face broke into a wide grin that instantly lightened Stephen's mood.

Miss Schofield studied him head to toe. Stephen found himself shifting slightly in his chair, unsure of where to put his hands, or whether to cross his legs. Her gaze went back and forth between him and the book, her hands running down the page. It was not the same forbidding look his father gave him while he was drilling some new lesson about duty and responsibility. Nor was it like the harried stares of his neighbors who forced an uneasy smile on their faces as they rushed by. This was something else. Something new. Someone who was interested in Stephen, the man, not Stephen, the marquess. Someone who wanted to help him. And somehow, he wanted to believe that she could.

"Well, your eyebrows don't meet at your nose, and your ears appear to be in the proper place." She looked down at the book again. "Any hair under your tongue?"

Stephen contemplated sticking it out at her, then decided it would not be gentlemanly. Instead, he opened his mouth and curled his tongue back. "Sthee?"

"No? Fine. Next, please get up and walk across the room," Miss Schofield said, then added quickly, "my lord."

"I don't understand."

"Do you want to get to the bottom of this beast business or not? I don't know about you, but it would get awfully tiresome for me." He didn't appreciate her chiding tone, but she was right. It was awfully tiresome. He got out of the chair, walked about ten paces then back.

"Well? May I sit down?"

"Of course," she said with a small laugh that invited a smile in return. "You will be pleased to know that you do not have a sloping walk whatsoever."

"My tutors would be happy to hear. Anything else?" She was curious, this one. And fun. He hadn't had fun in such a very long time.

"Well, I don't suppose you noticed any hair on the underside of your skin when you've cut yourself?"

"No!" The very idea sounded ridiculous. And uncomfortable.

"Very well. In any case I would think that would be terribly itchy." She turned back to her book. "You can cure it, you know. Have you ever said any devotions to St. Hubert?"

"As I said, just the Virgin Mary. One might assume that's going over his head."

"Well, it couldn't hurt perhaps. There are a few other remedies, but none seem terribly pleasant." She rested the book in her lap. "But it doesn't make any sense. You have no memory of your rampages. And, relatively speaking, they are quite tame compared with what were-wolves are capable of."

"I destroyed a man's dog and thirty of his chickens, Miss Schofield."

"Yes, but you didn't destroy *him*. Or his wife." Miss Schofield pushed the book in his direction.

"But my mother, Catherine—"

"My understanding," she faltered a moment, "is that the Beast did not emerge in its current form until after the death of your wife, correct?"

"Yes, but—"

"And they died of other causes. Natural, if tragic, ones. Look at that picture, my lord." Miss Schofield pointed at the illustration. "Were-wolves are indiscriminate killers. So much so they suffer from nervous depression when they are in human form, from guilt. I would think that suffering from a pricked conscience requires you to be fully aware of your deeds, and you are not." Miss Schofield closed the book and leaned forward, thoughtful. Perhaps, damn it all, a little sympathetic. "Though it is clear you do carry a tremendous amount of guilt with you. Do you suffer nervous depression?"

"It is not fitting for a person of my station to display any weakness," he replied, perhaps a little too gruffly, but she cut a little too close to the bone. Guilt was his constant companion. The memory of him standing at his mother and Imogene's grave, desperately trying to keep his eyes dry for his father, came rushing back.

"I see. Peers of the Realm don't suffer from afflictions like nervous depression?"

"Of course not."

"But you can suffer from the curses of miserable old women? If that was the case, I would think the Kingdom would be at the mercy of every old woman hard done by a nobleman. You'd all be running around the countryside, and England would cease to have any chickens."

"Are you mocking me, Miss Schofield? You have not seen the damage I have caused. The blood on my hands." The litany of sins he'd committed that cast a shadow over Barronsfield and half of Yorkshire. His frantic attempts to continue, to break the curse, do to his duty, and produce an heir?

"I am trying to help you, my lord. I thought—"

He stood, incredulous, desperation driving him. "Do you want to help me, Miss Schofield? Marry me. Give me an heir so my line can continue."

The girl stiffened, as if on her guard. "I can't do that, my lord. You know why."

"Some imagined slight against your dignity."

"Imagined?" Her voice cracked with indignation, and she shot up, dropped the book on the chair, and pointed a finger straight at his chest. "Who here is imagining things? Who am I to argue with a marquess who knows everything except what is happening to his own body for hours at a time?"

"You do not believe me." Stephen took a step back, uncomprehending. He'd lived with this so long. He had made one horrible mistake that set his path. One horrible mistake that had cost him dearly. The curse was known from Cornwall to Scotland. "There has been much I have questioned, Miss Schofield. I have harbored my own doubts, only to have them ripped away. If there is one thing I am sure of, it is that I am to blame. I cannot hurt any more people. If I can at least sire an heir, then my line will continue." In that part of his duty, he could not fail.

"Marrying you helps no one. Not me, and especially not you." Her voice was soft, but the note of pity in her tone rankled.

A knock at the door interrupted them. Expecting to see Hanley, Stephen was surprised as Reginald Schofield entered the room, his manner uncharacteristically unsettled. Of course, being here, found alone with his steward's niece in her uncle's presence was enough to make Stephen unsettled as well.

"Rosalind! There you are. I must have word with you at—" Schofield stopped, no doubt surprised at the sight of his niece not a foot away from Stephen. "My lord! Forgive me for intruding."

"Uncle," Miss Schofield replied, her countenance only a little betrayed by the color in her cheeks. "Lord Barronsfield invited me to see his library. He just now came to inquire after my health."

"That was very generous indeed," Schofield said, an undeniable strain in his voice. "However, I must ask you to return to the cottage directly. Mrs. Irving will be waiting for you."

"But—"

"My lord, I must speak with you directly," the steward continued, his gaze bouncing from Stephen to Miss Schofield.

"Of course, Schofield. Go to my study. I shall join you there."

Schofield bowed, but rather than leave as he'd been directed, he tarried a moment, looking past Stephen to his niece. Something was amiss, and from Schofield's bearing it was difficult to tell if his concern was regarding protection of his ward, or something else.

"Miss Schofield, please help yourself to the red book and any other volume," Stephen said in his most officious voice, then lowered his voice, and spoke to her as softly as he dared. "Excuse my outburst, I beg you. The library is at your disposal—please use it. It stands empty most of the time."

He watched her as she considered his words. He wasn't good with words anymore. At one time he'd been full of flowery speeches that turned the head and softened the glance of many a lady, but he was past that now. He had become a man of few words, mostly hard and critical phrases which were his best defense to keep the attentions of society at bay. Now, as she shook her head and gave him a smile laced with a hint of sadness, he wished his words were capable of more.

"I really must go." With that, she went to her uncle, exchanged a few words, and left.

Though it was still filled with thousands of volumes and the same comfortable chairs, the room felt empty once she'd gone.

"This way, Schofield," he gestured to a bookcase near the hearth which swung open. His steward walked through the entry way and into Stephen's study, taking his seat opposite the large desk where Stephen conducted his business. "What is the news?"

Schofield took his seat and leaned forward, raking his finger through his gray hair. "My lord, Sally Coles has been found."

Stephen scanned his memory. The scullery maid who'd disappeared nearly four days ago. It had become harder and harder to keep servants. As Schofield rubbed his beard, a sickening feeling crept into Stephen's chest. "Tell me."

"Her body was found near the ruin, my lord." Schofield swallowed hard. "I spoke with Doctor Brayden not thirty minutes ago. He said her wounds were very severe. Like she had tangled with a wild animal."

Stephen sat back, the blood rushing in his temples, his stomach tightening into a knot. Perhaps Miss Schofield was satisfied he was not a were-wolf. And maybe she was right on that score.

Maybe he was just a monster.

CHAPTER 9

osalind's boots clicked as she raced down the stone steps of Barronsfield Manor. Uncle Reginald's rather direct request that she return to the cottage, coupled with the undeniable unease in his eyes made Rosalind wonder if she'd stepped over the line of propriety. She had taken a few steps out the library door when Hanley returned with her pelisse and bonnet and showed her out the front entrance.

Dear heavens, what if Uncle Reginald insisted the marquess marry her? Or would she be sent directly to London? The cool autumn breeze brought a relief from the rush of panic that prickled under her skin. Uncle Reginald couldn't send her away. A heavy weight formed in the pit of her stomach. The thought was nearly unbearable.

Marrying the marquess was the only sensible choice of the two options, if she was even presented with a choice. Lord Barronsfield was rich, powerful and handsome. He was also incredibly vulnerable. He used his so-called aristocratic sensibilities as armor, like the ancient metal suit that stood guard at the bottom of his grand staircase, yet the desperation of his renewed proposal only reminded Rosalind of how much fear and doubt lingered below his hard surface. She'd lived in a house most of her life where she'd been unloved. Now that she'd had a taste of something else, to go back to that—even in the grand trappings of Barronsfield, even with that most beautiful and perfect of libraries—was impossible.

"Miss Schofield!"

The sound of her name pulled Rosalind out of her thoughts. She stopped at the bottom of the steps and turned, surprised to see Mr. Geoffrey Pembroke bounding down the steps toward her, walking stick in one hand, waving with the other. His wind-tossed hair and warm smile was an immediate antidote to her uncertainty and doubt, and she smiled in return.

"Good morning, Mr. Pembroke."

"Good morning, Miss Schofield. It is a delight as always to see you."

A delight. The pit in Rosalind's stomach faded, filled instead with butterflies.

"This is an unexpected pleasure, sir," she replied. "But I am afraid I must be on my way. My uncle has begged my immediate return to the steward's cottage."

"Of course. In that case I will accompany you."

Rosalind shook her head. "I thank you, but there is no need to trouble yourself. It is not far."

"Under the circumstances I really must insist, Miss Schofield," he replied. "And it is no trouble. Although I have an ulterior motive, going for a morning walk is one of my favorite diversions."

Rosalind looked him up and down, noting the haste with which he was dressed, and the hazy look in his eyes. How many mornings had he ever seen? But she didn't want to be rude, and he was so incredibly pleasant. And so happy to see her.

Mr. Pembroke gestured to her arm. "May I?"

His request surprised Rosalind, but she let him take her by the arm. Soon, they were walking in step, casually heading out of the park and down the lane toward the cottage.

"I am sorry I missed you at Barronsfield, Miss Schofield. I didn't expect to see you at such an hour."

She hesitated a moment, unsure of exactly what she should reveal. "I was visiting the library," she said at last.

"So you are a reader then! I myself do not mind the odd word or two," he said. "I hope you weren't alone. I don't know how safe Barronsfield or anywhere is these days."

"Mr. Pembroke, what on earth has happened? My uncle bid me return to the cottage, and there was something in his countenance that felt out of character."

"I am loath to share it, especially with a member of the fairer sex." He paused a moment, then leaned in uncomfortably close. "The body of a young woman was found late yesterday near the ruin. The girl was one of the scullery maids here at Barronsfield Manor."

"No!" Rosalind recalled the look in her uncle's eye as he came in search of her. "And do you mean to say it was—"

"The Beast? Well, according to the doctor she'd been dead for several days at least, and the nature of her wounds—" he looked at Rosalind and swallowed deeply.

"This is terrible! Does his lordship know?"

"I suspect if your uncle is with the marquess, he does now." He pursed his lips, as if choosing his words carefully. "I do not envy Mr. Schofield. He has been in the service of this estate for many a year. My uncle—the 5th Marquess of Barronsfield—commanded the respect and love of the entire county. The estate and its reputation have crumbled under my cousin's rule. He has suffered the effects of the curse since he was a boy, and it has distracted him from his duties. After his wife Catherine died, things became much worse. They say he cursed the old witch in his grief and this—the horrible transformation into the Beast—was the result. Half of the household left after that. You've seen the manor. It is a shadow of what it should be."

Rosalind could hear the edge in Mr. Pembroke's voice as he spoke those last few words.

"You believe the curse is real."

Mr. Pembroke looked carefully in every direction before speaking. "I wanted to make certain we were not being watched before I reveal my tale. I have good cause to believe, Miss Schofield. I have seen the Beast."

His confessions stopped Rosalind in her tracks. "When?"

"Six years ago. Not long after Catherine's death. She was Barronsfield's wife. We were there for the funeral, you see, and I stayed on a little longer to keep my poor cousin company, as he was nearly out of his mind with grief. It was a clear night and the moon lit up the night, like a great chandelier." He paused, as if recalling something so painful it took a moment to collect his thoughts, then continued.

"I'd come in after a late evening of visiting. I was in my room, having a brandy before bed when I heard the most incredible howl. Truly, it made my blood run cold. I looked out my window and saw nothing. Then I realized, to my horror, the sound was coming from *inside* the manor."

Rosalind put a hand up to her mouth in shock. Mr. Pembroke continued.

"I ran out of my room, down the hall. As I did so, I could hear a ferocious scream, like a trapped animal. There was a great commotion, and it was all coming from my cousin's bedchamber. Half the household was up, and standing outside Barronsfield's door. We were terrified some kind of large animal was in my cousin's room, tearing him to pieces. The noise from inside the room was horrible—I will never forget it." He looked away at that moment, and it seemed to Rosalind a shudder went through him. "I had my pistol with me, ready to fire, and opened the door. But there was no animal. Just Barronsfield. And not Barronsfield."

"I don't…"

"His form was changing even as we saw him. One moment he was like nothing I can really describe—like something out of a nightmare. His eyes were red and full of hatred, his face was that of an animal, not a man's. His hands were gnarled into claws, and a line of fur ran down his back, like a dog with his hackles up. And then, before our eyes, he became again the Barronsfield we all knew."

Rosalind looked at Mr. Pembroke for some hint that he was having her along, but he remained deadly serious. She started walking again, as she slowly digested his tale. Question upon question started to brim up in her mind.

"Was my uncle with you?"

Mr. Pembroke nodded his head, falling back in step with her. "He arrived only a minute after it happened. He saw the aftermath, but not the Beast itself. There were a few others too—the cook, Hanley, and a couple of footman I believe."

"Did they all see…him?"

"I don't think anyone had a full view but me. I went in first, as I was armed. It was dark and there was so much confusion, but I will never forget it."

"I thought you said it was bright—there was a full moon."

"His curtains were half drawn, and he'd knocked the candles to the ground. He's lucky he didn't burn down the place."

"Did you tell anyone?"

"So many questions, Miss Schofield!" He patted her hand, and chuckled under his breath, then because serious. "You, of all people, should be aware of the danger, given your proximity to him. At first I doubted my own eyes—and as for telling the others, they were more likely to think I was mad." Pembroke shrugged. "But it was only the beginning. Many atrocities followed."

"Surely that is a strong word, Mr. Pembroke."

"Tell that to the Wickwire family."

"Who?"

"Anne Wickwire was Barronsfield's intended after Catherine."

"Yes, I have heard of her. I was told she died in a carriage accident."

"It may have been an accident that the carriage went off the road, but something more sinister took her life." Mr. Pembroke's voice was barely above a whisper, and he leaned in so close Rosalind almost felt a need to step back.

"Mr. Pembroke!" She could not believe it. What he was insinuating was something much more horrible than she found herself wanting to believe.

"I saw her body after the accident. It was broken in a way I have never seen." The color drained from his face as he spoke.

Rosalind was silent, confronting her lingering doubts and confusion. Mr. Pembroke seemed so genuine in telling his tale. Could it be true? And if so, why did she not want to believe it?

"Perhaps...you have not many victims of such an accident to compare it to," she said when she finally found her voice.

"Maybe you are right, Miss Schofield. It was terribly hushed, and I am sorry for my part in helping to keep it that way. Miss Wickwire's body was spirited away and she was buried quickly, at her parent's home. And my cousin was nowhere to be seen the night she died. Until he appeared later, the next day, bloodied and half out of his mind."

"Out of his mind—in grief?" Rosalind supposed. "Over losing his beloved?"

"Anne never loved him," he replied, distain in his voice that took Rosalind aback.

"Could he explain his whereabouts?" She asked the question already knowing—and dreading—the answer.

"No. He never can. But in his heart, he knows."

On that point Rosalind found she could not argue. The marquess wore his guilt like a mantle.

"About the poor girl they found—the maid. Do they know for certain it was the Beast? Were there any witnesses?" Rosalind asked. "Was she a very beautiful woman?"

"Apparently the girl disappeared the night the vicar's livestock was destroyed. Perhaps she merely got in his way—the wrong place at the wrong time. As to her beauty, I cannot say."

"Perhaps the Darlings saw something," she continued, barely hearing him now. Rosalind thought back to her arrival in Elmsdale, and the scene at the Darling's where so much of the horrible events occurred. She retraced her steps in her memory—the strewn carcass of fowl, the smell. The muddied purse she'd found. "But they didn't, did they? They awoke to it, but it was already done. If the Beast makes so much noise, as you say, why did no one hear it?"

Her question seemed to catch Mr. Pembroke off guard.

"I don't—I don't know. Perhaps they are sound sleepers? Or perhaps they were afraid, and stayed in their beds until the commotion was gone."

"Mr. Pembroke—"

"I know, Miss Schofield, it's all so terrible. Let's move on to more pleasant subjects, shall we?" he asked with what looked like a forced smile. Perhaps he felt it was for her benefit, but his sudden interest in changing the subject confounded her.

"Of course," she replied at last. She would save her questions for her uncle. Or Eleanore.

"I hope you are still intent on coming to the assembly tomorrow evening, Miss Schofield," Mr. Pembroke said brightly.

"Yes, of course. I promised Miss Martin, and my uncle has consented, so there is no impediment in my way. Do you think the assembly will continue, considering the circumstances?"

"Your concern does you credit, but I see no reason why it wouldn't. It was only a pot scrubber, after all."

Rosalind glanced away, embarrassed by his carelessness with regard to the girl who'd been murdered. The difference in society between the scullery maid and Rosalind was far less than the difference between Rosalind and the marquess, or even Mr. Pembroke.

Obviously mistaking her gesture for something else, he stopped, took her elbow and gently turned her toward him, fixing his blue eyes on hers. "Fear not Miss Schofield, I take a great personal interest in your safety."

Rosalind remained speechless for a moment, befuddled by Mr. Pembroke's touch and the depth of his stare, though his eyes were a tad less dazzling now than a few moments ago.

Her mind raced for a suitable answer. "Thank you. That is very generous."

They continued on their walk, and Mr. Pembroke drifted off into other subjects, as light and full of mirth as if the darker parts of their conversation had never come to pass. Before she knew it, they were standing at the small gate that led to the cottage.

"Here we are! I thank you for the walk, Mr. Pembroke" she said.

"Thank you. You are lovely company, as always," he took her hand and kissed it, lingering for an awkward amount of time. "I am truly looking forward to our dances tomorrow night."

She smiled as he finally let go of her hand, then escaped to the cottage, where Dreyfus came to meet her. She gave him a quick pat, and from the safe distance of a window in her uncle's small study, watched Mr. Pembroke continue on his way. Hopefully her uncle would be back soon. She had so many questions, but her first order of business was to apologize for going to the marquess's library alone. Or rather, for being alone in the library with the marquess.

Perhaps that was the least of his worries now. A girl was dead, and too many people were pointing fingers at Lord Barronsfield, including Mr. Pembroke—an educated man living within the marquess's inner circle. They were a puzzle, those two. Lord Barronsfield was so staid in his manner, shunning much of society who shunned him in return, though he seemed to be an honorable man. Mr. Pembroke on the other hand, was all frivolity and friendliness, with an easiness of character that was everything his cousin was not. And yet, something lay hidden. She sensed it, just under the surface, in both of them. It made her doubt her feelings on either account.

Pots clanged in the kitchen. Emily might have some more insights into what happened, Rosalind thought. She rushed out, her skirts brushing the edge of her uncle's desk and knocking some papers onto the floor. She stooped to pick them off the faded floor cloth, and was about to place them back on the desk when the word "Halifax" caught her eye, making her stop and take a second glance. The note was unfinished, and written in a hasty hand.

Admiral Hart,

I am writing to give you news of my ward, Rosalind Schofield, who is the daughter of your dear friend and my brother Captain John Schofield. I beg your indulgence on a matter of great importance. I promised my dear brother I would keep Rosalind safe always, but circumstances here have made this very difficult at the moment. I beg you—

"Miss Schofield dear, is that you?"

Emily's voice rang out from the kitchen door, and hastily Rosalind gathered the papers and returned them to her uncle's desk. She swallowed deeply and dabbed the corners of her eyes to stifle the tears that had formed. Letting out a long breath, she went to greet the housekeeper, and uttered a silent prayer that she might find an answer to the curse before her uncle could send her away.

Stephen retreated to his library, brandy in one hand, rubbing his temple with the other. He didn't know whether to be angry or sick. Sally Coles. Truth be told, he could barely picture her. To think he might have had her blood on his hands—it was almost too much. And yet, this did not feel right. Not this time.

Schofield had clearly been shaken by the news, but of course he would have hired the girl. He'd burst into the library looking for his ward and found her nearly nose to nose with Stephen. Was Schofield worried she was in the same room as a killer? Though the man's bearing was impeccable as always, there Stephen detected, in the split second before he spoke, a look of doubt, and possibly fear, across Schofield's brow. Of course, the steward was no longer solely the protector of Barronsfield, but of something perhaps more precious to him. Rosalind Schofield.

Stephen had sent Schofield away with directions to see to the servant's family if she had one, arrange for a burial and some kind of assistance. Schofield and Stephen would meet again later today to further discuss any developments and news. He needed to know more.

Light spilled from the large windows of the library, bathing Miss Schofield's ancient red book in warmth. Stephen grabbed the tome and sat down in the chair where she'd sat moments ago. There remained a hint of her perfume about the place.

Stephen turned to the page where the image of the were-wolf lay, and started reading, but the image of the horrid creature on the oppo-site page won his attention. Maybe he was looking at himself. If there had been any doubt left in Elmsdale about the Beast of Barronsfield,

Stephen was certain that they died when Sally Coles's body was found.

"Am I interrupting?"

Stephen looked up to see Edmund coming in the room. "Yes."

"Good. You looked far too morose for your own good. Like you've swallowed a pile of undercooked tripe." Edmund took a seat near the hearth, opposite Stephen. "You worry me, cousin."

"Worry you?" Stephen took another rather large sip of brandy and savored the burn in his throat. "You are looking at the worry of most of Yorkshire."

"Stephen, you have no idea if you had anything to do with that girl's death."

"How do you know about that?"

"Your steward informed me. He's troubled about the whole thing."

"I am sure he is. You should have seen the look on his face when he found me in the same room with Miss Schofield."

Edmund leaned forward, his normal carefree manner replaced with concern. "Who was this girl?"

"Sally Coles—worked in the kitchen. Schofield told me something of her." Stephen set the glass down on a small table beside him, and rested his head back on the chair. "Her death makes no sense to me, Edmund. None at all."

"In what way?"

"I barely knew her. Whether she was a pretty girl or not, I couldn't say." And he did not meddle with servants. "Her circumstances do not fit with the others."

"Maybe someone else killed her, and used what happened at the vicarage to cover up their crime," Edmund said. "She wouldn't be the first young girl, I'm sorry to say, to disappear at the hands of some n'er do well."

"The Beast does provide the perfect scapegoat. I'd thought of that. Schofield will bring back more information this afternoon. We might get some answers then." Stephen stretched out his legs, and stared into the hearth. "I have to meet with the servants this afternoon. They are no doubt frightened. I have no idea what I'm going to say."

"You'll be fine, Stephen. You'll find the right words when the time comes."

The two men sat in comfortable silence for a little while, the only sound the crackle in the hearth and the scuffle of Hanley's feet as he brought in a small tray of food.

"I saw Miss Schofield leaving with Geoffrey not that long before I came in," Edmund said between bites of his sandwich. "What was she doing here?"

Geoffrey? That rankled. "She is a bookish sort of a female, her uncle informed me. I thought she might like to see the library."

"You *invited* her? Here? And she came?" Edmund looked at Stephen with a faint sort of amusement on his face.

"She has no particular fear of my reputation. She's a different sort of female. Rather different, actually." Stephen caught himself thinking about the morning he'd found her among his beloved roses, her eyes wide, a thick plait of hair running down her back. Only Miss Schofield could make a conversation about were-wolves and curses seem like a pleasant way to spend an hour.

"Well, I like different females. I really do need to meet her," Edmund replied, enjoying this far too much for Stephen's liking.

"Do not read anything into it but simple obligation. Schofield has been a loyal servant since you were in swaddling clothes. Some small gesture to his niece is nothing but that—a gesture."

"Whatever you say." Edmund pulled a book off the shelf and took the chair opposite Stephen. "I wouldn't think an heiress would need too much reading to attract a husband. Too much might scare them away."

"I don't think Miss Schofield is particularly concerned with marriage." *At least not with me.* "She enjoys reading. I have a library. Somebody might as well enjoy it. Besides me, it gets no use."

"I haven't met a girl yet who's not interested in marriage. On the contrary," Edmund muttered as he grabbed an apple, prepared to take a bite. "The ones I meet are all extraordinarily preoccupied with the notion."

"Miss Schofield made it quite clear to me that because of her fortune, she may never be inclined to marry."

"I didn't realize you had feelings for her."

"I haven't. It's convenient for both of us—I merely failed in convincing her of that."

"You're probably the richest man north of Lincolnshire. Why wouldn't she?" Edmund eyed the book in Stephen's lap, still open to that ghastly page. "You said she's not afraid of the curse?"

"Hardly. In fact, I pointed out to her she had nothing at all to fear from it."

Edmund slouched back into the chair and rolled his eyes. "You didn't."

Stephen only nodded.

"You do have the manners of a bear. And she refused you."

Stephen nodded again, a tad more sheepish this time.

"Can't say I blame her. What on earth were you thinking?"

"I was thinking that if I married her, the curse—wouldn't kill her. Is that such a horrible thing? I need an heir, Edmund. I can't have this estate fall into Thomas—" Stephen closed his eyes, remembering who he was speaking to. Thomas Pembroke was a bastard, but he was still Edmund's father.

Edmund held up his hands. "On your last point, you will hear no argument from me. But with regards to Miss Schofield, do you hear yourself? You take yourself entirely too seriously."

"You are the second person to tell me that today."

"Really?"

"Miss Schofield said the same in so many words."

"Then I confess I like her already." Edmund paused. "Do you?"

"Do I what?"

"Like her."

"Who? Miss Schofield?"

"Were we speaking of someone else? I suppose you do if you want to marry her. But why her? Why not find some desperate girl in need of a fortune?"

"Well, at the risk of seeming terribly pathetic, I've not been able to find a girl desperate enough."

"If you asked my mother, she'd tell you it's because you haven't been looking."

"You may give my regards to my aunt, and perhaps she is right." With few exceptions, Stephen did not go to public events since Anne's death. It was too bloody uncomfortable for everyone, especially him. "Miss Schofield is here, she practically fell into my lap. I'd like to think somehow that means something. Besides, she is…" What? Intelligent, lively. And her eyes were quite striking. And the freckles across her nose were almost pretty, if he had bothered to consider it. Her smile. Her smile was like sunshine. "She is an interesting, lively sort of person."

"From that smile on your face I was expecting more than 'interesting.'"

He was smiling?

"Are you planning on going to the assembly tomorrow?" Edmund asked.

Stephen shook his head. "After the discovery this morning? I hate to disappoint you, but the dear people of Elmsdale have already been treated to one of my outings in this past week, and I would be very surprised if they are in any mood to see me in such a venue any time soon. Besides," he grumbled, "I don't dance."

"Barronsfield, far be it from me, a lowly second son, to lecture the Marquess of Barronsfield on duty—"

"Then don't."

"—but given what's happened, it would not only be a good gesture, but your *duty* as marquess to attend and support this assembly. Sometimes doing your duty means having a little bit of fun."

Stephen raked a hand through is hair, and gazed down at that awful woodcut image of the were-wolf. The last time he'd attended a public assembly was during his engagement to Anne. About five years ago, before the Beast started terrorizing his neighbors in earnest. Still, as much as he disliked crowds, staying at home might fuel the rumor mills and cement his guilt.

Stephen shut the book. He couldn't look at that damned picture anymore.

"Very well, Edmund. I'll consider it."

"Excellent." Edmund rose, adjusted his coat, and headed for the door. "And, it is your duty to introduce me to every lovely face in the room. And the interesting people too." Edmund paused, giving Stephen a look that said he enjoyed his cousin's discomfort. "*Especially* the interesting ones."

CHAPTER 10

After Rosalind broke the news to Emily about Sally Coles, the housekeeper made haste for the manor to comfort the younger staff and help out where needed. For Rosalind, the rest of the day stretched on interminably. She had a dress she'd attempted to fix for the assembly, but sitting in one place with a needle and thread was not a good pastime for Rosalind at the best of times, and this was not the best of times. Instead, she went for a long, rambling walk with Dreyfus through the wooded paths around Barronsfield. As the naked branches on the trees swayed in the cool autumn breeze, the idea that her uncle might send her away from here, where she was free to be herself, only added to her anxiousness. It seemed like such a selfish thing, given a girl had been found murdered. When Emily returned to the cottage at last, it was well after sunset. Despite Emily's long day at Barronsfield—or perhaps because of it, the housekeeper had little to say about Sally Coles, and given the weariness in her expression, Rosalind had no heart to press her on the subject.

The next day, a note arrived at the cottage inviting Rosalind to come to the vicarage, where she would have tea and get ready for the assembly. Her uncle, perhaps feeling some time away from Barronsfield was in order, thought it was a capital idea. After tea, Mrs. Darling left Eleanore and Rosalind to get ready. Once alone Rosalind asked Eleanore for news. Word of Sally Cole's death had made its rounds through Elmsdale.

"The Darlings have told me very little, except that the girl had family nearby."

"Do they have any clues as to what happened?" Rosalind thought of the marquess. "I found a little reticule in the mud at the vicarage the day I arrived here. Was it hers?"

Eleanore nodded, her expression troubled. "It was sent home to her family along with the body. They had to bury her right away. Mr. Darling went yesterday to perform the burial."

Rosalind's lips pulled into a tight grimace. She must have been dead for four or five days before her body was found. Her poor family. She shook her head, driving the horrible thought from her mind, and focused back on the purse she'd found. She needed to find out what had happened.

"Was there anything in the purse to give an indication she might have been out to meet someone?" she asked.

"Just a few coins and a little cloth bundled around a few black seeds."

"Seeds?" Rosalind said. "What kind?"

Eleanore shrugged. "I don't know. Mrs. Darling couldn't identify them. She thought they might have been mustard seeds, but it was hard to tell."

"Why would Sally carry a bundle of seeds?" Rosalind asked.

"Mustard seeds are considered good luck by some. Perhaps that's what they were."

They clearly didn't help the poor girl. Nor Lord Barronsfield. "What about the marquess?" Rosalind asked. "What are people saying?"

Eleanore sat forward, thoughtful. "It does look bad, does it not? For all that has happened, this feels different. People are frightened, because they don't know what else to be."

Rosalind could imagine the talk. The hatred directed at her uncle those first few moments after they'd arrived in Elmsdale still loomed in her memory.

"Was she a remarkable looking girl?" She asked it aloud, fully knowing that Eleanore probably couldn't answer. It was possible Lord Barronsfield could have been having a dalliance with his servant— though an unpalatable thought, it was certainly not uncommon for powerful men to prey upon their female staff. But if she was not particularly beautiful, then her death at the hands of the Beast did not make any sense.

Whether it was the restless air, or the news about the servant girl making Rosalind feel that way, it was hard for her to tell. She went to the window, where a heavy blanket of gray cloud settled in the sky and a tempestuous breeze whipped leaves from their branches. The day had started out pleasant enough, but a scorching red sunrise, coupled with an earlier complaint from Emily about her creaking elbows, had convinced the housekeeper rain was coming. By four o'clock, Rosalind was sure Emily was right.

The clock chimed the hour, bringing Mrs. Darling into the parlor.

"Well now, I think it is high time you girls went upstairs and got yourselves ready. Rosalind, your uncle will be sending the carriage for us in no time, and he'll be eager to see you both."

Rosalind and Eleanore went upstairs, where Mrs. Darling had put out their dresses. A simple but elegant, blue muslin gown meant for Eleanore hung on one hook. She took it down and held it up to herself in the mirror.

"It is very pretty, isn't it?"

"Very pretty," Rosalind replied, fingering the fine muslin. While Rosalind was certainly not an expert on matters of fashion, it looked new, and she could not help but wonder where a parlor-boarder might find such a gown.

"Mrs. Darling claims it came from her cousin in the next town." Eleanore turned, carefully placed the dress on the bed, and, almost under her breath, added. "Of course, many of the things I receive come from her cousin in the next town."

Rosalind had wanted to ask Eleanore about her parentage, but given their short acquaintance, thought it impertinent. It was obvious to Rosalind that her young friend knew Mrs. Darling's 'cousin' was just as likely to be some minor lord, looking after their ill-gotten progeny from afar. The girl was sixteen, but she was not foolish.

Eleanore picked through a basket of ribbons and other fripperies, tugging out a ribbon or two that would look 'perfect', only to find another that was 'more perfect.' Rosalind could only smile to herself. Though the events of the past day had no doubt unnerved Eleanore, youthful anticipation of attending her first assembly, clothed in such a lovely dress, was winning over the fear.

Rosalind crossed her arms and let go a breath as she glanced up at her gown, hanging from a second hook on the door. A cast off from a friend of her aunt's, it was a sad grayish-purple thing with a stomacher that pinched in some places yet managed to gape in others. She'd wished she'd had time to find something new, or even had discovered time and skill to fix this one, especially for the first assembly in which she had a dance partner. Perhaps, it didn't matter. This might be her last assembly in Elmsdale if her uncle believed she was in danger.

"You must be excited, Rosalind. To have secured the first two dances from Mr. Pembroke!" Eleanore sat on the bed, silk strands in a dozen colors trailing down her arm. "But then, you have attended so many assemblies. You probably think I am very silly."

Rosalind could faithfully recall the covering on every wall of every assembly hall in Halifax, but she was not going to douse her friend's excitement. "Not at all! We are going to have a lovely time, and I suspect there will be many a young man well pleased to dance with you."

The corners of Eleanore's mouth turned up in a thoughtful smile, giving a hint of familiarity that made Rosalind start. Before she could ponder it further, Mrs. Darling bustled into the room, a parcel in her arms.

"Miss Schofield, if you'll pardon me. This arrived just now."

"For me?" Rosalind asked.

Eleanore and Rosalind bounded off the bed, making room for a large bundle wrapped in linen. Rosalind gingerly pulled away the cloth, revealing a beautiful green gown.

"Oh Rosalind!" Eleanore squealed in a tone that matched the delight bubbling inside Rosalind as she slowly freed the gown from its protective layer. Brilliant green silk tumbled onto the floor.

"Where on earth did this come from?" Rosalind asked, looking to Mrs. Darling, who's only answer was a big smile and a slight shake of her head.

Rosalind held the dress to her body in front of the mirror. The color suited her perfectly. It was unornamented except for the smallest bit of delicate French lace around the neckline, and the cut and the fabric of the dress was exceptionally fine. Uncle Reginald. It had to be. No one else here would do this for her. Her eyes began to glisten. No one had ever done anything like this for her.

Mrs. Darling had one housemaid who dressed the girls' hair, then helped each of them into their gowns. Around her neck Rosalind wore a simple locket that her parents had given her. Eleanore looked a vision in her light blue gown. Rosalind had loaned her a strand of pearls that complimented her dress.

"Eleanore, Miss Schofield!" Mrs. Darling called from down the hall. "I believe Mr. Schofield has arrived with the carriage."

Rosalind lingered a moment in front of the mirror at her dressing table, almost not recognizing herself in her pretty green gown, her hair elegantly, yet softly dressed. A nervous excitement grew inside, starting at her slippered feet. Was it too much to hope for new possibilities? When the night was over, Rosalind was determined to speak to her uncle, beg if necessary. There was no way on earth she was going back to her old life. And if she needed to prove to him that the marquess was not the cause of the girl's death, she would find a way to do it.

CHAPTER 11

Reginald Schofield's face glowed as Rosalind came down the stairs. His cheeks were flushed, and his gray eyes bright with a sheen of unshed tears. His own hair was hidden underneath a well brushed wig that was still the fashion for older men, and he wore his best dark green coat. A small twinge of sadness squeezed Rosalind's heart as she descended, and she found herself trying very hard not to dwell on the fact that had the fates been different, her father would have accompanied her at a moment like this. From the look on her uncle's face, it was apparent he was keenly aware of it too.

"Rosalind, dear, you look lovely. Just lovely." He took her by her gloved hands and kissed her cheek. "I am sorry for the circumstances that brought you here, but I am so very glad you have come to me."

"As am I, Uncle." She cleared her throat, determined to bid the melancholy away. "The dress is beautiful. Thank you, you really shouldn't have gone to all the trouble."

Her uncle paused a moment, pursing his lips slightly, and simply shook his head.

"To see you here, looking as pretty as you are, I think was worth the effort," he replied, then turned to Eleanore. "And you too, Miss

Martin. You are quite lovely as well. I think the young men of Elmsdale will be fighting over which one of you to dance with first!"

"Miss Schofield will already be dancing with Mr. Geoffrey Pembroke!" Eleanore replied gaily.

"Mr. Pembroke? Truthfully, Rosalind?" Uncle Reginald looked at Rosalind with what she thought was an undue amount of care.

"I'm sorry, Uncle, for not telling you earlier. There has been so much excitement this past week it escaped my memory." It wasn't exactly truthful, but given all that had happened, even since yesterday, everyone had been preoccupied.

They all loaded into the carriage. All the way to the hall, there was not one ounce of discussion about Sally Coles or even the marquess. Her uncle, it seemed, was determined to focus on the evening in front of them, and given that he had no doubt been focused on little else of late that was pleasant, Rosalind could hardly blame him. He also gave her no hint about the letter to Admiral Hart. Though she dearly wanted to ask him about it, there was no way for Rosalind to raise the subject privately in the carriage with the Darlings and Eleanore present.

By the time they arrived at the hall, the assembly was already underway. The room, which showed its Tudor heritage, was tastefully decorated with flourishes that marked the end of the harvest. A lively reel filled the air, immediately putting Rosalind in a good mood and helping her to overcome the last bit of trepidation she'd felt as they got out of the carriage. Despite recent events, the hall was a crush of people. Between the sound of the music, the clapping, laughing and cheers of the crowd, Rosalind had to lean in close to hear her uncle as he spoke.

"It seems the people of Elmsdale are in good form tonight, my dear. Let's go introduce you to our neighbors, shall we?" Uncle Reginald's smile betrayed no hint of trepidation. Her uncle, of course, was as much a symbol of the troubles at Barronsfield as the marquess himself—and subject to some of the same scrutiny. As they crossed the room, Rosalind couldn't help but wonder if any of the men present shared the same sentiment as those she'd heard at the vicarage. As she took in the myriad of new faces about the room, she noticed the smiles, the glances filled with unabashed curiosity, and the whispers from onlookers.

Eleanore stuck to Rosalind like glue, the Darlings trailing behind. In a moment, there were not one, but two young men who approached Mr. Darling, asking to be introduced, hoping for a dance with Eleanore. Rosalind sighed inwardly. Eleanore was beautiful. And young. Maybe this would feel like home all over again.

"My dear Miss Schofield," came a familiar voice.

Or maybe not.

"Mr. Pembroke!" Rosalind bowed slightly as her dance partner approached, trying hard not to look overly eager at his attentions. Remembering her manners, she gestured to her uncle. "Uncle Reginald, please let me introduce Mr. Geoffrey Pembroke."

"Mr. Pembroke, sir," her uncle said steadily. "It is very good to see you here this evening. I did not realize you were a fan of public assemblies."

"Come, come, Schofield! I'm not that high in the step. I take what amusements where I can, and this seems like a jolly enough way to spend an evening."

Geoffrey Pembroke was exquisitely dressed—easily outmoding everyone in the room by his choice of coat, which was of the finest wool. He cut a very fine figure, something that had not gone without notice by many of the young ladies—or their mothers—in the room. But his eyes, for the moment, were solely on Rosalind, and she found it difficult not to be intoxicated by the novelty of the attention.

"I was fortunate enough to secure the first two dances with Miss Schofield," Mr. Pembroke said to her uncle. "If you have no objections, Schofield, I have been waiting most anxiously for her arrival."

Rosalind waited as patiently as she dared for her uncle's assent, which took more deliberation than she would have thought. Perhaps Uncle Reginald was simply being careful. This was his first outing as her protector, and he was in a precarious position. Mr. Pembroke was the cousin of his employer, the grandson of a marquess. Her uncle was at best gently born and worked for a living.

"I thank you for your attentions to my niece, Mr. Pembroke, sir," he said at length. Her uncle smiled, but Rosalind could see past her uncle's politeness, certain he was biting his tongue.

"Your uncle is a good fellow. Very protective too, I see," Mr. Pembroke said as he led her to the dance floor. Obviously it had not escaped his notice either.

"He is new to his duty as my protector. I—" her thoughts instantly scattered, conscious of Mr. Pembroke's touch as he walked with her to the dance floor. Had he noticed that his arm had brushed up so close to her bosom? He was so careless with his manner, so free, and the ballroom was so crowded, it must have been a mistake. Collecting herself, she continued. "I think he is unsure of how to direct me."

"He will learn his place soon enough," he smiled down at her, his eyes dazzling, but his words stunned Rosalind. As the music began, she nearly forgot to move as she turned over his words in her head. *What was he implying, exactly?*

Over the course of the two dances, through the pleasant conversation, the dazzling smiles and the string of innuendos Mr. Pembroke spun about Rosalind's beauty, Rosalind smiled. She even laughed. But there was scarcely a moment to speak. Scarcely a moment to think. Mr. Pembroke had spent the hour being so gracious and playful and dazzling that Rosalind decided she needed a rest. It was as if she'd dined on a huge piece of cake with far too much icing.

At first she worried about how she might escape him in a room of such a modest size. However, the assembly was also full of single girls and their mothers who, seeing a new and very eligible gentleman in the place, Rosalind's getaway into the crowd was less difficult than she had feared.

Dancing in an overcrowded and sweltering assembly hall left Rosalind parched, and she went in search of the refreshment table. As she walked, she found herself scanning the room for Lord Barronsfield. He was nowhere to be found, of course. His absence was not a surprise, but her disappointment because of it was unexpected. Not that she could blame him—she'd heard plenty a wild tale and even worse, accusations that involved his name since she'd arrived.

Near a large pitcher of lemonade she met a handsome young man, finely dressed. He had warm, rich brown hair cut in the latest fashion, and his clothes, though not foppish, were of the finest cut. His eyes were blue and lit up his face when he smiled. He bore a strong resemblance to Mr. Pembroke, though younger—perhaps a little more than twenty, and far less affected in his manner.

"May I fetch you a glass of lemonade?" he asked.

"Thank you, sir."

"I ask only a small price," he replied as he ladled the tart liquid into a glass. He held it up, but kept the glass out of her reach.

"And that would be?" After an hour of being 'charmed' by Mr. Pembroke, she really wanted a glass of lemonade.

"Your name, my lady. And the pleasure of a turn about the room with you."

She must have looked uneasy, for he followed with, "I promise to deliver you safely back into the hands of your uncle. I crave new acquaintances you see, and I have not yet had the pleasure."

Rosalind could not help but relent at the warmth of his address. She nodded and he put the cup into her hand, being careful not to let go.

"Rosalind Schofield."

"Your reward." He let go of the cup. "My name is Edmund. Edmund Pembroke."

"I had guessed you might be a relation of Mr. Pembroke. The resemblance to your brother is unmistakable."

He looked almost wounded by her words. "I suppose Geoffrey's a handsome enough fellow, so I should take that as a compliment."

"It was meant thus, sir." She paused for a moment, thinking back to their words only a few seconds ago. "I believe you must have been joking with me."

"I don't understand."

"You said you would deliver me safely back to my uncle. You must have known who I was, or that was the most lucky of guesses."

"Barronsfield was right! You are an intelligent creature."

Rosalind nearly choked on her lemonade. "The marquess said I was intelligent?" Well, she knew he didn't consider her a beauty. Still, it was a compliment. From him.

"He did indeed, only today. I have to say that our conversation made me quite impatient to meet you. Besides, I make it my business to become acquainted with all lovely young ladies as soon as possible."

Rosalind could not help but smile at the flattery that slipped so easily off his tongue. It must run in the family. But she found herself temporarily distracted by the idea that the marquess had been talking about her with his younger cousin. She could imagine what a fine topic of conversation she was.

"Do you and your brother often visit at Barronsfield?" she asked.

"My brother prefers London to the wilds of Yorkshire. He has not been here in several years," he replied. "For myself, I come as often as time permits and my cousin puts up with me long enough for both our tastes. I try to visit at least once a year. Sometimes two. The shooting is excellent, and my cousin is amiable enough company. And I get to see Barronsfield Manor, which is a treat unto itself."

"I thought the marquess preferred his time alone. But then, you know his habits." She took a sip of lemonade, unsure why she felt the need to know more about him.

"As well as he lets anyone, I dare say."

She opened her mouth, ready to ask another question, but thought the better of it. Edmund Pembroke, however, must have sensed her hesitation, for he spoke up.

"My cousin has a certain interest in you, and I have to admit that was, in part, my motivation to meet you."

Rosalind started, and took another sip of her lemonade to disguise the fact that her jaw had dropped at Mr. Edmund Pembroke's declaration. He was so guileless and open with his cousin's opinions. She wondered what Lord Barronsfield would think. But this was also an opportunity. Perhaps he would be honest with her. "I have heard so many stories about him."

"Don't tell me—the dreaded Beast of Barronsfield?" He said with a comically dramatic air.

Rosalind nodded and stifled a laugh.

"My cousin is a troubled man, Miss Schofield. Despite the rumors, he is not a violent one, but he has grown morose and even bitter on occasion. He is only thirty you know, but he seems much older at times."

"And the curse? Can any of that be true?"

"Miss Schofield, do not disappoint me," he admonished playfully.

"So you do not believe in the curse either?" Rosalind asked, relieved she was not alone in her convictions.

He shook his head. "Let's just say I think there may be other forces at work here," he replied. "Though I've not lived through the horrors of late that have plagued him, belief is a powerful magic of its own—for good or ill."

"A magic to which none of us are immune." She smiled at him, but there must have been enough doubt in her eyes for Mr. Pembroke to notice. His playful manner faded, replaced by a more earnest, almost serious countenance.

"My cousin has planted roses everywhere at Barronsfield, and they are beautiful when they are in full bloom. They have yet to wilt in his presence. I promise you, he may gnash his teeth, but he doesn't bite. For his own preservation, if nothing else, my cousin has taught himself not to see a pretty thing even if it is right in front of him."

Rosalind didn't know what to say. My dear, were all the marquess's relations so charming? She looked over her shoulder, where she could see her uncle taking his place on the dance floor with Eleanore, and Mr. Geoffrey Pembroke in an animated conversation with several young people.

"Would you honor me with a dance, Miss Schofield?" Mr. Edmund Pembroke leaned in, almost conspiratorially, his easy manner returning once more. "I promise not to trample over your feet if you promise to avoid mine."

"I believe I can honor that promise, Mr. Pembroke. I would love a dance."

STEPHEN'S CARRIAGE came to a stop in front of the assembly hall. As he gazed through the carriage window up to the hall entryway, unease pricked at the back of his neck, and kept him frozen in his seat even as the carriage door opened. Assemblies such as these had never been his forte. Still, he had squeezed into his best black coat, and it would have been a waste of poor Hanley's efforts if he turned around and went home now. Besides, Miss Schofield was in there somewhere. And so was Geoffrey, no doubt doing his best to fawn over her. The very notion was enough to drive away any lingering doubts about his presence here, though it did plenty to confuse him about his true motivation in attending.

A light rain had begun to fall. Taking a deep breath, Stephen stepped onto the road, an audible hush from the few onlookers stinging his ears. He nodded calmly to those around him, adjusted his waistcoat and marched to the front of the assembly hall, as nervous as a young student going before the examiners. It had been five years since he had been to a public gathering such as this. The musicians inside played a fast moving jig, and the jolly melody, melding with enthusiastic hand clapping and the stomping of dancing feet on the wooden floor lightened his trepidation. He tried very hard to remember that once upon a time, he'd enjoyed a setting like this. And tried very hard to forget how lonely this made him feel.

Heads turned as he came out of the shadows and approached the entrance. Forcing a smile to mask his unease, he walked in and caught the naked surprise on the faces of those who noticed him. Indeed, it was not two minutes before word of his arrival had gone right around the room. From the lowliest servant up to some of his most well-to-do neighbors, he saw a mix of shock, confusion and even a hint of fear.

If they only knew their dread was a merely shadow of his own.

The crowd parted as he strode into the room. Chandlers burned brightly overhead and the white-washed room and colorful gowns provided a respite from the blackness of the evening. The air was thick with the smell of perfumes and wax. The music that had welcomed him as he entered halted abruptly as dancers stopped the quadrille and watched with unguarded amazement, as he came into the hall.

"My lord!" came a voice from the crowd. An older, well dressed man appeared out of the mass of people to Stephen's right and approached him. It was Mr. Battersby, a local squire whose small property was nearly three miles from Barronsfield. Stephen could see his appearance flustered the man, but not in an unflattering way. "Welcome to our assembly, my lord! This is a most unexpected pleasure."

"Mr. Battersby, sir." Stephen raised his voice so everyone could hear him. "I beg you, do not stop the amusements on my behalf. I have come to enjoy the evening, not interrupt it." With his words, Mr. Battersby gestured to the crowd, and the music started again.

"I am very pleased to see you here, my lord," the old squire said. "It has been too long."

"I cannot help but agree, though I am concerned my presence might be an obstacle to the general amusement."

"I think you can see that is not the case, my lord." The old squire gestured to the rest of the room, but the expressions of many around him seemed to negate his words. He continued, however, unfazed. "And Misters Geoffrey and Edmund Pembroke have been busy keeping the ladies engaged. Mr. Geoffrey Pembroke is quite the sensation tonight, quite a favorite with the ladies."

"I am sure he is," Stephen muttered under his breath. He saw Pembroke in among a small crowd of ladies, flanked by each of the Perkins girls, clearly enjoying being the object of so many adoring women. Miss Schofield was nowhere to be seen.

He stood to one side, talking to the squire and a few others of the lesser gentry from the surrounding estates. Even the vicar came up to shake his hand. Not all the crowd was so inviting—there were more than a few harsh stares and whispers to endure. No one would dare challenge him publicly. It was the gift—and the curse—of being who he was.

As he scanned the room and found Miss Schofield, nimbly dancing her way through the set with Edmund, Stephen knew it was worth the trial. Her form, he noted, was actually quite fine. Not the epitome of grace, but full of a natural liveliness that became her. The warm green silk suited Miss Schofield—it was alive, refreshing, and a fair contrast to her hair, which warmed to a rather remarkable chestnut color in the candlelit hall. When Stephen had overheard Mrs. Irving speaking with his steward about how Miss Schofield didn't have a proper dress for the assembly, he wasn't sure Reginald would accept his offer to help. Looking at Miss Schofield now, Stephen was glad Schofield had consented, and Mrs. Darling did a fine and discreet job of securing a gown. He was inexplicably pleased Miss Schofield looked so well in it.

Quite well, in fact.

Twice he caught her eye, and she graced him with a shy smile that gave birth to a giddy sort of happiness not terribly becoming for a man of his rank. Nor deserved of a man who'd trampled so freely over her feelings.

The set ended, and the crowds departed the dance floor. Stephen's anticipation at being able to speak with Miss Schofield was somewhat disconcerting. She caught his eye and smiled, before her expression changed, as if suddenly fearful of being seen. A gloved had went up as she waved, then appeared to be gesturing behind him.

"Decided to come out among the crowds, Barronsfield?" came Geoffrey's voice from behind him. Geoffrey's interruption stole his attention. A second later, she flashed him a disarmingly amiable if apologetic smile, and disappeared into the crowd.

Was Miss Schofield avoiding Geoffrey? The idea brought him more satisfaction than it should. Enough, perhaps, to get him through the next few minutes of his cousin's boorish company. He pasted on a smile. "Pembroke. Enjoying the evening, I see?"

"Quite. A remarkable neighborhood, if I must say. Such charming ladies," Geoffrey strolled up from behind him. "A few quite spectacular ones, in fact. Miss Schofield is looking particularly lovely this evening. And quite an excellent dancer."

Stephen was overcome by the need to wipe the stupid, leering smile of Geoffrey's right off his face. Of course, having an indication that Miss Schofield did not welcome Pembroke's attentions made it easier for him to be bold.

"Then I shall have to determine that for myself. I shall ensure I have the first of the next set with her."

Geoffrey raised his glass, his normally charming expression wearing a decidedly sour note before he recovered himself and moved on, to the great delight of a nearby group of ladies determined to have his attention.

For the next hour, Stephen engrossed himself in conversation with several of the gentleman in the room, taking time to shake hands with the few townspeople who actually seemed eager to have the honor of speaking with him. Still, the ghost of Sally Coles and the Beast hung in the room, as lace fans provided cover for whispers and intrigues that were thick in the corners of the assembly hall.

"Not quite the cataclysmic event you thought it would be?" Edmund said when it was finally the two of them alone. He presented Stephen with a glass of wine.

"I suppose not," Stephen replied. "Although I cannot help but wonder at what tales will be told tomorrow."

"Come, Stephen. England survives on gossip as much as it does on mutton and ale. It's the great leveler. Prince or pauper, a tall tale is enjoyed by all."

Stephen's lips pressed into a thin line. *Not by me.*

"No doubt it would help matters if you were not looking so incredibly dour." Edmund held up his wine glass, gesturing across the crowded assembly hall. "Besides, you are being usurped as the topic of gossip by Geoffrey. He's making quite the to-do, it would seem."

Stephen took a long sip of his wine, which tasted uncommonly bitter as it rolled over his tongue. In another corner of the room, Pembroke appeared to be happily entertaining several young ladies and gentlemen, Eleanore Martin among them, which did nothing to improve his mood. Off to one side was Rosalind Schofield, keeping an ever-watchful eye.

So that was where she had hid herself. As if sensing his gaze, she turned her head ever so slightly, catching his eye and smiled. He nodded his head in acknowledgement.

"Ah! I see you have found Miss Schofield. I wondered why you were looking so recovered," Edmund said.

"Let me commend you on your excellent eyesight," Stephen grumbled, turning his attention back to his company.

"She favored me with a turn about the room," Edmund continued. "She is a very thoughtful woman. Very—what was the word? Ah, yes. Interesting."

"What in the blazes is your brother doing?" Stephen asked, ignoring his cousin's last jibe. Geoffrey had gone and taken Miss Schofield by the hand, clearly teasing her to join him and his crowd.

"Doing his absolute best to keep Schofield's charge in his attentions. He's already danced with her twice. Maybe he's aiming for a third set." Edmund replied. "But I am certain Miss Schofield is far too sensible to fall for his charms."

As Stephen watched Miss Schofield laugh at whatever jokes Geoffrey was telling, he wondered about that. This was a girl who he had found wandering in his orangery in the heavy dawn mists. Who argued with the local bookseller because he denied her a book about mythical beasts. Who openly questioned his curse. Who refused the offer of marriage to a marquess. "Sensible" was not the first word he would ascribe to Rosalind Schofield.

Of course, the constricted feeling in his throat as he watched his cousin fawn over her wasn't entirely sensible either. She relented at last, and joined Geoffrey at his side as they wandered back into his clutch of hangers-on.

"Where the hell is Schofield?"

"For heaven's sake Barronsfield, stop grimacing."

"It's this wine." He stared into the ruby liquid in his glass. "Where on earth did they find this bitter draught?" Stephen made a mental note to have Schofield oversee the procurement of wine for all future assemblies.

"It tastes fine to my inferior palate," Edmund said.

He continued to extol the virtues of the libations as Stephen's attentions drifted back across the room. To her. Amazing how such an ordinary girl could catch his interest. When she laughed, he couldn't help but notice how she would raise one of her hands to her chest and rest it on her bosom.

Perhaps he should join them. That's what people did at assemblies, did they not? They danced, they laughed, they talked, and they enjoyed themselves. Riveted where he was, he realized he had forgotten all of that. Or—as he thought back to the endless lessons about decorum from his tutors, from his father—perhaps he had never really learned how.

"Barronsfield? Stephen?"

"Ummm?" Stephen looked over to a mystified and amused Edmund. "Yes?"

Edmund laughed. "Never mind. I am sorry cousin, but with so many pretty girls to be had, I can no longer content myself with your company, as stimulating as it may be." And with that, he disappeared into the crowd.

Stephen drained his glass, and with equal determination, decided to join Miss Schofield, who stood far too close to his cousin for his liking. The fact that Geoffrey seemed to be helping himself to generous glances at Miss Schofield's bosom only spurred his resolve.

"Barronsfield!" Geoffrey called out. "Come join us."

Not that he needed Geoffrey's invitation, but he strode over, placing himself between his cousin and Miss Schofield. The sour expression on Geoffrey's face as he did so gave Stephen a certain measure of satisfaction.

Miss Schofield's cheeks were flushed, and while it was very close in the room, Stephen was not certain the heat was the culprit. She toyed with the locket around her neck. Was she nervous? He could hardly imagine her so. While she wasn't a typical beauty she did have a way about her that was pleasing. And by no means had he fallen head over heels in love in with her.

She was safe. And so was he.

As Geoffrey nattered on about fencing at Oxford—which he never did—or his impressions of Walpole's *Castle of Otranto*—Geoffrey hated to read—Stephen found himself fixated on the idea of dancing with Miss Schofield, and at the same time, dreading asking her. After such a disastrous marriage proposal, she might well assume that standing up with him in a public assembly room might be considered only a slightly lesser insult. Only, he didn't want it to be. He was ready to make his excuses and remove himself from the party, if only to escape the rather schoolboyish nerves that were besetting him.

But he'd already declared to Geoffrey that the next dance with Miss Schofield would be his. As notes from the musicians signaled another set was about to begin, Stephen saw Geoffrey making overtures, as if testing Stephen. Swallowing any doubt that he might insult her, he pulled down on his waistcoat, let out a breath, and turned to her.

"Miss Schofield," he blurted out, "if you are not otherwise engaged, would you care to dance the next with me?"

He could see the uncertainty in her eyes. He was putting her on the spot, he knew very well. She stared at him for what seemed like a very long time, and then a curious thing happened.

"I would indeed, my lord. Thank you."

A murmur of frantic gossip rose over the din in the room as he escorted her to the dance floor. The idea that Miss Schofield might be censured for standing up with him gripped Stephen. He lowered his voice, speaking barely above a whisper.

"I am sorry if I am embarrassing you."

"Do not be, my lord. If anyone should be embarrassed here, it is the so-called polite society in this room."

And then, standing nearby as they took their places, Edmund started clapping loudly. Before long, Mr. Battersby, the Darlings and others joined him, braved the crowd and made their approval known.

Miss Schofield stood opposite him, smiling. If she had opened her mouth and spoken the words "I told you so", it would have not have been any more understood than her countenance at that moment.

"I am surprised you did not refuse me, Miss Schofield," he said as the music finally began.

"As am I, my lord."

"Then, may I ask why you accepted?"

"Perhaps it was the lesser of two evils," she said as she turned in Geoffrey's direction.

"For a moment I thought perhaps you were trying to escape me."

"You?" She looked clearly surprised. "I would never run from you. Except, perhaps, when you are making an as—excuse me, an idiot of yourself."

"Congratulations on your restraint in your choice of nouns, Miss Schofield."

"Thank you," she replied.

"My God," he said under his breath, somewhat panic stricken. He'd forgotten.

"What is it?" Miss Schofield asked, alarm widening her eyes.

He almost couldn't say it. Taking a look to his left and right, he leaned in. "It has been some time since I have been on a dance floor. I don't know if I can recall the steps."

She gave him the most endearing look. Surely his heart would have melted if he had any feelings for her. "We shall make the best of it, and have a little fun. Just mind my toes."

He smiled back and started to wonder about her toes.

The music started, and thankfully, it was a quadrille. Though he took a misstep once or twice, it came back to him quick enough, and the pleasure of being just another person in the room—even if he knew that wasn't completely true—allowed him to relax a little. And the stolen glances and brief touches from Miss Schofield, even through gloved hands, made the moment as perfect as it could have been.

"I am almost afraid to say it, my lord," Miss Schofield began.

"What?" his curiosity peaked.

"You appear to be enjoying yourself."

"And so I am, Miss Schofield," he replied. *Thanks to you.* "I hope you will not spoil it by lecturing me."

She put on a look of false indignation. "Me? Never. At least not in public. I'll save it for your library, if you like."

"I would like that. Very much." The conviction in his voice

surprised himself, and from the look on her face, Miss Schofield as well.

A sense of euphoria crashed over him in the next moment, a fit of laughter seizing him. Before him, Miss Schofield's smile change into confusion, then concern. Was it something he had said?

He tried to speak, but his tongue failed him. And in the next moment, as the room began to turn and he could feel the sickly familiar feeling of blood rushing through his body, he realized it was happening again.

Dear God. Not now.

CHAPTER 12

"My lord?"

Rosalind stopped dancing.

Lord Barronsfield's expression went from amusement, to a bizarre outburst of laughter, to utter panic. His body swayed even though his feet were frozen in place. The skin around his eyes started to flush, and he looked about the room as if he was suddenly unsure of his surroundings.

"Lord Barronsfield." She stepped toward him and took his shaking hand into her own. His actions were beginning to attract attention, but Rosalind ignored the curious stares of those immediately next to them. "What is the matter? Are you unwell?"

His face contorted, and the unnerving expression stopped Rosalind from taking another step closer. It was as if he was fighting with his own body for control, and it was a fight he was losing.

"I haf to leafff, Mizz Schofield," he said at last, his voice thick and clumsy. He sounded like he was foxed, but he had been perfectly sober a moment ago. He placed an unsteady hand on her arm, pressing down on her with almost all his weight in a desperate bid to keep himself upright.

Alarmed, Rosalind searched frantically about the room for her uncle or Edmund Pembroke. Instead, she saw Eleanore rushing up to her.

"Stay away from me!"

The roar exploded from the marquess, who lurched away wildly when he saw Eleanore approach them. The girl stood fast in her tracks.

"Get my uncle directly!" Rosalind called out to her, all the while trying to hold the marquess steady. The music had abruptly stopped, and the dancers and onlookers stepped back, gawking in fascinated horror. Eleanore blinked, in shock, but then disappeared into the crowd.

"I have t' get out, get out," he rambled on, nearly incoherent now.

"Don't worry my lord. My uncle is coming."

The marquess's movements became ever more erratic as he pushed through the crowd in a frantic effort to get to the door. Rosalind still propped him up, but with every step it became more and more difficult.

"Miss Schofield!"

Geoffrey Pembroke appeared out of nowhere, and in one fluid motion, pulled her away from Lord Barronsfield's grasp. The marquess's balance, already precarious, deserted him, and he fell face first, a gasp rising from the throng at the sickening sound of his head smashing against the hard wooden floor.

Rosalind looked back at Mr. Pembroke in confusion, then back down at the marquess. Blood poured from his nose as he tried desperately to get up. A second later, her uncle and Edmund were at his side, pulling Lord Barronsfield onto his feet. Just as they managed to get him upright, the marquess thrashed violently about and they were both immediately thrown to the floor. Before they or Rosalind could reach him, he stormed past them, out into the night.

The room descended into chaos, assembly goers running in all directions, uncertain whether it was safer to stay where they were or brave the night, where the marquess had gone, raving like a madman and, according to belief, about to shed his human guise for a more beastly form. The angry threats of those louts who'd confronted her uncle at the vicarage came back to her, filling her with a sickening sense of dread. Would they go out looking for the marquess, ready to reap their own rough justice?

"Uncle Reginald! Mr. Pembroke!" Rosalind struggled to push her way through the anxious crowd, toward Edmund and Uncle Reginald, who were bounding for the door in pursuit. She took no more than a couple of steps before she was pulled back.

"Where on earth do you think you are going?" Geoffrey Pembroke asked, his voice a mix of incredulity and panic as he kept a firm grip on her arm. "Can you not see what is happening to him? It is not safe out there, Miss Schofield. Not with that monster lurking about. Let me protect you from his madness."

"The marquess—your cousin—is in obvious distress, Mr. Pembroke. We must help him, before he does himself, or anyone else, harm." She raised her voice over the cacophony in the room and tried to pull free from Geoffrey Pembroke's increasingly uncomfortable grasp. "He is in danger. My uncle—"

"Miss Schofield, I think you would be far better off staying here, under my protection. Or, if you prefer, I can escort you home," he said, a notable amount of urgency in his voice.

"Mr. Pembroke—"

"You must heed me. The last woman he chased after in the night came home a corpse."

His words made her start. Did Mr. Pembroke truly believe she was in danger? If anyone was at risk right now, it was the marquess. Of that she was sure.

The pleading in Mr. Pembroke's eyes receded as Rosalind stopped pulling away. Her apparent second thoughts must have been enough for him to relax, for when she looked for any sign of his concern, she found none. He seemed steadfast on the idea of keeping her within his sights, which made her equally determined to get past them.

Out of the corner of her eye, she spotted Eleanore, still looking dazed by the whole affair. Rosalind was shocked by the fierceness of the marquess's reaction to the girl, but poor Eleanore appeared as if she would not recover from it. If anyone needed an escort home, she did. Which gave Rosalind an idea.

"Mr. Pembroke sir, you are very generous. I have been extremely short sighted. I think the excitement of the evening has clouded my good sense." Wasn't that what women were supposed to say? Apparently so, for Mr. Pembroke's look softened as she spoke. "I would ask if you could escort me home. But first I must see to Miss Martin. I will join you shortly."

"I will find you here when I return?" He asked in an untroubled tone that sounded terribly out of place at the moment.

"Eagerly awaiting you, yes." She smiled, and hoped it didn't look as false as she felt doing it. Walking away, she tried to shake off the uncomfortable feeling that he was watching her every move. Fortunately the chaos in the room made it easy for her to disappear. It also made it difficult to find Eleanore again, but after several minutes, she saw her friend, looking quite bereft and so very, very young.

"My dear Eleanore!"

Eleanore nodded but seemed to have lost her voice. Rosalind wrapped her arms around her and gave her a squeeze. In doing so she heard her friend cough back a small sob.

"Where are the vicar and Mrs. Darling?" Rosalind dug out her handkerchief and dabbed her friend's eyes. "I am so sorry your first assembly ended so horribly for you."

"For us all, I would say." She smiled sadly.

"He wasn't in his right mind when he left, Eleanore."

"I know. It must be the curse. Oh Rosalind, what if it is all true?"

"We shall find him and worry about the rest later."

"Eleanore, my dear." Mrs. Darling pushed through the crowd, folding her charge into a strong embrace. "That must have been terrifying."

Rosalind, content to see Eleanore would be looked after, turned away. She had only gone a few steps before Eleanore caught her hand.

"Rosalind," Eleanore said. "Where are you going?"

Rosalind shook her head, her sense of urgency growing with every passing moment. "I must go." Looking past her friend, she saw Geoffrey Pembroke scanning the crowd looking for her. "Eleanore, I must ask you to do me a great favor."

"Anything."

"Mr. Geoffrey Pembroke might come back looking for me. If he inquires, you must tell him that I have gone in search of him. Can you do that?"

"Where are you going?"

"To find Lord Barronsfield."

"Rosalind, you cannot! It is dangerous."

"Eleanore, Lord Barronsfield is more a danger to himself in his current state than to me or anyone else. Besides, my uncle and Edmund Pembroke are out there looking for him as well. I will be safe —I promise you."

Her young friend must have caught the determination in her eye, for she said nothing more. Lines of worry strung across her young face, Eleanore pulled Rosalind close to give her a small hug, then let her go. Without further discussion, Rosalind disappeared into the crowd.

She found the servants' entrance. Grabbing a heavy cloak and a lantern, she made her way out the door and into the alley. It was dark, and light rain left a sheen over the stone buildings. Thunder rumbled in the distance and the wind whipped around her, as if channeling the chaos and fear of the people inside the assembly hall. A nervous shiver ran through her as she looked to her left, then right, not completely certain of where she was going or how she would find the marquess.

She ran down the cobblestone road, conscious of the sound of her slippers scuffing on the stone. The buildings in the narrow lane seem to close in on her from above, and clouds overhead raced as if the very night was closing in on her from all sides. The sound of a cart, its wheels rumbling furiously over the uneven road, emerged from behind. They grew louder, though the darkness obscured its approach. They sprang into view at almost the last second, and Rosalind, heart pounding, dove for the side of the building just before the beasts could trample her. In the next second horses whinnied and hooves skidded on stone as the driver pulled the cart to a rough stop only a few feet from where Rosalind hid in the shadows of the buildings, hiding the lamp in the folds of her cape.

"Son of a bitch, where'd he go?"

Not daring to give herself away, Rosalind strained to listen to the voice not ten feet away.

"Too bloody dark," another voice spat. "I vote we head for Barronsfield. He's probably headed home."

"We'll need to get 'im before he gets there, or it'll be our necks."

They were after him, just as she'd feared. The first voice she recognized from the vicar's yard. How on earth could they have gathered so quickly? How could they have guessed this would happen to Lord Barronsfield tonight?

Unless they didn't have to guess at all.

"What about the steward? I say we pay him a visit," came a third voice.

Rosalind held her breath.

"First things first. That's not part of the plan right now, see? We can't be lollyin' around here all night! Tom, get a move on."

A crack of the reins and the cart lumbered away.

She waited until they were safely out of view, then burst into a run. She needed to find the marquess, even as uncertainty gripped her about what she might discover. But she had to get to him before they did.

Her feet pounded on the hard stone, while her thoughts moved even faster than her feet. There was *something* wrong with him. His flushed skin, his slurred speech. He was clearly under the influence of something—but a curse? No.

Thunder rumbled again, louder, announcing its approach. She came to the end of the lane and found herself on a larger road that led out of town. The road toward Barronsfield. Would the marquess go there? Rosalind had no idea, though it seemed logical. Listening for any signs of the men she'd seen earlier, the only sounds she heard were her own breath, and the wind rising. Rosalind continued on, stopping every few minutes to catch her breath and look out on the horizon. She needed another way back there, a faster way.

She stumbled through the darkness for what felt like a long time. The weathered buildings and overgrown hedges of Elmsdale had slipped away into the distance some time ago, the road ahead stretched into the interminable blackness. The landscape was still new to her, which made her journey all the more taxing. The moon and stars were buried in cloud, leaving Rosalind only her lamp to guide her. Her feet ached from running on the stone with nothing but thin slippers on her feet. The marquess had disappeared, and even her uncle and Edmund were nowhere to be found. Standing alone in the middle of a long, bleak stretch of road, she deliberated heading back to the assembly hall, or walking on to Barronsfield, which she guessed was still at least another mile down the road. In the dark. The daring that had sent her into the night started to desert her. She looked up into the sky, hoping for a trace of starlight, but there was none to be found.

Praying that it wasn't delusion forcing her on a wild goose chase, Rosalind made for Barronsfield. The road was becoming rutted as the rain fell a little harder now, obscuring her vision and drowning her spirits. What on earth was she doing? How was one woman of ordinary size with no particular talent going to help the marquess? This night was like no tale she'd read, nor even one she'd dreamed for herself.

The skies opened and pelting rain replaced the light drizzle. She held up her lamp, its meager light trying to cut through the wet night. Her eyes scanned the horizon once more. Through the darkness, she could make out the forms of the gates leading into Barronsfield. A flash of lightening cut across the stone pillars, monuments to the grandeur of the park they guarded.

Monuments. In a moment, Rosalind knew where the marquess was going. The place where he went for solace. The place she'd found him only a few nights ago, baring his soul to the dead. To the orangery, where his beloved roses were ensconced in glass, so they would never fade. Last time, she'd found it only by accident. She'd have to make it back to the manor, and find Hanley. She could get that far at least. Her feet squishing in the muddy road, she continued on.

Just before the large gates that led into the estate Rosalind stopped to catch her breath, which hung in chilled night air. Her legs ached, and her hand was sore and freezing from clutching the lamp. Rosalind bent down, setting the lamp on the ground to give her hand a rest. Flexing her fingers, she shoved her hand under her arm to warm it up again. Rain pelted her, and the chill from the earth reached easily through the thin, mud soaked fabric of her slippers. She had to keep moving, not just to find the marquess, but to get warm.

She bent down to retrieve the lamp, and caught the shadowed indent of footprints in the mud. Standing, hunched over, focused on the road, more of what looked like a track of prints, made by a man's boots, led away from the gate, following a cattle path that led behind the estate. Rosalind followed, the storm at her heels, but hope that the marquess might be close by drove her on. Before long, the storm caught up with her.

She started to whistle, as loud as she dared, recalling a story her father had told her about how his ship had been caught in thick fog off Sable Island. He'd used dead reckoning and a lead line to find their way back. Slowly, surely, looking ahead to mark which direction to go. Holding out her lamp, swallowing her fear, she started ahead, using what meager light she had to guide herself as he had.

A clap of thunder came much louder this time, and with it, lightening cut through the darkness, revealing a small stone wall to her right. Beyond it was the orangery. She continued along the path until the stone and glass structure was almost next to her.

"Lord Barronsfield!" she called out as loudly as she could. There was no response.

"Lord Barronsfield!"

Still nothing. Picking up her now drenched skirts, she ran her hand along the stone exterior wall, hoping to find the entrance. The ground quickly became soft under her feet, and every step took more and more effort to ensure she didn't slip.

"Lord Barronsfield!"

She held the lamp in front of her, straining to see through the dark and the rain. A second later, lightening bristled in the air, allowing her eyes to focus in on the frantic figure of the marquess, standing not ten feet away from her, his hands clawing at the glass annex to the hot house.

"Lord Barronsfield!"

Another brilliant flash cut through the blackness when she saw him. A silent gasp caught in her throat. Eyes wild, tearing at his chest, spewing a litany of curses and incomprehensible babble, the marquess contorted as if his own body was on fire. Filth was smeared across his face and soiled his shirt, which, along with his waistcoat, was torn open. His coat was gone, lost perhaps, to the mud. He seemed totally unaware of anyone or anything surrounding him. Whether he could not hear her above the storm, or whether he simply didn't understand her, she couldn't tell.

She looked about, dearly wishing her uncle would appear. The marquess was nearly a foot taller and broader than her by a half; there was not a hope she could bring him back to the manor in his current state. Though they weren't far from the manor, the small wooded lanes that led to this spot would soon be little more than muddy rivers. She had to figure out a way to lead him back to safety.

Carefully Rosalind made her way closer. Her feet slipped on slick ground, and she tried not to focus on the unsettling sounds coming from Lord Barronsfield. At one moment he spoke softly, but to whom, she could not make out. At other moments he screamed in such agony as to freeze her in her tracks.

Taking cautious steps, her skirts dragging behind her, she bent to set the lamp down. As she stood, she met the wild stare of Lord Barronsfield, his eyes as black as they had ever been.

A clap of thunder overhead drowned out Rosalind's scream. He was a dangerous combination of aggression and fear, more wounded animal than man. And yet, despite his beastly appearance, a man he was still.

Rosalind closed her eyes and bucked up courage.

"Lord Barronsfield." she spoke the words gently, and he started at the sound of his name, though whether he recognized it as such, she didn't know. Rosalind waited, but he did nothing. "It is I, Rosalind Schofield. Do you know me?"

In the shadows, Rosalind found it nearly impossible to decipher his expression, but his attention remained fixed on her. Whether that was for good or ill, she couldn't be completely certain. Wounded animals were dangerous.

"You need help, my lord. I must get you to safety." Even as she uttered the words, she realized she had spoken them before.

He staggered toward her, his manner so lumbering she instinctively staggered back, stopped by one of the glass walls that encased the rose bush behind her. "Please, my lord. I am here to help you. I must get you back to the manor."

A second later, he nearly fell on top of her, holding onto her shoulders as if trying to steady himself.

"My lord!" she yelled, unabashed in her fear. She turned her head away, waiting for a blow.

"Rozlin." It came out as a low clumsy slur—the same way he had been at the assembly hall.

Rosalind swallowed hard, then opened her eyes. "Yes, my lord."

"Pleash help me fine Rozlin." He shook her gently, but it was a plea for help, not the action of anger. "I need to fine her."

"I am right here, Lord Barronsfield. Rosalind is here. I am she."

He looked up at that moment, releasing her in a rough movement that almost caused her to fall at his feet. Quickly, he became agitated again, and started backing away. She turned to look over her shoulder, to the place that had caught Lord Barronsfield's attention. There, past him, was the distant glimmer of lights. Hoping against hope they signaled the help she needed, and not the hooligans out to harm him, she determined to keep Lord Barronsfield in this spot until they arrived. If the marquess ran off now, she would never find him again.

Screwing up her courage—what little she had left—she started walking toward him, speaking as calmly as she could manage.

"Stephen, please. It's Miss Schofield. It's Rosalind. I am here to help you."

He shook his head, muttering to himself. Rosalind saw the lamps straying off in another direction. Impulsively she yelled out to them, which only seemed to make the marquess more agitated.

"What you are doing to her, Barronsfield?"

Rosalind looked over her shoulder to another form that had approached from out of the night. Geoffrey Pembroke.

"Mr. Pembroke, thank goodness. Please help me." She was relieved to see him, but the anger in the man's voice gave her pause.

"Back away, Miss Schofield!" he yelled out to her. "He is too dangerous!"

"Please sir! He is in great distress. I am unharmed, as you see," she shouted back, the rain and wind whipping her words away into the blackness.

"Barronsfield! Answer me, you devil!"

Rosalind's eyes widened as she saw Pembroke raise his arms over his head, a large piece of stone in his hands, aimed squarely at his cousin. Utterly panicked, she cried out, "What are you doing? Mr. Pembroke, stop!"

But he wouldn't. And as the lightning crackled in the air above them, Rosalind saw madness.

"My lord. Stephen! Look out!"

At that moment, Barronsfield turned around and lurched toward his attacker, but he was too slow. Rashly, she tried to push the marquess out of the way, slipping on the muddy ground before Mr. Pembroke could deliver his blow.

Rosalind hit the ground so hard the wind was knocked out of her, and she strained to get her breath. She lay there, trying to recover from the shock and the force of the blow, feeling nothing but the rain pelting on her, and the cold wet ground under her body.

A moment later, she was aware she was being picked up, cradled, by the marquess.

"All is well now," she said through chattering teeth, holding onto him.

A grip of panic came upon her as she remembered that Geoffrey Pembroke must be nearby. She lifted her head, straining to see. A second later, she was blinded by light shining a few feet away.

"My lord! Lord Barronsfield!"

"Stephen! It is Edmund! Answer if you can!"

The sound of her uncle's and Edmund's voices brought a rush of relief. "Over here!" she cried out, before turning her attention to the marquess. "My lord, help is come."

She looked into his eyes which, for a brief moment, seemed clear and aware. "Edmund and my Uncle Reginald are coming. Let them help you. We will take you home."

"Please," he sobbed, his voice thick and rough. "Please stay with me."

"Uncle," she called out through chattered teeth. "Mr. Pembroke—"

"Rosalind," her uncle replied as he approached. He pulled her to her feet and pushed the hair out of her face. "There now my girl, you are fine now."

Her teeth chattered so wildly it was nearly impossible to speak. She looked for Geoffrey Pembroke, but he'd seemed to have disappeared into the shadows. Where had he gone?

Lord Barronsfield was calm, if disoriented at first, then, as the realization that she was no longer with him seemed to sink in, he became agitated once again. He called out into the night for her, his voice cracking with fear.

"Uncle, please, let me go to him," she begged, the sound of the marquess's frantic calls driving into her heart. "I can help him. He will listen to me."

"Rosalind my dear, he is too dangerous. He doesn't hear you. I can't risk it." Her uncle swallowed deeply, and even through the rain and wind she heard the fear in his voice. "We have people here to help us. As much as he is my lord and master, I cannot risk you."

A moment later, she stood alone, watching helplessly as her uncle, Edmund and four other men managed to wrestle the marquess into a cart. They tied him down like an animal in a desperate bid to keep him from hurting himself or killing one of them. She choked back her sadness, and for the first time that evening, Rosalind was grateful for the rain.

CHAPTER 13

It took Edmund, Rosalind's uncle, and three footmen to bring the marquess from the carriage back to his bedchamber. Lord Barronsfield fought them so violently that by the time they got him through the door and to his bed, it took three more men to keep him there. After a great deal of struggle, they'd managed to tie him down. The doctor had been summoned, but in this weather, it would be sometime before he would arrive. In the few moments Rosalind could stand to tear her eyes away from Lord Barronsfield, she discovered several of the maids standing in the shadows just outside the door, sometimes peeking in at the spectacle, then looking away, their faces uncertain, whispering among themselves. Each of them wondering, no doubt, who the marquess had attacked tonight, and if that person would end up like Sally Coles.

Once Lord Barronsfield was secured, her uncle went to reassure and direct the servants, then returned to the room and took Rosalind's ice cold hand in his own.

"My dear girl, we need to get you into dry clothes before you catch your death."

Rosalind nodded, realizing how loud her teeth were chattering. Her slippers were soaked through, her beautiful silk dress ruined, and

141

her entire body stiff and sore. On another night, a cup of hot chocolate and her bed would have probably done her a world of good. But this was not any other night. The marquess moved between unconsciousness and violent semi-wakefulness, his body mud soaked, tied down for his own good. Every time he tried to claw at his own skin, she could barely stand to watch. Though the room was filled with people, Lord Barronsfield laid there, alone. Helplessness tormented her.

"Can we not find a way to help him? Surely this has happened before," she pleaded with her uncle. "There must be a remedy for his ills. We cannot leave him like this."

"We have summoned the doctor, and that is all we can do right now. I think you need to get some rest, my dear. Tending to the marquess is not your responsibility," her uncle said. He reached up and pulled her hair gently out of her face, and cast a wary glance to one side of Rosalind's head. "What have we here?"

Instinctively she put her fingers to her cheek. The skin was tender, and she could feel a small cut. There had been so much commotion she had barely been aware of it.

"It is nothing, Uncle. I slipped in the mud just before you found me." Eager to direct her uncle's attention back the marquess, she cleared her throat and pointed at toward the bed where Lord Barronsfield lay. "If you could have someone fetch me some clean clothes, and a basin of water, I would be happy to stay with you and Edmund. I think it would be safer for him."

"Rosalind, I don't—"

"Please." Wracked by a need she didn't understand, she found it difficult to control the edge threatening to creep into her voice. "We cannot leave him alone. Can we not wait for the physician? I beg you, let me stay and be of use. Besides, maybe the marquess will say something that will give us a clue as to what happened. Uncle, you must consider that as horrible as this looks, we have learned something important. Something positive."

"What on earth is good about this?" He turned to look upon his master, mud caked, a bloodied face, pulling against the restraints.

"We know he isn't a monster, Uncle. He didn't turn into any sort of creature. He is just a man." A man who was perfectly fine one minute, and not the next. Was it illness? Or something else?

Water squelched from her sodden slippers as Rosalind bounced up and down on her toes, watching her uncle deliberate. The man was clearly torn between the needs of his master and his duty as her guardian.

Thunder crashed again. Uncle Reginald beckoned her out to the hall. "Rosalind, my dear, as much as I know you want to be here, I must look after you too. I could not live with myself if you fell ill. You've already been hurt. Lord Barronsfield does not even know you are here." He regarded her with such a gentle, heartfelt expression. "But you will stay at the manor tonight. No charge of mine will be going anywhere in this weather."

He turned to one of the servants close by. "Bess, take Miss Schofield to the Green room and see to it that she gets warm and into some clean, dry clothes. There should be something there she can wear."

The girl, plainly relieved at not having to go into the marquess's room, nodded, and escorted Rosalind down the long hall. Paying attention to little but the candle light coming from the maid ahead, Rosalind followed in silence. Shadows sliced up the walls, and eyes from the portraits peered out as they walked past. From behind her, an agonized howl she recognized as the marquess echoed in the long halls. If this was the sound that haunted the corridors of Barronsfield Manor at night, it was little wonder why so many of the servants had left.

Soon they arrived at the room that would be Rosalind's bedchamber for the night. Stale air filled Rosalind's nose as she entered. The room must not have been used in quite some time. Soon candles were lit and a fire crackled in the grate, burning away the mustiness in the air.

"You're chilled to the bone, miss! Sit here by the fire, and cover yourself with this." Bess handed Rosalind a heavy blanket of finely spun wool, and removed her mud soaked slippers. "I'll be back in a few moments with some water." As she stood, the sound of another scream echoed in the distance, and the young girl stood up with a start.

"Don't be frightened," Rosalind said. "He sounds scary, but he is ill, that's all."

"But the Beast—?"

"I have been with him all evening, Bess. I watched him fall ill, but there was neither fangs nor claws nor anything else unnatural."

"But Sally—" The girl's eyes widened before she looked away and busied herself by seeing to the fire.

"What happened to her was terrible. Were you friends?"

Bess turned to face Rosalind, and nodded. "Aye. Not close, mind. We were friendly."

"Emily said she was a smart girl."

"She was quick, that's for sure. 'Cept she went and got herself a crush on Jack Gates. That was none too smart." Bess shook her head sadly. "That boy's an arse if there ever was one."

"Jack Gates? Does he live in the village?"

"Aye—works at the mill alongside his dad, Tom. The Gateses is all a tough bunch. Certainly give us here at Barronsfield a hard enough time." Bess walked to an ornate wardrobe, the doors creaking slightly as she opened them. She pulled out a chemise, shook it out and brought it back to the hearth, where she carefully laid it out to air out and warm the fabric.

Rosalind stood close to the fire, watching Bess, letting the flames' heat seep through her heavy layers of wet clothes. "In what way do they give you a hard time?"

"They said the master destroyed part of their livestock, not long after Miss Wickwire passed." Bess started to pace, fumbling a bit with her apron. Her voice shook ever so slightly. "They've always been stir-ring up folks, sayin' us at Barronsfield is siding with the devil. Mr. Schofield has told us never pay them much attention, but after what happened to Sally—"

Rosalind reached out to the servant, and took her hand. "I would be scared too. But I promise you, I saw nothing any reasonable person would call devilry. No spell, no curse. Just a man who's fallen ill." Deathly ill, in fact, but she didn't want to give voice to her own fears. "What's happening to your master is frightening, but do not be scared of him. If anything you should be scared *for* him."

Bess gave Rosalind a cautious smile, then stooped to gather up Rosalind's sodden cape. "I'll be back with some warm water directly."

The girl left, leaving Rosalind to her own thoughts. *Gates.* The name 'Tom Gates' had been whispered in the dark by those men when she'd gone in search of the marquess. A man named Tom had accosted her uncle the day she'd arrived. It was perhaps not terribly Christian of her to think ill of a man she'd never met, but there it was.

A shudder shook her body. The fire was warming, yes, but her dress was still cold and wet. And ruined. As she inspected the hem she could see mud caked heavily at the bottom. Her white stockings underneath were also not fit for wearing. Unable to wait for Bess to return, she rose, dropped the blanket on the floor, and started to pull at her dress. After some minutes of wriggling, she managed to pull off her gown. Her heart sank a little as the once pristine silk, now heavy with water and mud, fell in a heap at her feet. Gingerly she picked it up and draped it over a wooden chair. She untied her stays, and peeled off her stockings, leaving her in naught save her shift, which was also wet. She removed it and donned the chemise Bess had laid out for her. Pulling the blanket around her once more, she started to feel a little more comfortable.

What a miserable night. If any good could be said, it was that those horrible men from the village hadn't found the marquess or her uncle. Lord Barronsfield had barely left the assembly hall when they were out on the roads giving chase. While she didn't doubt that word of Lord Barronsfield's madness would have spread quickly, how did they know of it and gather in pursuit mere minutes after it had began? It was as if they'd known something was going to happen.

Taking a candle, she went to the wardrobe, looking for a dressing gown or robe to better cover her. The door creaked as she opened it, revealing a closet bursting with dresses. Even in the dim light, she could tell they were of the finest fabric. She was running her fingers over the dresses when the door to the room flew open. Geoffrey Pembroke raced in, sodden and agitated.

"Mr. Pembroke!"

"My dear Miss Schofield, I could not tarry a moment longer." He strode over and stood much too close for her liking. She stepped back, her body recoiling from his presence, but with the armoire at her back, she had nowhere to go. All she could do was pull the wool blanket tight around her body.

"Mr. Pembroke! You will leave immediately. This is highly improper."

"Concern for your wellbeing has bade me throw caution to the wind." He began touching her hair, putting his hands on her shoulders, holding her fast. The madness she'd seen in his eyes earlier had vanished, replaced with something just as terrifying—desperation.

"Mr. Pembroke! Please!" Apprehension crept into her belly, and only with effort could she keep her mortification in check. "I appreciate your concern, but I insist you leave at once. I would be happy to meet with you on the morrow, when we are both rested and properly attired."

He showed no signs of even hearing her. Instead, he zeroed in on her face, lifting her bruised cheek to the candlelight. She winced at his touch.

"That devil. What has he done to you?"

She brushed his hand away. "He has done nothing, Mr. Pembroke. You did this. What were you trying to do, kill him?"

"You were in danger, Miss Schofield. Mortal danger," he replied. "He's killed three women already."

"The marquess posed no threat to me."

"Clearly the excitement of the night has overcome you." He regarded her with unflinching condescension. "It is only natural, after all that has happened."

"But—"

"Shhhh." He placed a hand over her lips, speaking to her as if she were a small child, reminding Rosalind of her aunt. It only served to make her more furious, but the memory of his anger toward the marquess brought a fear that trapped her breath in her throat. "There now, Miss Schofield. It's over now. You are overwrought. So much unpleasantness after what should have been a lovely evening for us."

"For us?" Rosalind sputtered, her heart beating faster "Please, Mr. Pembroke. This entire evening has been unpleasant. If you have any concern for me, please leave."

"I fear I cannot. I think too highly of you to put this matter to rest. He has wrought too much havoc. I will not let him damage you as well."

Before Rosalind could get in another word, he planted a hard kiss on her lips. She nearly choked as she felt his tongue push past her lips.

"I'm here with your water, miss, at last."

Rosalind's heart leaped into her throat when she heard Bess's voice. Mr. Pembroke halted his advances. The blanket she'd held around herself had fallen loose to the floor leaving Rosalind clad in only her thin shift. She was for all purposes, nearly naked. Instinctively, she crossed her hands over her chest and ignored the look of frustration on Mr. Pembroke's face.

"Bess! Thank you! Mr. Pembroke was just leaving."

"I'm sorry, Miss Schofield," he said, his voice remorseful. "The excitement of the evening has overwhelmed me. I will check on you in the morning, and see that you are well. Good evening." He stood there for another moment, the fire light dancing off his face. And then, as abruptly as he arrived, he left.

As the door closed behind them, Rosalind's knees threatened to buckle under her. With a large intake of breath, she bent down to retrieve the blanket at her feet. In a moment, Beth was there, wrapping it tightly around her shoulders. She led her to a seat close to the fire. Rosalind, desperate to get warm and rid herself Geoffrey Pembroke's intrusion, wiped her mouth with the corner of the blanket. *Are all of the men in this household mad?* She looked up to Bess, who placed her hands over Rosalind's arms, rubbing them briskly in an effort to get her blood flowing. "Your timing was brilliant. Thank you."

"I'm sorry I left you, miss," Bess said. "Shall I ask Hanley to bring you some brandy, miss? You're shaking something fierce."

"There is no need for apologies. You had your duties to attend to," Rosalind replied. The poor girl looked more worried than when Rosalind first seen her, scared out of her wits outside Lord Barronsfield's room. "Did you see my uncle? Has the doctor arrived?" She needed to think about anything else, and the wellbeing of Stephen Pembroke was of most immediate concern.

Bess, in the no-nonsense manner of an experienced servant, prepared the water for Rosalind's ablutions. "I spoke with one of the footmen. His lordship is more settled now, but he is not well."

Bess put a chair in front of the fire, and Rosalind sat. One by one, Bess pulled out the pins from what remained of Rosalind's chignon and gently untangled her hair.

"Bess, about what happened here, with Mr. Pembroke—I don't wish for my uncle to be concerned about this. He has enough on his mind right now." She'd probably return to the steward's cottage to find her bags already packed and a carriage ordered to take her to safety if Uncle Reginald knew the man who might be his future master was trifling with her. Or worse, he might force Mr. Pembroke do to something 'honorable.' She shuddered at the idea.

Future master. Rosalind grimaced at the thought. She could barely imagine Geoffrey Pembroke as marquess, and Rosalind credited herself with an excellent imagination. The scene at the ballroom when he'd pulled her back from Lord Barronsfield, allowing the marquess to crash to the floor, betrayed an element of cruelty deeper than a well-timed barb. Never mind the spark of madness when he stood at the ruin, prepared to bash in Lord Barronsfield's skull with a stone. Did he truly fancy himself as her savior? Desperate to save her from the ravages of his cousin? In his own mind perhaps. And what went on in Geoffrey Pembroke's head was beginning to scare her.

Rosalind lowered her head over a large tin basin, and soon warm water cascaded over her hair. The vessel soon filled with water colored by the mud that had caked in her hair. Carefully, the touch of

Bess's fingers and the squish of soap ran over her head, and for a moment, the gentle touch allowed her to relax.

As the last of the soap and dirt was rinsed away, Rosalind squeezed the rest of the water from her hair, and began drying it in front of the fire when a knock came to the door. She locked gazes with Bess.

"Don't worry miss," the servant whispered. "I won't let Mr. Pembroke in."

Their fears were allayed, however, when the visitor in question turned out to be Rosalind's uncle.

"Forgive the intrusion, my girl," he said. "I wanted to make sure you were comfortable before you settled in."

Rosalind rushed to him, faltered a moment, then pulled him close.

"I'm fine now," she replied after releasing him from their embrace. "Bess has been taking excellent care of me. I don't need to sleep. I—" she faltered slightly, almost embarrassed by her need. "I would like to enquire after the marquess."

"There is nothing that can be done until the doctor arrives," he replied. "And you must have your rest."

Uncle Reginald lingered a few minutes longer, then left to attend to his master. Wind and rain still battered the windows as Rosalind finally crawled under the covers. Bess had freshened the bed and put a warming pan between the covers while Rosalind had bathed, so by the time she got in, it was toasty warm.

Rosalind laid there, a single candle burning on the table by the side of her bed. The clock on the mantle chimed midnight. Despite the grandness of the room, and the comfort of a lush bed, freshly warmed, the disturbing events of the evening kept sleep at bay. Her thoughts drifted back to the assembly, which seemed a long time ago, instead of a few hours. The dance with the marquess—the touch of his hand, the intensity of his looks and the strangely sweet trepidation in which he approached her, was everything that her dance with Mr. Pembroke was not. For a moment, she had actually enjoyed herself. And, she dared to think, he had too. Edmund Pembroke had revealed as much, and even discounting Edmund's words, she saw it in the way the marquess's dark eyes shone when she'd agreed to dance with him.

Rosalind squeezed her eyes shut, her hands balling into fists under the covers. She needed to dislike him. Or, at least, not to like him very much. She could never, ever allow herself to be with someone who didn't love her. She'd had far too many years of that already. With his preposterous proposal in the carriage, the marquess had offered just that, hadn't he? Marriage without love. A marriage that would cost Rosalind her self-respect.

Except practically everything he did since that day made her doubt her belief. Lord Barronsfield listened to her, even if he didn't like what she had to say. He cared about the people around him. Despite his occasional bluster, the man was mortified at the idea of hurting anyone. So he'd shut himself off from the world, and in doing so, he was lonely. And even if she didn't come from nobility, even if she was easy with her manners— even if she was *"just Rosalind"* as she could hear her Aunt Stanhope say—she knew what it meant to feel lonely too.

As she lay there in the massive wooden bed, in absolute comfort, she knew he was in another part of the house, in absolute misery. And Rosalind found she could not bear the idea.

A minute later, her feet hit the floor. She went to the armoire and dug out the simplest frock she could find. She couldn't walk down the hall in naught but her dressing gown, after all. Especially if Geoffrey Pembroke was about.

Maybe there *was* a beast in Barronsfield, but it wasn't the man tied down to his bed on the other side of the manor.

CHAPTER 14

*R*osalind held her breath and curled her fingers around the curved brass door handle that led to Lord Barronsfield's chamber. All but the loudest of the marquess's outbursts were shielded by the heavy oak door. As she stood there, deathly still, an unwanted memory pushed its way to the center of Rosalind's thoughts, tightening her throat. Another time, a not so ornate door handle, and a much thinner door, separating a young girl from her mother. A mother whose chest rattled with infection until she fell into a feverish stupor that silenced her forever. They'd kept young Rosalind away then, too. But she wasn't little anymore. Letting go an exhale, Rosalind pushed down on the door handle and slipped into Lord Barronsfield's bedchamber.

A faint stench of vomit hung in the room. The marquess lay on his bed, cleaned up as best as anyone could manage, which, given the state of him, was not very well. He strained against the leather straps that kept him secured to his bed. Around him were Mr. Edmund Pembroke and her uncle, who had their backs to the door, apparently unaware of her presence. The doctor stood on the other side of the bed, a hand on the marquess's head, bending down to check his breathing, which was as erratic as the rest of his movements. His chest heaved so much that even from where she stood, Rosalind could almost see his heart beating through his ribs. In another time and place, she thought, they would be exorcizing him for demons.

"Is there nothing we can do for him?" her uncle asked in an urgent hush barely audible over the moans and incoherent babble coming Lord Barronsfield.

"He will have to be watched quite closely, but there is little we can do for him except wait," the doctor said, his expression grim.

Uncle Reginald nodded. "I must go see to the servants. We will need to set up a watch. Mr. Pembroke, can you stay with the doctor until I return?"

Her uncle's declaration put her on her guard. She ducked back out the door and into a dark corner of the corridor, her fingers pressing hard against the wood. To her relief, he headed in the opposite direction. When the sound of his shoes on the floor disappeared, she went back into the marquess's room where Edmund Pembroke and the doctor remained, deep in conversation.

"Can we at least give him something for his relief? Some laudanum, perhaps," Mr. Edmund Pembroke said, raking a hand through his hair and pacing back and forth at the foot of his cousin's bed. Rosalind was struck by how young he sounded. He was out his depths, and racked with worry.

The doctor shook his head. "Until we know what is wrong with him, that would be unwise. Can you describe when his affliction started?"

"I can."

At Rosalind's declaration, both men turned in her direction.

She cleared her throat and squared her shoulders, all too aware that her presence was unexpected, and in any other situation, beyond any semblance of propriety. "Forgive my intrusion. I had heard the doctor had arrived, and I wished to be of use, if possible," she said, as if that was the only explanation she needed. It was all she was prepared to give.

The doctor gave Edmund a quick glance, then adjusted his spectacles. "If you would be so kind, Miss Schofield. The more information I have, the better it would be for his lordship,"

She took a few cautious steps forward, and forced her attention away from Lord Barronsfield as she addressed the physician. "At the assembly this evening, sir. We'd been dancing for perhaps five minutes, when rather suddenly, Lord Barronsfield looked at me with an expression of panic. He muttered something, though I couldn't tell what, because his speech was slurred. At first I thought he'd had too much drink, but he'd been fine the moment before. Then he fell forward, as if his legs were having trouble supporting him."

"And did you see him earlier?"

Rosalind shook her head, and immediately Edmund spoke up.

"I was with him for some part of the afternoon. He seemed fine." Mr. Pembroke's voice wavered.

"Did he have anything to eat or drink before this attack?" the doctor continued.

Mr. Pembroke shook his head. "Don't know. We didn't arrive together. I was as surprised as any when he walked in. He and I had a glass of wine together once he arrived, but we both drank it."

The doctor was clearly at a loss. "I will consult with some of my texts, but for the moment there is nothing more to be done here. Watch him for the next twelve hours, and alert me as soon as he is awake."

"Of course." Rosalind and Edmund Pembroke locked gazes, having both responded.

"This is my fault," Edmund said, his voice cracking slightly. "I will stay with him."

"Very well." The doctor began packing up his things. "I hope we don't have to bleed him. Have someone come for me directly if the situation changes." He gave Rosalind and Edmund direction about what to watch for, and took his leave.

Mr. Pembroke sank down into a chair next to his cousin, head in his hands.

"Mr. Pembroke, he is going to be all right. He's strong. No doubt he has been through this before."

"Edmund." He nodded formally, as if they were being reintroduced. "'Mr. Pembroke' is a title that reminds me far too much of my father. I would like us to be friends."

Rosalind smiled. Edmund looked like he needed a friend, and she was happy to count him as one.

A small moan escaped from their charge on the bed. "Please, Miss Walton. Please help her." The marquess's voice was low and urgent, and sounded young. He wore a tortured expression and tears streamed down his cheek. "I'm sorry about your flowers."

Rosalind's gaze went from Edmund to the marquess, whose face would be still one moment then contort in a manner she found difficult to watch. It was pain, fear, horror, all at once. Each time it happened, it sent a stab of sorrow through her. No wonder the marquess was the way he was. No wonder he chose to hide himself away. And suffer, alone.

But he was not alone now.

"Miss Walton?" Rosalind asked Edmund. "Is this the old woman who cursed him? Haddie Walton?"

Edmund nodded, barely acknowledging her question. He ran his fingers through his hair. "I am not sure how to help him. I've never—I mean I haven't—"

"You've never seen him like this before."

He shook his head, and looked even more woebegone. On a small side table Rosalind spotted a decanter of spirits—brandy it looked to be—and some glasses. Just what the doctor ordered.

"Well, neither have I, so let's think on it together. But, first order of business." She walked to the side table and poured a generous portion of brandy into a fine crystal glass, then pushed it into one of Edmund's hands. "Drink this."

He accepted it willingly, gave her a wry smile, then swallowed its contents. Rosalind walked to the end of the bed, hands on her hips.

"We need to get him out of his wet clothes, before he catches his death. Hanley will no doubt be here soon enough, but we can get started." She walked to the end of the bed and began working at the bindings around his ankles, loosening their grip. "Could you help me remove his boots? We need to make him more comfortable."

Edmund obliged her and stood by, stifling a yawn. "This is my fault. I should have let him be."

"Edmund, please," she replied as she freed one of the marquess's legs from the straps. "How on earth is any of this your fault? His lordship, I imagine, does not do anything he doesn't want to. You must know that."

"I suppose." He grunted as he tugged on one of the mud caked black boots still firmly attached to the marquess's foot.

"It's a good thing you're a gentleman," Rosalind said, unable to stifle a giggle as she watched Edmund struggle with one boot, then the other. "Your career as a valet would be a short one, I think."

As the second boot came off—nearly causing Edmund to land on his backside—he shook his head. "No wonder he likes you."

"Excuse me?" If the circumstances were different perhaps, she would have enjoyed Edmund's declaration more. But it caught her off guard nonetheless.

"You do not let him get overly morose. You are exactly what he needs, Miss Schofield. Someone to take the piss—excuse me— someone who can make sure he isn't feeling sorry for himself."

"Perhaps." She cast a glance at Edmund who was leaning against one of the bed posts, eyes drooping. "Now, Edmund, pray go and get some sleep. You look as though you are ready to sleep on your feet."

"Rosalind," he protested, swaying on his feet even as he did so.

"I'm fine. I will ring if I need anything." She gestured to the velvet pull near the marquess's bed, where the Lord Barronsfield lay, sleeping a little less fitfully now. "Besides, Hanley will be here any moment. And no doubt you will be needed in the morning. You'll be of no use to anyone if you are sick yourself."

Her last comment must have made an impression, because he went to his cousin's side, said a few quiet words, then left.

A gentle whoosh of air and the slight click of the door closing behind Edmund, left Rosalind alone with the marquess. The rain pounded anew on the windows, whipped into a frenzy by the harsh north wind that rattled the sashes and sent a shiver down Rosalind's back.

Rosalind's confidence faltered as Lord Barronsfield's head flailed from side to side on his pillows. The marquess was still in the wet clothes he'd worn outside, and while some of the mud and filth had been wiped away he was in desperate need of dry clothes and clean sheets.

He no longer strained against his bindings, but not even in her most optimistic assessment of him could she report he was lying peacefully. Whatever this was—sickness, or something more sinister —still had its claws firmly in him. And now she was standing beside him, alone, useless. On the precipice of failure. What on earth did she think she could do for him?

Rosalind's mother had died slowly, the victim of illness, and Rosalind could only watch her mama's strength being bled away. Her father had died so far away, and she'd been powerless to help either of them. As she stood, gripping one of the posts at the end of his bed, her throat tightening, and heaviness in her chest, she knew she could not abide that helplessness again. She didn't know what she should be doing, but she was certain of one thing: 'nothing' wasn't it.

In some vain hope she'd calm the both of them, she started to make conversation with him. Decidedly one-sided conversation.

"Well, my lord," she began, as if they were meeting over tea. Except, perhaps for the quiver in her voice. "This has been quite the evening, wouldn't you say?"

There, was that so hard? Except it wasn't easy. So she kept moving, and pretended it could be easy.

"Now, Lord Barronsfield, I'm going to untie your arms." Unsure if he could even hear her, Rosalind kept her voice as light as she could manage as she approached one side of the bed. "I hope you're not going to thrash about or do anything else silly. I've already spoiled one dress tonight on your behalf."

A small grunt emanated from her patient, and he stirred a moment, then became still again.

"There, that's better, is it not?" She placed his newly freed arm down at his side, then repeated the gesture for his other hand, gently rubbing out some of the marks on his wrists.

Rosalind found water in the pitcher at a nearby washstand, and poured some into a small basin. Dampening a sponge, she gently started to clean the mud and dried blood from his face. Except for the occasional small movement, he hardly moved, and his breathing became ever more measured, but she couldn't tell if he was asleep or had slid deeper in the grip of whatever illness had befallen him. He seemed relatively peaceful at least. She wasn't the least bit sure about herself.

Unable to resist, she ran her fingers through his thick hair, stroked his cheek and let the rough growth on his chin bristle under her skin. He was beautiful, even dirty and with a swollen nose. A queer feeling gripped at her chest. *Too beautiful for me.*

Backing away, she shook her head in an attempt to rid herself of the sensation. Even if she had agreed to marry the marquess, he would never love her, would he? He had been plain on that score. Even if he did *like* her, as Edmund suggested, settling for a loveless marriage would be nothing short of painful.

His skin was still an unnatural shade of red, as if he had baked in the sun too long, and she could feel his heart thumping wildly in his chest. She was amazed he could lie still at all. He started to cough, short little bursts in his throat. Rosalind froze, panic rising in her chest. He was still in his damp clothes. Where was Hanley? They had to get him warm and dry. Or else...Rosalind couldn't bring herself to think about that.

Flexing her fingers, she looked away and started to undo the buttons on his breeches.

"Excuse me, Miss. Perhaps it would be better if I did that."

Rosalind's attentions snapped to the door, where Hanley stood, accompanied by three servants. One of them was Bess, loaded down with linen, the others were two footmen, carrying steaming buckets of water. Rosalind pulled her hands to her side, then crossed them in front of her, keenly aware of how wildly inappropriate this looked. Hanley, if he had an opinion about what he walked in on, gave nary a sign of it. At the smallest nod of Hanley's head, the servants went into action, performing what Rosalind realized was a well rehearsed scene, gently taking care of their master.

"I wanted to get him out of his wet things." She pulled her lips back in a sheepish, pleading smile. "I was worried—about fever. He started coughing."

"Of course, Miss Schofield," he said. He looked to his master, carefully examining him with a tenderness that bordered on devotion. Rosalind knew, of course, the marquess would be in good hands.

"Hanley, I know this is not my place perhaps, but if his lordship gets worse, or if you need help, will you please—" Her words stumbled, unable to give meaning to her feelings, as she could barely sort them out herself. Panic whelmed inside. "My mother died of fever. Alone. I don't—" She looked away, horrified at her outburst.

"I will have Bess send for you directly," Hanley said.

Rosalind nodded her thanks, cast one more glance at the marquess, and left.

STEPHEN WAS NOT sure how long he had slept, or if he was still sleeping now. The line between fantasy and reality had been obliterated, as it always was when the Beast was on him. The memories were disjointed, but he recalled running from the assembly hall in a panic after lashing out at poor Eleanore. She'd been horrified. He saw it, even in his confusion and panic of the moment. That, at least, was for her own protection. If anything had happened to her, he didn't know how he could bear it.

The Beast had been with him, the fierce madness coursing through him. He'd tried to fight it, though he hadn't been sure if it was real. Or if he'd been fighting himself.

Rosalind Schofield had been there too. He saw her, her light piercing the pitch dark of that god-awful night. He felt her. Remembered holding onto her as if his very life depended upon it. Had that been real? He didn't know. At least now she couldn't doubt him anymore, he supposed. As he lay there, he realized being right wasn't nearly as satisfying as it should have been.

The pounding in his head was real enough, and the sick feeling in his throat. He wanted to open his eyes, yet feared the stabbing pain in his eyes the light would bring. Even more perhaps, he dreaded what he would see. Dragging a leaden arm to his face, he shielded his eyes, and opened them ever so slightly, which expended far more energy than such a task should.

Darkness greeted him. The room was still and peaceful, as if it was any another morning. Strange, since it hadn't been any another night before. But no strong smells assaulted his nose. As he pulled his hand down from his forehead, he realized they were clean. No stale gore. Not even a drop of mud. He was almost astonished that he lay in his own bed, in fresh sheets.

With some effort he pulled himself up on his elbows, a move his body did not appreciate. Thunder rolled across his brow and his stomach protested.

"Here."

A hand guided him by the back of his head toward a porcelain chamber pot as he wretched.

"I know it is awful now, but you'll probably feel much better when you have this out of you."

He knew that voice, and despite the pounding in his head and the burning in his throat, he relaxed. If he'd had more of his wits about him, he might not know whether to be embarrassed or thankful. Usually Hanley handled these things. What on earth was she doing here?

Barely having time to look up, he was greeted by a cold cloth wiping his face.

"Do you think you are done then?" There was a slight pause from Miss Schofield, then, "Because if you are, I'll place this outside for now."

He laid back down, thankful for the darkness. Then, a second later, he was blinded.

"Bloody hell!" What was she doing here? Torturing him.

"Is there something the matter, my lord?"

"I can't see is what's the matter!"

"Sorry. Just a moment."

He heard the rustling of fabric and the sound of someone struggling with a window.

"Any better?"

Before he even opened his eyes, he could tell that not all the curtains had been closed. "No. The light hurts my eyes."

"You are quite contrary when you are ill, do you know that?" He heard more curtains being pulled, and then liquid being dispensed into a cup. "Of course, you can be contrary when you are not, so maybe it can't be helped."

"What are you doing here? Where's Hanley?"

"Hanley is tending to his other duties. I, on the other hand, am having the time of my life cleaning up the spew of the Marquess of Barronsfield, if you haven't deduced that already." Despite the clip in her words, she handled him gently as she attempted to raise him up to the glass she held in her hand. "Have some more ginger water. It will help your stomach."

He drank as though he had not seen a drop of water in weeks. She lowered him back down, and resting again, he was somewhat mollified.

"My apologies, Miss Schofield. I am feeling like the devil at the moment."

"Well, you don't look like him." She smiled at him, and for a moment he felt lighter.

She wore a plain yellow frock, covered by an apron. Her hair was pulled back into a simple knot, but several tendrils had fallen along the side of her face. He could tell by the rumples in her dress she had probably slept in it.

"You have been here all night?"

She shook her head. "We've been taking turns. My uncle and the servants have been here at night, and Emily, Edmund and I are here during the day. Our schedules have all been a little upside down of late."

It took a moment to understand what she had said.

"How long have I been like this?"

"Nearly three days, my lord. It is Tuesday."

"Three days?" He sat up quickly. Probably too quickly. He put a hand up to his eyes, which felt like they were about to pop out of his skull. "Bugger."

"You really should not exert yourself so."

"I have been lying here for too long, Miss Schofield." Damn the light. "I don't think I've been doing much of anything."

From behind him he could hear her fussing with pillows. He caught the scent of her perfume as she moved about, softly whistling. Roses. She smelled like roses after a summer rain. The aroma rang through his memories: a wooden sword, smashed blossoms at his feet. An old woman's harsh words. As he watched Rosalind Schofield move around him, painful as it was to keep his eyes open, the sensation of fear and penance gave way to something new. Something that bordered on comfort. Maybe even happiness.

"There now. Sit back. Gently—gently! No wonder your body is disagreeing with you." She held onto the back of his neck, her fingers laced in his hair. Her touch relaxed him, and he felt himself melting into her. "Now, try to open your eyes. It's really not that bright."

"I prefer the dark," he protested.

"Yes, well, as my mother used to say, you may prefer cakes to parsnips, but that doesn't mean it's good for you."

Her words piqued him, and in spite of himself, he opened his eyes wider, taking a moment to adjust to the light, dim as it was. Miss Schofield was tidying up around his bed. She wore the smile he was coming to enjoy so much, but there was something else there too. A distant sadness. *Her mother died of fever.* How did he know that?

"Do you have memories of your mother?"

"A very few." She took a chair beside him, and he found himself wishing she would sit closer. "I have a small picture of her. She died when I was six."

"I'm sorry. That is very young to lose a mother." Too young.

"Yes, I suppose it is." She paused, as if trying to sort out her thoughts. It seemed to him she was trying not to dwell on the memory overmuch. "But the world is full of orphans, Lord Barronsfield. Many who are far less fortunate than I. At least I had a loving father, and my mother's sister, who agreed to raise me while my father sailed."

"Do you miss her? Your mother?"

"Of course. Though in a distant sort of way."

"And your aunt…she raised you well?"

"I think she did the best she could with an extra mouth to feed. Of course, my father helped to support me, but his duties kept him away most of the time. I did my best to be helpful to her. To be helpful to all of them, and not be underfoot. My uncle was rarely home. He was a busy man, an important man." She laughed at herself, which crinkled her nose in such a way that made him feel curious. Curious, perhaps, about how it might feel to kiss her. "Well, as important a man as one can be in a colonial town on the other side of the ocean. That seems so far away now." She sounded far away as she said it.

"I don't think I have appreciated how different and difficult all of this has been for you." He looked about the room, his head starting to clear. "And this certainly can't be any help."

"I find myself at odds with my own feelings a lot of late."

He shuffled under the sheets, waiting for her to continue. Instead, she stood up.

"Would you like another glass of ginger water?" she said in what sounded like an overly cheerful tone. The kind one uses when they clearly want to change the subject.

"I think I would like some brandy."

"Perhaps, but this is better." She placed a glass into his hand.

He drank eagerly, and she poured him another glass which he gulped down as well.

"Better?"

He nodded. His head did seem to be clearing and his stomach a little more settled. As he sat back, about to relax, a breeze shifted the drapes, pushing them away and exposing a brilliant crack of sunshine.

"Could you *please* shut the window!" He shielded his eyes from the nearly unbearable brightness.

"Hmmm. Would you humor me for but a moment?"

"What are you going to do to me?" Not that he was nervous. Well, perhaps a little nervous.

"I'm going to open the curtains—"

"Are you so intent on torturing me?"

"Hardly. It wouldn't be any fun at all without an audience." She was smiling. He could barely see her, but somehow he knew. Her voice grew more serious. "I promise. This will only take a moment, and I'll do my best to keep your discomfort to a minimum. I want to test a theory."

He gave her a curt nod.

"Right then. Close your eyes."

He did as he was bidden, and he heard the slight rustle of curtains.

"Now let me look at you." Miss Schofield sat on the bed next to him, holding his face in her hands. Her skin was smooth to the touch. "Can you open your eyes?"

As he did, he focused slowly on hers. She looked intently at him, moving in and out of the light, all the while looking into his eyes, and forcing him to keep them open. He flinched despite her best efforts to keep him still. She crossed her arms, her brow creased.

"Strange."

"What?"

"Your eyes. Are they always this sensitive to the light after…"

He could tell she struggled to find the right words.

"After the Beast comes? Always."

"I hate to be the bearer of bad news, my lord, but there was no beast."

What? "That's impossible. I felt the curse taking me. Right in the middle of our set."

"Well, you were gripped by something," she replied, matter-of-factly. "But there was no fur, no fangs, nothing. Just rain, mud, and you."

"Nothing? That's impossible. It all felt the same." Worse, actually, he thought. In all the times the curse took him, he had never been unaware for so long.

"You can sit there and look at me like that all you want, but I'm telling you the truth," she said.

"I don't understand," he said, ignoring the jibe. "What happened to me?"

For the first time in memory, Miss Schofield didn't look eager to speak. Instead, she took her chair and placed it a closer to the side the bed, then began to fuss with the hem of her apron.

"Please tell me," he asked.

"You just went…mad. Like you'd lost control of your body."

She looked away, and for the first time he noticed an ugly purplish yellow bruise on the side of her face. A stone dropped in his stomach, and he reached over and gently cupped her cheek.

"Did I—?"

"No." She reached for his hand, which sent the smallest shiver of desire down his back, followed by a pang of disappointment as she smoothly rested it back at his side. "I managed to find you in the little churchyard. As I came to you, Mr. Pembroke surprised us. I slipped on the mud and fell."

"Edmund?"

She shook her head. "Mr. Geoffrey Pembroke." He spotted a hint of distaste in the corners of her mouth as she corrected him.

He found himself trying his damndest to pull through his memories of the evening, as broken and distorted as they were. He remembered being in the hothouse. He remembered Miss Schofield being there—pulling her away from some ungodly creature that had been only a figment of his imagination. He could have killed Pembroke. Or had he?

"Geoffrey?" he panicked. "I didn't do anything to him?"

"No. He is quite in one piece."

They both sat, quiet, her hand holding his.

"How did you know I would be there?" He was on the edge of something dangerous, he knew, and yet powerless to release himself from her touch.

"I thought it would be a place you'd go to seek solace. It was a lucky guess." Her voice was little more than a whisper.

Stephen lay there, absorbing her story. The news cast him strangely adrift, and his one anchor was the sensation of his hand in hers. He lifted it so he could see, really see, each little detail of her fingers. He began tracing the little lines on her knuckles, the outline of each of her fingers, the tiny perfect ridges of her fingernails.

Deftly, gently, he brought her hand to his mouth, gently kissing each finger tip, then curled her fingers forward, pressing his lips, rough and parched, to her knuckles, savoring her touch like a balm to his unsettled thoughts. He marveled at the sensation of both the softness of her flesh and the strength of her hands. His blood rushed through his body, but unlike the violent and sickening effects of the curse, this sensation, this stirring was new. And wonderful.

Hungry for more, he struggled to control his appetites. Parting his lips, he turned her hand over, bringing his mouth to the delicate skin on the inside of her wrist. With each ragged breath, he could hear her body's desire as he caressed her. He so dearly wanted more, but this was all he dared.

Abruptly she pulled away, jumped up from the bed and began looking anywhere but at him. Her cheeks flushed, and he could see the anger and embarrassment on her face. He wanted to ask what was wrong, when a quick look down at himself, blankets fallen to his waist, told him all he had to know.

"I have no clothes on," he blurted out, his voice cracking. He pulled the covers up to his chest.

"Of course you don't. Did you want to die of lung fever lying there in mud soaked clothes?"

"Did you—"

"Of course not. I untied your bindings. Hanley and the servants did the rest."

"Untie my bindings? What on earth were you thinking? I could have hurt you." He could barely imagine it.

"It had to be done. I did it."

"It wasn't your place."

"You did ask me to be your wife not long ago, if you recall." Her voice rose, and she gripped the post of the bed even tighter. "If I had been so foolish as to say yes, looking after you would have been my place, so you shouldn't be having a fit about it now."

He bit back a curse. Why did women always have to throw things in your face like that?

"Even if you were my wife, that would not be your duty," he said, exasperated.

She looked at him as if he had come from the moon. "Caring for someone is not simply a duty. When you went out to speak with Mr. Darling the first day I arrived, that was more than duty."

"It was exactly that, Miss Schofield. My duty as a good lord."

"Yes, but you could have sent my uncle or someone else to dispense your duty and clean up his chickens and fix his fence. There was no requirement of duty for you to ride in to see Mr. Darling, to speak with him and see that his fears were eased." Her hands twisted the edges of her apron. "That is more than being a good lord. That is being a good man."

Silence hung in the air, when at last, she spoke again.

"I will send a servant in to tend to you."

"I didn't say you had to leave," he said with all of the dignity of a petulant child.

"Why do you want me to stay?"

"Because—" Why? He didn't know. Well, perhaps he did. There was something about her that was becoming more and more necessary. The notion should have been a little frightening, but it wasn't. Strange. "Because I feel safe with you, and—"

"Safe?"

The word broke under the emotion in her voice, taking Stephen aback. Her shoulders sagged, and if he didn't know better, he was sure Miss Schofield was going to cry. What the devil had he said?

"Are you well?"

"I am tired, is all," she said, clearing her throat. "I must go."

He pushed himself forward in bed, feeling a strange sort of urgency to get himself to her, but a fresh wave of dizziness and nausea forced him back into his pillows. Pillows that still held the lingering scent of roses.

She paused at the door, turning in his direction but never quite catching his gaze. "I will send for a servant. No doubt the doctor will want to examine you." And then, with a quiet click of the door, she was gone.

A moment later, as Miss Schofield had promised, a servant came into his room with a fresh pot of ginger tea. The woman tended to his fire, and found a nightshirt to cover him before he dismissed her.

Why in the blazes could he not have blustered through after Miss Schofield had interrupted him? Why couldn't he tell her needed her to stay?

He sank back into his pillows, staring aimlessly into the rich patterns of the fabric overhead, feeling much less safe, and far more lonely.

CHAPTER 15

*R*osalind bolted from the servant's entrance of Barronsfield Manor, the crisp autumn breeze brushing against her face. Sun spilled down onto the landscape, and gold leaves blazed against the brilliant blue sky. The brisk air energized her senses, providing something of an antidote to the unwanted melancholy swirling inside her. Bounding down the stone steps and onto the path, she emerged from the shadow of the house, lifted up her face to the sun and let out a long, low breath.

Safe? Hadn't he just kissed her? The sensation of his lips tenderly brushing every finger, the feel of his breath on the sensitive skin on her wrist, still lingered. He'd only given her the most gentle of kisses and even though their lips didn't touch, nothing about it felt innocent. Nothing about it was at all safe. At least not for her. Did he even have the slightest clue what he was doing to her? Probably not. Not a single clue that with the first touch of his lips, he'd opened up a floodgate of uncomfortable emotions, pushing and pulling at her like a ship being tossed at sea.

Gravel crunched under her feet as she stomped along, propelling herself away from the manor and him. The marquess wasn't worth the trouble of being hurt. She wasn't going to marry him. Whether he cared for her or not didn't matter.

Except it did, actually. That was the sorry part of it all. He mattered far too much for a man that would never look on her except as a means to keep his estate going. She rubbed her hands on her apron in a futile attempt to erase his touch, even as her stomach fluttered again at the memory of it.

The cottage appeared as she rounded a wooded corner, and her heart lightened a bit. This place was becoming home in a way that Aunt and Uncle Stanhope's house never had. Rosalind wondered how much it would cost to recreate such a pleasant little cottage in another part of Yorkshire. Preferably the corner furthest from Barronsfield. Except all the things that made the steward's cottage truly a home— her uncle, Emily, and even Eleanore—wouldn't be there.

If one good thing came out of Lord Barronsfield's troubles, it was that the distress of her uncle's unfinished letter had receded. Now that the marquess was awake and hopefully on the road to recovery, her uncle might finish it, no doubt more determined than ever to get her to safety. But the last thing on earth Rosalind wanted to be, was safe.

Emily was in the front yard, digging turnips out from the small kitchen garden near the faded flower beds.

"Good morning!" Rosalind called out, determined to be cheerful for Emily.

The housekeeper stood and wiped her hands on her apron. "Good afternoon, actually, Miss Schofield. How is the master?"

Good afternoon? Three full days and sleepless nights worrying about Lord Barronsfield, her uncle, and everyone else at Barronsfield were taking their toll. Heavens. "Awake and starting to mend," Rosalind grimaced. "In fact, I would say the marquess is well on his way to getting back to being his charming self." She may have rolled her eyes when she said that.

"Right then." Emily raised her eyebrows, but thankfully said nothing more on the subject.

"I'll take these in for you." Rosalind scooped up the small basket at Emily's feet. "Is there anything you need for me to do here?"

Emily shook her head. "I'm fine, dear. Eleanore's inside. She called after you about an hour ago. When I said you were still at the manor, she asked if she might help out here, so she's baking some scones. Mrs. Darling's recipe, and there's none finer in Yorkshire." Brushing the last of the soil from her hands, Emily walked with Rosalind toward the door. "I didn't want her near the kitchen, but she wouldn't hear of it! Fancy that. I hope she finds a good man sometime, that child. She deserves it, lord knows."

"I'll see her directly," Rosalind replied.

Emily rested a hand on her hip and looked Rosalind up and down. "You've barely slept these past few days. I have it on Mr. Schofield's orders to make sure you get yourself a decent rest."

"Well, I'll check on Eleanore first. I am sure some good company and a fresh scone will help me sleep all the better." That, and hearing any village news from Eleanore. They hadn't spoken since the assembly. Though she'd heard bits and pieces of gossip, little of it was useful, and even less appeared to be told with any care as to the truth of what happened.

The girl was exactly where Emily said she would be, pulling a fresh pan of scones out of the oven. Rosalind stood at the kitchen door, taking in a generous breath.

"This is a glorious smell indeed."

"Rosalind!" Eleanore put down the pan and reached out for a friendly embrace. Rosalind hugged her tight.

"How are you, Eleanore? I was worried about you after all that upset at the assembly."

"It was fine," she said. "What of you? Mr. Pembroke nearly went mad looking for you after you left."

I'm sure he did. "Yes, well, suffice it to say that I am quite well."

"Are you certain?" A hint of doubt crossed Eleanore's brow as her eyes fell on Rosalind's bruised cheek.

Rosalind shook her head. "It is nothing, really. I was caught between Lord Barronsfield and Geoffrey Pembroke. Don't worry about me, I am quite—*safe.*" Rosalind popped one of the warm scones on a plate. "And you? Lord Barronsfield—clearly he was not himself when he reacted to you so strongly that night," Rosalind said. He'd been almost primal, in fact.

Eleanore pulled her lips into a tight line, her brow furrowed. From a stoneware jug, she poured out a glass of lemonade for herself and one for Rosalind. "I don't know what to think of that, honestly. Mr. and Mrs. Darling told me not to dwell on it."

Clearly it did play on the girl's mind. Unable to abide her being troubled, Rosalind changed the subject. "How was the dancing at the assembly before the night took its awful turn?"

Eleanore was silent for a moment, still scrutinizing, but soon gave in to more youthful excitement. "It was so much fun. Wasn't it? If I looked half as well pleased as you did when you were dancing with Lord Barronsfield, then I was having the time of my life."

Rosalind nearly choked on her lemonade. "Excuse me?"

"Well, you did seem to be enjoying his company, and he looked happy enough. Of course, I really don't know either of you particularly well, but if appearances are anything to go by—"

"They're not." By the expression on Eleanore's face she realized her words must have come out much more clipped than she'd meant. "My apologies, Eleanore. I guess I'm more tired than I thought. I haven't slept well the past few days."

"Have you been at the manor this entire time?"

"Back and forth." But sleepless either place. Worry had stolen her rest.

"Well, you did look very happy that night." Eleanore added, looking over at her with a sly smile on her face. "Sometimes I like to dream that a handsome prince would look at me that way. Or at least a duke."

"Between your pretty face and your cooking, you shall have no end of suitors. And I wouldn't bother with a duke or a prince." Rosalind smeared butter on the scone, all the while thinking back to her marriage proposal. It felt like a long time ago now, even though it was a little less than a fortnight. "The marquess made it quite clear to me that in better society, people marry to protect inheritance, and never, ever for love."

"Really?" Eleanore asked, a rather coy expression on her face. "When did he say that?"

"Oh—a little while ago. Just conversation," Rosalind replied, taking a bite of scone and anxious to change the subject. "These are excellent, Eleanore."

"What else did the marquess have to say about marriage?"

"Nothing." Rosalind's gaze went from the small, sunny kitchen window to the servant's staircase that led to her bedchamber. She was still in the same dress and shift she'd been in since yesterday. She popped the last bit of scone in her mouth, then washed it down with the glass of lemonade. "I think a short rest and a change of clothes would do me a world of good," Rosalind said, wiping her fingers on her rumpled apron.

"I think so too. Go on—I'll see you later." Eleanore waved the backs of her hands at Rosalind, practically shooing her out of the kitchen.

Rosalind happily obliged. The bench scraped across the wooden floor as she pushed herself away from the table, then climbed up the stairs to her room, her legs heavy by the time she reached the upper floor. As the door clicked shut behind her, Rosalind let go a sigh of relief. *Home.*

She shuffled to the window and pulled it open to invite in a bit of fresh air. Barronsfield was stale. Lifeless. Except for the marquess and the few servants scurrying around the place, it was but a shell of a home. Even the rose bush in the hothouse felt more like a monument than a living thing. The only place that seemed to have any vibrancy was the library Lord Barronsfield loved so much. It embodied the last bit of him that the curse had left unspoiled. Rosalind's lips curled up in a wistful smile. Maybe, aside from the towering shelves laden with volumes and the magnificent carpets and soaring windows, maybe what she loved so much about the library was that it reminded her so much of him. The best of him.

She let her shoulders droop and leaned her forehead against the cool glass of the window pane. Outside, she spied the spot beside the apple tree where the marquess had stood nearly a week ago, an invitation in his hand. He had been so out of sorts. So intent on making his apologies. He was such a puzzle, Lord Barronsfield. A puzzle that would be the undoing of her if she wasn't careful.

Rosalind plodded across the room, pulled off her pinafore and threw it over the chair near her dressing table. Out of the pocket tumbled a small wad of cloth, landing on the floor near her feet. She picked it up, but it pricked her skin, and she immediately loosened her grip. Carefully, she unwrapped the old linen which covered a light green husk, covered in long spines. It reminded her something of a horse chestnut, but with longer prickles.

Where did that come from? She was tempted to ask Emily, but right now she was too tired and a little too heart sick to bother. Instead, she placed it on her dressing table, plunked herself down on the bed, and started pulling off her boots.

Life had been easier when she was ignored. When she knew her place. Every moment she spent with Lord Barronsfield, she drifted farther from understanding where exactly her place was. He hadn't of course. In his eyes, she was safe.

Tears stung her eyes. She had to stop this. Rosalind Schofield didn't cry over men. She'd laughed about them, and occasionally she'd even sighed over one. But she'd managed never, ever, to care for one. After years of going unnoticed, it had become painful to entertain such expectations. She used to be quite fine about being overlooked. Now, it felt a little hollow, like a fairy story she didn't believe in anymore.

Eager to push away the tumult of feeling and the unwanted tears forming in her eyes, she sat on the edge of her bed, let go a long breath, and crawled under the quilt on her bed. Eleanore was right. She was exhausted. No one could think straight when they were tired, could they?

The song of chirping sparrows nesting in a nearby oak wafted in on the breeze. The sound of life soothed her. It was practically absent at Barronsfield. Every window was shut. Every curtain drawn. The marquess lived in a tomb of his own creation. If she were mistress of Barronsfield, that would change instantly. But she wasn't, and wouldn't be. She was safe, but being safe wasn't what she wanted. She wanted to be loved.

Rosalind pulled the thick quilt over her, and let the mattress and pillows cradle her body. Drinking in the stillness, she finally surrendered to the weariness that came from sleeping in one very expensive, but rather uncomfortable chair several nights in a row. Sleep took her quickly.

It just didn't last.

Rosalind opened her eyes to darkness—a darkness so black she wasn't sure her eyes were open. At her feet appeared the soft glow of candle light. She squinted in the dim light.

"Eleanore?"

"Ah! There you are." A wizened voice answered from somewhere in the darkness. Rosalind's eyes opened wide, and her heart skipped a beat before she sprang up, swinging her legs over the edge of a small cot she was lying on. Except for a small fire in the hearth and a candle sitting on a table in the middle of the room, it was dark, but the place felt modest in size. On the table, near the candle, sat a small delft bowl that brimmed with the fullest dark pink roses Rosalind had ever seen.

"Where am I?" she asked, almost under her breath.

"You're dreaming of course," replied the no-nonsense voice from the other side of the room. "You don't actually think any of this is real, do you?"

Rosalind stood, banging her head on an iron pot hanging from a beam above her.

"Ow!" She rubbed her head. "It feels real enough."

Her eyes slowly adjusted to the light. On the other side of the wooden table stood a stout woman easily old enough to be Rosalind's grandmother. The woman turned to poke at the hearth, seeing to some concoction that bubbled in the iron pot over the fire. She was simply dressed, her wild, gray hair barely contained in a mob cap, and she moved around very well for a woman of such an advanced age.

"Can I ask where I am?" Rosalind said.

"You just did," the older woman humphed. "Now then, let's go."

Rosalind followed, ducking through the maze of pots, dried plants, and ephemera that filled the small space. Impatient, the old woman beckoned

Rosalind to hasten her step all the while gesturing to the door. Rosalind stepped through it, blinded again, this time by the most dazzling sunlight.

"Come, come!" The woman took her by the hand, her touch light as a feather and as cold as December.

Once Rosalind's eyes became accustomed to the brightness, she saw she stood in a lush forest, filled with trees that stretched to incredible heights in the sky, and a floor carpeted with a layer of bluebells. Sunlight poked through the verdant canopy, strong pinpoints of light dancing over the landscape.

"We have but a moment," the woman stated, desperation in her eyes.

"Could you at least tell me your name," Rosalind said, walking as quickly as she could to keep up. "And why you were waiting for me?"

"Haddie. My name's Haddie," she replied. "There is something you need to see, and I'm the one to show it to you."

"Is this about the marquess and his curse?"

The woman turned around and looked at Rosalind with an expression so full of sorrow and regret Rosalind wanted to apologize for asking. Haddie nodded at last, then moved on, scanning the woods with all the intentness of a falcon on the hunt.

"So it is real? Is that what this is about?"

"You ask a lot of questions for so young a thing," Haddie replied with a huff.

"The marquess isn't really cursed."

A small smile crept across the old woman's lips. She came to a stop so abrupt Rosalind nearly banged into her. Unconcerned, she peered into the verge, then rubbed her hands, as if about to feast. "Ah! Here it is."

"What is it?" Rosalind bent down beside the woman who was examining a rather ordinary looking, leafy green plant with long, white flowers that reminded her of the flowering squash plants back in her aunt's garden.

"A pretty but dangerous little thing, my dear." She picked off a prickly round husk from the plant, and placed it in Rosalind's hands. "If you are going to help him, you need to know about this."

"What is it?"

"You will have to find out for yourself. I am only given leave to show you this small thing. You are a smart girl, so I am told, and you will know what to do."

"So there is a curse?"

"Only of a man's own making, but I am sorry for my part in it." The woman looked over to her right, then motioned to an unseen presence before she turned back to Rosalind. "I am out of time. Be careful, dear. There is a darkness in Barronsfield. Do not let it take you."

Rosalind reached out to her, but in the next moment the woman, and the dream, were gone.

Rosalind lay on her side, shivering from the chill. Dull light gave a subtle glow around her window, and she guessed it was morning. She was under a few more quilts, and a quick check over her shoulder confirmed the window had been closed. Emily must have checked in on her last evening. She sat up and stretched as best she could, given the confines of the dress she still wore from when she went to bed. She rose just as she heard a knock at the door.

"Miss Schofield, dear?"

"Come in, Emily."

Emily bustled in with a large pitcher of water she poured into a porcelain bowl. "I came up last night, but you were sleeping so peacefully I didn't have the heart to wake you."

"Thank you. With all that's happened, I think I needed it."

With Emily's help, Rosalind changed into a clean shift and a serviceable frock. Despite the dream, Rosalind felt rested for the first time in days. The weariness had dissipated, replaced with the need to hold on to the dream as it threatened to slip away from her memory. Haddie's insistence on showing her the plant reminded Rosalind of the husk she'd found in her apron. Carefully she took the green prickled sphere and held it up for Emily's inspection.

"Do you know what it is?" Rosalind asked.

"I don't really know, child. Old Haddie Walton—now, if she were still living, she could tell you. Plants and medicines, that was her domain. But a lot of that knowledge went with her to the grave."

Or into Rosalind's dreams, perhaps. She stared at the thorny little orb in her hand. Haddie was a healer. The plant was a clue. It was dangerous, she said, and Rosalind had little doubt it involved the marquess. Rosalind needed to unlock its secrets—including how it got into her possession in the first place. Was someone trying to help her? Someone afraid of being caught?

"Does Elmsdale have an apothecary?" Rosalind continued. She needed to know what the plant did.

Emily shook her head. "You'd have to go all the way to Pickering for that."

"What about the doctor? Surely he might have an idea?"

Emily opened her mouth about to answer, when the sound of the front door below jarred Rosalind's attention. Heavy footfalls on the wood floor below announced her uncle's return. Quickly, she wrapped up the husk and pattered down the stairs, eager to see him. She'd not spoken with him about the letter or anything else, save the marquess's condition, since the night of the assembly.

"Rosalind my dear," he said, taking her hands into his and giving her an affectionate squeeze. Worry and fatigue bested his attempt at a smile. "Are you rested?"

"Since I went to bed before supper, I should hope so. You look so tired. Let's go get you some breakfast, shall we?" Rosalind started toward the kitchen. "I wanted to speak with you actually. I have a few questions about—"

"I must speak with you."

The edge in his tone stopped Rosalind in her tracks, the floor creaking uncomfortably under her feet. She closed her eyes, not wanting to turn around. Clearing her throat, she asked in a voice far too light for her heavy mood, "Shall I bring you some hot chocolate, or coffee first? I thought you'd like a little refreshment."

"Come, Rosalind." He opened the door to his study and gestured for her to follow.

Rosalind forced herself to turn away from the kitchen and entered the study. It was the first time she could recall her uncle's company as unwelcome.

Her uncle sank heavily into his chair, and leaned forward, his elbows on his desk. He rubbed his temples, burdening the oak with what seemed to be the weight of many troubles. Rosalind took a seat opposite him, fiddling with the balled handkerchief in her hand, and praying that the dim morning light hid the blood she felt rushing up her neck and into her cheeks.

"Bess Hargrove has disappeared."

What? "Bess—the servant?"

Her uncle nodded, his lips tightly shut.

"When?"

"No one has seen her since yesterday. She told no one where she went. I have a few of the lads from the stables out combing the area for her."

"Perhaps she ran away? Frightened?"

"Perhaps. But her disappearance is a harsh reminder. It was folly to bring you here—putting my own needs and wishes ahead of your safety. My dear Rosalind, if anything should happen to you, I couldn't forgive myself."

"Uncle—"

"That is not all."

Rosalind's heart sank.

"Another body has been found."

"You don't think—"

"We don't know. I don't know anything yet."

"Uncle, I followed the marquess that night," Rosalind said, hand in a fist in her lap, leaning forward and using every bit of decorum she had left not to jump from her chair and raise her voice. "It could not have been him."

"All hell broke loose after he left. It took us some time to find him. Did you actually see him from the time he left?"

Rosalind shook her head, and slumped back a bit in the stiff chair. She'd only found the marquess much later. The two sat in mutual silence while the steady tick-tick-tick of the clock on the mantle pushed time forward. Uncle Reginald rubbed his face in his hands, then looked up at Rosalind with an expression of heartbreaking tenderness.

"In all my time, I never expected I would be in the position I am in now," he began, his voice a soft rumble. "My parents were of modest means, Rosalind. Your grandfather was a lawyer—a hard working man who did well for himself, but because of his birth, not considered equal to half the ne'er do wells with titles to their name and little else to recommend them. Your grandmother had the great misfortune to fall in love with him, and though she said father's love was a gift, she was spurned by her family for marrying beneath her. Mother, God rest her soul, never made us feel that your brother and I were less than anyone else."

Rosalind sat perfectly still. Her father had rarely mentioned his family. Both his parents were dead before she was born.

"I had long given up the idea of having a family of my own," he continued. "After your mother died, I offered to take you if arrangements with your mother's family could not be made. My position here at Barronsfield was secure, though I knew I could not offer you the same bonds of family that living with two guardians and other children could offer you."

Rosalind sat deathly still. If she moved, even breathed, she feared the tears she held back would fall freely.

"That you would be coming to stay with me, if only for a short while before you marry, was the only thing that dulled John's loss. I had hoped your stay here might be of some duration, though I was perfectly happy to accept that you might be more eager to go to London, where you would start a life of your own."

"Uncle," Rosalind burst out, tears catching in her throat. "You have been so very kind to me, kinder in fact than anyone I have ever known. Indeed, I have no desire to marry at this time. For the first time ever, I feel like I do have a life of my own, and it is here, with you, that I want to live it."

"You have no idea how happy that makes me, and how sad."

"No. Uncle, please." She struggled to keep her voice strong. "You cannot send me away."

"Not forever. I have already sent a letter to Admiral Hart, a friend and colleague of your father's, who has a house in London. I expect an answer from him any day now."

"Uncle Reginald, no!" Rosalind stood, hands balled in fists at her side.

"Rosalind, Admiral Hart can offer you protection that I cannot, including falling prey to fortune hunters, though perhaps, you've already met the worst of them." Her uncle didn't utter Geoffrey Pembroke's name, but Rosalind had no doubt this was who he spoke of.

Desperation drove her to ignore good manners and possibly good sense, but she was not giving up without a fight. "When I spoke with Bess the night of the assembly, she told me that Tom Gates and his family gave the servants here at Barronsfield a hard time. And she told me that Sally was seeing one of the sons—Jim, John—"

"Jack. Jack Gates."

Rosalind nodded her head, thrilled to have her uncle's interest. "Maybe they have something to do with Bess running away. After the marquess left the assembly, he was chased by men in a cart. I overheard them outside the hall. One of them was Tom Gates."

"Bloody hell." Uncle Reginald cleared his throat. "Sorry, my dear."

"Uncle, if we can find Bess…if we can find out what is happening to the marquess, please, I beg you to reconsider. Please. Whatever is happening to the marquess is not supernatural. Evil is being done to him, Uncle, but he is not evil. You know this. There is no way he is responsible for Bess's disappearance, any more than he was responsible for Sally's. I am in no danger here. Not from him."

"I can make no promises. There is still something amiss, and whatever that is, I cannot risk putting you in its way." Her uncle gazed up at her, a little less world weary than when he walked in. "If we can put a stop to this madness, and soon…" He shook his head. "But until that time, I must be firm in this."

Rosalind nodded, biting on her bottom lip. Everyone was so keen to have her safe—her uncle, the marquess, even Geoffrey Pembroke in his queer way. But none of them had the good sense to realize that the last thing Rosalind wanted or needed was their version of safety.

Precious seconds passed before Stephen could focus on the timepiece on his mantle. Ten o'clock. Half the morning already gone. The door to his bedchamber clicked shut, leaving him alone to digest the news his steward had delivered. Bad news of course. Was there any other kind of late? Stephen pushed away his fatigue, urgency banishing the clumsiness in his limbs. The wooliness in his head was replaced with the blinding need to discover what had happened to his maid, and if the body of the unfortunate soul found in a back alley in Elmsdale was somehow connected to him.

"Damn," he cursed under his breath. Whatever sleeping draught the doctor had ordered, it had worked far too well. He flung out his arm, grasped for the bell pull and heaved on it, as if wrenching harder would make Hanley instantly appear. Incapable of waiting, Stephen pushed himself out of bed, his body coursing with ripples of nervous energy that tightened his throat and twisted in his gut.

The windows in his room shuddered from the blustery late October wind. A slate gray sky greeted him as he pushed the curtains open, the landscape as dull as his mood. He placed a hand on the glass, savoring the cold as it ran through his fingers. What he wouldn't give to feel alive again. Instinctively, his gaze went past the fading gardens toward the wooded lane, then beyond the trees to where the steward's cottage sat. He squinted through the mottled glass and found himself wishing he was back under the apple tree in his steward's front garden, his hands on Rosalind Schofield's waist, arguing over fairy tales while trying to count the freckles on her nose. The thought of it was enough to pull his lips up ever so slightly into a brief smile before the upheaval of her uncle's report crashed down on him again. He pulled his hand away, the curtains falling shut once more.

The door clicked open, and Hanley shuffled in with a footman behind him, carrying a tray with a small pot of coffee.

"You have callers, my lord," Hanley said as he poured out a cup. "Mr. Geoffrey Pembroke and Sir Walter Perkins are below. They wish to speak with you."

If Stephen had entertained even for a moment the thought that the day could not get any worse, he banished the idea at Hanley's announcement. Pembroke always did have a remarkable sense of timing. Stephen inhaled deeply, swallowed his disgust, then turned to his butler.

"Very well. Direct them to my study, then wait for me," Stephen directed. "And send word to have my horse ready when I am done with them." Schofield had told Stephen that Doctor Brayden had the body for examination at the infirmary. Stephen had every intention of leaving directly to see the good doctor, but Pembroke's arrival put those plans on hold for the moment.

Hanley nodded, then left. Silently, the footman helped Stephen dress. Of all the people Stephen wished to lay eyes on, Pembroke would be at the bottom of his list. As the footman helped Stephen with his waistcoat and cravat, Stephen turned over Hanley's announcement in his head. Pembroke was *calling* on him. Hadn't he been living in the manor for the last bloody week? And why the devil would Perkins be with him? Something was afoot. The footman had barely slipped Stephen's bottle green coat over his shoulders before Stephen walked out the door and headed for his study.

Hanley was waiting outside the study door when he arrived. The old man answered Stephen's wordless question with a simple nod, indicating his visitors were inside. Stephen adjusted his collar, squared his shoulders, and entered the room, not bothering to acknowledge Pembroke or Perkins until he sat down at his father's ancient oak desk. Beast or not, Stephen was still in charge and they were about to be reminded of that fact.

The men stood. Perkins's shoulders were hunched forward, and he gripped the brim of his tri-corn. Pembroke leaned heavily on a cane, his face marred by cuts and bruises, like he'd seen the working end of a cricket bat.

"Good lord, Pembroke. What the hell happened to you?"

"That is what we are here to discuss, Barronsfield."

Stephen watched Pembroke carefully ease himself into his chair on the other side of the oak desk. He caught the hint of a smirk on Geoffrey's face as their eyes met. It was all Stephen needed not to feel sorry for him.

"Difficult few days, Pembroke?" Stephen asked.

Geoffrey whipped off his gloves, waving off Stephen's words like he would dismiss a servant. "Not as difficult as yours will soon be, Barronsfield."

"I suppose you are here, expecting an apology for injuries I have allegedly given you?" Stephen knew he was on the attack, but displaying any weakness to Geoffrey would only feed his cousin's fire.

"Not alleged, Barronsfield. I have several witnesses. But I am not here on my own behalf. No. I am here because of another you claim to have under your protection."

Stephen sat up. "Who? Miss Schofield? I have already spoken with her and she assures me—"

"I am sure you have," Geoffrey interjected, his voice booming with confidence, "and I am also certain, in some misguided need to protect her uncle, and maybe even you, she has denied it. She would do anything to protect her uncle," Pembroke said, and Stephen found he could not disagree. Pembroke cleared his throat and continued. "I understand from some of your long suffering tenants that the body count in Elmsdale is rising again. I think the business of the curse—

and the future of the estate—must be addressed before others are hurt by your depravity."

"So here it is then." Somewhere deep inside him, Stephen had known that it would all come to this.

"For years, Barronsfield, the good people of Elmsdale have lived in fear of you. You can barely keep a servant in the house. The eastern wing of this great manor is closed, and soon it will crumble if it is not given the proper attention. The name of Barronsfield is now associated not with greatness, but with fear and devilry. What have you to say to that?" Geoffrey sat back, arms crossed, a smug satisfaction pasted on his face.

Stephen gripped the arms of his chair, listening to Geoffrey's barrage of accusations. Each and every one of them he'd considered himself. Each and every time the Beast appeared, he found them harder to counter. Still, Rosalind Schofield had refuted them all, and her belief in him was a powerful antidote to his doubts.

"Consider your options, Barronsfield," his cousin continued.

"And what might they be, Geoffrey?" Stephen spat as he fought to keep his anger in check. "It is very convenient that you should level this charge, considering you stand to benefit from its outcome. Though you know I simply cannot give away my title."

"Do you take me for a fool? Do you think all I care for is a title?" Geoffrey charged back. "But at least if the estate came under my father's oversight, the ancestral home could be revived, rather than allowed to decay further. Think of that, cousin. Think of something beyond your own desire to hold on to a crumbling estate. Consider the people who depend on Barronsfield for their livelihood."

Being lectured by Geoffrey on any subject even remotely related to responsibility was beyond galling. Stephen clutched the polished wood arms of his chair before leaning forward and looking Geoffrey square in the eye. "I would rather hand it over to Schofield. He at least knows something about how to run affairs on this scale. Your father can barely manage you." It was a petty shot, but satisfying nonetheless.

Geoffrey reddened, but his voice remained even. "Do not stray from the facts, Stephen. Sir Walter Perkins will attest to my injuries. If not for his hospitality, I might be dead now. Which, I think, would have been very convenient *for you.*"

"Perkins?" Stephen turned his attentions to the man who fidgeted in his seat every time his name was mentioned. "What do you have to say to this?"

"Y-your Lordship, sir," Perkins's eyes seemed to dart in a thousand directions, loath to meet his host's. "Your neighbors, your tenants... they are witnessing the decline of a great family. It bodes ill for all of us. It grieves me to say it. Your father was a great man."

The mention of his father caused Stephen to start a little. The idea that he was denigrating his father's memory was hard to hear.

"That he was," Stephen replied, managing to sound as detached as if he were speaking about crop rotation or the color of the brocade on the chairs in the dining room. The ability to quash his feelings, to bury his emotion, was a gift from his father. The irony that he was using it now, in this way, was not lost on Stephen. "Still, I believe he would not wish me simply to relinquish Barronsfield without a fight. At this point, it is still your word against mine, Geoffrey. Perkins saw nothing."

"At least a hundred of the good people of Elmsdale saw you leave the assembly that night, ranting like a maniac," Pembroke said.

"But I was quite human, if somewhat—incapacitated. What have you to say to that?" In his darkest hour, that revelation was a gift, and Stephen seized it, but his small triumph was short lived.

Pembroke opened his mouth when the sound of the door opening silenced him. Edmund crept in, shoulders hunched, hands shoved in his pockets, avoiding the gaze of nearly everyone in the room. Pembroke, however, broke into a smile at the sight of his younger brother, which only served to make Stephen wonder what was up Geoffrey's sleeve. Or on Edmund's conscience.

"No." Geoffrey said. "To that, Edmund can attest. Surely his word means something to you."

Stephen shot a hard stare at Edmund.

"Edmund, pray, tell me what happened. And why, perhaps, you did not enlighten me to your brother's condition before this moment."

Edmund stood silent for what felt like a very long time.

"I'm sorry, Stephen," he said in a wooden tone Stephen barely recognized. "I—did not wish to burden you when you were not well."

"Neither my feelings, nor my own personal wellbeing, can be at issue when the right thing must be done." He took cold comfort in the measured words he had heard his father say many times in his youth. And for once, he was glad for the harsh, chilled tones his father had instructed him with. "Is what your brother says true? Did you see me beat him within an inch of his life?"

Edmund nodded. "By the time I arrived, Geoffrey was on the ground, and the monster—you—seemed intent on killing him."

"The monster?" his voice fell to a whisper before he recovered. "You saw me in an unnatural form?"

Edmund nodded stiffly.

Stephen's gazed fixed on him. An uncomfortable prickly heat crawled up Stephen's back. He swallowed deeply, wanting time to choose his words.

"What of Schofield? I understood that he was with you the entire time."

"He's older, Stephen, less steady on his feet in the dark. I ran on ahead, and he came but a few moments later, as you were already changing. There were several who went out in search of you. You had collapsed by the time Schofield found you. I carried Geoffrey out of harm's way, and a villager took him to Perkins. We wrestled you into a cart and took you back here."

Impossible. It seemed impossible. Miss Schofield had said so, and suddenly, that was good enough for him.

"Miss Schofield…where was she?"

"You struck her senseless, Barronsfield." Geoffrey spoke up now, anger seeping into his voice. "You were going to kill her. That was when you turned on me."

Stephen shook his head. "No. I asked her about this. Why would she lie?"

"Perhaps to save your feelings. Perhaps out of fear. She is under your protection, at the moment. Although that could change." Geoffrey answered.

Stephen's eyes narrowed. "Edmund, you have spoken to her. You know she would not spare me from this to save my feelings. Nor is she afraid of me." He thought back to their numerous exchanges. The remarkable thing about Rosalind Schofield, besides the way the she crinkled her nose when she smiled, or the bounce in her step as she walked, was that she had never once feared him.

"Her uncle is in your employ, Stephen," Edmund replied, his voice low. "It is possible that she would not want to risk his position."

"Right." Stephen opened the ledger in front of him to a page at random, not bothering to look up. His eyes scanned over meaningless numbers as he practiced careless disregard while his insides battled to keep control. Edmund *was* lying, and worse, lying to support Geoffrey's dubious cause. Why? Stephen looked up and his younger cousin, looking so bloody uncomfortable in his own skin. Geoffrey must have something over him.

After a few excruciating minutes, Stephen addressed his audience. "Well, gentleman. Thank you, for sharing your concerns about my abilities. Geoffrey, I assume that your gambling debts are getting out of hand again. What's that, Perkins? Yes, my cousin tries his luck at piquet and hazard. Often loses, which is the rub, even for the son of a viscountess."

"Barronsfield!" Pembroke slammed his fist on the desk.

"Good to know I didn't break your arms, Geoffrey," he replied in his haughtiest tone. "Perhaps next time, eh?"

"You dare to mock me? Your neighbors are readying themselves to deal with you!"

"Is there a party? No matter, I abhor the tedium of such soirees."

"My lord," Perkins cleared his throat, as if suddenly obligated to speak. "They are speaking of petitioning the King to force you to hand the stewardship of Barronsfield to your uncle. The Bishop has also been consulted, given your, ahem, extensive history of engaging magicians and priests of many faiths to excise whatever devilry that has befallen you."

"Really?" Stephen stood up to his full height, and peered down at Perkins with his most impervious gaze. "Was this your idea, sir? I believe there is no such precedent in law, so good luck to you. I was unaware that you had such serious grievances, or that until this moment, no one had the spine to address them with me."

Perkins swallowed deeply, and looked over to Pembroke. This entire farce must have been Geoffrey's idea. He looked past the two of them to Edmund, who stood arms crossed, avoiding his gaze.

"How many times do you need to hear this, Stephen?" Geoffrey said. "My God, man, you have avoided society for years, except when the Beast preys on the poor people of this town. How many times have you awoken to clean up the mess? A dozen? You know in your heart of hearts that you must confront this truth. Why put yourself through the indignity when your sense of honor and duty knows what is best for Barronsfield?"

All the words made sense. He had said them to himself a thousand times. But he knew what was best for Barronsfield. And it wasn't Geoffrey Pembroke. He needed to talk to Schofield and discover what truth was in Edmund's claim, if any. "What time does the witch hunt begin?"

"On the morrow. I'd hoped not to do things this way. Pray reconsider, Stephen," Geoffrey said. His manner was cold as he rose, and leaned on his cane. "Think of your father. He would want what was best for Barronsfield."

"Do *not*," Stephen said, his voice deadly cold, "tell me to think of my father. There is not a moment when I do not think of him. Do you understand me?"

Geoffrey nodded, then left, Perkins in tow. Edmund tarried for a moment, about to leave, when Stephen noticed his hesitation and called him back.

"Edmund, a moment."

Edmund stopped, and turned slightly, not quite meeting Stephen's eye.

"Why did you not tell me about your brother and what you saw?" Stephen asked.

"Stephen…" He seemed to search for an answer. "You were ill."

"When the right thing needs to be done, it must be done immediately. That is a weak answer and you know it."

"I am not weak!" Edmund's voice filled the room, nearly taking Stephen aback. The anger and fear in his cousin's eyes were unmistakable. Someone must have gotten to him. Geoffrey, no doubt. What on earth did he have over his younger brother?

"I have always known you to be a thoughtful, insightful man." Stephen took a more conciliatory tone. Nothing would be gained by forcing Edmund into a corner. "I need to know why you waited until now to tell me this. And if you knew about this meeting your brother has arranged."

"Perkins called for this meeting." Edmund edged toward the door as they spoke.

"Perkins's a simple-headed fool. Your brother must have put him up to it."

"No."

"You are willing to believe that none of this is Geoffrey's doing? That I am a monster than needs to be thrown out of his castle to save Barronsfield?"

Edmund looked so damned forlorn. "He is my brother, Stephen. That must count for something."

"I suppose it should," Stephen replied. "Will you be attending this… meeting? Or Miss Schofield?"

"Miss Schofield does not know of it."

"I see. So who are the others to be at this gathering?"

"I do not know. I am not a part of it."

"How can you not be? Your story is rather important to Geoffrey's case, I would think."

"I—just—I don't—" Edmund turned away, unable to hold Stephen's gaze.

"Edmund, please—"

"Leave me out of this, Barronsfield." He swung the door open and bolted.

Stephen sank back into his chair and closed his eyes. His heart raged in his chest, and for a moment he thought he'd forgotten how to breathe. Barronsfield was all he had left. He could not lose it. Even if, perhaps, he had not always done what was needed to keep it.

Stephen poured himself a generous helping of brandy. He rarely took spirits in the morning, but his encounter with Geoffrey, coupled with the distressing news from Schofield earlier, called for it. He took a few minutes to collect his thoughts while he savored the harsh burn of the liquor in his throat. Geoffrey had no doubt already spread word to the discontents in the neighborhood, likely with promises of favors, and like crows they would be gathering to feast on his downfall. Stephen had to deny them their prize—and the truth was the only means to do it. He'd start with the infirmary, and then find Schofield.

Stephen threw open the door of his study, and walked along the dark corridors of Barronsfield Manor. There was little point in lighting all the lanterns in the manor. Aside from a few servants, he was the only one to grace its halls.

Wood floors creaked under his boots. Half of the rooms seemed inhabited by ghosts, the contents hidden under yards of white fabric, looking sad and forgotten.

Was this his legacy to Barronsfield? A massive, empty house? No children to run its halls. No sons to run amok in the orchard, no daughters to watch dance in the ballroom. No neighbors and tenants being feted and thanked at the harvest.

A weight like a hundred stones pressed down on his chest as he turned a corner, only to come face to face with his father. The eyes from the portrait starred out at him. They were as he remembered. Detached. Powerful. Sad.

He stalked away, and called for Hanley to bring his gloves and cloak. While he waited in the empty foyer, he caught a glimpse of himself in the mirror. In the lamplight, he caught his own reflection. Detached. Powerful. Sad.

So much of his father's later life was spent alone. His wife had been taken from him. Did he blame Stephen for that? Stephen had never told him about the curse. Never told him about Haddie

Walton's roses. He could never bring himself to do it. Maybe he was a coward, too.

But as cold as he had been, his father had known love. He had known companionship. Stephen never would. Maybe that was his curse. Still, he could not indulge himself by dwelling on it now.

Minutes later, he was out the door, his heavy black cloak catching in the breeze. His mount waited for him. He cast one last glance back at the manor, then spurred the beast on toward Elmsdale. Self-doubt was a luxury he could no longer afford.

The journey to Yorkshire had been tedious, but Thomas Pembroke had waited far too long to be deprived of this moment. The walls were closing in on his nephew, and he was going to make damn certain Barronsfield would be buried by them.

In the tight quarters of his room, Thomas sat facing both his sons.

"Geoffrey," Thomas began, "are you healing well since your ordeal?"

"Well enough, sir."

"And how did you fare with your cousin?" Thomas spoke to Geoffrey, but cast a sideways glance at Edmund, who was unusually sullen. From the look of him, Edmund must have done as he was told. Thomas didn't know whether to be happy at the boy's displeasure, or disgusted the deed took so much out of him.

"You should have seen the look on Barronsfield's face when Edmund spoke up." Geoffrey beamed at his younger brother, sparing Edmund an unusual bit of warmth.

Edmund pulled a hand through his hair, which was more unkempt than usual, then glowered at his brother before casting a pleading glance at Thomas. "He reacted as if I'd struck him."

"You confronted him with the truth. Sometimes the truth is… uncomfortable." Thomas ran his tongue over his teeth, his eyes fixed on his younger son, and saw doubt linger in Edmund's eyes.

"Is it?" Edmund leaned forward, turning to his brother. "Is it the truth?"

"Are you doubting me?" Geoffrey replied, taking in a breath.

Thomas couldn't help but admire Geoffrey's performance. He looked positively wounded by Edmund's insinuation.

"That's not what I'm saying, Geoffrey," Edmund countered, then lowered his voice. "You're my brother."

"This is not a scheme, Edmund." Geoffrey's mouth twisted into a scowl. "Stephen nearly killed me. Just because you were inconveniently absent when I needed you—as usual—doesn't mean it didn't happen. The least you can do for me is defend me after the fact."

Geoffrey was such an excellent liar, Thomas owned. If he could have spared his eldest a smile, he would have. But the gesture would only alienate Edmund further, and as much as Thomas hated the idea, he needed the boy on his side, even if it was unwillingly.

"Look at your brother, Edmund. Do you think any man would inflict such horrible injuries on himself?" Thomas watched Edmund shift uncomfortably in his seat. Doubt lingered in his eyes. Edmund lacked so many of the qualities his brother possessed, but he wasn't stupid.

"You have always followed Barronsfield around like a lost puppy, Edmund. You would rather trust a monster than your own blood," Geoffrey said, his eyes narrowed. He crossed his arms and turned away from Edmund.

"That is not what I am saying!" Edmund's voice rose, his cheeks flushing. "But I have never seen this creature you purport Stephen to be. Not once in all the times I have been at Barronsfield have I seen any evidence of it. To suggest such a story is true based on—"

"Based on the word of your brother. That should be enough for you." Thomas spoke. "You are a member of this family, though you seem to forget it when it suits you."

"Father, you know I wish to support my family. But telling such a falsehood—"

"It is not a falsehood," Geoffrey spat.

"Right then," Edmund continued, pressing his temples with his fingertips. "This false witness, or whatever the hell you want to call it —it feels wrong."

Damn Edmund and his sense of honor. It was time for Thomas to end this. He softened his manner, lowering his voice the way he might speak to a young child. He needed to feed Edmund the smallest bit of the balm he knew the boy sought from him—his attention.

"Edmund, my boy, think for a moment. What other explanation could there be? There has been so much terror in Barronsfield that has been unexplainable save for this awful curse. You may not have wanted to see it. I understand that. That makes it all the more important that you stand up for what is right. Stand up for your family. You wouldn't want to explain to your mother why you allowed your brother's injuries to go unanswered? Or, perhaps you would rather explain to her how you nearly killed a man in a duel after being caught between his wife's legs?"

The fight leeched out of Edmund's shoulders, just as Thomas knew it would. The boy dropped his chin to his chest, and shook his head.

"I have done everything you have asked of me," he said. "I made one mistake. I didn't know who she was."

"That is because you are a young fool, Edmund, who acts before he thinks. It cost your mother her health, and it is all I can do to make sure this news doesn't reach her. It would finish her."

Edmund kept his gaze fixed straight ahead and swallowed deeply.

"How is mother, sir?" It was Geoffrey who piped up now, as if on cue. It was a dance Geoffrey and Thomas played whenever Edmund's compliance was required. Now, it was essential.

"I visited Lowry Hill on my way from London. Your poor mother is a little somber, as she always is at this time of year. Perhaps a little more despondent than usual," he offered with as much false concern as he could manage without falling over into theatrics.

The injuries his wife had suffered to her legs years ago came when the fool had tried to save Edmund as he'd dashed out in front of a carriage in a London street. Her legs, badly broken, had left her a convalescent, unable to participate in society. It was quite a satisfactory arrangement for Thomas; she was far too fragile to host expensive parties, and too isolated to know about his mistresses or his use of her fortune. Sequestered in the country with a few servants and companions, she was out of the public eye much of the time. Even better, Thomas had long been able to exploit Edmund's soft nature and guilt over being the cause of his mother's situation. That Evelyn loved Edmund dearly and without malice, was the ironic frosting on the entire situation.

"I fear for her if news of Barronsfield's assault on Geoffrey reaches her ears—she is so delicate. I think, Edmund," he turned to his youngest, "if by some unfortunate occurrence that it does happen, your support of your brother at this time will provide her some much needed solace."

Edmund's head snapped up. "Perhaps I should remove myself and be with her, sir."

Thomas pulled his cheeks back into a thin smile. "Admirable, Edmund, but as usual you have thoroughly misjudged what is required of you. You need to be here, close by, to defend your brother's honor if the need arises."

"What if they know I didn't actually see the Beast?" Edmund looked his brother over, then turned back to Thomas.

"They will not find out, will they?" Thomas replied, his voice hardening again. "You will straighten your shoulders and pretend to be a man. Have I made myself clear?"

The boy was silent, sullen, but there was a spark of steel in Edmund's eyes Thomas had not seen before. It gave him pause. But then, as always, it melted away.

"Completely." Edmund pulled himself up and glared at Geoffrey. "At least one of us can play the part of a loving brother."

He cast one last look at both of them, then slammed the door behind him.

"Do you think he'll spill his guts to Barronsfield?" Geoffrey gestured with a quick sideways nod toward the door, then wiped his hands against his breeches.

Thomas waved off his concerns. "Your brother is the least of my worries. He has a certain credibility in Barronsfield. Perkins, the fool, was easy enough to satisfy." The promise of marriage to one of his hapless daughters to Geoffrey was all he required. "With Gates firmly in our pocket, some untidy secrets to keep our man at Barronsfield in line, and a promise from an insider at St. James Court to entertain the petition, the title will be in our hands by the new year, if not sooner." Thomas had nearly bankrupted the family to do it, but at last he would finally have his due. "Edmund's story will make it complete, correct? No loose ends?"

At that moment, Geoffrey paled, and started pulling at his cravat. Thomas examined his son's every movement, looking for that twitch in his cheek. Geoffrey could be as smooth as the finest Chinese silks, even with the bruises and cuts that marred his face. But the minute a corner of his mouth pulled back slightly, causing his cheek to twitch ever so slightly, Thomas knew desperation lurked beneath his son's calm expression.

Desperation was never a good state for Geoffrey. He became foolish, reckless, and maybe even a little dangerous. When Barronsfield's fiancé had decided not to have Geoffrey even as a lover, Geoffrey's desperation had morphed into madness, and Anne Wickwire's pretty neck was broken. The only advantage to that disaster was that it gave them the perfect opportunity to cement Stephen's reputation as the Beast of Barronsfield.

Geoffrey started rubbing his hands on his thighs. Slowly. Methodically.

"No loose ends," Thomas repeated, his voice low, allowing a bit of an edge. "Is that correct?"

Geoffrey swallowed, his head shaking back and forth too emphatically for Thomas's liking.

"No, sir." And then, as if expecting to be caught, Geoffrey turned away. But not before Thomas caught the shudder in his son's cheek.

"Who?" he shouted.

"Schofield's niece. She saw me that night, before this." He gestured to his battered face. "Her and the maid. She's gone—the maid, that is. Ran off. It shouldn't be a problem." Geoffrey started running off at the mouth, baring his teeth in a forced smile while his tongue wagged all the faster. "Schofield has forbidden her from going anywhere near the manor. This will be all over before she has a chance to say anything."

Thomas shut his eyes, his fingers curling into fists. It was all he could do not to strike Geoffrey.

Thomas opened his eyes. "You know damn well that word of your story will reach her, and when it does she will challenge it and our cause will be damaged." Thomas's knuckles on his right hand crackled as he clenched his fingers. Small beads of sweat gathered on his son's brow. "You've got to fix this Geoffrey."

"She's got ten thousand pounds, father. We could use that."

"You sort it out. Either she is your wife, or she is a corpse, but deal with it. Or I will."

CHAPTER 17

$\mathcal{U}$ncle Reginald's warning to stay at the cottage threatened to drive Rosalind mad. There had been no news about Bess. The girl's disappearance had clearly distracted the housekeeper, so the two furiously scrubbed walls, beat rugs and baked pies. Anything to make the time go by. Every once in a while Rosalind would stop and catch her breath, and her thoughts would wander to the great house and its Lord. She thought of him sitting alone in his library, cut off from the world, so grateful for every spare glance of kindness. She paused, remembering the touch of his skin as he'd laced his fingers in hers. The panic in his eyes at the assembly when he'd thought he'd forgotten how to dance, and the joy in her heart when they fumbled along together. And it was joy. It was too spectacular to be anything less.

At last, a knock on the door came. Rosalind ran to answer it. She pulled the door open, and a smile froze on her face.

Geoffrey Pembroke. Rosalind gaped at his battered appearance.

"Mr. Pembroke! Have you been in an accident?"

"Miss Schofield!" He smiled, though the expression did not quite reach his eyes. "May I come in?"

She stepped aside, shock fixing her where she stood as Mr. Pembroke hobbled into to the parlor and helped himself to a seat.

Rosalind closed the door and went to take a seat next to him.

"Thank you for seeing me. Your very presence helps me to rally."

"What happened?"

"This is the work of the devil, Miss Schofield. Or my cousin, when he is under the devil's curse." He said it so matter-of-factly, and without bothering to lower his voice, it took Rosalind aback. "He beat me within an inch of my life, as you can see."

"When?" The bruises on his face were still purple, and the cut on his cheek was freshly made. When she'd left the marquess yesterday, he'd still been abed and far from well enough to engage in any fisticuffs.

"The night of the assembly, my dear Miss Schofield. Of course, you may not remember, after the Beast struck you. You did not stir for some time."

Rosalind's eyes widened, and the back of her neck began to tingle. "My memories of that night are clear, sir."

"I believe it is normal for women in times of stress to have bouts of hysteria that can affect their memories." He went to her and patted her hand, his expression soft as if he were speaking to a small child. "It is all for the best, perhaps, considering the feminine constitution."

Rosalind swallowed her anger at his condescension. "You came to my room. Do you not remember? You were uninjured. I saw you." Dread tightened her throat. Bess Hargrove did too, didn't she? And she had disappeared. Rosalind stared at him anew, alarm bells ringing in her head.

He smiled blithely, but his hand shook ever so slightly as he smoothed the front of his coat. "As I said, you were no doubt over-come by the horror of the evening. Edmund found me, then put me into the hands of one of Walter Perkins's servants, who took me back to his master's house." His eyebrows rose suddenly, as if he was engaging in a dare. "It is lucky I did not die of pleurisy."

"Lucky," Rosalind echoed. He seemed to be watching her every move, which made her nervous.

"But it is your wellbeing that concerns me most." He lowered his voice and reached out for her hand, which she moved under the pretense of wiping a stray lock of her hair. "You must know, Miss Schofield, that you are my particular concern."

Rosalind pulled her lips back in a smile, inwardly shuddering at his flattery. She couldn't help but recall the first time she'd met Geoffrey Pembroke in the square. She'd groaned at the sight of the marquess coming toward them, his dark eyes troubled, hair glinting in the sun, and interrupting their foolish chatter about assemblies. If only he would interrupt them again.

"I thank you, but, Mr. Pembroke, I must be clear. I may have been unconscious at the ruins, as you say, but I was quite awake when you were in my room later on." She lowered her voice to a whisper, lest Emily hear. "You tried to kiss me!"

"Dreams are powerful things, especially after such a night as that," he said, using the same tone of voice that had bewitched her in Dalrymple's as she tried on bonnets for him. But the magic no longer held its sway over her. "I am quite flattered I featured in your dream so …intimately."

Rosalind was dumbstruck. What did she say to that?

"Mr. Pembroke—"

"But I have come to you to speak on more pleasant business." He moved so quickly, Rosalind held out her hands, sure he was about to fall. Instead, he landed in front of her. On one knee.

Rosalind was about to be ill.

"Miss Schofield—Rosalind—I feel that fate has brought us together. And fate nearly took you from me a few nights ago." He reached for her hands, grasping them before she could pull away.

"Mr. Pembroke, I don't—"

"Please, you must call me Geoffrey. I know this is sudden, but you have been the light that has sustained me through these past days. Indeed, it has been those very trials that have taught me that life is precious, and I have no time to waste to secure my happiness. And yours as well, of course. Rosalind, I want—nay—I need you to accept my proposal."

Rosalind stopped breathing. Did he—

"You want me to marry you?"

He broke into a smile, but desperation widened his eyes. He barely blinked.

"From that first moment I saw you, I knew I needed to have you. Surely, you have felt it."

The memory of that initial attraction turned her stomach. "I don't know what to say." In truth, she knew exactly what to say, but answering the question felt dangerous.

"Say you will marry me." In a movement so very quick for a man who'd walked in with the use of a cane, he rose again, holding her with one hand and gesturing with the other. "We could go to Scotland. It is impulsive, perhaps, but I cannot contain my passion much longer. Life is so fleeting."

"Mr. Pembroke, this is so unexpected." And he looked so terribly unhinged. "I—"

A loud knocking at the door brought Rosalind a welcome reprieve.

"Excuse me, Mr. Pembroke, please. The place has been quite busy with visitors, what with all that is happening at Barronsfield." That was a lie, but a convenient one.

"Ah—of course," he said as if he'd awoken from a trance.

Rosalind gently but firmly untangled her hands from Mr. Pembroke's grip. She turned away and made for the door, all the while feeling his gaze on her. What sort of dark mischief was Mr. Pembroke about? Did her uncle know about it? Did Lord Barronsfield? Mr. Pembroke had no doubt spread his story to every sympathetic ear in Elmsdale—like his confession to Rosalind about seeing the Beast for the first time.

Rosalind opened the door to see the vicar standing there. Salvation indeed.

"Mr. Darling! Come in!" Rosalind all but pulled the man inside.

"A pleasure, Miss Schofield, but I am here on business I'm afraid," he said in a low voice. "Your uncle sent me here, and there will be others coming behind me. It's about the business with Miss Hargrove."

"Of course. Please come in." She led the vicar to her parlor, where Geoffrey still stood.

"Mr. Pembroke, this is an unexpected pleasure." The vicar held out his hand, though the vicar's countenance seemed strained as the two recognized each other.

"I could say the same, thank you. I wanted to ensure Miss Schofield was improving after the horrible events of late," Geoffrey Pembroke replied, his charm and ease of delivery rapidly disappearing. They all stood in agonizing silence, before Mr. Pembroke walked to Rosalind, leaning heavily on his cane once more, took her hand and kissed it. "I must go. But I will be seeing you again soon, I hope."

"Thank you for your visit, Mr. Pembroke," she replied. If not for Mr. Darling being present, she would have slumped on the settee in relief. Instead, Rosalind raced to the window, where she watched Mr. Pembroke's stride change from a hobble to a hurried walk as he made his way back to a waiting carriage.

"Are you well, Miss Schofield?" The vicar asked, concern in his voice.

"I am now, thank you." Rosalind, satisfied Geoffrey Pembroke had gone, turned away from the window as Emily bustled in with a tray of tea. "Is there news of Bess Hargrove?"

"No." He accepted a cup of tea from Emily. "I have just been to bury the poor soul found this morning. And while this is probably not a terribly Christian thing to say, you may find some relief that it was not Miss Hargrove."

"You said my uncle will return?"

"Soon. On orders of the marquess he is sending a man to London. Your uncle believes that there are some villagers who may be working against the marquess, so he felt it safer to meet here."

Rosalind excused herself and bolted up the stairs to her room, her body a bundle of nerves her after her encounter with Geoffrey Pembroke. She picked up the husk she'd found earlier in her apron, and wrapped it back up in the linen cloth. Lord Barronsfield needed to know about Geoffrey Pembroke's lie, and she needed to find out more about Haddie's clue. Somewhere in the great library in Barronsfield Manor, between the books on were-wolves and the sermons by Fordyce, there must be a book on botany, or medicine. Or poison.

Rosalind raced back into the kitchen, tossing her cloak over her shoulders, Dreyfus yapping furiously at her feet. Emily entered, drawn no doubt by the dog's barking.

"Miss Schofield, your uncle—"

Rosalind clipped her cloak around her neck. "I must go to Barronsfield Manor at once. If I miss my uncle, can you give him a message when he returns?"

"Of course dear."

"I fear Geoffrey Pembroke is telling a falsehood about the marquess." Rosalind gripped the edges of her cloak. "He claims he received his injuries from the marquess the night Lord Barronsfield took ill at the assembly. But I know that is untrue. I just need to prove it."

Emily pulled Rosalind into a hug. "Be careful."

Rosalind flung open the kitchen door, sparing but a moment to glance up at the heavy, dark gray sky. She had barely taken two steps out into the lane leading to the manor when the clouds made good on their threat and opened, pouring down on the bleak landscape. Wind tossed the trees, bringing down the leaves, baring the twisted gray and brown branches to the harsh weather. Rosalind picked up her skirts and ran for the great house.

Never did she fear the marquess's curse, or cower at the idea of a Beast. What scared Rosalind was the way the man himself was beginning to capture her heart. Whether he realized it or not, Lord Barronsfield needed her. If only he wanted her too.

The stone edifice of the manor stretched toward the sky, as dark and ominous as the clouds above. Only a few of the manor windows were lit. The rain fell, cold and thick, each drop reaching down through Rosalind's heavy cloak, past the dark blue muslin of her dress and chemise, through to her skin. Hand on the iron knocker, she tapped, then pounded at the front door for what felt like a long time. At last, the door opened, Hanley standing on the other side. Rosalind dashed across the threshold.

"I must speak with my uncle at once. Or the marquess, if he is well enough," Rosalind blurted out, before recovering her manners. "And I need to use the library—if it would be of no trouble."

Hanley nodded and raised his bushy white eyebrows ever so slightly, betraying only the slightest reaction to her outburst.

"Neither his lordship nor the steward have yet returned, Miss Schofield," Hanley said in a clear, measured tone. "I will take you to the library and inform them of your arrival when they return."

A few of the sconces on the wall in the entryway were lit, their meager light making the manor only slightly more inviting on the inside than on the outside. A shame, really. The intricately cut wooden floors beneath her feet and the winding stair in front of her would have dazzled if the massive chandelier soaring above her head was alight.

Hanley took Rosalind's cloak, now heavy from the rain. The tremendous hearth in the entryway lay dark, even though the inclement weather and the damp air begged for it to be put to use. She hugged herself to stifle a shiver. He prepared to lead her up the main staircase when she put a hand on his arm.

"I can find my way, Hanley. Thank you." She dashed up the stairs.

"Hot chocolate, Miss?" The butler's voice broke her concentration.

"That would be grand, thank you," she called over her shoulder.

In contrast to the entry, the library was almost completely lit, and a fire blazed in the hearth, as if she'd been expected. She walked the length of the room, her fingers running along the shelves of books, scanning the spines as she did so. Her gaze followed shelf upon shelf, row upon row of books. Where would she ever find what she was looking for? There were probably hundreds, if not thousands, of volumes on these shelves.

She stopped at the fireplace, allowing the heat to sink into her body. The clock on the mantle chimed four o'clock. She wanted to linger near the fire until she'd chased the last bit of the damp from her bones, but there was no time. Three solid walls of books confronted her. She did not even know where to start.

The door opened and Hanley returned with a fine woolen shawl and a steaming pot of chocolate.

"Thank you." She accepted the rich, soft material and pulled its comforting weight around her shoulders. "Can I ask you one more question?"

"Yes, miss."

"Do you know where the volumes on botany might be found in this library? Or natural history, perhaps?"

"I am afraid not, miss," he said, leaving her alone again.

Rosalind scanned the shelves, overwhelmed by the sheer number of books. Between the massive cases were portraits of the former occupants of the manor, less formal that those in the main corridor, their likenesses captured by a master's brush at the height of their glory. A few of them bore a strong resemblance to the marquess. One shared the same careless expression as Geoffrey Pembroke. But the small portrait of a woman, sitting unobtrusively to one side of the hearth caught her eye. The shape of the green eyes looking back at her. The mouth, turned ever so slightly up on the right side.

"For heaven's sake, Rosalind, remember why you're here," she admonished herself, and returned to the bookshelves, which started to move before her eyes. Her breath caught and she jumped back, only to see the marquess emerge from the other side of the wall.

"Good afternoon, Miss Schofield."

"What on earth?" She looked behind him to the bookshelf that looked as solid as it had before he'd walked through it. "You are full of secrets, my lord."

A forbidden longing stirred inside Rosalind as Lord Barronsfield stood before her. His shirt was missing his cravat, and though he wore his coat, his waistcoat was unbuttoned, and his hair was damp. "And you are managing to uncover them. This leads to my study—and on a simple hinge. Not nearly as mysterious as it appears. I'm glad you're here."

Something like expectation rose in Rosalind's chest, and she couldn't fight the smile forming on her lips. "Really?"

"I visited with Doctor Brayden earlier today—I am sure you heard about the second body discovered at the ruin."

"Of course." Dead bodies. Rosalind kept her smile pasted on her face. Sharing news of corpses was always a good reason for a man to be excited by her presence. "And?"

"It wasn't Bess—no one knows who is it, I'm afraid. The good doctor believes he died a few days ago. Not right after the assembly."

Rosalind nodded, happy at both the news and the relief that Bess might still be in one piece and still likely to be found.

"I also learned that Sally Coles may have died in a similar fashion and that her body was left there, evidently to be found." He wiped his forehead with the back of his hand and gestured to his informal appearance. "Excuse me for not receiving you properly. Hanley said you wished to speak with me and I didn't want to keep you waiting."

"I do." Gathering a breath, she tried to calm the nervous sensation growing inside of her. "I'm not sure how to say this best, so I am just going to do it. Mr. Geoffrey Pembroke showed up at my door, not fifteen minutes ago. He walked with a cane, and sported several large bruises. He claimed you gave them to him the night of the assembly, at the churchyard."

"I saw him earlier today. Your assessment of his injuries is correct."

"Then he must have sought me out to ensure his version of what happened to him has been properly circulated. He's lying."

His eyes narrowed and he put his hands on his hips. "How do you know this?"

"I saw him that night—later, after everything had happened. He was uninjured."

"Later? When in the blazes were you talking to Pembroke?" The marquess stepped closer, and put his hand on her shoulder. Then, as if he had done something wrong, let his arm drop back down to his side.

"After you'd been brought back to the manor. I was given a room in the house, because of the bad weather." The marquess's dark eyes were fixed on her, his gaze so intense the blood flushed into her cheeks. "He claimed he was coming to check on me, to make sure I hadn't been hurt. There was not a mark on him, and he walked in and out without aid."

"He was in your room? *Alone?*"

"Are you not listening to what I am saying?" Why was he so concerned about propriety now?

"Of course I am. The bastard—excuse me—Pembroke, was in your rooms with you, *alone*," he spat. He looked away and uttered what sounded to Rosalind like a low curse before recovering himself. "Did he touch you?"

Rosalind opened her mouth, then closed it again. Heat rushed into her cheeks. "He—"

"He did. Bloody hell." He raked his hand through his hair, and let out a low, exasperated sigh. "I hope he did not impose himself—"

"My virtue was quite intact when he left the room."

He did not appear to relax at her declaration.

"I am here with you now, quite alone, unchaperoned," she challenged.

"That's different."

"Very different," she uttered quickly then turned away as heat prickled through her body, her hands balling into fists.

"Is something the matter, Miss Schofield?"

"No," she lied. The urgency of her quest had to be enough to keep her from dwelling on how much she hated that she was *safe* with Lord Barronsfield.

"Are you certain? I should not be so callous as to bring up unwanted memories from that night."

Not unwanted memories. Unwanted feelings perhaps.

"Everything about that night bothers me, my lord, though perhaps not in the way you imagine." She started pacing, pushing her feelings aside. "First, let us consider that the Beast—in whatever supernatural form—does not exist. What happened to you was shocking, I admit, but it was also—what's the word?"

"Disgusting."

"Convenient."

"You are confusing me. Again."

"To have the curse come upon you like that, in the middle of a crowd? For you to run off into a stormy night, moonless, so dark you could barely be seen? Yes, I think that is terribly convenient." The weight of her convictions chased away her nerves. She grasped her shawl with one hand while she gestured wildly with the other. "So this —whatever this is—does not make any sense to me. Never in any fairy tale I've read is love the means to an ill end. On the contrary. Love breaks spells and curses. It sets the cursed one free."

"Is this why you are here? Looking for a book of fairy tales?"

She turned back to the shelves, and placed her hand on her hip. "No. I need a book on botany. I think you are being poisoned."

There. She said it.

"Poison?" He put a hand to his face, absentmindedly stroking his chin. "How do you know?"

Rosalind produced the thorny husk, which Lord Barronsfield took into his own hands and examined. "I found this in my apron yesterday. I think someone left it for me, hoping I'd discover what it is, so here I am. There are some extractions, my lord, which can cause a person to see things that are not real, and to remember things that never actually happened. There is something about this entire affair that isn't right. Many things, actually. At first, it was small things here and there, like a little pebble in my shoe. Enough to make me stop and look. After today," she paused, catching herself fidgeting, "well, I am convinced."

"Your certainty is admirable." He studied the plant in his hand, then handed it back to her. "Pray, tell me your theory."

"First, we need a bit of proof." She folded the husk back up in the linen cloth and placed it on the mantle over the hearth. Then gestured to the shelves around them. "I'd hoped I'd find something to identify the plant in among your collection."

Lord Barronsfield came to her side, and held out his hand. Her breath catching, she swallowed her trepidation and caught his intense gaze, softened by a tender smile that she'd seen once before in the vicar's front yard. Wrapping her fingers around his, a shiver of excitement flowed through her as he led her to one of the towering bookcases.

Lord Barronsfield cleared his throat. "You are looking for a particular volume?"

He gestured toward the shelf of books. She tried to think of small talk, all the while attempting to ignore his strong masculine presence so close by.

"I don't know exactly. Do you have anything on flora identification?" There were so many volumes, even on this one subject. Some titles were in English, some Latin, and Greek.

He reached up and pulled a large blue book off the shelf and handed it to Rosalind. *Coloured Figures of Rare and Exotic Plants.*

"Aha! This looks promising." Satisfied, she headed back toward the hearth. As she started thinking about her theories, her confidence rose, along with her curiosity.

She scooped up the linen cloth with the husk and plopped down into a smaller chair and started leafing through the drawings in the blue cloth-bound book in her lap.

Concentrating on each page was no small feat while the marquess paced in front of the fire, watching her intently. The book was filled with beautifully illustrated plates. At last she found one with a drawing of a round, prickly husk. "Here it is!"

She rose and motioned for him to sit, which he did without delay. Unceremoniously she dropped the book in his lap, and hand resting on the arm of the chair, she leaned over to point out the entry. Ignoring the surprised look on his face, the searching in his eyes, the scent of his skin, and the sensation of his body so close to hers, she continued her explanations.

"*Datura stramonium.* It isn't terribly widespread in northern England, but common enough in other places. It has some medicinal properties, but if you look down here," she dared to lean in farther, suddenly aware of the heat in her cheeks, the fluttering in her chest, and how incredibly out of place her hair was at the moment. "The seeds of the plant are quite dangerous. They can cause madness, an aversion to sunlight, insatiable thirst, flushed skin. They can also make it difficult to..." She paused while she tried to find a delicate way to talk to the marquess about his toileting habits. Turning to him, she found his face only inches from hers. His suggested he was enjoying her discomfort.

This was positively nerve-wracking.

"To what, Miss Schofield?"

"Conduct your, ah, private business." She turned away, aware that his eyes were still on her. "You don't need to answer that."

"I won't, thank you," he said. "But, if this is so..."

"Then the Beast has been a lie."

CHAPTER 19

A lie. Years of wrangling with nightmares, frightened villagers, and vicious rumors that made him afraid to be seen out in the light of day. Years of searching for false hope, bloodletting, rituals —all in search of a cure that could never come. And guilt. So much of that.

Poison. Simple, and yet devastatingly effective. A trick that allowed everyone—himself included—to see exactly what they wanted to see. And it was all *a lie*.

Stephen shifted in his seat, using every ounce of his deportment to remain calm as the idea settled heavy in his gut. The rain, whipped around outside by a growing, angry wind, matched the turmoil inside him.

"I don't think you are the Beast of Barronsfield," Miss Schofield said softly. "Haddie Walton wouldn't have been so vindictive to a small boy."

He sprang out of his chair, leaving the book on the seat behind him, and walked to the hearth. Resting his elbow on the stone mantle, he drew his hand slowly down over his face then turned to Miss Schofield, who stood near. "How can this be? I have caused too much pain. I brought the curse into Barronsfield. I watched my mother and sister die, even as I begged for their protection. And Catherine, and the babe too. It was my duty to protect them. And I could not."

He stopped then, using every ounce of control he had left to keep his emotions from spilling over. She reached out and took his hand in hers.

"You cannot protect everyone all the time. That is not a failure of duty. That you feel their loss is a testament to you as a loving son, husband, a father. As a man." He savored the warmth and compassion of her touch. Her eyes were bright with a sheen of unshed tears. "My lord, I am sorry that you lost so many that you loved. I have lost a mother and a father, both of whom I loved very much. And I do not think I am cursed. It is just the way things happen sometimes. I cannot speak to what happened between you and Haddie Walton all those years ago, but I am certain she would be sorry you have lived with this guilt for so long."

They stood in comfortable silence for a moment, the only noise between them the crackling of the fire.

"Who would do such a thing?" he blurted out at last, the enormity of the crime angering him. The words had hardly escaped his mouth when he had an excellent idea of the answer.

Stephen had seen Geoffrey reckless in the past—but he'd always led with his fists. This was more. This was devious. Geoffrey had his reasons to despise Stephen, but for this level of insanity, his Uncle Thomas must be instrumental. Only Thomas could find the right way to twist Edmund to his bidding. And Thomas, not Geoffrey, was the most immediate benefactor of Stephen's misfortunes.

"My uncle," Stephen answered for her benefit. "Geoffrey's father. A positively Machiavellian man. I have no idea how he hatched this plot, but I am confident he is behind it."

"Has your uncle always known of the curse? Perhaps your father may have told him about your encounter with Miss Walton?" She put her hand to her mouth before reaching out to him, resting her hand on his arm. "I'm sorry. Perhaps you do not wish to speak of it."

Warmth radiated from where her hand lay, and as he looked down, she must have mistaken his surprise for something else—disdain maybe?—and drew it back quickly with an apologetic smile. But the echo of her touch lingered, and he found himself grateful for it. He let out a long slow breath.

"My apologies, Miss Schofield. I have not spoken of this in many years," he said, recovering himself. "Before the Beast, my uncle didn't know of the curse. Even my father was unaware. I was never brave enough to tell him. Only your uncle knew the truth of it." Stephen thought back to the day Reginald Schofield found him on Haddie Walton's front porch as Stephen pounded on her door, face hot with tears, begging her to release his mother from the curse. Imogene, too little to fight the disease, had died first. Haddie Walton was nowhere to be found. Schofield had scooped young Stephen up and brought him home, without revealing to anyone where Stephen had gone and why. Stephen had never breathed a word about it to another soul. Except...

Another memory, dimmed by time and far too much wine, became clear.

"Geoffrey." The name came out is a rush of breath. He released her hand, and started pacing. "We were sitting in my study the night before I married Catherine. I'd boasted about it, that I'd beaten the curse. I told him about Haddie Walton, the roses—everything. He laughed about it, and told me I was mad to believe in such hocus pocus."

"Mr. Pembroke told me he saw you change into the Beast after your wife and child died."

"What?" Stephen stalled in his tracks.

"He said he saw you, that night, after your wife died. He and your cook."

"Well, he is right about one thing," he said. "That was the first night that something happened to me. The night the Beast, as the villagers would know it, was born—real or otherwise. And the day after I wished I was dead, too."

His mind raced back to that terrible night after their death. Stephen was positive the curse had killed them, like it had his mother and sister. He'd been so angry, and said some horrible things in his anger—both to Haddie Walton, wherever she was, and to God. The following night the curse twisted horribly, and the Beast appeared for the first of several times, wreaking havoc in the village. Stephen's secrets about Haddie Walton and his mother's death were secrets no more.

Despite this, Stephen was determined to give Barronsfield an heir, and nearly two years later asked Anne Wickwire to marry him. He'd had no idea Geoffrey wanted her. Anne had accepted Stephen's offer, despite the rumors of the curse she may have heard. He was marquess, Geoffrey wasn't, and Anne was ambitious. Geoffrey never really forgave him for that, and her death only made the animosity between them worse. The Beast was blamed for that too, and sealed his fate. No woman would have him after that.

He'd been left unable to produce an heir, and his title in jeopardy.

My God, how could he not see it? The veil of guilt that had clouded Stephen's vision began to lift. "I think this so-called beating Geoffrey claims I inflicted may be the lie too many. He was a little too smug, even for him."

"I'm worried for Bess." Miss Schofield twisted a lock of her hair in her fingers in a most distracting manner. "She was with me, that night, when Mr. Pembroke came into my room. She could attest to the state of his health. Having her disappear like this must be by design, my lord."

Before he realized what he was doing, he stopped in front of her, taking one of her hands in his own. His world was spinning. He needed something to hold on to. He needed her.

"Stephen."

"Excuse me?" Her question was barely above a whisper.

"Please, call me Stephen. I rarely hear my own name. Sometimes I'm afraid I'm going to forget who I actually am." He looked over and caught an expression on her face that was hard to make out. Had he imposed himself too much?

THE WARMTH of his touch and the depth of his plea nearly stopped

Rosalind's breath, echoing from another place and time. She'd dreamed that plea. The man that had spoken those words in her dreams had wanted her. She wanted to close her eyes and capture this moment—the sensation of his masculine touch, the soft intensity in his dark eyes.

"Unless," he said, "you would rather not."

"No." She nodded her head and broke into a smile. "I would like that very much. You may call me Rosalind."

"Thank you. And thank you for believing in my innocence for so long. Believing in me."

The door opened, interrupting them, and Rosalind was grateful they stood by the fire to disguise the heat flooding in to her cheeks.

"Excuse the intrusion, my lord," Hanley said, entering the room, a servant behind him carrying a large silver tray. "We thought you might be in need of nourishment."

"You do not mind eating informally?" Stephen asked her.

"No! This is lovely."

The servant set the tray down on a table between the two chairs near the hearth. Even under the cover of silver services, the smell of thyme and sage tickled her nose, and her stomach began to grumble in spite of herself. She smiled as she sat down and the servant handed her and Stephen a plate before leaving them alone again. "This is very good," she said after a few bites of pigeon.

"The feast before us is the debut meal of one of my kitchen servants. At least until I can find a new cook," he said. "Hanley informed me earlier that the chef has to resigned his post with me as of this morning."

She paused, her fork halfway to her mouth. "Had your cook been with you as long as Hanley, or my uncle?"

"No one has been here as long as Hanley," Stephen smiled. "The cook came not long after I married Catherine." Stephen put down his fork, and looked at his plate as if he had not seen it before. "You don't think..."

"The cook has been a convenient witness to back your cousin's story about your transformation into the Beast. And, though it could be anyone, he does have the best access to your food," Rosalind said. "Do you normally dine alone?"

"Yes, but not the night of the assembly. Of course, knowing my uncle, he probably has several men in his purse. He'd have to in order keep this going."

Rosalind was certain of at least one of them. "A man named Tom Gates threatened my uncle within minutes of my arrival here—at the Darling's yard, the day after the Beast supposedly attacked. Emily told me that he's happily spread tales about the Beast through the village. He was out hunting for you the night of the assembly—with help of course. And Bess told me Sally Coles was out with his son, Jack. Perhaps the poor girl discovered their involvement?"

"I asked the doctor about Jack—his father claimed the lad saw the Beast and was lucky to get away with his life. If Jack was hurt, he never sought Brayden's help. It was probably another false story." Stephen sat back in his chair, a look of remorse about him. "Your uncle never told me that Gates was giving him such grief. He's a good man, your uncle, but he takes too much upon himself."

Rosalind picked up her fork and pointed it in Stephen's direction. "If there is any curse around Barronsfield, it's good men who take too much upon themselves."

"Your uncle is a good man, Rosalind. The very best in fact. If I find he has been ill used or handled roughly by Mr. Gates…" he trailed off, but Rosalind caught the edge in his voice. That Uncle Reginald meant so much to Stephen—that meant the world to her.

Stephen rose, and pulled on the bell rope. A few moments later, Hanley appeared, and Stephen asked for the magistrate to be summoned. While he spoke with the butler, Rosalind found she was unable to draw her attention away from him. Perhaps it was the way he cocked his head to the side when speaking, or where he rested his hands on his hips, or even how perfectly his buckskin breeches fit over his solid, muscular legs, but it distracted her. This was most definitely not the time to be thinking such things, she admonished herself, even though it was difficult not to.

They were so close to finding the answer, and then her uncle couldn't send her away, could he? She could spend all her days here, and see Barronsfield Manor the way it should be. See Stephen Pembroke happy. The way he should be.

An unwelcome thought settled in, threatening to chase away her appetite. Once they'd found the answer, once they solved the mystery of the Beast of Barronsfield, Stephen Pembroke would be free to marry whomever he wished. Would he wish it was her? Why was she suddenly wishing it was her?

Lost in her own thoughts, she hardly noticed Hanley leaving. It was only after the clicking of the library door as it closed that she noticed Stephen standing there, staring at her, with a most peculiar look on his face. She was about to ask him about it when the words caught in her throat. The look in his eyes reminded her of when they were on the dance floor in the assembly hall, before all hell broke loose. Eleanore Martin had commented on how happy Rosalind had been.

"Eleanore Martin." The name escaped her in a flash of inspiration.

"Excuse me?" he asked as if she had taken leave of her senses. "What does she have to do with anything?"

Putting her plate aside, she hopped up out of her chair and returned to the portrait that had captured her attention after she'd come to the library. With fresh eyes, she stared at the face. Looking back at her was Eleanore Martin.

A RATHER UNCOMFORTABLE sensation gripped Stephen as he watched Rosalind peer at the tiny painting. And this time, it had nothing to do with the way her hair glowed in the firelight.

"It's been bothering me since I first looked at this portrait. I couldn't place it at first." She looked back at him, beckoning him closer. "The hair is a little darker, and the face a little older, but the resemblance is undeniable."

Was Rosalind Schofield the first to notice the curious similarity between Olivia Pembroke and Mrs. Darling's parlor-boarder? His father had laid out specific instructions in his will to see to both the comfort of Eleanore and to keep her parentage secret from everyone. Stephen had done his duty. To do more might have put her in danger too. Unless—he paused, gazing at the book lying on the floor near Rosalind's chair—there was no curse.

"She is your sister, isn't she?"

Stephen nodded.

"And Miss Martin knows nothing of the connection between you."

He turned to her. "It is for the best she does not."

"Because of the curse? But what about all we just discussed?" She prodded, gesturing to the book. "Then what?"

He did not know. He could not imagine a life other than the one he had lived for so long.

"She is your sister." The rebuke in her voice was as plain as the disappointment on her face. "She deserves more than a bucket of coal for the winter and a new frock every year."

"I have blessed little family left," he said. He'd had a sister, and he'd lost her long ago. "I will not lose any more."

Rosalind threw up her hands. "After all that we have spoken of, you cannot believe this fantasy. You are an educated, learned man."

How could he explain that lingering fear? That despite everything —Uncle Thomas's plot, the poison, the lies—the dread still existed that he might have the power to end a beautiful woman's life by loving her. "There are two elements of this curse. One involves the possibility of poison, I grant you, and if so, then wonderful. I am no longer the Beast of Barronsfield. I am no longer this thing that has terrorized the neighborhood. But before the Beast, there was something else, and it involves a dead woman's roses."

"Stephen, I know this is difficult, but look around you. You are alone. Eleanore is your flesh and blood."

"Eleanore is also growing into a very pretty young woman. I cannot risk it."

"I do not understand you."

"I never asked you—or anyone—to try." She didn't understand him? At the moment he barely understood himself.

She sat down again. The glow from the hearth lit her face and caught the red and gold in her hair as she stared off into the fire. For a moment she reminded him of one of the fairy tale princesses from those stories she so loved to read.

"It has been a very long day," she said after an agonizing moment of silence. "I should leave."

Stephen was searching for a reason why she shouldn't when the doors of the library opened and Hanley returned.

"My lord, the wind and rain has downed several trees, making travel extremely hazardous. It would be advisable to wait until the storm lets up before sending a runner for the magistrate."

Damn. That was going to make it nearly impossible for Stephen to meet up with Schofield and the others before Geoffrey landed on his doorstep in the morning. Of course, Stephen's one consolation might be that it would slow his cousin down as well. And if Geoffrey was on the loose and had any idea of Rosalind's theories, then the safest place for her to be was here at Barronsfield where Stephen would be nearby.

"Shall I prepare a room for Miss Schofield?" Hanley asked.

Rosalind knit her eyebrows together, her gaze going from Stephen to Hanley, and back again. Stephen was not a betting man, but he was willing to lay a fiver she was counting to ten.

"Miss Schofield, as you know, Hanley is a man of impeccable veracity," Stephen continued. "We will be unable to send a runner until the rain has passed at the very least. And if it is too dangerous for me to send a runner out, it is too dangerous for you. I cannot risk it, nor the safety of one of my servants to accompany you." He laced his declaration with his best aristocratic tone. If there was any benefit at all to being a marquess, he had to be able to get his way with her at least some of the time.

And this was one of those times.

"Hanley's word is good enough for me," she said at last. She gave the old man such a warm smile that Stephen found himself a bit envious.

"This way, Miss Schofield," the man gestured to her.

"You may take a book or two to read, if you like," Stephen added, gesturing to the shelves, desperate to mend the awkwardness between them.

"This will do." She held out the blue book in her hands, then followed the butler without a backward glance.

"I have been alone in my thoughts for so long," he blurted out before she reached the door. She stopped, then slowly spun around on her heel, her mouth in a firm line. "I cannot discard my fears like a worn coat. They have become comfortable in their own way."

"Loneliness should not be such a comfortable thing," she replied. "There are people here who wish to be near you. To love you, if you would give them half a chance."

Her eyes widened, and her shoulders hunched slightly, before she whipped around and disappeared out the door, leaving Stephen alone. Wishing he could be near her.

Rosalind gripped one of the posts on the corner of the bed in the room where Hanley had brought her. Letting go a long, steady breath of exasperation, she rested her forehead against the rich wood. Stephen Pembroke was without a doubt the most stubborn man ever to be born. Despite all they'd discussed, despite all they'd discovered, an undercurrent of fear still over shadowed his logic.

Maybe she expected too much of him, too soon. And maybe she had too much at stake as far as the curse was concerned, and the stakes were conflicting. Proving it a myth would allow her to stay where she had finally found a home. It would also make the marquess an extremely eligible man. Maybe he would seek out someone to be his wife. Someone else. Which should have been perfect, except she was falling in love with him. She buried her head in her hands, embarrassment prickling her skin. She'd practically declared it in front of him, hadn't she? She shook her head, wanting to shake loose the memory of what she'd done. What foolishness had inspired her to do that?

He couldn't love her back. He'd made that plain in his marriage proposal. What had her aunt said to her once? Handsome enough for a profession, but not for a title. When she'd pointed out that Uncle Stanhope was a barrister and not a Baron, she had been confined to her room for a week. She had learned to count to ten during her punishment.

Letting go of the bedpost, she sat near the fire. The room she occupied was not as large as the one where she'd had her encounter with Geoffrey Pembroke, but much more agreeable. Drapes in a rich floral pattern hung from the tall windows on the other side of the heavy oak bed, which also had curtains. All in all, it was a pleasant room. It would have been much more pleasant if Rosalind wasn't feeling so off kilter.

A servant arrived with fresh towels and a warm basin of water, and helped Rosalind prepare for bed. After the servant left, Rosalind re-read the short but instructive entry on datura. Though there were other plants with a similar effect—nightshade, foxglove—none of them looked like the thornapple husk she'd found in her apron.

At last, when the fire was dying and the chill became too uncomfortable, Rosalind slid underneath the warm linen covers of her bed. Leaning over, she blew out the candle, leaving only the fading glow of the fire for light.

She closed her eyes, mulling over everything that had happened that evening. Perhaps, whatever happened, her feelings for Stephen would be like the fire in the hearth, and slowly cool and fade away with time. A dull ache twisted inside her. Either way, she would fade away from him into nothing. And the thought was somehow unbearable.

Fatigue taking control at last, Rosalind sank into a deep slumber.

A loud, low bang, like a great door slamming shut, shook Rosalind awake. Her eyes were blinded by a bright light that forced her to shield them. Slowly, painfully, her surroundings came into view. She stood in the middle of a vast, ancient cathedral, its vaulted ceilings soaring high overhead. An organ droned from somewhere in the distance, playing a fugue. The notes were off key, and the tempo was too fast. Her shoulders were weighted down by the most elaborate gown she had ever worn. Covered in jewels and beads, it bordered on garish.

Edmund stood beside her. His eyes were dull and expressionless. He held her by the arm, and as they began to move, a clanking sound added to the discord of the music. He wore a large, heavy chain around his middle. It dragged across the stone floor behind him.

"Edmund," she whispered, "what is happening?"

"You are getting married," he said in a tone that matched the low, stilted pitch of the music.

Panicked, she looked down the aisle, where a clergyman stood in front of the altar, which was bedecked in roses. The rest of the cathedral was empty. The music lumbered through the air, and the hackles rose on the back of her neck. Edmund continued moving relentlessly to the front, and dragged her along with him.

"Edmund, please..." Her voice cracked, and left her unable to control the fear coursing in her veins. Her efforts to pull herself free were fruitless and her ears filled with the sound of Edmund's clanging chains and the organ music that grew louder with each passing moment.

"Let me go!" She was screaming now, but neither Edmund nor the dour bishop at the altar took any notice of her terror.

In the next minute, Edmund was gone. The music disappeared and the cathedral was deathly quiet. She was alone. Rosalind's ragged breath caught, unsure if she should be more afraid, or less. There was a lone figure in the room with her. He stood behind her, whispering into her ear. The voice was utterly cold, his presence like a creeping dread moving over her body.

"Wake up, Rosalind," she told herself. "This is a dream. A dream."

"It is a nightmare," hissed the voice, and a hand snaked around her throat.

"Wake up, Rosalind. You're dreaming. Wake up!"

Rosalind's eyes flew open, only to see another dark pair of eyes staring directly into her own, his hands on her shoulders. She let out a scream and flailed her arms, knocking the unwanted guest off her bed and onto the floor. In a flash she hopped out of the bed, grabbed a heavy candlestick and prepared to put it to the crown of whoever it was in her chamber.

"It's me!" came a very loud, very indignant voice. "For heaven's sake, it's me."

She stood over him for a few seconds, eyes wide, heart pounding, until she realized it was Stephen speaking to her.

"What in the blazes are you doing here?" Slowly she lowered the candlestick, which he took from her shaking hands, and set it on the dressing table.

"I heard your cries from down the hall. I thought you were being attacked in your sleep."

Rosalind nodded, her panic subsiding. Stephen watched her, concern evident in his gaze. His hair was damp, and he wore little but loose breeches and a dressing gown, which had gaped enough for her to catch a glimpse of his chest. It served to remind her of how little she wore. Horrified, she threw her hands up over her chest, then cast about the room for her robe. "Turn around."

"What?" He sounded confused.

"Turn around." She made a circular motion with her wrist.

"Oh for heaven's—you just tried to brain me with my own candlestick. You're lucky I can stand."

"If you were a gentleman, you would turn around."

Looking disarmingly boyish as he made a face, he turned to the wall while she covered herself with the blue silken robe.

"It's fine," she replied. "You can turn back around. I'm sorry if I disturbed you. I didn't realize I was so loud in my sleep."

"I was not that far away when I heard your screams. You sounded like you were in great distress."

"It was only a nightmare. A really unpleasant one."

"Nightmares generally are."

"I don't have them often, though I admit my dreams of late have been—strange. But this one…" She shook her head, trying to drive the sense of dread from her bones.

"Stay here, I shall return in but a moment." He disappeared as quickly as he'd arrived.

Rosalind poked at the fire, and added some more wood, bringing it back to life. She sat on a nearby settee, her knees tucked under her chin. Images from her dream turned over in her head. The mysterious presence at the very end—so cold, so calculating. It was but a shadow in her earliest dreams after she had first met Stephen. That it had stood so close to her, touched her...she shivered again. For the first time, she'd felt truly afraid, though of what, she could not say. To pass the time, she took her candle and started flipping through the pages of the blue botany book, and tried to bury her fears until Stephen returned.

At last he returned, carrying a tray with hot chocolate, a small dark bottle, and a plate of biscuits. He set it down on a small table by the settee, and sat beside her.

"I hope you don't mind my service. Hanley is far better at this, but at this hour I don't have the heart to wake him. You will have to contend with my sloppy pouring."

"Thank you, this is very kind." Rosalind watched him pour a small drop of a golden liquor into the cup, then fill it with the steaming chocolate.

"A little fortification against the damp conditions and nightmares." He held out a fine, tall porcelain cup, which she took, deliberately ignoring the small jolt of electricity when her fingers grazed against his. She took a long, slow sip of the dark, sumptuous drink, its flavor made all the richer by the nutty notes of the liquor.

"You will spoil me for this."

"You're rich now," he replied, with an easy smile. "You could drink this morning, noon and night if you choose."

"Perhaps you are right. I shall spend my fortune in cocoa beans." She looked up from over the rim of her cup. "You might be wise to invest in them."

"I think I will take your advice on that."

"It's probably un-English to say so, but I do not understand the fuss over tea," she said, her eyes lingering over the bare skin peeking out from under his dark silk robe.

"Perhaps because it's not as extraordinary as hot chocolate, don't you think? Not as satisfying." The sound of his voice seemed hypnotic, robbing her of her words. All she could do was nod.

She took another sip. Whether it was the liqueur in the chocolate, or the marquess sitting next to her, a pleasurable heat started to swirl in her belly, reaching down between her legs. She lowered the cup and set it down on the silver tray in front of them.

"Wait." He put his finger under her chin and gently turned her face to his. His eyes shone in the firelight like obsidian—black, and wanting. "You have a smudge of chocolate right here." With an achingly slow movement, he ran his thumb over her lips, and in a moment every muscle in her body felt like it was melting. Then, too quickly, he pulled his hand away. "I shouldn't be doing this."

On impulse Rosalind caught his hand and laced her fingers between his, daring to match his gaze. This was wrong. Dangerous, in fact. Her breath quickened as this new sensation, this desire, began to overrule reason. Soon she would be sent away, or he would be married to another, and the end result would be the same—she would be alone. But he was here, and so was she, and for once, Rosalind was going to have this small bit of adventure and keep it for herself. Pulling his hand to her mouth, she placed a lingering kiss on each finger. A low growl escaped from his lips.

His fingers brushed across her cheeks, around her hairline, sending a tingling sensation coursing through her. Her entire being focused on his touch, and her body was alive in a way that was new and wonderful. As his fingers moved down on her throat, she closed her eyes and leaned her head back in invitation. An invitation he accepted.

SHE TASTED like chocolate and felt like heaven.

Every touch told Stephen that Rosalind's body was on fire, like the beautiful mane of hair streaming down her back. Each sharp intake of breath she took, each gasp of pleasure, only spurred him on.

Hungrily, he pushed his lips onto hers, lips that first taunted him weeks ago. Her fingers curled in his hair, pulling him down to return the full force of his kiss. Opening her mouth wide, he explored her more deeply, the kisses more intense, his need meeting hers. Deftly, he slid his hand down along her front, letting loose the knot on her robe that covered her. When he'd first seen her in it, his mouth nearly went dry. The fabric shimmered over her body, hinting at her curves. Now it was simply a layer of fabric in his way. Every inch of his body yearned to envelope hers.

The robe fell open, and he moved his hand to her bosom, gently cupping her left breast. She let out a low moan which nearly finished him before he had even started. He grazed his thumb over the thin cotton of her chemise, teasing her nipple to a tight point. She broke the kiss, overcome with a deep throaty sigh and looked at him with wide eyes that betrayed surprise and arousal.

Driven by her response, his kisses moved down her throat, over her shoulders, and down to her bosom, relishing the taste of her skin. He pulled the delicate blue ribbon on her shift, letting it fall loose. The glow from the fire fell on the most perfect set of breasts he had ever seen. Neither too big, nor too small. Just perfect. And as he took each nipple into his mouth, teasing each one with his tongue, he was certain they tasted perfect too.

She wriggled under his touch, brushing against his erection with her leg, which only served to drive him wild. All of the nervous energy, the sharp wit, the occasional fire of her temper—it burst from every part of her. And, selfishly, he wanted it all.

"I didn't know it was possible to feel this way," she gasped.

Funny, Stephen thought. He didn't think it was possible to either. He also knew he was heading into territory nearly beyond the point of no return. Gently he pulled away—barely able to hold his own lust at bay, but knowing he had to, for her sake.

"I cannot do this to you. I should stop, before—"

"No." Her eyes were intent, direct, and he could feel her fingers curling into the skin on his arms. "No, you shouldn't."

He hesitated only a moment, then scooped her up in his arms. He brought her to the bed, the sheets already in disarray from when he'd woken her. As he laid her down, she trembled beside him.

"Nervous?"

"Cold."

He smiled wickedly. "I will take care of that."

Shedding his robe, he pulled the blankets up over them, and pulled her close.

"Better?"

She nodded, already preoccupied with running her fingers down his chest, sending waves of pleasure straight to his core. She mimicked him and playfully licked one of his nipples, and for a moment he thought he'd go out of his mind with lust. Lust he allowed to overrule his reason.

Her sensuous mouth—when had it become sensuous—her smooth, silky skin, and her most perfect breasts would have been more than any man could resist, and it had been too long. Far too long. It was the only thing that made sense—this unfettered need for her. As her hands and mouth explored his ears, his neck and his mouth, she gave him more and more to need.

Disappearing under the sheets, he straddled her, and once again paid due attention to her breasts, which made her squirm and squeal with a playful, lusty laugh. As he moved lower, letting his erection brush up against her belly, down to the achingly soft skin of her inner thighs, the giggles disappeared, replaced by deeper, throaty gasps. Rosalind was loud and active. And he loved it.

Burying himself even deeper in the sheets, he let his hands and mouth explore every inch of her body. The slight curve of her hips, the softness of her belly, the delicate shape of her calves. He suddenly yearned to light every candle in the place so he could take in every inch of her with his eyes. Occasionally he would look up to see the expression on her face as she bit her lip and reached furiously for him, bringing him back to her mouth for the longest and most luscious of kisses. As she did so the last time, he ran his fingers up to her hot core, which was already slick. That she was so ready only drove his need, and he found himself stroking her faster and faster, feeling her hips push up against his in an instinctive rhythm when she found her release.

Hips lifting off the bed, she frantically grabbed at his hand, pushing it against her in a futile effort to fulfill the need her body demanded of him.

"Stephen!" she called out breathlessly. "What's happening to me?"

"Pleasure. Oblivion."

Tears ran down her face, as her hands dug into the sheets and held on as the waves of her orgasm crashed down.

"I know what you want. Are you certain?" It would be the longest, coldest walk he'd had in a while if she was not.

She nodded wildly.

"I will try and be gentle."

"Does it hurt?" she asked, sobering slightly.

"So I am told, but not much, and only the first time," he said, trying to remain calm in his speech while the rest of his body was on fire.

Slowly, deftly, he guided himself into the soft, wet folds of her body. He watched as her body tensed slightly, and then with a sharp push, he broke through the last vestiges of her innocence. A sharp gasp—this one not of pleasure—escaped her.

"Are you all right?"

"I think so."

As he gently stroked himself back and forth within her, he watched her intently, looking for any signs of discomfort. She betrayed none. Instead, to his utter delight, he could feel her hips shifting with his, moving up to reach his length. Each stroke was like ambrosia, but it was getting hard and harder to contain his release. And he would have to.

With a strength of will he didn't know he had, he pulled out of her, releasing himself beside her. It was bad enough he had taken her virginity. To leave her with a child, especially, heaven forbid, a daughter...

He gazed down on Rosalind, who wore an expectant smile. Her freckles lightly speckled across her face, her hair spread across the pillow, and her eyes bright. She looked straight out of any man's fantasy, and yet to him she had become so much more. She saw only possibilities, not obstacles. She had a sharp mind, and a smile that warmed his soul. He didn't know the exact moment that he began to anticipate seeing her, but her presence gave him something to look forward to like nothing or no one ever had before. Everything about her was bright and alive.

Everything about her was beautiful, he thought, as his heart flipped over in his chest.

And froze.

Beautiful.

CHAPTER 21

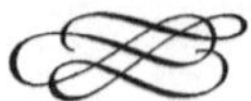

osalind's stomach lurched as he remained above her, frozen, looking as though he'd swallowed something distasteful. Then, he slid out of the bed, nearly tripping over his own feet as he did so.

"Is something the matter?" she dared to ask, barely above a whisper. The bliss and intimacy between her and Stephen evaporated before her eyes.

"I—I must go." His voice broke through the uneasy silence, hurried. His gaze darted from the floor to the bed, to the ceiling, but most decidedly not at her. He grabbed his robe and covered himself, then snatched up his drawers in his hand.

Rosalind pulled herself up, holding the blankets up to her neck. If there was a fire in the room, he could scarcely have moved quicker. Was sharing a bed with her so disgusting?

"Stephen, please. What's the—"

"Nothing's the matter. I'll send a servant—they'll make sure you return home safely." He walked to the door, sparing her a look one might give to a rock wedged in a shoe.

"What are you doing?" She shot up and stood by the bed, covered only in bed linen. Outrage helped put her shame at bay. "You claim

230

friendship, honor, kindness and duty, and yet you use me and dispose of me like a child does with a toy they no longer find amusing."

Stephen was silent, his eyes fixed on her, his expression unreadable. She wanted to see anger, outrage or hurt at her accusation. He gave her nothing. *Nothing.* He turned and walked out.

Rosalind stared at the door, her throat tightening, bile catching in her throat. He'd come back, wouldn't he? He had to. Time stood still. There was no sound, save the dying embers of the fire. The door remained closed.

He'd found their lovemaking unseemly. Ugly. Something to be swept under the carpet and not talked of again. She slumped on the bed, releasing traces of sweat, sex and his scent from the sheets. Suddenly she wanted to be clean of both the smells and the memory of the event that had so disgusted him.

How could she have allowed herself to think, for even a moment, that he had really wanted her? That she was the type of woman who could inspire great passion? The only thing she inspired was regret—for both of them.

Moments later, a servant walked in as promised, her stiff skirts swishing on the carpet. Though Rosalind composed herself as best she could, she kept her gaze down. As the maid helped Rosalind wash and dress, the full implication of her intimacy with the marquess, and what that would mean for her, tore at her heart.

"I must speak with Mr. Hanley. Would you like me to bring you some hot chocolate, Miss?" the servant asked.

"No, thank you," Rosalind replied at last, then added softly, "I think I've lost my taste for it."

Closing her eyes, she stifled the tears long enough for the servant to leave, then put her head down and released the hurt and humiliation from every pore. "Stupid, stupid girl."

She couldn't stay here. What if Stephen came back? Rosalind had barely been able to look at herself in the mirror when the servant tied up her hair. There was no way she could face him again. She had to leave. Unceremoniously she blew her nose in her handkerchief, stood up, straightened her shoulders, and went to the door.

It was still early—barely six o'clock. Her liaison with Stephen would be through Barronsfield Manor before sunrise, and her uncle would soon uncover her secret. After this, maybe he wouldn't even want her to stay anymore. Had she ruined him too? The one place she'd actually wanted to call home would be taken away, and she would have hurt the one person on earth who loved her. She gulped back panic along with her tears.

Maybe she could leave. Leave this godforsaken place and her folly behind. Her ruin was payment, she supposed, for one moment of wretched foolishness, one moment of believing that perhaps she deserved something more than what everyone expected of her. Who was she to want for more? Instead, she would go to London as her father had wished, with her ten thousand pounds, and find someone a little interested in her and a lot interested in her money. Someone desperate enough to marry a plain woman past marriageable age. Damaged goods. She closed her eyes and pressed her lips together, forcing back a sob. How distasteful the idea had once been. Now it was to become her lifeboat.

With all the composure she could muster, she opened the door, and stuck her head out into the corridor, relieved to find it empty. If Stephen had bothered to send someone to accompany her home, she was not about to wait. Taking a candle, she stepped out into the long hallway. In the dark, every foot fall on the hard wood floors echoed. Feeling the heat rise in her cheeks and her bottom lip quiver slightly, she picked up the pace.

"Miss Schofield, a moment."

She hesitated, then turned to see Hanley hobbling toward her, a book in his hands.

"You've forgotten this," the old butler said with a kind, sad, smile.

"It isn't mine. I came with nothing," Rosalind said, confused.

"But you cannot leave that way. Please." He pushed the blue botany book into Rosalind's hands.

"I don't understand."

"He is afraid, you see. Afraid for you."

Afraid? A coward maybe. "Hanley, that's—"

They were interrupted by two younger men running toward them. By their dress, she assumed they must work in the stables.

"Mr. Hanley, sir!" One of them doffed his cap quickly, breathless. "I send word from Mr. Schofield, sir. We must find his lordship straight away."

"What is the matter? Where is my uncle?" Rosalind asked, gripped by fear made only more pressing by the urgency in the boy's voice.

"Beg 'pardon, Miss. There's a crowd coming. Practically on our heels. Mr. Schofield is on his way as well, along with help, but I don't know if they'll get here in time."

"What on earth are people doing gathering at such an hour?" Rosalind asked, fear cracking her words.

"Don't know exactly, except it has to do with the master's curse and all," the stable boy replied.

"Right." The softness in Hanley's voice disappeared and he took on a sharper, younger tone. "Miss Schofield, I beg you to go to the library. You will be safer there, given the circumstances." His ancient hands, which had spent a lifetime in service to this family, took hers, and squeezed them gently. "Don't give up on him."

Well, Stephen had certainly given up on her, hadn't he? Rosalind returned a mirthless smile. There were so many things she was feeling, but pity for Stephen Pembroke was right down on the bottom of the list. She allowed a little for herself. But it was fear for her uncle that ruled her now.

Rosalind watched Hanley and the two young men go. The library was the last place she wanted to be, but she could think of no better place to for her at the moment. She needed her uncle, and he was coming straight to her. If she could discover where the poison was hidden—the one that created the mythical Beast of Barronsfield, Geoffrey Pembroke would be exposed and her uncle would be safe. It had to be in the manor somewhere. Heading for the library, she rounded a corner and bumped headlong into Edmund, who landed promptly on his backside.

"Edmund!" Rosalind blinked her eyes. The gentleman looked drawn, and he had at least a day's growth of beard on his face. His clothes were disheveled, like he'd slept in them, though the dark circles under his eyes suggested that he may not have done that, either. She put a hand out to help him up. The odor of stale brandy assaulted her nose as he rose to his feet.

"Are you foxed?"

"Not as much as yesterday."

"It's only been today for a few hours, Edmund."

"Well then, I am behind."

She shook her head. "This entire household is mad." Rosalind continued on her way, leaving him behind. The last thing she needed at the moment was another Pembroke.

"Where are you going?" he called after her.

She answered by entering the library and then slamming the door shut behind her.

Ignoring the hurt that enveloped her as she entered the dark room, she made her way to the fireplace and lit a few more of the candles. The sky outside was a dull gray-purple, which only served to deepen her gloom. In the distance, she could see the faint glow of fire, little red pin pricks in the pre-dawn light. They were coming.

She closed her eyes, allowing a moment to steady herself. What had gone so wrong?

Hanley said Stephen was afraid. *Afraid for her.* Rosalind sniffed, fearful a new rush of tears would stream down her cheeks. Afraid that he'd ruined his steward's ward, perhaps. The only people who had to fear the so-called curse were beautiful women. Rosalind wasn't a beauty. Everyone knew that. Stephen had just proved it in devastating fashion.

The door swung open, and Edmund emerged from the shadows, frantic and disheveled.

"What do you want?" Rosalind asked, more than a little perturbed that he'd followed her.

"I spoke with Hanley. My God, I didn't think it would all come to this." He paced up and down. "I don't know what to do. I don't know how to help him." He looked at her expectantly, and must have been taken aback by her undoubtedly puffy eyes and lack of empathy. He sobered, his gaze softening. "You've had a falling out with him."

Rosalind only nodded.

He stepped closer, taking her by the hands. "You're in love with him."

Heaven help me, yes. "I don't wish to speak of it. I am here to secure my uncle's safety, and that is all. And then I am leaving. The marquess does not want my help."

"You can't leave him now. You're his only friend." His expression looked particularly miserable as he spoke that phrase.

"No, it would seem that I am not," she said, anger rising.

"I don't understand."

"He sent me away."

"Excuse me?" He blinked.

"He does not want me. The only reason I am here talking to you is because of this mess about to land on his doorstep. Which is fine." She fought back tears with anger. There was no counting to ten this time. "I will be happy to leave this wretched place, and that awful man, and every other living soul on this estate who tiptoes around and lets him indulge in his own bloody misery." The swearing, which appeared to take Edmund aback, was satisfying. "And what does it matter? Soon I'll be in London. I have a good fortune. This can be nothing more than a dim memory."

Funny. That last part was supposed to make her feel better. Instead, she suddenly felt as if she was taking her first step into a big, black hole.

"You can't leave him," Edmund pleaded, taking her by the hand. "He will be alone."

She shook her head. "He is a grown man. A marquess, as he likes to keep reminding me. He chooses to be alone."

Edmund let her go, and slumped into a nearby chair. "They are coming to take it away from him. The estate, and possibly his good name. Maybe even his freedom. Geoffrey's been telling anyone who'll listen Stephen nearly killed you both the night of the assembly."

Rosalind shook her head, incredulous he was still speaking about that ridiculous story. How could anyone believe it now? "Edmund, he did not touch me or your brother. You know this."

His face fell, and he looked as miserable as she had ever seen a man, and the awful truth dawned on her.

"You have supported your brother's story."

"I've been a fool." Edmund raked his fingers through his hair, so morose she almost feared for his state of mind. "I ran into a little trouble in London. Like a good father, he held it over my head. And like a wretched man, I've let him."

"We can fix this." She rummaged through a small pocket in her skirt and pulled out the thornapple, still wrapped up in her handkerchief, and shoved it under Edmund's nose. "He's being poisoned."

"What is it?" he asked.

"It's what makes the Beast seem real, at least to him. It's the fruit from this plant." Dropping the plant in his hands, grabbed the blue book and flipped through the pages until she came to the picture of the thornapple. "Look here."

Edmund came over, and squinted at the print.

"All of Lord Barronsfield's behavior the night of the assembly, and every other night the so-called beast appears—the Beast that only your brother and the chef have actually seen—can be explained by this."

"Datura."

"What?" Rosalind looked up. Edmund staggered back at bit.

"Datura—Devil's Tulip. I've seen this before."

"Where?"

"My father's green house." His voice was so low, Rosalind strained to hear him. He looked past Rosalind, his face white. Swallowing deeply, he turned to Rosalind. "I must go. Please. Do not leave. Not yet. I beg of you."

"Where are you going?" Rosalind reached out to him, but he was already pulling away, making like lightening for the door. "Edmund please." She grabbed the book and ran after him, but he was taller; every stride he took was nearly two of hers. By the time she had reached the stairs, he had disappeared.

Except for the deaths of her parents, Rosalind could scarcely recall a time in her life when she was more confused, upset, or unsure of herself. Before coming to Barronsfield, she'd lived a hum-drum life pricked by a countless number of petty disappointments when it came to matters of the heart. Sometimes she'd dream about a new life for herself, filled with adventures, filled with promise, and when she dared to allow it, filled with love. Perhaps she'd been wrong to believe Stephen could give her all three things.

She gripped the book under her arm, her whole body teeming with raw, nervous energy. Leaving Stephen Pembroke's fate to a lie was not going to make her pain go away. It would definitely make life more difficult for her uncle, for Hanley, and every other servant forced to serve Geoffrey's father.

She flew down the stairs, chasing after Edmund.

STEPHEN HAD BEEN on his way to the rose garden in the orangery, determined to face his damnable fears when he caught the first glimpse of Geoffrey's mob coming in the distance. Suddenly, he had no time to indulge in thoughts of Haddie Walton, or the rose bush he'd foolishly nurtured as some sort of penance. Or even how he'd hurt the person who, he now realized, meant more to him than anyone.

Stephen stood now on the steps of Barronsfield Manor, watching the approaching crowd. The sound of men and carriage wheels broke through the early morning silence, and the glow from lamps and torches grew brighter with each passing moment. If Rosalind were here now she'd be giving him words of encouragement, or at the very least, filling him with hope by standing beside him. A vision of her in their last moment together played in his memory, and he clasped a hand to his face and indulged in the sting of remorse. Rosalind *was* beautiful—heart wrenchingly so—and the idea had shot fear through his heart. A fear, he owned, that made the moment he was about to face pale in comparison.

Pulling away from her was pure instinct. And pure cowardice. Not just because she was beautiful, but because he loved her. If he managed to get through the morning, perhaps he could find a way to persuade her to forgive him.

When he saw the approaching rabble, Stephen sent word with a servant to have all the rooms in the front of the house lit, and already the glow rained down on the lawn below. It was the first time Barronsfield Manor had looked so alive since the night of his infamous engagement party to Anne Wickwire.

Stephen pulled his heavy dark cloak over him and stamped his booted feet on the cold stone steps. He wanted to hunch his shoulders, to protect himself from the cool mist of the pre-dawn, but he forced himself to stand straight and damn the discomfort.

The clatter of many pairs of boots scuffling over gravel provided a strange sort of relief, allowing him to focus on matters other than his abominable exit from Rosalind's bed. Among the men on foot was a carriage, which pulled ahead and stopped at the bottom of the steps. A group of men, perhaps fifty in number, gathered around it. Looking out into the throng, he recognized a mix of farmers, laborers and tradesmen from Elmsdale.

"What brings you to my doorstep at this hour, when you should be home in your own beds?" Stephen called out into the crowd, coming down a couple steps to meet them.

The door of the carriage swung open, and out came Geoffrey, Perkins, and the magistrate. The latter two remained near the carriage while Geoffrey climbed the stairs, leaning more heavily on the walking stick now than yesterday. Even in the dim light, Stephen saw confidence radiating from his cousin. Geoffrey stopped on the landing, stood next to Stephen, then turned to the men below.

"My good folk, calm yourselves." His cousin held up a gloved hand, as a conductor might to give cues to a symphony. The crowd was loud and agitated, but for now, under some semblance of control. Geoffrey's control.

"Justice!" came a determined cry from a few loud and angry voices in the crowd. Stephen squinted in their direction. Tom Gates was at the center of them. Of course.

"Geoffrey, what madness is this?" Stephen said in a harsh whisper. "Did you rile up this crowd on purpose to scare the rest of my household away? For I swear if any of your men touch any of them—"

"Do not threaten me," Geoffrey replied loud enough for all to hear. "We are finished with your threats and violence against the good people of Elmsdale."

The mob erupted into a mix of jeers and taunts, fists raised. Stones hurled at a window nearby shattered glass, exciting the crowd even more.

"Stop!" Stephen shouted, his blood rising. The fierceness of his order subdued the men, if only temporarily. "If you have an argument with me, then you will take it up with me alone. Not the innocent people inside who are under my protection. If they are hurt, there will be consequences."

"That is quite the declaration, cousin, given the hardship and torment unleashed by you upon the people you proclaim to protect," Geoffrey replied aloud. "As promised, we have brought the magistrate to discuss the charges."

"You might have done this privately," Stephen said, deliberately keeping his voice calm.

"It was my wish to do so, but when word of your deeds reached the ears of your neighbors, the anger grew to such a state I could not stop them from coming."

"I bet you couldn't," Stephen spat. "What are the charges?"

"Attempted murder, for one. Two counts."

Stephen raised his voice to ensure he was heard, and he did not bother to disguise his contempt. "I am not guilty, and you know it. You have wild accusations, but that is all."

"And you have nothing. Look at you, Stephen. A Peer of the Realm, alone, defending his estate. Where are your supporters? You should have at least three dozen servants here. They are gone, left, and why? Because you have failed. Failed in your duty."

Stephen stood ramrod straight, hands clenched behind his back.

"And what would you have me do, Pembroke? What is the pound

of flesh in exchange for these trumped up charges and your non-existent witnesses?"

"Edmund has provided Mr. Perkins with a sworn account of how you attacked me and Miss Schofield." Dramatically brandishing a piece of paper, he handed it to the magistrate who stood with Perkins two steps below them.

"I would not harm her!" A rush of anger pushed through his attempt at calm, and he grabbed Geoffrey by the lapels. The mob erupted below, rushing toward them. Only the shouts from the magistrate, brandishing a musket, held them back. Stephen released Geoffrey.

"You can barely control yourself, even now." Geoffrey's face hardened and Stephen cursed himself for giving his cousin exactly the reaction he'd wanted. "Barronsfield cannot continue with an animal as its Lord."

His cousin looked out over the crowd, crossing his arms, his chest out. Triumphant. Stephen looked at his cousin anew. He took a step forward, and deliberately faced Geoffrey, blocking his view of the crowd below.

"This isn't about the charges, is it?" Stephen stood nearly nose to nose with Geoffrey. "Not about the people of Elmsdale, or Miss Schofield. It's about you and your father wanting control of Barronsfield."

"Father's agenda is his own," Geoffrey hissed. "I want justice for the woman I loved."

Stephen blinked. Anne. This was about Anne. It was about losing her to the man Geoffrey had always resented. A woman endowed with physical beauty and little else.

"Geoffrey, I never killed her." As the words left his mouth, Stephen truly believed it for the first time. "It was a wretched accident."

"You forced her into a marriage she didn't want."

"I made an offer. She accepted. She wanted the title, Geoffrey. That's all she wanted from me. Nothing more. It could have been anyone."

"It could have been me," Geoffrey's eyes were like steel. "It should have been me."

"This game you are playing is dangerous, Pembroke." Stephen gestured to the crowd. "Threatening my household is not justice. It is thuggery. And what will you gain when this is done?"

Geoffrey leaned in close, his voice a harsh, low whisper. "I will watch you suffer. That is enough for me."

CHAPTER 22

Rosalind chased after Edmund, her feet pounding on the wooden floors. He was a dozen steps ahead of her, running headlong for the front door, desperate to rescue his cousin. The sound of glass breaking from close by rattled her, but drove her even faster. Edmund's hand was on the door when she caught up with him, desperate to stop him before he did something foolish. Stephen's voice was audible, if muffled, through the thick oak doors, but she could tell he was trying to calm the throng, which sounded ready to tear someone to pieces.

"Edmund!" Rosalind snapped, her nerves starting to get the best of her. She reached out and held onto his wrist. "You need proof if that crowd is going to believe you."

"I have all the proof anyone requires," he spat, his hand gripping the massive door handle. "Fool. I am a bloody fool."

Rosalind shook her head. "Unless you have the substance, it is your word against your brother's. A brother who has gone out of his way to charm half the neighborhood, and a public who has learned to fear Lord Barronsfield. We must act if we wish to help him. Facing that mob without the poison is foolhardy."

Edmund's shoulders sagged and he shook his head. From outside, angry shouts and jeers grew louder. Rosalind jumped, releasing her grip on Edmund's arm. Would they come through the doors? She hugged the book in her arms to steady herself.

"If you wish to redeem yourself, help me now. I have an idea of where to look." She started off toward the kitchen, pulling Edmund along with her.

A massive hearth and an array of pots, ladles and spoons greeted them when they arrived. To her relief, the kitchen was empty. No doubt the staff had been marshaled to their posts by Hanley. Rosalind wondered if they were frightened. She was.

"Where would someone hide such a thing?" Rosalind's gaze darted around the room. *Calm down and think, Rosalind.* She laid open the botany book on a large wooden table, flipped to the page on datura, and scanned the text. "According to this, you can use the leaves or the seeds, but the seeds are more potent. If you were going to hide them in food, you'd have to crush them."

"Spices," Edmund said. "They would be locked up."

"Hanley would have a key."

"Right. Stay here."

Edmund disappeared for a few minutes, and returned with the butler. "He insisted on coming. He wouldn't give up the keys."

"Of course he wouldn't." Without thinking she reached out and gave Hanley a hug, his presence an island of measured calm.

Hanley led them to the pantry that adjoined the kitchen. There stood a tall cupboard, guarded with a single lock. From his massive ring of keys, he slid a long brass one into the lock, which opened with a definite click.

A heavy scent of cloves and cardamom mixed with the sweet aromatic tones of nutmeg and savory rosemary filled the air. On shelf after shelf, there were little boxes and jars—powders and pods, seeds and leaves in bright oranges, muted yellows and deep greens. Few were labeled, and most were in French. Rosalind's heart sank. Going through them all was going to take forever.

As if reading her mind, Edmund shook his head, then began rifling through them, smelling each one.

"According to the book, it doesn't really have an odor. Just a bitter taste," Rosalind said, emotion cracking in her voice as she reached past Edmund to grab a small armload of containers. Anything brightly colored or strongly scented she dropped at her feet. "We don't have time to be neat about this."

Edmund's eyes narrowed. "The night of the assembly he complained about the taste of his wine. Claimed it was bitter."

"Who gave it to him?"

"I did. I was talking with Geoffrey when Stephen arrived. Geoffrey asked a servant to fetch another glass." Edmund shook his head in disgust. "Geoffrey. I am going to kill him."

There was entirely too much conviction in his statement for Rosalind's liking.

A low rumble of discontent rose in the distance. Even in the bowels of Barronsfield Manor, the anger of the crowd outside was audible. A shiver ran down Rosalind's spine. Time was running out. She dropped another box of powder to her feet when inspiration struck her. She scrambled to find a small wooden stool, which she placed in front of the cupboard and held out her hand to Edmund. "I have an idea! Help me up."

"What are you thinking?"

"That if I kept poison in the pantry, it wouldn't be in easy reach." Peering over the top shelf, nothing stood out as the jar in question. So she went through them all, one by one, as quickly as she dared.

"Maybe we're looking in the wrong place." Edmund pulled a face as he sniffed the contents of another jar.

Rosalind reached far into the back and pulled out a small wooden box. She opened it to find a cache of small black seeds. She put her nose to it and inhaled deeply. It was odorless. "I think this is it!"

Forcing her hands to be still, she cradled the box in her palms, then rushed to the table where the book lay. Rosalind emptied a few of the seeds on the counter, and hunched over them, trying to quell her anticipation as she studied every detail. The shape, the color, the size all looked like a match. With the slightest bit of hesitation she put one of the seeds in her mouth and crushed it between her teeth, releasing a sharp bitter taste. Pulling a face, she turned and spit into a handkerchief Hanley magically produced before her. "This is the poison! I'm sure of it."

Carefully she scooped up the small flat black seeds and put them back in the box, and handed it to Edmund. The muffled din of the mob outside rose like the growl of a dog about to attack.

"Let's go."

ANGRY FACES SURROUNDED Stephen on every side, hidden in the shadows or glowing red from torches and lamps. Men shook their fists and jeered him. Despair threatened Stephen's will to endure their anger, but he remained, soaking in the ill will as penance for every horrible thing he'd ever done. For stealing those roses. For leaving Rosalind Schofield alone, without explanation, exposing her to ruin, because he'd been too afraid to confront his own demons. He would face all of them now.

Geoffrey stood next to him, clearly savoring every curse hurled Stephen's way. It was time to put an end to this, once and for all.

"Men of Elmsdale! Cease this madness!" Stephen's voice rose loud and rough over the fray. "Do not let yourself become pawns of a mad man's schemes as I have!"

His words caught the attention of the crowd, some of whom quieted.

"My friends, tenants and neighbors, I stand here now, admitting that I have failed you as Marquess of Barronsfield. I have stood by and allowed fear, suspicion and malice to divide us, to turn neighbor against neighbor, and men against their lord."

The men became unsettled, and jeers rose up. A single voice rose among them.

"Quiet down you fools, and let his lordship speak!"

Stephen peered into the throng, and saw Harrison, the man who'd dared to speak plainly with him in the vicar's field, doff his cap to him. Alongside the man was his son, Charlie.

"Thank you, Harrison." Stephen continued. "Men of Elmsdale, hear me. It has been my fear, my weakness that has allowed this to continue for far too long. The moment I allowed others to use those fears against me, was the day I failed you in my duty. For it is the day the fallacy of the Beast of Barronsfield was born and used to do all of us ill. It is for that I beg your forgiveness, and for that alone. In return, I promise to work to return Elmsdale and Barronsfield to its full potential, with your help. I cannot do it alone, and I know I have no right to ask for your help."

"You shall have it my lord!"

The sky brightened as the sun peeked over the horizon when Stephen saw Reginald Schofield, his voice booming loud enough to rival any sergeant-major, as he bounded out from the crowd. Behind him were half a dozen others, Mister Darling and Doctor Brayden among them. Below, another scattered bunch of local craftspeople and farmers congregated around them. Schofield stepped up to Stephen, bowed, and pushed a scroll into Stephen's hand before returning to his place a few steps below.

He nodded to his steward, and glanced at the contents of the parchment before turning his voice to the mob below. "I dare any of you to step forward and make a claim on Mr. Darling's Bible that they have seen in the flesh, the Beast of Barronsfield, fangs, claws and all."

Thomas Gates stepped forward, but before he opened his mouth, Schofield cut him off.

"You, Mr. Gates, had better think very carefully about what you are about to say." Schofield's eyes narrowed, and Stephen saw there was more between these two than a simple disagreement. "I happen to have brought with me the local haberdasher, who's informed me that for a mill worker you've come into some rather expensive tastes in boots and coats in the past six months. What say you?"

Gates opened his mouth, flicked a quick glance toward Geoffrey, then replied, just as bombastic, "That's none of your business, Mr. Schofield. We know you're paid to protect his lordship."

"So you're paid to protect someone then, eh Tom?"

"That's not what I'm sayin'!" The man's face reddened, and Stephen could see, for the first time, the anger in the crowd give way to a sliver of doubt.

"And once we are done here, we can ask the magistrate to speak to your son, Jack, about his whereabouts the night Sally Coles disappeared," Schofield continued.

"You keep my boy out of this!"

"Your *boy*, sir, is up to his neck in this," Schofield scowled, "and apparently he suffers from having an even bigger mouth than yours. A few people wish to talk to the magistrate about what they overhead in the pub two nights ago with regard to the body found behind the assembly hall."

At Schofield's proclamation, the crowd fell into chaos. Geoffrey remained stone silent.

"Mr. Pembroke can bear testament to witnessing the Beast, and more than once." Perkins interrupted once again, though with less assurance than before. "And you know well the cost in blood to the marquess's own family. He can never hope to provide an heir, given his history."

"A little convenient," Stephen answered over the crowd, "considering Barronsfield and my title passes to my uncle, and therefore this gentleman before you. Congratulations on finding yourself a lap dog, Geoffrey." Stephen motioned to Sir Walter Perkins, standing a few steps below. "So Perkins, what did my cousin promise you? A parcel of Barronsfield's best land? Studding rights on my best horses? Or perhaps, an engagement for Miss Perkins and a suite on the 2nd floor?"

Perkins, looking horror struck, started blustering something unintelligible, although Stephen could make out something about damaged reputations and pride.

"Well done, cousin." Geoffrey spoke up through gritted teeth. "Except I do have witnesses."

"If you are thinking of Miss Schofield, I have spoken with her," Stephen countered, feeling like the worst sort of cad for invoking her name in his defense. "She claims she saw you later that night, and your normally charming face had nary a scratch on it."

"She was half out of her mind with fear that night, after you struck her," Pembroke replied. "You know how women can be when they get hysterical."

"Schofield can attest to her claims. I would give him full rights to shoot me if I had ever conducted myself in this way." Stephen looked down at his steward.

"Indeed, my lord," Schofield replied, "I have been told that my niece was complaining about falsehoods being spoken on her behalf."

A low murmur went through the crowd.

"Schofield is your employee, Barronsfield," Pembroke called, his confidence still not shaken. "A servant. Of course he would support your word."

"If I may, I will speak for myself on this matter."

Stephen's heart leaped into his throat at the sound of Rosalind's voice, which brought even the biggest blowhards in the crowd to heel. She slipped through the crowd and went straight to her uncle, and stood beside him, as regal and stately as any who would grace the court at St. James.

"My dear," Schofield said, the worry across his brow plain. "This is a dangerous place to be."

"I am quite safe, and happy, knowing you are well." She turned to the magistrate, her voice clear and loud. She spared Stephen not a glance. "Sir, I would like to make a statement as to the veracity of Mr. Geoffrey Pembroke's charges regarding what happened on the night Saturday past. I was at the orangery, as Mr. Pembroke suggested. He was the only one in hysterics. He tried to bash Lord Barronsfield's head in with a rock while the marquess was taken ill."

The crowd went wild before the magistrate bellowed out for calm. Rosalind continued.

"Then, later that night, after the marquess was back in Barronsfield, I was brought to a room to recover from the events earlier. Mr. Pembroke came to see me, in an effort to make me believe that I had gone into hysterics and could not remember what happened. But I do. I also remember Mr. Pembroke was uninjured when he spoke to me."

"You are Schofield's niece. Of course you would protect him," the magistrate countered, "as well as his position here with the marquess."

"I owe the marquess nothing."

The coolness in her voice as she spoke did not escape Stephen's notice. Nor did he think for a moment it was for show.

"I might ask you to consider, sir, the risk to my reputation by admitting his presence in my chamber to an audience." Rosalind looked coolly at Geoffrey. "I might be forced to marry such a gentleman."

Stephen cast a glance at Geoffrey, then back to Rosalind. *Over my dead body.* Of course, after this morning, Stephen had no right to her at all.

"Bess Hargrove, a servant at Barronsfield, was also present," Rosalind continued. "Though, most convenient for Mr. Pembroke, she has disappeared."

Geoffrey's turned a hateful eye to her, but stayed fixed in place. He continued on, determined, like an actor with a script. "But it is not just I!" Geoffrey shouted, clearly distracted now by Rosalind's story and the change of mood in the crowd. "There are the villagers in Elmsdale who have lost livestock and buildings to your devilry. These men here," he motioned out to the crowd where Gates stood, "can provide testament to these accusations. They can tell us how the very symbol of protection in his part of the country has turned into a thing to be feared and loathed."

Stephen held up the scroll that Schofield handed him earlier. "My steward has provided me the names of at least fifteen so-called victims who will testify that while there was damage, there were no sightings of a beast." He opened it up and scanned the contents in the growing morning light. "In fact, upon further inquiry, there is a curious coincidence between the nights I was supposedly out marauding the countryside as the Beast. There was no moon, or there was fog so thick that no proper identifica-tion of any perpetrator—human or otherwise—could be identified."

"I have seen the Beast." Geoffrey insisted, the last vestige of his calm now gone. "Half the bloody village saw you go mad last week."

Stephen watched the crowd consider this. "Was my back covered in fur? Did I howl at the moon? When I was found, Schofield, what did you see?"

"You were out of sorts for certain, My lord. But nothing *unnatural,*" Schofield replied, eyeing Perkins so coldly it forced the man to turn away. The men in the crowd exchanging critical glances and whispers.

"Then it is the word of two men against you," Geoffrey replied. "Edmund will also testify to this story's truthfulness."

"No, he will not," came a loud voice, cutting through the din. Stephen turned to see Edmund emerge from the crowd, and bounded up the stairs to him. "Stephen, forgive me. I have been made a fool and played the part exquisitely. Allow me to make amends."

He saw the pain in his young cousin's eyes, and held out his hand. "I am glad to have you at my side."

Edmund turned to the crowd, and gave Geoffrey such a cold, angry stare it forced him to step back.

"I found Lord Barronsfield, barely conscious, lying in the mud soaked field, looking like he needed his bed, but none the worse for wear." He dug into his pocket and held up a crumpled envelope. "Two days later, I received an express post from my father, urging me, as a good, obedient son, to support my brother's accusations against the marquess."

Geoffrey stood stone-faced.

"And, thanks to a little deductive work, we've found the agent that brought on Lord Barronsfield's delirium the night of the assembly." He took the small wooden box out of his pocket. "We found this only minutes ago, in the cook's personal spice cupboard. Is the physician here?"

"Mr. Pembroke." Doctor Brayden made his way through the crowd to where Edmund stood.

"Doctor, can you identify this substance?"

The man took the box, beckoned for a lamp and examined the contents. He picked out a few seeds, held them up to his nose, then carefully bit one before quickly spitting out the contents into an handkerchief. His eyes opened slightly in surprise, then threw a cautious, but appreciative look at Stephen, before replying. "This is datura. Thornapple, it is sometimes called."

"And what is datura, doctor?"

"A poison."

The crowd became thunderous.

"Silence!" Stephen boomed.

"Does it have any other uses?" Edmund persisted.

"It has been known to relieve pain, and be useful for some breathing problems. But it is also a powerful hallucinogen. It must be handled very carefully."

"According to my information, it causes memory loss, sensitivity to light, and madness." Edmund turned to the throng. "The marquess has been the victim of poisoning for years. It happened the night of the assembly. And you all have played your part in this scheme—a scheme orchestrated by my father."

"Edmund!" Geoffrey's voice cracked, and he looked as though he wanted to tear out his brother's throat. "What are you doing?"

"I am waking up to the insanity of this plan of father's to remove Stephen and take control of Barronsfield," Edmund replied. "I shall not be a party to this disgraceful, treasonous madness. And I would like to apologize to my cousin in public view for this entire affair, in part helped by my failure to stand up for the truth."

The crowd erupted, and in the time it took for the excitement to subside, Stephen allowed himself a moment to let this all sink in. The madness was over. Instinctively, he searched for Rosalind, but she stood far from him, on the other side of her uncle, clutching his hand. He caught her eye, but her face hardened, and she turned away.

"So, Perkins," Stephen said, forcing his attention back to the matter at hand. "Do you want to proceed with this farce, or do you wish to suggest that perhaps you were pressed by Mr. Pembroke and my uncle to support you in this scheme."

"I don't—" he turned to Geoffrey. "I don't know what to say."

"Do you agree to drop the charges?" asked the magistrate.

Perkins looked to Geoffrey, then nodded and beat a hasty retreat to his carriage.

Laughter at Perkin's expense peppered the crowd, before all heads turned back to Geoffrey. Ashen, but composed, he shoved his hands into his pockets.

"And you Geoffrey," Stephen said in a low, steady voice. "What punishment do you and your father deserve for stealing five years of my life? For inducing fear and distrust into Elmsdale? For wreaking havoc on the wellbeing of my servants, my tenants? Should the authorities be called in, do you think? Or do we solve this as gentlemen?"

"I'm a good shot, Stephen, you know it," Geoffrey said, the quiver in his voice belying his attempt at nonchalance.

"And I'm a better one," Edmund spoke up.

"Even if I did shoot you, the head of this beast would still be happily sitting in his lair at Notley house." Stephen paced around Geoffrey, circling him, selfishly enjoying every nervous twitch his cousin betrayed. "Perhaps the best thing to do is make this whole sordid affair public, and let society deal with you. Having no reputation to speak of, I have little to lose. But there are few who are going to release their daughters or their dowries to a traitorous n'er do well with little to show for himself but a fine suit. What say you, gentlemen?"

After due deliberation, those present agreed with Stephen.

"You may take the few others in town who assisted you with this ruse. Once Schofield finds their names, I am sure the residents of this area might make their continued stay...uncomfortable." Stephen looked to Schofield and cracked a smile before turning back to his cousin. "You may find yourself the nearest carriage back to London from here, Geoffrey. I will send your things along to you. Neither you nor my uncle will darken the doors of Barronsfield again."

"You can't do this to me!" Geoffrey protested, his voice cracking a bit. "I am not some common peasant, to be tossed away."

"No, you are less than that." Stephen turned to him, swallowing back his hate. He faced his cousin, nearly nose to nose, so close he could see the beads of sweat forming along Geoffrey's brow. "You should hang. And if I hear another word out of you, by God, I will see to it that you do."

He stood a moment longer, staring hard into Geoffrey's face, struggling to get his own anger under control, all the while savoring Geoffrey's fear. Before Stephen acted foolishly, he turned, adjusted his coat. "Now go and join your man Perkins, before I kick you down the steps myself. And the rest of you," he shouted out to the men below, "those of you duped by suspicion and fear, I beg you go home. Leave now, be peaceful, and no harm will come to you."

Geoffrey scrambled down the steps and disappeared into the carriage, leaving the larger part of the crowd to disperse. Stephen walked down to thank the men in the crowd who'd come to support him. The sun's brilliance finally broke over the horizon, reflecting pools of blue and gold on the ground where last night's rains had not yet evaporated. He took a deep breath. The smell of wood fire mixed with damp ground thickened the air, and he drew in every bit of it. Today might be the start of something new. Turning his gaze to the steps where Schofield stood, he couldn't help but notice Rosalind had gone. His shoulders slumped as disappointment settled on him like a mantle, robbing him of the victory that was supposed to arrive with Geoffrey's defeat.

It took nearly an hour before the last of the hangers-on started to straggle back to Elmsdale. A town he had played in as a boy, visited as a youth, and feared as a man. There had been so much fear. And until this morning, when the curse was finally exposed for the lie it was, he hadn't realized how much.

"Stephen." Edmund stood behind him, hands shoved in his pockets, looking uncertain. "I—"

"Do not apologize to me again. I accepted it the minute I saw you."

"They played me for a fool. Even Geoffrey—" his voice broke slightly here, "has lived too long and hard under the fist of our father. I know you cannot forgive him, but when you live with a monster like our father, it is hard not to emulate that."

"Yet you managed to remain a sane human being," Stephen replied.

Edmund said nothing for a few moments, and they walked along the park in comfortable silence. "You should speak to Miss Schofield, Stephen."

He gave a curt nod. "I have been the worst sort of coward, Edmund. I imagine she must despise me." Whether she could forgive him was another story. He'd only tried to beg forgiveness once before, and to no avail. Melancholy crept into his chest. How could he ever explain himself to her?

Edmund took Stephen by his shoulders. "She is leaving Barronsfield. I would not be surprised if her plans were already fixed."

Stephen stood silent a moment, savoring the fierceness of the emotion building inside him. "No. I will not let her go." He stalked off toward the orangery, purpose fueling his steps.

"Where are you going? The cottage is that way!" Edmund pointed in another direction.

"There is something I need to do first," Stephen called out. For years he'd tended Haddie's roses like a shrine. A testimony to his guilt.

No longer. Today, for the first time in twenty years, he hoped they might be a testimony to his love. His walk broke into a run.

One last dragon to slay. One princess to win.

CHAPTER 23

osalind stood in the small entry way of the cottage, surrounded by silence, her feet weighted down by gloom. The moment when Geoffrey Pembroke's plot had been revealed was supposed to have been a happy one—her uncle would remain at Barronsfield, and she would have a home with him. A home where she would be appreciated and loved. And maybe, the man she'd come to love, Stephen Pembroke, might have found a way to love her back. It just didn't work out that way.

True, the myth of the Beast of Barronsfield had been put to rest, and the men threatening her uncle and the others had been exposed. She and Edmund might have made this right for Stephen, but nothing was right for her. After Geoffrey Pembroke's story was discredited and the crowd began to disperse, she'd fled to the cottage. Her courage was spent, and so was her heart.

Emily was nowhere to be found—no doubt she'd gone to the manor, where an impromptu celebration had broken out. Willing her feet to move, Rosalind went to the parlor and lit a fire in the hearth. Had her uncle already discovered her shame? Maybe he would demand that Stephen marry her, salvaging her reputation and making her a marchioness in the bargain. The irony of it, considering

Stephen's original proposal, put a grim smile on her face. Either way, she would be tied to a man repulsed by her. It was just as distasteful an idea now as when he'd first proposed. Maybe it was worse, because now she loved him.

Rosalind wiped away the unwanted tears, then stood, her back ramrod straight. She had to get away. When she'd first arrived at Barronsfield, her dream was to be on her own. Of course, that was before she had an inkling of what it meant to have a real home. But if Admiral and Mrs. Hart were willing to help her uncle by allowing her to stay in London while she found a husband, they might entertain the idea of finding suitable lodging for her there until she figured out where she would go next. She just needed to do it before her reputation caught up with her.

Going to her uncle's desk, she composed the letter, then walked to the stables with Dreyfus. There she found a boy willing to take the message into town where it could be sent by special post to London.

The dog wagged his tail as they rambled along the soggy lanes back to the cottage. The sun was out now, and though the weather was damp, it had enough strength to warm Rosalind's face.

"I will send for you if I am able," she said to the pup. "I do not know if the Harts care for dogs, and it would be less than polite to invite you somewhere you might not be wanted." As she well knew. "Besides, Emily will take good care of you, and I am sure it will be much nicer here than being limited to parlors and sidewalks." *Like I will be.* Her heart lurched at the idea of being confined once more.

The dog tore off ahead to where the sound of cart wheels rumbled nearby. Rounding the bend, Rosalind spied Eleanore on a small cart, her red cape flapping in the breeze as she approached the cottage.

"Ahoy there!" Eleanore called, then jumped down.

"Eleanore!" Rosalind said, Dreyfus at her heels. "Mind his paws— he is learning not to jump, but he forgets himself." She held out her arms and gave Eleanore a good hug, then took her friend by the arm and walked into the house.

"I assume you've heard the news."

"About the marquess and his curse?" Rosalind replied, trying her best to be enthusiastic.

"Actually, it's about Bess Hargrove."

Rosalind's breath caught for a moment. "I haven't. It's good I hope?"

"She's been found! She went into hiding after Mr. Pembroke threatened her. He tried to buy her off apparently, but she didn't trust him, especially after what happened to Sally Coles. She hid in the closed down wing of Barronsfield Manor, right under everyone's noses," Eleanore replied. "Both she and Sally had suspicions about the plants used to poison the marquess. She said she sneaked one into your apron, hoping you would find it."

"What a smart girl!" Rosalind broke into a smile. Relief flooded through her. "Wonderful! No, I hadn't heard."

"I would have thought you'd have been at the manor, actually. I looked for you for some time." Eleanore regarded Rosalind carefully. "Why are you here by yourself?"

Rosalind took a deep breath, her lips pressed together as she opened the door to the cottage. "It has been an exhausting few days, and I needed some time to myself. Besides, I have some news of my own."

Eleanore waited, an expectant look on her face.

"I will be heading to London after all."

"London? When?" Eleanore's brows dipped, and the corners of her lips fell into a frown.

"As soon as possible. I've sent a runner in to see what arrangements can be made on my behalf. I hope to hear back by tomorrow."

"So soon?"

"This is what my father planned for me all along." Rosalind led Eleanore into the kitchen and hefted a kettle onto the stove.

Eleanore fetched the prized tin of tea, then carefully spooned a heaping measure of dark aromatic leaves into a dainty yellow pot. "I can't help but wonder why you are leaving so soon, Rosalind. The last time we talked about London, we could have been talking about the plague for all the appeal it had for you."

Rosalind moved around the kitchen, grabbing plates and digging for teacakes. The dishes clattered in her hands, lids on canisters banged as she looked for butter and honey. "I've tarried too long here. And I'm not as young or as beautiful as you are, Eleanore. No one will seek me out as a wife unless I help it along a bit. London is the place to do that." She looked up after her flurry of activity, extremely satisfied with how reasonable she sounded, when a cup slipped from her hand and the crash of porcelain smashing at her feet froze the smile on her face.

"You should not say such things about yourself. And besides, you are seven and twenty, not seventy." Eleanore scolded as she bent over to help her friend clean up the mess. Her manner reminded Rosalind a little too much of the girl's half brother. "Mrs. Darling says to me all the time what a lively, pretty woman you are, and she is right."

They cleaned up the rest of the mess in silence, Rosalind unwilling to speak lest she lose the last of her self-possession. Eleanore got another cup, poured the tea, and the two went into the parlor. Dreyfus followed, curling up by the fire as the ladies seated themselves.

Settled, they conversed for the better part of the morning, and for a good portion of it, Rosalind managed to forget about Stephen, about London, about everything. They laughed about hairstyles and dresses, gossiped about village news, and even fantasized about Rosalind's cottage and the book shop she thought she might open one day. Eleanore had already agreed to work in it.

A loud knock at the door interrupted their chatter. Rosalind opened it to see Geoffrey Pembroke on the other side. A small but fine black coach waited beyond him by the gate.

"Mr. Pembroke!" Rosalind exclaimed, startled by his appearance on her doorstep. She stepped back, fearful of the unfocused, nervous way he held himself.

"Miss Schofield," Geoffrey tipped his hat, and fidgeted with his pocket watch. "I understand you are leaving Barronsfield. As it happens, so am I. I think perhaps a little visit to Scotland would be lovely, don't you think?" He moved toward her, and smiled in a most unnerving way.

"That is kind of you." Rosalind gripped the door handle, prepared to close the door. "But I am not at liberty to take my leave. I am sorry."

"I would be sorry for your trouble, if I were you." He pulled on the door, ripping it away from her and grasping her wrist before Rosalind could react. "You have ruined me, Miss Schofield. But I am a generous man, and will allow you to make amends."

"Rosalind?" Eleanore's voice called from somewhere behind her.

He dropped his voice. "Come now, and she'll keep her throat intact."

Rosalind froze, watching Geoffrey strain to see beyond her shoulder to where Eleanore was speaking. Her mind raced. If he was capable of harming Stephen, who knew what he'd do to a poor girl like Eleanore.

She swallowed deeply, and nodded. "Do not harm her. She is no threat to you." Her voice registered barely above a whisper.

Dreyfus bolted to the door, barking madly at her feet.

"Shut that mutt up."

She picked up the dog and met Eleanore, who was coming to the entry way.

"Rosalind, what is happening?"

"Eleanore!" She turned, trying hard not to betray her fear. "It seems my plans have changed."

"I don't—"

"Mr. Pembroke has kindly offered me passage back to London. I could be there in a few days rather than a week." She handed the dog to a rather confused looking Eleanore, and leaned in and kissed her cheek. "I must go."

"What about your uncle? Or Lord Barronsfield?"

"Tell my uncle I love him, and I will write as soon as I am able. And tell Lord Barronsfield..." her mind raced. Tell him what? Her eyes widened slightly as a desperate thought came into her head. "Tell him I am going to visit with the kelpies."

Rosalind's heart leaped into her throat at the sound of Geoffrey's footsteps crossing the threshold. She whipped around and met him at the door, grabbed her cloak, and was roughly pushed off the step by her captor. As soon as the door closed behind them, he turned, so close to her the rankness of his breath brushed up against the back of her neck. She wanted to ask him if he was mad, but the question was moot. He opened the door of the carriage, and pushed her inside it, sitting her on the red velvet bench before taking the seat opposite her.

"Where are you taking me?"

"You need a husband, Miss Schofield. And I need ten thousand pounds. Compensation for ruining my father's plans to rid Barrons-field of its current master."

"Your father?"

"He's planning the wedding. Let's go meet him, shall we?"

Stephen stood in the orangery, an axe in his hand. Before him stood Haddie Walton's glistening rose bush, its lush blooms mocking the cold air on the other side of the glass. The first time Stephen had dared to steal these roses, he was a boy. Two days later, his mother and little sister lay dying with typhus. But the distant pain of losing his family was supplanted with another memory—one far fresher and just as painful. The despair on Rosalind's face as he deserted her.

Fingers coiled around the wooden handle, he lifted the blade, prepared at last to strike the rosebush down, and clear its damnable presence from his life. Stephen closed his eyes, the palms of his hands growing damp as he began to swing. It was the last time he would allow Haddie Walton's roses to ruin his life. His life been shaped by these flowers, and his belief in the curse. And for so long, he'd been content to have it so.

The blade stopped.

Stephen opened his eyes, and loosened his grip on the axe. Sun poured through the glass, brightening the already impossibly pinkish-red flowers. The roses were brilliant, and this particular species was rare in this part of the world. But despite their shimmering beauty, they were just flowers. Not magical. Not cursed. Just like him. They were no more responsible for the ills in his life than the heather that grew around Yorkshire.

A bitter chuckle escaped his lips. So much energy wasted. And they could be better used for a more worthy purpose. Instead of serving the roses, the roses were going to serve him.

Stephen put the axe away, and found a freshly sharpened set of pruners. Heart in his throat, he prepared to clip the freshest, most perfect blossoms. They were the only ones worthy for the task. Hopefully, somewhere between the hot house and the steward's cottage he would find the words that would convince Rosalind to forgive him and condescend to be his wife.

As the first bloom fell into his hand, he was interrupted by the sound of his name. It was Edmund, pulling up on a cart, calling from the other side of the glass. The frantic tone raised the hackles on the back of Stephen's neck as he dropped the pruners and strode outside to meet him.

"Stephen," Edmund blurted out again as he brought the cart to a halt. He jumped down and helped Eleanore Martin, who accompanied him.

"What's the matter?" The panic on Edmund's face jarred Stephen further, dread gripping at his throat. "What happened?"

"Mr. Pembroke took her—Miss Schofield. It looked like she was to elope with him." Eleanore spoke up.

Stephen glared at Edmund. "Did you know about this?"

Eleanore stepped in front of Edmund, looking squarely at Stephen. Suddenly, the young girl seemed neither meek nor fragile. "Her manner was strange when he came, and she left with nothing but her cloak. I think she was spirited away, my lord, under force."

"I swear to God under heaven, Stephen. I had no idea of his plan," Edmund said.

A hint of the old familiar fear rose, and Stephen tasted bitterness in his throat. He put a hand to the back of his neck, now exposed to the cool breeze that rustled against him, sending a shiver down his spine. The faint hint of roses caught in the air, reminding him of the flower still in his grasp. Rosalind had never given up on him. He swallowed the bitterness. He would be damned if he gave up on her.

"Eleanore," Stephen turned to her, clearly surprising the girl by addressing her so. "Did Rosalind give you any indication of where Pembroke was taking her?"

"She said she was going to London with Mr. Pembroke, and to tell you she was going to visit with the Kelpies," she replied. "Perhaps we can write them and ask them to look for her."

Kelpies?

"Thank you." He had a million things to say to her, but they would wait.

"We need to find Schofield," Stephen climbed up on the cart. Edmund and Eleanore scrambled up with him.

"I'm going with you," Edmund said. "This is as much my doing as anyone's. And if they're headed to London, they could be anywhere."

Stephen shook his head. "Kelpies are mythical creatures from Scotland. That's where he's taking Rosalind. He's going to marry her." Stephen's heart sank as he spoke. Geoffrey couldn't have Anne, so he would take Rosalind instead. And she had something Geoffrey always needed. Money.

"If they are going to Scotland, my grandmother's family has a small estate there, near Coldstream."

It was at least a day and night's ride to Scotland. This time, he didn't fear the darkness. Time was his enemy now. And if they found them—*when* they found them—Stephen vowed that if Geoffrey or Uncle Thomas had laid so much as a finger on Rosalind, they would find out for themselves exactly how much of a beast Stephen could be.

CHAPTER 24

Rosalind stood in a small chapel that was deserted except for herself, her captors, and a pallid clergyman standing near the altar. The richest gown she'd ever worn hung heavy off her shoulders. It was a most putrid shade of purple, though she might have looked upon it a little more kindly if the circumstance for wearing it were anything less than ghastly. Her hair was hidden under an ornate wig that itched her scalp. Hemp fibers bit into her wrists as she struggled against the rope binding her hands fast. Flexing her fingers to force blood into her hands, they ached and prickled with pins and needles.

The entire scene was a cruel reminder that sometimes the dreams that come true are nightmares.

She wanted to go home. And home, she knew, was Barronsfield. Where she was loved, and had made real friends. She thought about Hanley and Edmund, imploring her to stay. Stephen had been afraid, Hanley said. She replayed Stephen's ill-timed retreat from her. The blood draining from his face. The stillness in his body before, eyes wide, he bolted. He wasn't repulsed by her. He was *terrified*. Why? Because he thought he would hurt her. Because she was no longer *safe* with him.

Because, just perhaps, he thought she was beautiful.

Elation at the idea that fear, and not revulsion drove Stephen's retreat was smothered by the panic that settled in her chest and shallowed her breath. The dampness in the chapel forced a shiver down her back as regret, self-pity, and other unpleasant emotions threatened to take hold.

Geoffrey stood near the altar. It was mid-morning, and what little she'd eaten of her breakfast tumbled around in her stomach. The door to the chapel was filled by the same large man who'd guarded her door the night before.

No music played, no flowers adorned the chapel. The sky illuminated the one stained glass window that bore the wounds of Cromwell's wrath over a century ago. Broken shards of red, blue and yellow light stained the walls.

"Let's begin, shall we?" Thomas Pembroke stood behind her, his voice loud and urgent.

She felt herself planted where she stood.

"I will drag you up there, my dear," he snarled in her ear. "But it might be better for you if you don't make a scene."

Rosalind found her feet, swallowed hard, then walked with as much dignity as she could muster. She knew well that people often married for money, and affection came second. Still, she had held out the illusion she might have been happy. Now, that illusion was laid out as naked and bare as she felt under her gaudy, ill-fitting gown.

She would run. Run as far as she could. Geoffrey could have all of her money. She didn't care. Rosalind had never had it before, she would do without it now. She would run all the way back to her Aunt Stanhope if she had to. Even that life would be less wretched than this.

Too soon she reached Geoffrey, who took her bound hands in his own. "Don't worry, darling. I won't be the ogre my father is, I assure you."

If Rosalind's wrists were not bound, she would have reached up and throttled Geoffrey's neck.

"That is supposed to comfort me?" The words came out in a harsh whisper as she stood beside him. "You are a snake and a coward."

He only smiled at her. It was the same charming, and she realized now, thoroughly soulless expression that had so bedazzled her the first time she had met him. What would she give to see Stephen's haunted eyes, his hesitant smile, or even his infuriating haughtiness?

"Get on with it!" Thomas barked at the clergyman, breaking Rosalind out of her thoughts. He turned to Geoffrey, whispered into his son's ear, then disappeared into the vestry.

The drone of the clergyman began, but Rosalind barely heard a word.

Geoffrey grabbed her shaking hand, about to place the ring on her finger. She closed her eyes, unable to watch. "With this ring—"

"Pembroke! Stop this madness!"

Rosalind's eyes flew open, and she squinted hard, at first doubting her own senses. The rush of sunlight from the open door behind him obscured his features, but Rosalind knew that Stephen Pembroke stood at the rear of the chapel.

"What in the bloody hell are you doing here?" Geoffrey's tone crackled with indignation as Stephen marched toward them, stepping over the body of the goon now lying by the door. Rosalind's heart lurched, and she blinked to make sure her eyes were not playing tricks on her. Seeing the look of surprise across Geoffrey's brow, Rosalind sought to take advantage. Wrenching hard, she attempted to break his grip, only to have him swing her around and tighten his hold on her. Pulling her in front of him as a shield, the cold gnaw of fear grabbed her gut as he exposed her throat. From the corner of her eye she caught the glimpse of steel.

"Keep walking, Stephen," Geoffrey growled. "Keep walking and I will slit her throat."

"Let her go, Pembroke, and I'll let you out of here alive." Stephen walked slowly toward her, a musket in his hand, his eyes darting between Rosalind and Geoffrey. His stare hardened. He looked rough and ready, like he had spent a long time in the saddle. His hair was windblown, and at least a day's growth shadowed his hard jaw. Still, he was without a doubt, the most beautiful sight she had ever seen.

"How are you, Miss Schofield?" he asked, visibly softening as he spoke.

She smiled as best she could with Geoffrey's hand at her throat, and fought to keep her voice steady. "I am unhurt."

"And so you shall stay, I promise," Stephen replied, still approaching them. Though calm, Rosalind caught emotion in his voice. "Your uncle was not far behind me, with the constable."

"We are already married, Stephen. What do you say to that?" Geoffrey lied.

Rosalind looked straight at Stephen, imploring him to notice the slight shaking of her head.

"Is that all you want? Ten thousand pounds?" Stephen cried. "Let her go and you shall have it."

"You know damn well that is not all I want!"

Rosalind winced has she felt the sharp tip of the blade at her throat.

"Geoffrey, for Christ's sake, let her go!" Stephen yelled out, running toward him. "This madness must end."

Desperation pushed Rosalind to struggle against Geoffrey when she saw his father lurking behind Stephen. Eyes widening, she opened her mouth to warn him when Thomas grabbed Stephen and held him steadfast, a pistol to his temple.

"You are right, nephew. This madness must end, and it ends now."

THE COLD TIP of the musket pressed against Stephen's skin, but it was the hate ripping through his uncle's words that threatened to steal his nerve.

Fool, Stephen groaned inwardly. Did he think that after all the insane machinations his uncle had set in motion, he would allow Stephen to walk away with Rosalind?

"For God's sake, Thomas—murdering me will end both our lives, and the title goes back to the King. Geoffrey will get nothing."

Out of the corner of his eye, he could see his uncle's tortured expression. The musket barrel pushed harder against Stephen's head.

"Just walk away. You and Geoffrey," Stephen replied. "Edmund is close by. Go to him, and—"

"Edmund? Edmund is useless! Weak! Betraying his own blood for a nameless wench and a rich cousin. As far as he is concerned, he is not my son. You took my title, and then Edmund," Thomas seethed. "You shall have nothing more from me!"

Stephen heard the hammer on the pistol being pulled back. Rage and fear fired in his chest, and in one desperate act, he swung his elbow hard into his uncle's gut, which loosened his uncle's grip and sent Thomas crashing to the floor, knocked senseless. Grabbing the pistol, he rushed toward Geoffrey.

"No!" His cousin's voice crackled with anger as he held Rosalind against him, his grip tight at her throat. "You took the woman I loved from me. Now you will know how that feels."

Stephen held up his pistol. Rosalind stifled a sob, sending a rush of fear straight through his chest. "If you hurt her, Geoffrey, I will rip you apart."

"It would be so easy," Pembroke replied, his grip tightening on Rosalind's throat. "One quick snap, and she would be gone. Just like Anne."

It took precious seconds for Geoffrey's words to register in Stephen's consciousness. *Just like Anne.* Anne had died in a carriage accident, or so he'd understood. He had been under the influence of the Beast at the time. Or rather, Geoffrey's poison.

Stephen knew Geoffrey had a temper, but until now, he never appreciated that it could turn so deadly. But he needed answers, and a distraction while he figured out how to get Rosalind away from Geoffrey. Fanning Geoffrey's temper could mean Rosalind's end, so Stephen tried another tack. Softening his voice, he lowered his pistol. "Pray, tell me more about Anne. I had no idea she had flung you aside so callously."

Geoffrey's face contorted, his cheeks flushed with anger. "She was going to break off our arrangement. We were going to be lovers, after you were married. I promised her we'd be discreet. But it wasn't enough. I wasn't enough. I got so angry."

Stephen inched his way closer, and let Geoffrey keep talking.

"She was laughing at me. Laughing. At me. I couldn't listen to her anymore. She was tearing my heart out and laughing at me all the while. It was her fault. She made me so angry."

"So you killed her." Rage tightened Stephen's throat and quickened his blood. Geoffrey had killed Anne and framed him. What kind of twisted logic had fired Geoffrey's anger for Stephen when he'd taken her life with his own hands?

Geoffrey nodded, his body heaving as he sobbed, the dagger at Rosalind's throat lowered as his grip loosened. Stephen saw his opportunity. He started to move toward them, only to see Geoffrey's head snap up, a glimmer of madness in his eyes. Geoffrey's hand was firm on Rosalind's throat. Her eyes widened, and Stephen could see her struggle for breath.

Stephen took another step, swung his fist and slammed it into Geoffrey's jaw. The force of his blow knocked Geoffrey back, loosening his hold on Rosalind enough for Stephen to pull her free.

"I should kill you, you bastard," Stephen spat, his breathing labored as he stood over Geoffrey, who lay up against the altar, blood gushing from his nose. Stephen's pistol pointed at Geoffrey's chest. "But I have spent far too long living with the torture of believing I was responsible for so much death. I will not have your blood on my hands."

A rush of voices came through the door. Stephen cast a glance and caught a glimpse of Edmund and what must be the constable entering the church.

"You shall spend the rest of your days rotting in prison, unless the Wickwire family would prefer to see you swing." He walked away even as the constable came forward.

Stephen reached out for Rosalind and held her in a strong embrace, trying to calm the terror that still rippled through her body. The sound of a pistol's hammer being pulled back caught Stephen's attention and he looked up to see Thomas had pulled himself to his feet. He wore a wild expression on his face, and pointed a pistol at Rosalind's back. Stephen thrust Rosalind to the side, closed his eyes and tried to block out the sound of Rosalind's cry as the sound of a pistol exploded in the air.

Stephen opened his eyes and looked down, frantically pulling at his shirt, searching for the wound. Finding none, he looked up in time to see agonized shock on Thomas's face as his uncle sank to the stone floor, blood seeping through his jacket from his shoulder, the musket falling from his hand. Over his shoulder he saw Edmund, his face like stone, his arm still raised from where he had fired his gun.

Geoffrey pulled himself up, pushed away the Constable and rushed to his father.

"What the hell have you done?" he cried out at Edmund, his voice cracking.

Stephen picked up the musket where it had fallen to the floor.

"Schofield!" Stephen shouted above the din. Reginald already had his niece in his protective embrace. Rosalind was pale but still had her feet under her. "Get her outside. I will be there shortly." His steward nodded and escorted Rosalind out. Stephen stopped at his uncle's feet.

"I will call for a surgeon, which is more than you deserve. I want you well so you can take your time to rot in Newgate."

He strode away, the clamor of Geoffrey's cries and Thomas's cursing hanging in the air. He stopped only to grab Edmund, who stood motionless at the door.

"Come. This is over."

Edmund looked over at Stephen, his face full of self-loathing. Stephen recognized the expression, having seen it staring back at him from his own mirror.

"You did what was right, Edmund, and you saved my life."

"I wanted to kill him."

"But you did not. Do not forget that."

It took a moment until Edmund was able to turn his back on the howls and curses of those he'd left behind, but at last, the two walked away.

Stephen spied Rosalind by the horses, her uncle standing beside her. Her hands were untied, the wig lay in a lump at her feet, and she was frantically pulling pins out of her hair. Despite the aching in his legs from two days of hard riding, he ran across the open field to where she stood, looking wild, and beautiful. She looked up as he approached, tentative.

He opened his mouth, but there were no words. No words to capture the joy at seeing her again, and the sorrow he'd suffer if he'd lost her. She'd suffered so terribly because of him. Standing before her, he was suddenly afraid. He had saved her, yes, but only so that she might walk away from him forever.

The thought drove him to his knees.

CHAPTER 25

"What on earth are you doing?" Rosalind watched Stephen crumple to the ground before her eyes, her breath catching in her throat. "Are you hurt?"

"I don't know. I think I am begging for forgiveness. That, and I've ridden for nearly two days straight. My legs are bloody sore." He smiled and reached up for her, then stopped and pulled his fingers back, as if he'd overstepped an invisible boundary. Impulsively, she took his hand. As his fingers laced in hers, the warmth of his skin sent a rush of comfort through her, releasing the horror of the past two days. Sobs gripped her body so deeply they stole her breath. As Rosalind found herself gently pulled down and into Stephen's embrace, the tears flowed freely at last.

"Oh Rosalind, I am so sorry. I am so sorry for everything you've gone through." His voice cracked with emotion. He stroked her hair, then whispered in her ear. "You're beautiful, do you know that?"

She pulled away, eyeing him suspiciously. "Why are you saying that? What do you want from me?"

"Nothing. And everything." He held on to her hands as if his life depended on it, a sense of desperation in his eyes that almost took her aback. "I have been a fool, Rosalind. A complete and utter fool. I was, as you so ably tried to tell me, so busy creating my own misery, I could not see the misery I was creating in others. I was afraid. Afraid of a fairy tale of my own making. Let me try and rewrite the ending. Even though I have done little to deserve you."

"My lord—"

"Stephen." He squeezed her hand a little. "Just Stephen."

Fresh tears spilled over onto her cheeks, and she took a moment to savor both the fear and the comfort she felt in his arms. Was it fear that drove him away? She needed to know. To be sure. Because she didn't trust herself. "Maybe you think you feel this way, because of everything that has happened, and you pity me. And that's why you are here with me now, like this. And not—" *and not because you love me.*

"I did not trust my own heart, Rosalind. Nor did I trust in you, Eleanore, or even my servants and friends who stood by me when I did not bother to find the truth myself." He brushed the tears from her cheeks, stirring both torment and joy in Rosalind's belly. "That morning, after we laid together, I looked at you and realized how deeply I loved you. How beautiful you are. It terrified me. Because I thought I would lose you. And I couldn't." He turned his face away. "What a fool I have been."

Rosalind swallowed her tears, and pushed past the last vestige of her fear. "After today I have come to the conclusion that most men are fools, or mad. There is hope, at least, for the fools." She put a hand to his cheek, gently bringing his gaze back to her own. "I think I have loved you since you came to the cottage with the invitation for the library. And I have never stopped. So, who is the fool?"

He pulled her close, then gently kissed her forehead. She drank in his scent and the feeling of his rough beard against her face. A warm tingling feeling welled up inside her.

"We'd better move on." Stephen released her, rose, then helped her to her feet. "I can't wait to kiss your body in a thousand little places, but here is neither the place nor time."

Rosalind agreed, already eager for when he might kiss her again.

"I still can't believe you found me," she said. "I wasn't sure you'd even remember about the kelpies."

"You are many things, but forgettable is not one of them. We'll have to inform Mr. Turner you put the book to good use. I'm sure he'll be thrilled." He smiled at her with the same expression that had made her heart skip the first time she'd seen him. Stephen cast a glance up at the sun, then over to the other side of the church, where Edmund, Uncle Reginald and two constables had wrangled Geoffrey and Thomas into the back of a jailor's cart. Tension melted out of her shoulders as Stephen rose and helped her to her feet, then led her to the side of a large chestnut horse. He mounted the animal, then held out his hand, and pulled her up in front of him. She welcomed his solid, masculine form as he put his arms around her and grabbed the reins.

They stopped at a nearby inn to rest before the journey back to Barronsfield. Stephen helped her down from her mount and she rushed to her uncle. They embraced warmly, and in that moment, she thought she felt a little spark of her father there with them.

"My dear, it is a miracle to have you back. I don't know what I would have done if I were ever to lose you." Uncle Reginald looked her over, concern creasing his brow. "I think you will want a hot bath, and a rest. And I will speak to the innkeeper about fetching you something a little less fanciful to wear for the ride home." He gave her an affectionate kiss on her forehead. He turned to leave, then hesitated for a moment, before taking her hand.

"What is it?"

He shook his head softly. "It is not for me to say. I wish the best for you."

"Thank you." She wasn't sure what to make of her uncle's bittersweet expression.

"I need an ale, I'm not ashamed to say," her uncle recovered, more bombastic. "And by the look of Mr. Pembroke over there, I think he could stand to join me."

She caught sight of Edmund out with the horses, looking off, clearly wishing himself somewhere else.

"I will be but a moment." She ran outside and took a few hesitant steps toward the figure leaning against the tree.

"Edmund."

It took a moment, but he stirred, straightened and looked to her with a troubled smile.

"How are you?" she asked.

"I think I should be asking you that question, all things considering."

"I wanted to say thank you."

"You have nothing to thank me for, Rosalind." A new hardness edged his voice. "Except perhaps for turning a blind eye to my father's madness, or being too weak to stand up to him when it counted."

"Edmund, please. My words were earnestly meant."

His expression softened a little.

"We are friends, you and I," she continued. "And I know what you did was very difficult. I am sorry you were forced to act in such a way on my account."

"I almost had you tied to one of the most odious men in the Kingdom." He threw up his hands, clearly disgusted.

"Edmund," she pressed. "That your father is who he is, and that your brother chooses to follow—it is not your burden."

"Perhaps."

Rosalind could see he was not convinced. She straightened, putting her hands on her hips. "Edmund Pembroke—"

"Do you know how much I have come to despise that name?"

"Edmund?" Rosalind was not playing along. "I think it a rather nice name, actually."

"I was thinking of 'Pembroke.'" He looked away.

Rosalind crossed her arms and cocked an eyebrow. "I don't know about you, but I've had quite enough melancholy for one day. My uncle has seen fit to have a pint of ale, and he believes that you might like to join him."

At that, Edmund brightened, and Rosalind thought she could see a little of the gentleman she knew. "He is an astute man, that Schofield."

He held out his arm, and they walked inside the inn together. She deposited him beside her uncle in the great room, before a servant came and showed her to her chamber, where a hot bath waited.

The fire crackled and snapped in the small hearth, giving the room a pleasant warmth after the ride in the crisp autumn air. Plumes of steam rose from the tub, which carried the faint smell of roses through the air. Walking over to the water, she saw the faint, glimmering beads of what must have been rose oil floating on the water's surface. She took a deep breath, allowing the heavenly scent to lift her spirits.

"I can assist you, if you like," the servant said as she set a small tray down by the tub. Rosalind saw a small decanter, filled with what looked to be fortified wine.

Rosalind nodded and turned, facing the hearth. The heat from the fire caressed her skin. Fatigue creeping up on her, she closed her eyes, ready to let the servant undress her. From behind her, the door creaked open again, and closed, leaving the room quiet—the din of music and laughter from the great room muted by the heavy wooden door. She found herself in danger of nodding off even as she stood.

"How many of these little buttons are on this bloody frock?" came a grumble from behind her. A very familiar, very masculine grumble. Rosalind's fatigue disappeared.

"It's a good thing you were able to keep your title," she said, trying to fend off the butterflies in her belly at Stephen's touch. "I think being a ladies maid might prove to be a bit of a challenge."

"I shall have to practice, just in case." There was unmistakable hunger in his voice. It caught her breath and sent her blood rushing down to her most feminine places.

One by one he pulled out the rest of the pins from her hair, then gently ran his fingers through her locks.

"When you were in the library that evening, playing with a single lock of your hair, I was entranced. I wanted nothing more than to wrap my arms around you."

"I had no idea you thought of me in that way. I thought—" she faltered, reliving that horrible morning only a few days ago.

He turned her toward him, his shirt loosened, hesitating a moment before he started to speak. "You thought that I considered you unremarkable, as I encouraged you to. I lied to you. And to myself. I cannot bear to think of it without shame. You are the most remark-able woman I have ever known."

An incredible need filled her. She turned and raised herself up on her tip toes, gripped his shirt and pulled him down to her lips, where she kissed him as if her next breath depended on it. A low growl escaped him, and she felt his hands over her shoulders, pulling the dress away from her body. The sound of tearing seams caught her attention.

"You've ripped it," she said breathlessly between kisses.

"Ripped what?"

"My bodice," she replied, nibbling at his ear.

"You're right." He kissed all the way down her neck, which tickled and intoxicated her at the same time. "I would make a terrible ladies maid."

In an instant, he tore the rest of the gown away, leaving Rosalind in nothing but stays and stockings. "Let me look at you."

He took a step back, his hair in disarray, gazing at Rosalind with undisguised need. Rosalind's nervousness ended, overcome by the fire raging in her body. Every part of her longed to have him, to be stroked and kissed and nuzzled.

"Time for that bath, I think," he said, his voice thick with lust.

"A bath, now?"

"Hell, yes." He stepped forward, about to help her out of the rest of her clothes she stopped him.

"Wait." She held up a hand. "I'm not undressed yet. I don't want to get my underthings wet, do I?"

He looked at her curiously, then, as she started to unlace her stays, his face broke out in an appreciative grin. As the fabric dropped to the floor, she heard a quick intake of breath before another growl escape his lips. He pulled off her stockings, his touch along the inside of her legs sending rivers of heat through her body. He swooped her in his arms, and hungrily kissed her behind her ears, and around her neck. The feeling of his arms around her, touching parts of her body usually swaddled and constrained by fabric and whalebone was strange and wonderful and exciting. In a couple of strides he reached the bath, where he gently lowered her into the steamy water. It streamed over her body, enveloping her in warmth, tingling the already sensitive, private parts of her body.

He peeled off his shirt, and reached over her, grabbing the soap. He lathered the hard bar between his hands. "Perhaps I can bathe you. I think I might be better at that."

She nodded, breathless in anticipation. Kneeling beside the tub, he started with her arms, gently massaging the soap from her neck down along her arms to her finger tips. He was quiet and methodical in his movement. The stroke of his fingers, instead of relaxing her, put her on edge, making her want even more.

His hands moved up and over her collarbone. Her breasts, slick with soap, glistened in the firelight. His fingers ran over her nipples, now taut and pink, making her squirm with delight. He watched her intently, seeming to enjoy every squeal and breath she uttered.

"I want to touch you." She reached out with her hand, running her fingers over his arm, and across his chest. In response, he took her one of her hands and kissed each of her fingers before turning his attention back to her breasts.

"Me first," he replied playfully, before turning serious. "Let me do this for you."

He moved his hands down her belly and across her hips, then back and forth along the length of her inner thighs. Each time his hand moved up her leg, he grazed her folds with his thumb.

"You are being very naughty," she gasped between strokes, "teasing me like this."

"You have no idea how very naughty I can be." The dare in his voice thrilled her.

His thumb moved back up to her sex, fondling her with soft, rhythmic caresses that made her languid and wanton. She leaned her head back and closed her eyes, enjoying the sensation of the burning, sexual heat between her legs. It curled through her body, cresting in a wave of complete physical release she didn't want to end. Gripping the sides of the tub, she held on as a shudder of absolute pleasure ran through her body. It was a moment of utter contentment, followed by a moment of extreme need.

"Stephen, please." She reached out for his hands and placed them on her breasts, her body demanding still more of him. He brought his mouth down on them, suckling her nipples, lapping up the rivulets of water that ran along her skin.

He pulled her out of the water, wrapped her in a soft towel, and brought her to the bed. She could feel the fullness of his lust through his breeches, which he discarded the minute he laid her on the coverlet. Stephen straddled her, pulling the towel away and drying her off, bit by bit. As he did so, she felt the hardness of his erection against her legs and belly. She reached out to touch it, grazing the underside of him with her fingers. To her surprise he bucked a bit.

"Sorry." She pulled her hand back. "I didn't know that would hurt."

"It didn't, you minx. Quite the opposite."

She cocked an eyebrow, and suitably emboldened, touched him again, thrilled by the gasp he let out through gritted teeth. "I think it's only fair for teasing me so."

He brushed his lips against her neck and behind her ear. Heat ran down past her belly to between her legs, where his fingers brushed up against the damp curls of her sex. She let out a gasp of pleasure, which was answered with a low chuckle.

"What's the matter?" she asked.

"Nothing. I love your noises. When I first met you, I couldn't help but wonder if you were ever, ever quiet. How tiresome would that be?" He paused, and she felt kisses on her belly. "I love every squeal, every shudder, every gasp, every giggle that comes from that delectable, kissable mouth."

She answered with a deep throaty sigh as he ran his fingers between the wet folds of her sex, and she instinctively pushed against them, eager for more. She reached out and buried her hands in his thick wavy hair, and cried out as he brought her to climax for the second time.

"Rosalind," he gasped as he plunged into her, his voice low and rough. She lifted her bottom and locked her legs around him, reveling in the sensation of him moving inside her. They rocked in unison, his hairline damp with beads of sweat, the muscles in his arms hard. As she reached up and stroked one of his nipples with her tongue his body tensed, then he bore down on her with a hard, penetrating kiss.

STEPHEN FOUGHT for control of his body and his emotions as the orgasm rocked through him. It was beyond exhilaration. The first time he'd made love to Rosalind, he had held a part of himself back. Now, lying on top of her, cradled in her arms, feeling the warmth of her body mingling with his, he had unleashed it all, and it threatened to overwhelm him.

"What's wrong?" she asked.

He put his thumb and index finger up to his eyes, trying in vain to stem the flow of emotion. He shook his head. To speak threatened to unman him completely. But as he relished the comforting tingles from her fingers, gently running up and down his back, then playing with his hair, he lowered his hand. Pride be damned. A tear splashed down from his cheek onto hers, and she gave him such a tender expression he feared his chest would burst. The words he had so long denied, the words he'd feared for so long, demanded an audience.

"I love you."

Without missing a breath, she simply replied, "I love you too."

They lay quietly for a while longer, Stephen enjoying the sensation of her skin and her hair against his own. He traced his fingers along the curve of her hip when a small growling noise cut the silence.

"Sorry," Rosalind looked over at him with an embarrassed smile. "I haven't eaten much in the past two days."

"I didn't save you to starve you." He hugged her once more, then got to his feet. "I shall ring for supper, if you like."

"We should go down," Rosalind wrapped herself in one of the sheets and walked over to where a clean frock hung over a chair. "I don't want my uncle to miss me."

"Your uncle knows exactly where you are."

"What?" she exclaimed, looking horrified in a charming fit of modesty. "Does he know where *you* are?"

"He probably has an excellent idea," Stephen pulled his shirt over his head. "On our way here, I told him about my intentions toward you. My original intentions, which you quite deservedly threw back in my face."

He could see her redden, a look of embarrassment and horror. "I can't believe you would tell him that."

"I told him that, and much more. I told him that Rosalind Schofield was the most beautiful, intelligent woman I had ever laid eyes on. I said that she makes me laugh in spite of myself, has excellent taste in literature and has given me a decided affinity for hot chocolate. All qualities that would greatly enhance Barronsfield, if she would so do me the honor of becoming my wife." He hoped to heaven that sounded as earnest as he'd meant it. He could barely hear his own words over the pounding in his chest.

"Yes." She nodded, smiling broadly, before casting a look down at herself. "I feel so silly, wrapped in an innkeeper's sheet."

"I think you're overdressed as it is." He yanked on the soft fabric playfully, then took Rosalind up in his arms. "And I couldn't imagine you more beautiful than you are right now."

And he couldn't imagine being happier.

CHAPTER 26

Stephen paced in his study. Rosalind would return with Eleanore Martin and the Darlings at any moment. Together they would sit down, and Stephen would try to explain to a girl who thought she was a simple orphan living on the charity of an unknown benefactor, that she was so much more.

She was family.

"You look like you're about to give birth, Barronsfield," Edmund said as he came in the room. "What's the matter?"

"I'm expecting Eleanore any moment now." Edmund took a seat, but Stephen could not manage it at the moment. Only proposing to Rosalind had been more nerve-wracking.

"What do you plan on telling her?"

"The truth. What else is there? I expect her to be shocked. I hope she doesn't despise me."

Edmund pulled a face that suggested he thought Stephen had lost his mind.

"Yes, I suppose it's foolish." Stephen stopped and leaned on his desk. "In the past few days, I've gained a fiancé and now a sister. I suddenly have a real family again."

"Family," Edmund scoffed. "I am happy for you, Stephen. But I am more than happy to be rid of mine."

"You always have a home here, Edmund. In fact, I'd hoped you'd stay." There was no question of that. And no question that Edmund's ties—both financial and otherwise—to his father's estate were cut.

"And do what?" He shook his head. "I have no bloody purpose, except to play cards and parade around. Even your scullery maids wake up knowing what it is they must do."

"You can help me run the estate, until you decide," Stephen said. "Or visit with your mother's family. I am sure you would be welcome there."

Edmund sat for what seemed to Stephen to be a long time, lost in his own thoughts, before he rose. Resolution squared his shoulders, and he shook his head. "I want to grow up. I want to be of use in the world. And, no offense, be as far away from estates and titles as I can be. Maybe I'll go to the Canadas. Or India. Somewhere where I am just another face. Somewhere these hands can be put to good use."

"Edmund, you are a gentleman."

"Perhaps. But now I need to learn how to be a man."

"Then, allow me to do this for you." Stephen went into his desk and pulled out a small sealed envelope and pushed it toward Edmund.

"Stephen—"

"It's not a bank note," Stephen interjected before Edmund could protest further. "It is a letter of introduction to an old friend of my father, Sir Richard Hamilton. He works for the Home Office. Father helped him many years ago, and I've never known all the details, but he has remained a friend of Barronsfield. If you can't stay here, before you go carting yourself off to die of cholera in India, go see him. If you feel you owe me a debt, repay me by talking to him."

Edmund hesitated, then scooped up the parchment. "Thank you."

He shook Stephen's hand, then left.

A moment later, Stephen saw Rosalind in the doorway, clearly troubled.

"I said farewell to Edmund."

"For now," Stephen said. "I take it our guests have arrived?"

"I've taken them to the library. Hanley has laid down some tea, and I requested a little brandy as well."

"Do you think she's going to need it?"

"No, but you clearly do." She smiled and walked toward him. "Now, let's go meet your sister."

DAWN HAD NOT YET ARRIVED, but Rosalind lay in bed, awake. She was getting married in a few short hours to the man she'd come to love more than she could have ever dared to dream. Dreyfus lay on the floor next to the hearth, the gentle movement of his breath the only sound in the room.

She rolled over, forcing herself to rest when a noise at her window, like small pebbles pelting the glass, caught her attention. Uncertain if it was her imagination, she pulled off the covers, shaking off the rush of cool air as she did so, and made her way to the window. The glass tinkled again, and she peered into the darkness. Stephen stood near a horse, a lantern in his hand.

She pulled open the window.

"What are you doing?" she asked, her voice a hush. "I'm not supposed to see you on our wedding day. It's bad luck."

"First of all, it's not dawn yet, and second, I thought you didn't believe in superstitious things." From the glow of the lantern, she could just make out the boyish grin on his face. "I have something I want to show you."

Perplexed, she shut the window, pulled on her slippers and a robe, and went out to meet him. He pulled her up onto his mount, and they rode to the orangery. The glow from what must have been a dozen candles lit the glass enclosure over Haddie's roses. The beauty of it caught Rosalind's breath.

When they arrived, Stephen led her into the hot house, the pace of his footsteps betraying his own excitement as they moved through the maze of greenery to where the rose bush stood.

"I have something for you." He set down the lantern, then picked up a bouquet of roses, and placed them in her hands.

Rosalind's eyes widened. Each deep pink bloom, lush with petals and beautifully perfumed, dazzled her. Her gaze went from the bouquet, to the rose bush beside them, and back to Stephen.

"Are these…"

"Do they please you?" The urgency in his voice reached down into her heart. "I thought, if you liked them, perhaps you might like them for your wedding day. But if you would rather have different—"

She reached up, putting a hand to his shoulder, and kissed him. Softly at first, then deeper, trying to pour the ferocity of her love for him into this single act. At last she broke the kiss.

"I love them. And I love the man who picked them for me."

"I love you." He laced his fingers in her hers, then looked out the windows where the sky was beginning to brighten. "Now, I should return you to the cottage. We are getting married in a few hours."

"Suddenly, a few hours seem like an eternity."

"We have an eternity to be happy, don't you think?"

"Happily ever after?"

"Of course, darling. Isn't that how every fairy tale ends?"

THE END

TAKE A PEAK: NO PRINCE CHARMING

What happened to Edmund? Funny you should ask. Here's a teaser...

NO PRINCE CHARMING

CHAPTER ONE

Cumbria, August, 1795

An ordinary day for Lady Gwyneth Snowdon involved a little tea and much tedium, punctuated by her mother's not-so-occasional tantrum.

This was not an ordinary day.

Today she was well on her way to accomplishing one, if not two, incredible feats: saving the family's ailing fortunes, and, perhaps most extraordinary of all, making her mother happy—and doing both in style. All by embarking on a clandestine, impossibly romantic adventure to Scotland with a dashing European nobleman who would make her a princess before teatime tomorrow.

It was an extreme inconvenience to be sure, but it would all be worth it.

They'd ridden from her home in Warwickshire, through the western counties, and soon would be approaching the Scottish border. In a few short hours, she would accomplish all that mattered to a woman of gentle birth: an excellent name and a respectable fortune. She was going to be married. And not just *married*. Married to the man who, at the moment, gazed into her eyes from across the well-appointed coach. His eyes were the most remarkable shade of green and his hair was like spun gold. Adorned in the finest of buck-skin breeches and the smartest of woolen coats, he looked the very image of a fairy tale prince.

"My darling," Prince Henrich said, his rich accent adding a clip to his consonants that sounded as important as he looked. "Let me say again how honored I am you have consented to be my wife. When we return to Streichenstien, you will be the toast of Europe."

Gwynnie smiled at the compliment. Prince Henrich von Leuneburg was deliciously smooth in his address, and so incredibly dashing. The principality he was to rule was quite small, but sounded terribly important. He showered her with endless attentions and compliments; of course she was besotted with him. Mama approved of him unconditionally—which may have been a first in Gwynnie's memory. Her father, ill though he was, was thrilled with the match, and had bestowed on the prince as much condescension and flattery as he could manage. Of course, Papa had no idea that they had run off together. Her mouth fell into a small frown.

"Why the fretting, my pet?" Henrich smiled. A small rush of blood flooded into her cheeks as he reached forward and took her hand in his. "You will see...everything will be fine."

She pushed away the lingering niggle of doubt. She'd had more than a few niggles, actually, about this entire thing. But Mama had urged Gwynnie on, and if there was one person in her life she could not disappoint, it was her mother. Mama had been so excited about this elopement, Gwynnie had decided it was best to keep her doubts to herself. Besides, Mama had her sights set on her daughter becoming a princess, there was little anyone could do to stop her. Even the groom's parents.

"I just don't understand how your parents could be planning your wedding to another woman when they knew you were engaged to me," Gwynnie replied. "I'm the daughter of one of the kingdom's most ancient earldoms."

"Darling," he purred, nearly transfixing her with his emerald stare. "Our meeting, and the force of our love, was completely unexpected. My family promised my hand to the daughter of another noble family. I have written to them, explaining that I have met the loveliest, most noble creature in all of Europe and that I am making her my bride. But I do not trust to messengers and ships. I am not certain they would release me from that other obligation. So we shall marry now, so I will not lose you."

"Are you quite certain they would not disinherit you?"

"Disinherit…no. But they could threaten me with exile." Though his tone was light enough, the edge in his voice as he spoke those last words caught Gwynnie off-guard. His gaze flickered away from her for a moment.

Gwynnie's breath caught in her throat. An exiled princess? What kind of life was that?

He returned his attentions to her, a subtle command in his looks. "I will not lie to you, my dear. Breaking the engagement will test the alliances in the region, but with France in such turmoil, stability is required. A union from among the English Peerage will be seen as a positive move. And of course, I would never have suggested such a daring plan if I didn't want you so badly as my princess." He reached up and stroked her cheek, then put his lips to her hand and kissed her gloved fingers. "I am certain that when my parents see you, they will fall as deeply in love with you as I have. When we arrive in Streichenstien, we will have another ceremony. Big and grand, for the people. We could not deprive them of that. We will invite your family and all your friends. It will be splendid."

Friends. Gwynnie's lips pulled into a tight smile. Acquaintances she had in abundance. Friends? Only one name came to mind, and they had not been friends since the Boxfords had been sent away. Regret reached into Gwynnie's chest and squeezed. Even if she could find Kitty, the girl was a gamekeeper's daughter, not a lady. *Five thousand pounds too poor and a stone too heavy to marry well,* Mama had said.

You've no business consorting with the servants. Gwynnie shook off the memory and squared her shoulders, as if protecting herself from the onslaught of emotion that would come if she allowed herself to dwell on it. Kitty couldn't come to her wedding anyway. She would be so terribly out of place among society's elite. Gwynnie swallowed deeply, then turned her attention back to her fiancé.

"I still can't believe you went to Mama with your plan. Most elopements are secret," she said. Anyone who dared cross her mother, Lady Theodora Snowdon, was a brave person indeed. Gwynnie could never imagine it. Even her father, the earl, did not.

"Your mother wants to see her daughter a princess. And so do I." He released her hand and leaned back in his seat, a regal image of self-confidence. "Once the papers get wind of a European prince whisking away the beautiful Lady Gwyneth Snowdon, you will be the talk of all England and much of Europe, as well. You will have to order a hundred new gowns just to keep up with all the parties."

New gowns. Gwynnie nodded, took a deep breath, and settled into her seat. He was right. It was terribly romantic, wasn't it? He was so dashing, after all. And brave too, if he was willing to upset his family just so he could have her.

She took in a long breath, trapping the unease in her chest and forcing it deep into her belly. It was a familiar sensation since her mother and Henrich had first come to her with this plan two days ago. Two days ago, marrying a prince—or anyone good enough for her mother—had seemed an impossibility. But it was happening, and it had to be a good thing.

It had to be.

Her name and her princess-like comportment, Mama had said, would win over her new family. And Gwynnie had spent a lifetime honing those skills. She could walk as gracefully as a queen, knew the steps to every dance, and how to negotiate the politics of setting a table for a party. She'd spent years learning to be as perfect as possible, so she could be the perfect wife to the most well-titled husband she could attract. Marrying someone of Prince Henrich's standing had to be the reward.

As the setting sun flickered through the thick foliage of the countryside, another curious thought came to her.

Marriage would be culmination of her life's work.

At twenty-one. What then?

There would be balls and parties, and she liked those well enough. And she'd have the finest clothes, and she'd be on display all the time. She'd have her own household, so she'd not have to worry about stirring out of doors in the rain if she chose, or agonizing about being anything less than perfect. Although princesses were perfect, weren't they?

After marriage, of course, came children. A chill darted down her spine. The very notion did not appeal. She would hardly know what to do with a child. Of course, her mama had never bothered with her until she'd turned fourteen. Until then, nursemaids and governesses were her company—when she wasn't sneaking off with Kitty. Her dear father soothed her loneliness with all the gowns and slippers and ribbons a girl could want.

And Gwynnie wanted a lot. Still, a closet full of frocks and fripperies was not the most satisfying of companions.

Shouting and the loud whiny of horses, interrupted thoughts of silks and gown fittings. As Gwynnie strained to see what was amiss, the carriage heaved to one side. Gwynnie was thrown from her seat, against the hard wall, and into the prince's lap, banging her knees as she landed. He quickly scooped her up and set her back on the seat. Heart pounding, she took a second to realize the carriage was still.

She barely had a moment to collect herself when the carriage door flew open and she came nose to nose with a pistol.

"What is happening?" Gwynnie whispered as she fought to control her voice. She forced her gaze past the dark barrel to the man holding it, but the brim of his hat obscured his face.

"Sit down, my lady. I'm not here to hurt you," came the clipped reply. The ruffian turned to the prince, who immediately put up his hands. "You. Out."

"What is the meaning of this?" Prince Henrich asked, his eyes narrowing slightly.

A heavy sob caught in Gwynnie's throat, but anger forced it clear. "Don't you dare hurt him!"

"The prince and I have some business," the highwayman continued. "Whether he's hurt or not depends entirely on him."

"Darling." The prince turned to her, the authority in his voice providing some measure of comfort. "I am quite sure this gentleman and I can come to an arrangement." He grabbed her hand, kissed it, then jumped out of the carriage. "Whatever you do, do not run. You are safer here."

Gwynnie took a second hard glance at the highwayman and wasn't so sure.

EDMUND TRAINED his pistol on the golden man who hopped out of the carriage. He gestured to his captive, who, despite the long journey and being held at gunpoint, was decidedly unruffled. Over his target's shoulder, Edmund saw the curtain in the carriage window pulled back, and the most remarkable set of violet eyes looking back at him with a mix of fear and fury.

Edmund Pembroke, or rather Edmund Hanley, as he called himself now, had been on more dangerous missions for his employer, Sir Richard Hamilton. In the past five years he'd been shot at more times than he dared count, intercepted documents, planted fake maps and gathered secrets from the lowest of thieves to the House of Lords. It was the price Edmund was prepared to pay for anonymity, a roof over his head, and maybe even a bit of redemption.

Why he was here, along a deserted stretch of road twenty miles from the Cumbrian border with Scotland had more to do with family intrigues. Not his own, thank God. The now infamous scheme of his father Thomas and his older brother Geoffrey Pembroke, to steal the title and lands of his cousin, the Marquess of Barronsfield, had fueled the society gossip mills for months after it had been revealed. Edmund's foolish and unwitting complicity in it was, no doubt, laughed about in some of the finest ballrooms in the country. Did they talk about how he'd discovered the truth before the damage was done? How he betrayed Geoffrey and his father to do what was just?

No doubt, his cousin Stephen, the marquess, had spoken for him. Edmund had removed himself from ballrooms and gentleman's clubs. After his father and brother were caught, Edmund, unable to remain part of a society so fixated on power, had left it behind with barely a glance over his shoulder.

Right now, his employer needed a favor of a more personal nature. A favor so important he was prepared to dangle an irresistible carrot in front of Edmund's nose. The time spent waiting in the damp brush to save Sir Richard's goddaughter from an inconvenient marriage to a gold seeking imposter was a bargain. Edmund's orders had been simple. Intercept the carriage and take the girl back home. After his last assignment, nearly a year ago, to uncover evidence of a blackmailing scheme involving a Member of Parliament, this would be simple indeed.

"State your terms," the man on the other side of his pistol spat, hands on his hips, the very model of noble indignity. Edmund cocked an eyebrow, impressed. Years of living in the theatre no doubt helped Henry Fox—or Henrich von Leuneburg, as he'd been calling himself these days—pull off his ruse and snare the affections and the dowry of Lady Gwyneth Snowdon.

"I think we should move away from the carriage, your highness, so as not further distress the lady." Edmund's gaze moved past his target to the carriage. She was still there, still watching. The intensity never moved from him.

Fox nodded, and with affected Bavarian efficiency, he marched ahead toward the horses.

"You can stop right there, your highness," Edmund called out, fearing the man might try to run off.

Fox spun on his heel, facing Edmund, and put a monocle to his eye. He surveyed Edmund with the same practiced eye of the best Eton schoolmaster. Edmund was almost impressed.

Almost.

"What do you want? A jewel? A trinket? Will that be enough to get you on your way?" Fox asked, his accent firmly in place.

"I'm looking for something a little more substantial than that." Edmund raised his weapon. "You're going to release Lady Gwyneth to me."

Even in the dimming light, the change in Fox's countenance at the sound of the lady's name was apparent.

"And what on earth makes you think I would do any such thing?" Fox replied, his voice hitting a higher note. "What kind of gentleman would release such a lady to the custody of a criminal?"

Edmund held his pistol steady. "Curious. I thought you were the criminal here. An actor and a fraud, tricking Lady Gwyneth into marrying you. Tell me, what mythical kingdom did you tell her you'd rule over? Or were you saving that for the end of the grand tour?"

Fox stood straighter, apparently recovered from Edmund's challenge. "I have no idea what you are talking about, nor do I have the luxury of time to discuss these matters further." He put two fingers to his mouth and blew out a sharp whistle.

Out of the corner of his eye, Edmund saw the carriage driver stand in his perch, his weapon trained on him. "Do you think we travel these roads without protection?"

"Do you think I wouldn't expect that, Prince Henrich? Or should I say, Henry Fox?"

"Henry Fox?" Fox laughed, muttered a few couple of nonsensical German phrases, then continued, "I do not know a Henry Fox."

Edmund rushed the man, grabbing him by his collar. "I think you do."

As they struggled, Edmund heard the telltale click of a pistol being cocked.

"You'll never get a clean shot from there," he yelled up at the driver. "You're just as likely to get his head as mine."

"For God's sakes, stand down!" Fox hissed at the driver, both his noble demeanor and his Bavarian accent deserting him. His eyes narrowed and his mouth twisted into a sneer. "What the hell do you want?"

"I told you what I want. I want the girl."

"Who is she to you?"

"She is no one to me. But my current employer takes a great deal of interest in her future. And her future does not include you."

"Is it the father then? I should have known the old bastard would be trouble. She should have listened to me." Fox spoke quickly, his eyes darting from side to side, as if groping for his next move. Obviously, improvisation was not his forte as an actor. "Look, perhaps we can come to some sort of agreement."

Edmund paused. *Who* should have listened to him? Surely not Lady Gwyneth. Sir Richard had dispatched Edmund to intercept this plan, but it was hastily done, as the information had arrived late and was incomplete. The longer Fox spoke, the more Edmund suspected there was a grander scheme afoot than a simple plan for an actor to defraud an earl's daughter of her fortune. Edmund loosened his grip slightly, signaling his willingness to listen.

Fox's lips pulled back into a harried smile. "In a few days I'll be a very rich man, see? I can stand to part with a few pieces."

Edmund took a step back, keeping the pistol trained squarely at Fox's chest. The man was getting nervous. It offered Edmund opportunity to learn more about Fox's plans, but also greater opportunity for things to go awry. The driver's movements in the perch were twitchy—clearly he was out of his depth as well, which added to the danger. Fox, hands shaking slightly, reached into his jacket pocket and pulled out a small silk bag. He offered it to Edmund.

"Take it. There's a small fortune in there—enough to keep you in ale and women for a good while." He cocked his head toward the carriage. "All you have to do is walk away. Tell your boss you never found us. Disappear. From the looks of a man like you, that shouldn't be hard."

If the wretch only knew how hard it had been to disappear. After Edmund had left Barronsfield, he'd spent months working on shedding his identity and years trying to stay out of sight. Edmund lowered his pistol and pocketed the silk bag, signaling to the fake prince his acceptance of payment, then considered his next move.

"Do we have an agreement, then?" Fox asked.

The muffled sound of the woman's voice came from the carriage.
"Prince Henrich?"

Fox rolled his eyes, then forced a smile as he went back into character. "Do not worry, my dear," he called. "I am discussing a resolution
to our situation with this fine gentleman. Stay where it is warm."

Fox squared his shoulders and leaned in, wearing a confident smile
as he gestured toward Edmund's pocket and spoke once again in his
natural tongue. "You are a richer man than you were a moment ago,
and in a few days, I will be as well. Working men need to make a
living, too. And seeing how she's done nothing to deserve that money
except being born, I don't see why we don't deserve to take some of it
back." He rubbed his hands together, and took a step to leave. "Are we
done then?"

"We are done." Edmund whipped around, pulled a knife out of
his sleeve and hurled it at the carriage driver. The man cried out,
dropping his pistol to attend to where the blade had embedded in
his arm. Edmund turned and took a swing at Fox, his fist
connecting with the man's jaw. Fox staggered back, gazing up at
Edmund with a horrified awareness that Edmund would have
nothing to do with any proposed scheme. Whatever it was, Edmund
was certain that more than Lady Gwyneth's reputation and dowry
was at stake.

He raised his pistol and aimed it at Fox when someone jumped on
his back, throwing him off balance.

"What in the bloody—"

He threw the unwanted attacker off his shoulders, whirling
around with his pistol in his hands to see the lady in question, her
eyes wide with a mix of fear but unmistakable rage.

"Get back in the carriage," Edmund ordered. "I'll deal with
you later."

She pulled herself to her feet. "Leave him alone, you cretin. You
have no idea who he is! Or who I am."

"I have a perfectly good idea of who he is, my lady. You on the
other hand, might be misinformed."

"Your Highness," she called to Fox, care in her voice. Foolish woman. "Are you hurt?"

"I am well enough," Fox replied, his European accent returning, though lacking its former smoothness. "Do not worry, my pet. This ruffian has been hired by someone disloyal to my family who wishes to crush our happiness. I will not let that happen."

Lady Gwyneth rushed to his side, then lifted him up to his feet before throwing her venom back at Edmund. "What kind of coward would pull a gun on an unarmed man?"

"I told you to get back into the carriage. I suggest you do as I say."

"Are you going to shoot him?" she asked, standing between Fox and Edmund.

She might have been foolish, but her bravery was remarkable. Misplaced, but remarkable.

The second crack of a pistol broke through the chaos. Edmund heard the ball whiz by his head, thudding into the ground nearby. It was the carriage driver, who'd obviously managed to recover his pistol, though thankfully, not his aim.

"Don't shoot at her, you fool!" Fox snapped.

"Your highness?" The girl's eyes narrowed slightly and she stilled, no doubt caught unaware by Fox's command, given in clear, unaccented English, and the expression of mad desperation on his face.

Fox went to grab her, but Edmund pushed him onto the ground.

"Run!" he ground out.

Edmund was uncertain whether it was his warning or simply the violent chaos happening around her, but she bolted.

"Go after her!" Fox barked at the carriage driver, who had jumped down. "We need her alive! If you lose her, you can explain to my lady how you've ruined our plans."

Fox wheeled around, curling his hand into a fist, and landed a jab that clipped Edmund's jaw. Edmund reeled back, shook it off, and sent his own blow across his opponent's cheek. It was enough to stop the struggle, if only temporarily. Fox crumpled to the ground.

His companion ran toward the woods. Edmund pulled out his pistol and called out to him.

"Don't run. I never miss." It was part warning and all truth. He never did. It was part of what made him so valuable to Sir Richard. That, and a certain recklessness that came with a never-ending search for atonement.

The man paused long enough for Edmund to reach him. He tackled the driver to the ground, and kept him there with a knee to his throat, his hand pressed on the wounded arm.

"Who is this lady you speak of?"

"I can't...'e'll kill me."

"Not if I kill you first," Edmund growled, leaning on his prey's wounded arm. The man reached out for Edmund, writhing on the ground, hurling curses at him. After only a few seconds of this, he called out for Edmund to stop.

"I'll tell you, you bastard! Jus' let go me arm!"

Edmund released some of the pressure from his arm, but kept his knee firmly at the man's throat. "Who?"

"Lady Snowdon."

Edmund paused, uncertain he heard correctly. "Lady Snowdon. Do you mean the countess?"

"Aye!"

Edmund blinked, thrown by the man's words.

"Are you saying the girl's mother wishes her dead?"

"She wishes the girl gone. Fox was gonna take care of it for 'er." The driver shook his head violently, then struggled, grasping at Edmund's leg, trying to wrench himself free. Edmund pulled a length of cord from his coat, bound the man's hands, then gagged him with the man's own neck cloth.

Edmund stood, shaking his head as he looked to over Fox's form, stilled from his blow. A low, sickening feeling settled in Edmund's gut. He should have known Richard's price for this job would be high, though he doubted even his mentor would have dared to guess how steep.

It was time to earn it. Edmund went on the offensive. He had a new life to lead when this job was over. Not as the second son of a madman, nor the favored cousin of a marquess, nor even the sometime agent of a testy, enigmatic spymaster. Instead, he could slip into the life he'd been slowly building since he walked away from his name and society's trappings. Soon he would be simply Edmund Hanley, gamekeeper. A huntsman, free from the confinements of parlors, manners, and the power games of the titled.

There was only one thing between him and that promise, and she'd disappeared into the woods. But not for long.

GET the Book

CONNECT WITH MICHELLE

I hope you enjoyed reading **Not Your Average Beauty** as much as I enjoyed writing it. This book is the first in my *Enchanted Tales* Series.

Reviews, positive or negative, are welcome! Feel free to post one where you purchased the book, or on Goodreads.

My website is www.michellehelliwell.com. You can sign up for my newsletter and get a heads up on new releases.

You can also find me out and about on the web:

Facebook:

https://www.facebook.com/michellehelliwellhistoricalromance

Twitter: @mlhelliwell

Pinterest: https://www.pinterest.com/mlhelliwell/

Instagram: https://www.instagram.com/mlhelliwell/

After three torturous seasons, Lady Eleanore Pembroke is finished with husband hunting and happy ever after. Following the scandal of a broken engagement, eager to bury herself in her work at the local infirmary, she returns home shocked to discover their trusted physician gone, replaced by a dashing scoundrel. Bastien DuMont is a talented doctor, but Eleanore senses his restless heart. She's no longer prepared to risk hers, nor the trust of the people who've come to depend on him.

Caught up in a revolution that dissolved into terror, Bastien learned that devotion is for fools. On the run from a growing list of men who'd love to see him dead, he's forced out of the shadows and into the shoes of a respectable country physician, putting him under the scrutiny of Lady Eleanore, a local do-gooder immune to his roguish charms. When a mysterious figure emerges, threatening his life and the safety of those around him, can Bastien hunt down his opponent before he becomes the prey? Or is exposing his heart the greater danger?

Get the Book

ABOUT THE AUTHOR

Michelle Helliwell started writing her first novel, a time travel fantasy, when she was 15. She moved on to half-hearted attempts at something more literary, then nearly gave up on the writing all together until one fine day in 2005 a co-worker put a romance novel in her hands and told her to "get over yourself".

She did, and the rest, as they say, is history.

Michelle lives with her husband and two sons in Nova Scotia, Canada where moody weather and bagpipes are plentiful, but alas, guys in puffy shirts are too few.

Connect with me online!
www.michellehelliwell.com

9 780994 035738